THE HOLIDAY BROTHERS

WILLA NASH

THE HOLIDAY BROTHERS COMPLETE SERIES

Cover Artwork © Sarah Hansen, Okay Creations
www.okaycreations.com

OTHER TITLES

CALAMITY MONTANA SERIES

The Bribe

The Bluff

The Brazen

The Bully

The Brawl

The Brood

HOLIDAY BROTHERS SERIES

The Naughty, The Nice and The Nanny

Three Bells, Two Bows and One Brother's Best Friend

A Partridge and a Pregnancy

THE EDENS SERIES

Christmas in Quincy - Prequel

Indigo Ridge

Juniper Hill

Garnet Flats

Jasper Vale

CLIFTON FORGE SERIES

Steel King

Riven Knight

Stone Princess

Noble Prince

Fallen Jester

Tin Queen

JAMISON VALLEY SERIES

The Coppersmith Farmhouse

The Clover Chapel

The Lucky Heart

The Outpost

The Bitterroot Inn

The Candle Palace

MAYSEN JAR SERIES

The Birthday List

Letters to Molly

LARK COVE SERIES

Tattered

Timid

Tragic

Tinsel

Timeless

RUNAWAY SERIES

Runaway Road

Wild Highway

Quarter Miles

Forsaken Trail

Dotted Lines

STANDALONES

Ivy

Rifts and Refrains

A Little Too Wild

THE NAUGHTY, THE NICE AND THE NANNY

CHAPTER 1
NATALIE

"She's an angel."

"Aren't they all?" I deadpanned.

"Of course not," my boss muttered on the other end of our phone call. "Some kids are shitheads."

"Whoa." I giggled. "Cathy."

"Natalie, I know you're on vacation, and I know you're overdue for a break, but you're the only one available to take this job. You know I hate turning down clients."

I scrunched up my nose. Cathy hated turning down clients, and I hated turning down Cathy. But this was my vacation. The first vacation I'd had in ages, and one I'd purposefully timed to coincide with Christmas.

I was going to enjoy the holidays with my own family instead of caring for someone else's.

This morning I'd come downtown for a hearty breakfast of eggs and pancakes at Main Street Overeasy before setting out to do some last-minute gift shopping while enjoying the festive décor.

Enormous gold, red and green garlands were strung high

across the road, their strands twinkling beneath the clear blue sky. The trees, wrapped in tiny lights, glittered from last night's snow. Window displays were teeming with Santas, ornaments and intricately wrapped gifts. The morning sun was out, bright and cheery, warding off the winter chill. It was the perfect kickoff to my vacation.

"Cathy, I can't."

"Please," she begged. "The father sounded desperate. He's in town for the holidays. Sounded like the workaholic type. You'll be caring for his daughter during the day while he works. He mentioned a family holiday function as well, though I told him you were only obligated to work during the day. Apparently, his regular nanny walked out yesterday."

"I thought you said this girl was an angel. Nannies don't walk out on angels."

"He agreed to pay twice your regular rate."

I groaned. Of course, she'd tempt me with the money. "I never should have told you about Magdalena."

My beloved 1969 mint-green Volkswagen bus. Magdalena. Three weeks ago, her transmission had crapped out. The mechanic had ordered a new one from a parts store online that specialized in vintage Volkswagen parts, but with shipping, it was going to cost me over four thousand dollars.

I was a governess not a gazillionaire.

"And it's only for a week?" I asked.

"Yes. Just a week."

"Oh, stop your smiling. I asked a question. I didn't agree."

"How can you tell I'm smiling?"

I rolled my eyes. "You always smile when you get your way."

"So that's a yes?"

"Yes," I grumbled. "I'll do it."

"Excellent! Thank you. I'm sure this week will be a breeze." Cathy's famous last words.

She knew I preferred to work on long-term assignments. I'd been with my last family for three and a half years. The Scullys had been the best of the best family in Bozeman, Montana. Their kids were actual angels, sent from heaven to reward me for being the person Cathy could call upon for these *breezy* assignments.

The Scully boys had turned fourteen and sixteen this past year. Both were active in school, playing football, basketball and running track. Now that the oldest had his driver's license and they went to the same school, they didn't need me to shuffle them around from point A to point B.

My last day with them had been yesterday, and I'd cried like a baby while hugging them goodbye. They'd teased me mercilessly for my blubbering, and even though Instagram wasn't cool for kids these days, they'd promised to post a selfie every week as proof of life.

After New Year's, I'd be starting with another family. The kids were five and nine. Assuming we had a good vibe, I might be their nanny for years.

Short-term jobs, like the one she was pitching, were more like glorified babysitter gigs.

But for Magdalena, I'd be the babysitter.

"Send me the details," I said.

"Okay. They're expecting you by ten, so you'd better get going."

"Ten." My feet ground to a halt. "Today? I thought you'd at least give me one day off. Can I start tomorrow?"

"Um . . ."

"It's three days before Christmas. I haven't finished my shopping yet." Because I'd blocked off my vacation days to buy and wrap gifts. "You're killing me, Cath."

"The mall is open until nine."

"You know I hate the mall," I muttered.

This served me right for putting off my shopping. Every year I swore I'd start earlier. And every year, I procrastinated. The mall this close to Christmas Eve was a particularly sweltering level of hell.

"Thank you, Natalie. I can always count on you."

"If it wasn't for Magdalena . . ."

She was smiling again. I could practically hear the stretch of her lips. "You're the best."

"You'd better pick me as Employee of the Year."

"You were Employee of the Year last year. Everyone will think I'm playing favorites."

"Because I am your favorite and you do play favorites."

"True."

"Bye." I ended the call and checked the time.

Ten o'clock was in twenty minutes.

I spun around, retreating to my dad's Subaru parked in one of the lots off Main. He'd loaned it to me while Magdalena was in the shop.

Dad always said I was fiercely loyal. At the moment, I felt epically spineless. Cathy might believe she had no one else to call, but that was because she always called me first. For short-term engagements like this, when my primary family was on vacation, or for a weekend when a client needed additional help, I was usually her first request. And I'd always said yes.

But she'd earned my devotion by treating me right over the years and giving me the best families, like the Scullys.

Cathy owned a local nanny agency in Bozeman, and with the growing online services available to parents these days, she survived by setting herself and her staff apart. We were not the caliber of nannies you'd find scouring the classifieds. Our reputation was unmatched and new clientele was sent

6

through referrals only, hence the reason she hated to tell a prospect no.

This dad in desperate need of a holiday nanny for his *angel* probably hadn't blinked twice at a double-rate fee.

Magdalena, baby, this one is for you.

I reached the Subaru—*Barney? Barley?*—I was still in the process of picking the perfect name. My reflection in the car window had me whipping out my phone to call Cathy.

"If you're telling me you've changed your mind, you're too late," she answered. "I already called the father back and told him you were on the way."

"I don't have time to go home and change. Is there a dress code?"

"No dress code, but what are you wearing?"

"Blue turtleneck sweater. Ripped jeans. Duck boots." I was dressed for a day of shopping, not working. The Scullys hadn't had a dress code, but I never would have showed up in jeans with frayed knees. "I also haven't washed my hair yet."

"I'm sure it will be fine. I'll email him a note, letting him know that we've interrupted a personal day. If he has specific requests, he can let you know before tomorrow."

"Okay. Bye." I unlocked the car and got behind the wheel just as a text dinged from Cathy with the address. I punched it into my phone, then followed the GPS across town.

I'd lived in Bozeman for all of my twenty-nine years, and the fall after graduating from high school, I'd started working for Cathy.

As one of the fastest-growing cities in the country, Bozeman had transformed before my eyes and was no longer the town of my youth. Where there'd once been farmland, there were neighborhoods packed with new homes. Big-box stores were chasing out the small, local shops, and the number of new restaurants was staggering.

The directions took me to the outskirts of town, where the homes got larger and larger with every passing mile. As the mountain foothills neared, the properties sprawled and every private drive was blockaded by an iron gate.

"In one hundred yards, your destination is on the left." The navigation rang through the Subaru's Bluetooth.

Magdalena was too old for Bluetooth. I'd miss it—and these heated leather seats—when I returned the Subaru.

A log archway towered over the upcoming driveway entrance. The black metal gates were open as I eased onto a narrow lane lined with evergreens. Their limbs hid most of the house from sight until I rounded a gentle corner and then —*whoa.*

"Oh, hell. I definitely should have washed my hair."

It was a ski lodge masquerading as a family home.

With its dark wooden siding and red-trimmed windows, the house stood as proud and bold as the mountains at its back. The front door was wooden with a stained-glass window in its face. Where most porches would have a standard light, this home had two roaring gas lanterns, their flames flickering even during the day.

I'd been to many wealthy homes in my tenure as a nanny to Bozeman's elite but this one was the pinnacle. If Kevin Costner walked through the door and told me to get off the Dutton Ranch, I wouldn't be surprised. Only this wasn't the *Yellowstone* TV series, and as the clock on the dash glowed ten after ten, it was time for me to get to work.

Parking in the looped driveway that I suspected was for guests, I swiped up my purse from the passenger seat and checked my hair in the rearview. The blond waves I'd added this morning made my ponytail fancy—sort of.

The kid wouldn't care what I looked like, right? And the father, well . . . he'd have to deal with short-notice Natalie.

I stepped outside and hurried to the house, pressing the doorbell. Its chime was a familiar tune. Was that . . .

"We Wish You a Merry Christmas." I gave the door my best lip curl. That stupid song would be stuck in my head all damn day.

Footsteps sounded from inside and I put on my smile, ready to greet my new employer. The door flew open and—

"Hi—oh." My. God. Oh my God. Oh my God.

I'd just said *hi-oh* like one of Snow White's singing dwarves to Maddox Holiday.

The Maddox Holiday. The handsome boy turned *holy-shit-he-was-hot* man who'd once occupied each and every one of my teenage fantasies.

Maddox Holiday.

He'd been the most popular guy at Bozeman High. He'd been the boy every girl had shamelessly crushed on. He was the rich dad in need of an emergency nanny?

I definitely should have asked more questions before agreeing to this. I definitely should have washed my hair.

"Hi. Are you from Cathy Caron's agency?"

"Yes. Hi." I managed it without the oh. *Better.* "I'm Natalie Buchanan."

"Maddox Holiday." He waved me inside and closed the door behind us. "Nice to meet you, Natalie."

Wait. Nice to meet me? Seriously?

He'd already met me.

When. I. Was. Seven.

I stepped past him, wishing, hoping and praying that there'd be a faint flicker of recognition in his mesmerizing blue gaze. But . . . nothing.

The guy had no clue who I was. *Damn.*

Maddox was three years older than me, so it wasn't like we'd run in the same circles. But for many years, we'd gone to

9

the same schools. His twin brothers were my age. He should know me.

Still . . . nothing.

Fourteen-year-old me died a little inside. Her fantasy that one day Maddox Holiday would realize she was the love of his life went *poof* like a tuft of snow in the wind.

What was I doing here? When was I going to learn to tell Cathy no? For the next week, Maddox Holiday would essentially be my boss. And the man didn't have a clue that I'd once fallen off my skateboard and scraped my knee in his driveway.

"Thanks for coming on such short notice," he said.

"Sure." More wishing. More hoping. More praying.

Nope. Nada. He didn't recognize me.

Captain's log. December twenty-second. Today marks the most humiliating day of my life.

Should I tell him? Would that make it weird? Probably.

Magdalena was counting on me to rescue her from the mechanic, so I squared my shoulders, put on a smile and pretended that I was standing across from any other father who was paying me to care for his child.

"Did Cathy explain the position?" he asked.

"At the highest level." Though she'd left out his name, one I would have remembered. I suspected the full details about this position were in my email inbox. "You need a nanny for a week, correct?"

"A week. Your predecessor walked out yesterday." His jaw clenched, and *wowza*, it was chiseled. The corners were so sharp they deserved a snowman statue in their honor.

Just another dad. He's just another dad.

Okay, so maybe he wasn't exactly like other dads. None of the fathers I'd worked for in recent years were this insanely handsome. None had eyes like crystal-blue jewels. None had a gravelly voice that sent shivers down my spine.

Time had only improved Maddox Holiday.

He seemed taller now, standing a head over my five-foot eight. Maddox's face was clean-shaven, and his dark hair had been finger-combed away from his face. In high school, he'd kept his hair short, but if he would have had this hair, he would have had girls shoving their panties in his locker.

He probably already had.

Breathe, Natalie. It's just Maddox mega-hot Holiday. Focus on work. The job. The kid. "You have a daughter, correct?"

"I do. Violet." His gaze softened at his daughter's name. "She's seven. We're home for the holidays to visit my parents. This is their house, so I'm afraid there's never a quiet moment."

"Oh. Okay." The ski lodge belonged to Hannah and Keith? I wasn't sure why I was surprised. The Holidays were one of the most successful families in Bozeman.

Hannah was a real estate broker, and her face was on at least half of the for-sale signs around town. Her brokerage was the most well-known and most respected in the county, partly because she sold the best homes—those her husband built.

Keith Holiday was the most sought-after custom-home builder in the area. People paid a premium for a Holiday Home and were never disappointed.

Keith must have built this place. Even though I'd only seen the foyer, the interior was as grand and gorgeous as the exterior. A chandelier hung high above my head, its pendants refracting the light. Sunshine poured through the abundance of windows. The natural stone tiles beneath my boots were a beautiful shade of grayish blue.

It would not be hard to work in this house for a week.

When Maddox and his brothers been growing up, they'd lived in town. Two blocks over from my house.

Heath and Tobias used to ride their bikes past my childhood home on their way to our neighborhood park.

Wait. His brothers. Maddox might not remember me, but Heath and Tobias would. Were they going to be here?

"Is that okay?" Maddox asked.

"Huh?"

"You look worried." He studied my face, his eyes narrowing. "The extra people in and out. Will that be a problem?"

"Not a problem," I lied, fixing my smile.

"Good. I wish I had the week off work, but it's a critical time for my company. I'll be working in the house, upstairs in the office, in case anything comes up. But with the phone conferences and emails—"

"Adding a seven-year-old into the mix is too much."

"Exactly." He nodded. "I just need some help. My parents would normally jump in and watch her, but they're busy planning the annual party on Christmas Eve. Plus they're working this week too. I don't want Violet bouncing between us all, feeling lost. I want her to have some fun while we're here."

That was sweet. Then again, Maddox had always been sweet. It was the reason all the girls had crushed on him. He'd never let his popularity or good looks turn him into the arrogant playboy like so many other guys in his social circle.

"And Violet's mother?" I asked. Maddox hadn't mentioned a wife and there was no ring on his left hand. "Will she be here?"

"No, I'm divorced. She's in LA."

"Okay." Single dad. Grown-up Maddox just kept getting sexier.

"I'll let Violet give you the tour of the place. But please make yourself comfortable while you're here." Maddox studied me and for a moment my heart swelled. Did he remember me? Yes? Please? "Violet is probably in her room."

Gah. This guy sure knew how to crush a girl's ego. Not that I had an ego. Geeks who loved board games and volunteering at the senior center to call the Sunday bingo games couldn't afford egos.

While Maddox had been dominating the football field as quarterback and dating the head cheerleader, I'd spent my Friday nights in high school babysitting for the neighbors.

"Thank you again for coming." Maddox gave me a small smile that crinkled his eyes. Another improvement of man over boy. Except beneath the smile and rugged good looks, he looked . . . tired. I'd seen that type of exhaustion before in a lot of parents who'd brought in a nanny to help. Mostly it had been from mothers and fathers with demanding jobs who'd realized they couldn't do it all.

Natalie to the rescue.

"You're welcome. It'll be my pleasure. Cathy said she is an angel."

A flash of panic crossed his gaze. It was as telling as the previous nanny's hasty departure. "Let's, uh . . . let's go find Violet."

I followed him as he walked deeper into the house, doing my best not to stare at his firm ass in the best pair of jeans I'd seen in my life. His long legs moved with a natural swagger, the kind that most attractive men must have been taught in college.

Maddox glanced over his shoulder.

I tore my eyes away, barely in time, before he busted me staring at his behind. "It's a beautiful house."

Smooth, Natalie. Really smooth.

"My dad built it."

I forced my gaze to the house and off the man. "He did a fantastic job."

The walls were painted a soft white. The decorative wood accents gave the tall, open spaces warmth. The windows were a feature on their own, providing views at every angle of the sprawling snow-covered property beyond the glass.

13

Maddox led me past a living room full of cozy leather pieces. Red embers glowed in the stone fireplace. Past the hearth, a sweeping staircase with a beautiful, spindled railing led to the second floor.

"I'll get you the gate code for tomorrow morning in case it's closed," Maddox said, glancing over his shoulder as we started up the steps.

"I parked in the front loop. Is that okay or would you prefer I park in a different spot?"

"The front is fine. Mom hired a chef for the week so there's no need to cook for Violet. If you have any dietary restrictions, just let him know."

"None unless vegetables count. I trade vegetables for Christmas cookies this time of year."

Maddox chuckled and the smile that stretched across his face nearly sent me careening over the banister. Straight white teeth. Full lips. A dimple. I'd forgotten about that dimple over the years.

Boss. He's my boss-ish. Which was why I only stared at his ass for three stairs instead of five. In my defense, it was at eye level.

The second floor was as beautiful as the first. At the top of the stairs, a balcony overlooked the living room. Plush carpets padded our footsteps as we walked down a hallway.

Maddox stopped at the third door. "Violet?"

The bedroom was bigger than my living room. A fluffy, white bed sat in the center of the room, draped with a gauze canopy. The toy chest against the wall was open and the floor littered with books and stuffed animals and . . . was that a Nerf gun?

Excellent. I'd expected Barbies but Nerf guns were much better. After years with boys, I'd become a self-proclaimed sharpshooter.

"Violet," Maddox called again.

No answer.

"She was just in here." His forehead furrowed. "Violet, if you're hiding, please come out."

Silence.

"Violet." He marched into the en suite bathroom, coming out seconds later to check under the bed. "Maybe she went to the kitchen."

I followed as he led the way to the main floor. We'd just reached the living room when a crash echoed through the house.

"Shit." Maddox's steps hastened down one more hallway.

The scent of sugar and vanilla hit my nose. Cake. Or cookies, but I was guessing cake. When it came to sweets, I was also a self-proclaimed expert.

We rounded a corner and stepped into a wide kitchen I suspected most restaurateurs would drool over. Standing in front of a cluttered island, a red-faced man in a chef's coat was wiping a glob of chocolate cake batter off his neck.

His nostrils flared. His gaze was narrowed on a girl in the middle of the room.

She wore a red tutu and matching glitter slippers. In one hand, she held a wooden spoon. In the other, a butcher's knife.

"You must be Violet," I said.

The angel.

CHAPTER 2
MADDOX

"Hey." Heath strolled into my office. Without knocking. Did he not see me on the phone?

I held up a finger as he plopped into a leather chair in the corner of the room.

"Let me know after you talk to the owner," I told my assistant. "I'm willing to sign a seven-year lease, but I'd prefer five. Push for that."

"You got it."

"Thanks, John. Have a merry Christmas."

"Same to you, Maddox."

I ended the call and pinched the bridge of my nose. This headache wasn't going away, even after two aspirin and a jug of water. The throb had bloomed beneath my temples at exactly the same time I'd found Violet in the kitchen.

With a goddamn knife.

After hours of endless calls and back-to-back meetings, the pain had only grown. It was rare that I came to Montana, and the last thing I wanted to do was spend my vacation working.

But there were tasks to be done. Too much work to finish if I was actually going to move here.

I was in the middle of determining where and when I could set up a satellite office for my company. The employees who'd been open to a move to Montana would need a work space. Then there was building a house for Violet and me.

If it all came together, soon, Montana wouldn't just be a vacation destination. It would be home.

And instead of bothering me with endless texts and phone calls, my brothers would be able to interrupt my day in person.

"What do you want?" I barked at Heath.

"Someone's in the holiday spirit."

I shot him a glare. "Seriously. I have a million things to do before I'm done today. State your business."

"Did you ask him?" Tobias strolled into the room with a stack of cookies in his hand. Again, without a knock.

"Give me one of those."

"Say please."

"Please." I snapped my fingers. "Now."

"You're in a mood today." Tobias crossed the room and handed over a chocolate crinkle.

"I have a headache, and today's been a train wreck." I sighed, taking a bite of the cookie, hoping some sugar would improve my outlook. Was it too early for a drink? One o'clock was, well . . . one o'clock. Technically, I was on vacation.

"What's going on?" Heath asked.

"I'm having a hell of a time finding office space that's big enough, nice enough and an owner who doesn't think that because he googled my net worth, I'm willing to pay LA prices in Montana."

I'd made the initial calls myself, but after the third property owner had quoted me an exorbitant price, I'd delegated the task to John.

"The nanny I'd brought with me from LA decided to quit and enjoy a nice holiday vacation this week. After I flew her up here in my jet. Oh, and this morning I found my daughter in the kitchen with a knife."

"That's why we're here." Tobias took the matching leather chair beside Heath's. The look the twins shared had me sitting straighter.

"What?"

"When did you hire Natalie Buchanan?"

I blinked. "The nanny?"

"Told you he didn't recognize her." Heath swiped a cookie from Tobias's hand, chomping on the gingersnap. "Natalie Buchanan. She was in our class. Nice but sort of nerdy back then."

She had looked familiar, with blue eyes that had instantly drawn me in. But I'd been too busy trying not to stare at her long, slender legs to place her face.

"Definitely not nerdy now," Tobias said. "I haven't seen her in ages. She looks good."

Good was one word. Beautiful was another. But she was my employee and there was no way I would make that comment aloud.

"Leave her alone," I ordered. "She's here to watch Violet. I'm out of options so unless you want to be saddled with babysitting your niece for the next week, don't bother Natalie."

"Babysit Violet? Oh, hell no." Heath shot out of his chair and, as quickly as he'd come into the office, he disappeared.

"What was that supposed to mean?"

Tobias's gaze dropped to the floor. Then, like Heath, Tobias scurried away too.

So maybe Violet wasn't exactly an easygoing child. She wasn't a typical girl either, one who played with dollhouses and Barbies and makeup—assuming that's what other seven-year-old girls did. Besides Violet, I didn't have experience with other children.

Hence the nannies.

A whole fucking string of nannies.

Not even professionals seemed to have the capacity to handle my daughter. If Natalie survived the week, I'd be impressed.

In the past year, I'd had thirty-two nannies. The longest had stayed with us for seven weeks, probably because I'd scaled down her duties significantly. All she'd had to do was walk Violet to school in the morning, pick her up each afternoon, then spend three hours with her until I'd come home at six.

Apparently, three hours had been too much because on the day she'd quit, the woman had filled twenty minutes telling me everything that was wrong with my child.

Spoiled.

Unruly.

Naughty.

Not a single nanny out of thirty-two had enjoyed spending time with my daughter. It was like taking that goddamn butcher's knife she'd had this morning to the heart.

Violet was . . . difficult. The divorce had taken its toll. She acted out more often than normal. I wasn't blind or deaf to her antics. I just didn't know how to fix it.

Hopefully moving to Montana would be part of the answer.

But we weren't here yet. And at the moment, I simply wanted to survive Christmas unscathed. With any luck, Natalie could stick it out with Violet, at least through Mom and Dad's party. Once the party was over on Christmas Eve, Mom would have more free time to pitch in. At this point, if Natalie made it through today before she quit, I'd take it.

She was probably going to quit.

Natalie Buchanan.

Huh. Out of context, I hadn't recognized her name. She'd been the nanny from the agency, nothing more. I preferred using agencies because they did all the necessary background checks to vet caregivers before they came into my home, and after thirty-two nannies, the names had begun to blur.

But now that Heath and Tobias had pointed out who she was, I felt like a fool for missing it. Why hadn't she told me?

I shoved away from my desk, knowing I didn't have time for anything but work and Violet, but I took a minute anyway. Mom kept all our old yearbooks in this office, organized by year on the bottom row of a bookshelf. I plucked my senior yearbook out and brought it back to my desk.

The spine cracked as I flipped it open. The pages smelled like my senior year—football fields and keggers and sweet anticipation for the future. As I scanned the pages, I let myself be eighteen again. I forgot the burdens of a thirty-two-year-old single father and escaped to a time when my biggest worries were next week's game and my upcoming calculus exam.

The pages turned heavily, clinging to each other like magnets. The stupid smile on my face spread as I got deeper into the book, seeing group photos and club activities, all captured on the pages.

Then there she was. Standing in the back row of a group photo for the ten-person swim team. *Natalie Buchanan.*

Yeah, I definitely should have remembered her. She was a woman now, but her blond hair was the same, and so were her eyes. The pretty blues stood out from the photo, an electric color like the bulbs Mom had strung on the mini-Christmas tree in my bedroom.

Every room in the house had a tree, each with varying colors of lights and decorations. It would take her a month to stow it away. Each year she'd cuss and promise never to do so much decorating, but each year after Thanksgiving, she'd send me pictures of the trees, one by one as she put them up.

Tonight when I went to sleep, that tree's glow would make me think of Natalie.

Exactly the wrong person to think of when I was in bed.

Natalie Buchanan.

Damn, but she did look good. As a teenager, she'd been cute. As a grown woman, she was a stunner. I took another long look at her smile in the club photo, then flipped to the sophomore section and found her picture.

She was wearing a black turtleneck, the exact opposite of what the girls I'd dated had worn back then. They'd all pushed the boundaries of the school's dress code, seeing just how low those V-necks could stretch before getting called into the principal's office.

Natalie's hair was different in this picture than in the swim-team photo. She had bangs that nearly covered her eyebrows and were chopped in a harsh, straight line. Her smile looked wobbly and her eyes were squinted.

Bless those school photographers. They had a true talent for bringing out every teenager's inner awkward.

My phone rang, pulling me away from the yearbook. I set it aside and fit my earbuds into my ears before diving back into my workday. Jumping from call to call, I spent the next few hours giving my team rapid-fire instructions and hoping that if I delegated enough, I could take at least one day off during this trip. At the very least, not spend my evenings answering emails.

My mother would string me up with my blue Christmas tree lights if I missed a dinner. Not just because Violet was the world's pickiest eater, but because I hadn't seen my parents enough these past seven years. Once we moved here, we'd be making up for lost time.

For all of us. I'd missed my parents and my brothers. And I wanted them to have a stronger bond with my daughter.

But first, I needed a place to live.

Yesterday, I'd put an offer on a lot outside of town. It was fifty acres, giving me plenty of space between neighbors and lots of room for Violet to roam. There was a pond and direct access to a secluded mountain hiking trail.

The moment I'd seen it, even covered in snow, I'd jumped.

Dad and I had stayed up late last night discussing possibilities for a floor plan. As soon as I had the property, he'd pull some strings to get a crew over and break ground.

"What did they counter with?" I asked my realtor. This was our second conversation today.

"They want full ask."

"Of course, they do," I grumbled.

Dollar signs had likely flashed in their eyes at my name. But I hadn't made over a billion dollars by letting people push me into unfair prices. "Offer it. Remind their realtor this is a cash offer with a short close. If they squabble about anything, I'll walk. There are plenty of parcels in the Gallatin Valley these days."

Even though this was the one I wanted.

"Exactly," she said. "This is a smart move, Maddox. Really brilliant."

I rolled my eyes. She worked for Mom's company and had been a major kiss ass. But she was getting the job done so I'd been ignoring her over-the-top compliments. If not for the super-sweet sugary tone, her compliment probably wouldn't have bothered me at all. I was used to it.

Cece had perfected that tone years ago. She'd use it right before dropping a bomb in my lap.

"Email me a list of other options, just in case."

"Of course."

"Thanks." I ended the call and set my phone aside.

My stomach growled and another cookie beckoned.

Time for a break. I rubbed the nape of my neck, trying to work out what felt like a permanent knot, then picked up the yearbook and returned it to Mom's shelf. But before I walked away, curiosity got the better of me. I pulled out Heath and Tobias's senior year album, flipping through the pages.

And there she was again, on another swim-team photo.

Natalie's bangs had disappeared on her journey from freshman to senior. She was in the back row, standing amongst the boys. She was taller than the other girls, something I'd noticed earlier.

I was six-three, and most women I knew, other than Mom, had to crane their necks to meet my gaze. Not Natalie.

She wore a simple one-piece suit in the photo. In the freshman team picture, they'd all been in matching sweats and hoodies. But this swimsuit . . .

It all clicked into place.

"Damn." I chuckled. Yeah, I remembered Natalie.

I hadn't spent a lot of time by the pool at our high school, but for a few weeks during senior year, the normal entrance to our locker rooms had been closed. Before football practice, we'd had to use the swim side entrance.

One day when I'd gone through, Natalie had been in the pool. As I'd walked by, she'd shoved up and out of the water and no straight seventeen-year-old boy would have passed her without a double take.

Trim figure. Lush breasts. Taut nipples from the cold air. She'd been in a black swim cap, probably to protect those bangs from turning green. Why I remembered that cap I wasn't sure. Maybe because it shouldn't have been hot. But it was. *She* was.

And now she was basically an employee.

I slammed the book closed and shoved it back in the shelf.

23

Then I squeezed my eyes shut to brandish the image of Natalie, my new nanny, out of my head.

Employee. Off-limits.

And this was not the time nor place to get twisted up by a woman. Dealing with Cece was enough of a migraine.

"Hey." Heath strode into the office, again without a knock. "What are you doing? You looked her up, didn't you?"

"Yeah." I stood and moved away from the bookshelf. "What are you doing?"

He lifted a shoulder. "Nothing today."

"Don't you have to work?"

"It's called vacation. V-A-C-A-T-I-O-N. Ever heard of it?"

"Vaguely." I sighed and took one of the leather chairs.

Heath took the seat next to mine, bringing the coffee mug he'd brought to his lips. "The chef made Tom and Jerrys."

"Later. Still have some work to do." My phone vibrated in my pocket and I took it out to see a text from the realtor. The sellers had accepted my offer on the lot. "Looks like I've got property in Montana."

"Nice. That place with the pond?"

"Yeah. Cost a fortune."

"You can afford it. Dad and I talked today. I'm going to run lead on your build, if that's okay with you."

I nodded. "You bet."

Both Heath and Tobias worked for Dad's company. Heath oversaw the actual builds. Tobias was an architect. The twins had inherited our father's talent for design and management, and one day, they'd take over as owners of Holiday Homes.

"Mom was gossiping earlier about Cece," he said.

"Oh, hell." I groaned. "What now?"

My mother hated my ex-wife, something she didn't try to hide from anyone but Violet.

"Cece posted some selfie on Instagram from a beach."

24

"Sounds like Cece." I'd had to unfollow my ex because seeing her jaunting around the globe on my dime while missing weekends with Violet had made me homicidal.

Part of what made this move to Montana so appealing was that Bozeman was thousands of miles away from the city and Cece.

After the divorce three years ago, I'd stayed in LA. Partly for work. Partly with hope that Cece would decide to become a mother. Clearly, I'd been delusional.

Cece cared about Cece and Cece alone.

Violet needed more than me and a parade of nannies. She needed family. My family. She needed consistent affection from grandparents. Teasing and horsing around with her uncles.

Mom and Dad were over the moon that we were moving home. My brothers were wary of Violet at the moment, but eventually they'd warm up to her. If I was raising Violet alone, I was doing it in Montana, and Cece couldn't do a damn thing about it. Not anymore.

She cared more about her divorce settlement than our daughter.

The two of us had married young, a couple months after I'd graduated from college. When I'd made the announcement, Dad had pulled me aside and begged me to get a prenup. Luckily, I'd agreed.

When Keith Maddox gave advice, you were smart to listen.

Maybe he'd known I'd been destined for success. Maybe he'd seen Cece's true colors. Maybe both. Whatever the reason, we'd had one drawn up before our wedding. Cece hadn't liked it but she'd signed—something my attorney had reminded hers during the divorce negotiation.

I'd earned billions of dollars, and she hadn't been able to touch a penny.

But the prenup hadn't mattered. She'd had leverage. Violet.

What should have been a simple divorce had turned into a long, painful argument because I'd refused to give her part-time custody of our daughter. Cece had been a part-time parent to Violet, at best, while we'd been married. She'd also had the help of nannies, chefs and housekeepers. She didn't have the skill or the desire to care for our child.

But in the end, she'd won.

I agreed to pay her a ridiculous lump sum if she agreed to giving me full custody.

From that moment on, the divorce had moved like a hot knife through butter. Once the papers were signed, I'd said goodbye to my wife. And Violet had watched her mother disappear.

The nannies I'd hired couldn't fill a mother's shoes. I knew that. It had just been a bandage over a gushing wound, and it was time to get out the gauze and staunch the flow.

Mom would help. Montana would help too.

"Is Violet excited to move?" Heath asked.

"Not really. She's angry that she has to make new friends. She's mad that she has to start at a new school. Honestly, I don't blame her. But every damn time Cece lets her down, it gets harder. We have to get out of LA."

"She'll adjust. It's only second grade."

"Try telling that to Violet."

"Ha. I don't think so. No offense, Maddox, but your kid scares the shit out of me."

I chuckled. "When I brought Natalie in and gave her the quick tour, Violet was in the kitchen. She'd *accidentally* spilled a bowl of cake batter, and she'd gone for the chef's butcher knife so she could cut herself a piece of apple pie."

"I'm surprised Natalie didn't run for the door."

"Me too," I admitted.

Instead, she'd calmly crossed the room with a smile and taken the knife from Violet's hand, all while the chef had been ranting about his cake batter and I'd been struck dumbfounded.

"It's my fault," I told Heath. "I am sucking at this father gig."

"You've got a lot on your plate."

"Too much." I couldn't run my company in LA and be the full-time father Violet needed at the same time. It was time to offload some responsibilities to my staff. They could handle it.

The team I was hoping to bring to Montana were my elite. Each would get a considerable moving bonus and annual salary bump. They might have to tear some tasks out of my grasp—I'd warned them as such—but they were extremely capable.

Violet needed me more than Madcast.

We still had to return to LA after the holidays. I'd lined up a new nanny to start once we got back to LA. Hopefully my vivacious, beautiful daughter wouldn't send her racing for the door. But maybe once we actually moved to Bozeman, I wouldn't find a replacement. Maybe it could just be the two of us for a change.

Plus a chef because I was hopeless in the kitchen.

"Maybe I will have a Tom and Jerry. Are they good?" I asked my brother.

Heath answered by handing over his mug.

I took a sip, coughing at the burn. "Damn. That's got a kick."

"I already called dibs on a downstairs guest room tonight. No way I'm driving home after a few of these."

I stood, ready to hit the kitchen for a cocktail and another cookie, when a loud crash echoed through the house.

Heath shot to his feet.

I froze, waiting for the inevitable.

A loud gasp. A scream. A string of expletives.

Nothing came.

The house went eerily quiet, which only made my terror spike.

"Uh . . ." Heath looked to me.

I bolted out of the office, with Heath not far behind, rushing toward the balcony that overlooked the living room.

And there she was.

My beautiful girl.

Violet stood on top of the coffee table. Her arms were crossed over her chest. There was a scowl twisting her lips and the glare in her eyes was one I hoped she would use to keep boys away when she turned sixteen.

At the moment, that angry stare was aimed at the nanny.

Natalie's blond hair and blue sweater were dripping with water. Shards of a shattered white vase were at her feet along with two dozen red roses.

Flowers that I'd ordered for my mother yesterday.

I didn't need to ask what had happened. My guess was that Violet had *accidentally* tipped that vase over Natalie's head.

"Violet," I hissed.

My daughter's eyes snapped up to mine. The scowl didn't disappear. She didn't even look sorry.

"See? She's terrifying," Heath whispered, putting his hand on my shoulder. "I'm locking my bedroom door tonight."

"You're not helping." I brushed off his touch and stormed down the stairs, unsure whether I was more embarrassed or furious. Mortification won out.

"Dad—"

"I'll discuss this with you later," I told my daughter, then focused on Natalie. "I'm so sorry. I'll pay you for the entire week. I'll contact the agency and make sure they understand that the reason this didn't work out was in no way your fault."

Natalie, who had been staring at Violet as I spoke, finally

28

shifted her gaze. Those blue eyes met mine and the air rushed from my lungs. Not from the beauty of her face, but the smile that stretched across her mouth.

Though breathtaking, that smile was laced with malice. With revenge.

A wolf in a sexy nanny's body.

"Oh, I'm not leaving," she said, arching an eyebrow.

"You're not?"

"Nope." Natalie locked her own glare with Violet's, and in the space that separated them, the battle line was drawn.

Natalie reached for the hem of her sweater, dragging the soaked top off her body. Underneath she wore a thin white tank top that molded to her breasts and flat stomach. It was nearly as skintight as the wet swimsuit I'd seen her in years ago.

"Violet and I were just getting to know each other. Weren't we, Violet?"

Before my daughter could answer, Natalie rolled up her sweater, twisting it into a rope.

Then she raised her arms and wrung it out.

Over my daughter's head.

CHAPTER 3

NATALIE

"How did yesterday go?" Cathy asked, her voice booming through the Subaru's speakers.

"Great," I lied. "She's a sweetie."

Violet was a tutu-toting terrorist, but there was no way in hell a seven-year-old girl was going to best me.

That little brat.

Violet and I had ended yesterday in war.

I was still a bit mystified at the kid's strength. She'd picked up that full vase, water and all, and had *accidentally* dumped it on me. It was a miracle I hadn't gotten a thorn in my eye.

She'd bested me yesterday. I'd give her the point. But today, I was coming prepared. That was . . . if I'd be allowed to watch her again. Maddox might banish me from his parents' home, and though I'd hate not seeing him again, I wouldn't be heartbroken. I'd find another way to pay for Magdalena's repairs.

After the red roses incident yesterday, he'd stared at me like he'd seen the Ghost of Christmas Past. Immediately after I'd wrung my turtleneck out over Violet's head, she'd stomped upstairs in a furious flurry. I'd managed to force a polite smile for Maddox, all too aware that my white camisole had left little to the imagination, then had followed his daughter, soggy sweater in hand.

When five o'clock had rolled around, he'd found us both at the small table in Violet's room. She'd been coloring in a Santa book, holding the crayons so fiercely she'd broken the entire collection of reds.

Maddox had offered to walk me to the door, but I'd told him I could find my own way out. Then with a saccharine-sweet farewell to Violet, I'd escaped to the safety of my own home where I'd had to watch *Home Alone* twice to improve my mood. If I did get fired today, I'd already queued up *The Polar Express* and a pint of ice cream.

"Did you hear anything from Mr. Holiday?" I asked. Like how I'd lost my temper and drenched his daughter in rose-stem water.

"Uh, no. Should I expect to?"

"Nope," I said, too brightly. "It's all good."

"Thanks again for doing this. I'm off tomorrow and Saturday for Christmas but you have my cell if you need anything."

"Will do. Merry Christmas."

"Merry Christmas."

I ended the call, continuing down the road and turning onto the Holidays' private lane. The house was as impressive today as it had been yesterday, and when I parked in the front loop, I took a moment to appreciate the details I'd missed yesterday. The copper gutters. The carved gables. The driveway—heated, judging by the lack of snow and wisps of steam rising from the black surface.

What would it be like to have that kind of money? I doubted I'd ever know and that was all right by me. I'd grown up in a normal, three-bedroom, two-bathroom home full of love and laughter. That was a currency of its own, and in that regard, I was a wealthy woman.

Not that the Holiday house wasn't full of love. Yesterday, I'd bumped into both Heath and Tobias. With Bozeman growing like it was and our social circles running in opposite directions, I hadn't seen either of them in years.

The twins, like Maddox, had grown from the lanky boys I'd remembered in high school to incredibly handsome men, though not quite as good-looking as their older brother.

I climbed out of Dad's car, instantly missing the heated seats. Barney or Barley was growing on me with his modern comforts. *I still love you, Magdalena. Always.*

My breath billowed in a cloud as I opened the back door and retrieved my tote bag. The zipper bulged at the seam. This morning, I'd loaded every trick in my arsenal.

Bring it, Violet.

Squaring my shoulders, I headed for the porch, about to ring the bell when the heavy walnut door flung open and there he was.

Hello, Maddox Holiday.

Damn, but he was gorgeous.

"Morning," he said.

"Morning. Are you going to fire me?"

He laughed and that dazzling white smile with the dimple appeared. The flock of Christmas carolers who took up residence in a corner of my mind this time of year chorused, "Hal-le-lu-jah."

"Honestly, I'm in a bit of shock." He held the door for me as I stepped inside.

"So the jury's still out on me being fired?" I set my tote down to strip off my coat and hang it on a hook.

"No, shocked that you came back. Each one of your predecessors would have bailed."

"I'm not the bailing type. And today, I came prepared." I hefted up my bag and smacked its side.

"My parents are here today." Maddox led us to the living room. "I suspect my brothers will be around whenever their stomachs drive them here for sustenance. I'll be in the office most of the day but am available if you need anything."

"I'm sure we'll be fine. Where is Violet?" *Come out, come out, little one. It's time to play.*

Like she heard my silent summons, Violet trudged into the room. No tutu today. Instead she was wearing a pair of jeans and a fuzzy red sweater.

Red was most definitely her color, and not because there was a real possibility that she was Lucifer's spawn. It brought out the milk-chocolate strands in her long, brown hair. Her blue eyes popped, just like her father's. She'd be the most beautiful child in the world if not for that epic scowl.

We'd work on fixing that today.

"Hi, Violet." I smiled.

She glared.

I had to give this kid props. She was a formidable opponent, but I was not your typical nanny. I liked to think that Dad had raised me tougher than your average caretaker.

"Violet, Natalie said hello," Maddox said, a warning in his tone.

She crossed her arms over her chest and gave a harrumph.

Maddox's gaze, full of remorse, met mine.

"Don't worry." I winked. "We'll be fine."

"I can get my mom—"

"Nope." I cut him off when I saw a glint of hope in Violet's gaze. This was exactly what she wanted. "All good here. I'm here"—I locked eyes with Violet—"for the whole day. All. Day. Long."

Maddox looked between the two of us. "Um . . ."

"Should we head up to your room, Violet? I brought some things with me."

She glared at my bag. "What things?"

I didn't bother answering. I simply turned and walked to the staircase, my chin held high. When I heard the smack of her shoes on the wooden stairs behind me, I knew I'd won.

Maddox stared at us from the living room, his hands on his hips and a look of befuddlement on his handsome face.

Poor guy. His kid was walking all over him with those glitter slippers.

Yesterday, Violet had informed me that they were moving to Montana. She hadn't seemed happy about it. Maybe that was the reason for this attitude. Maybe it was Maddox's work schedule. Or maybe she was just used to getting her way.

Well, not with me. Not this week.

We reached the top of the stairs and headed down the hallway toward Violet's bedroom when a woman emerged from another room. I recognized Hannah Holiday immediately, not only from the plethora of real estate signs around town but from the woman I remembered cheering for her sons at high school football and basketball games.

She'd never once forgotten to bring an air horn.

"Oh, hello." She smiled. "You must be Natalie."

"I am." I smiled back. "We never formally met, but I graduated with Heath and Tobias."

"Yes, of course." Hannah nodded. "They told me last night. We had to get out the yearbooks."

"Ooof. Please tell me you didn't see evidence of the bang-pocalypse my sophomore year." And please tell me Maddox wasn't there too.

"That's an awkward age for everyone, dear."

I laughed as Violet stepped up to us, staring back and forth as we spoke.

Hannah touched her granddaughter's shoulder. "Baby, why don't you go get out something to play with while I visit with Natalie for a minute."

"But, Nana—"

"Off you go."

Violet frowned but obeyed.

When she disappeared into her bedroom, Hannah blew out a long breath. "That girl."

"She's got spirit."

"Ha!" Hannah laughed. "You're so polite."

"Who's polite?" Keith came striding our way from behind Hannah. He saluted me with his coffee cup. "Morning. You must be Natalie."

"Guilty."

"Good for you yesterday," he said. "I wish I would have been here to see it. Violet can be a little shi—"

"Keith." Hannah's elbow jabbed her husband's side.

"Hey." He frowned at his wife. "Sorry. What I meant to say was that Violet needs someone who will give her a dose of her own, er . . . sass."

"I might have gotten a little carried away."

He chuckled. "Nah."

"Okay." Hannah checked her watch, then looked to Keith. "We'd better get going. Our meeting is at nine and I want to swing by the office first."

"Every year I swear it's our last Christmas party and every year she convinces me to do it again." Keith sighed. "Good luck today, Natalie."

"Same to you." I smiled, then headed to Violet's room. No surprise, I caught her sprinting away from the doorway where she'd been eavesdropping. "I brought something for you."

"I don't want it." She plopped down at her desk and plucked a red marker from the pile. Then she began drawing.

On. The. Table.

Those markers were washable and it wouldn't take more than a wet cloth to clean the surface, but when her blue eyes flickered my way, I shrugged, feigning indifference as I went to the bed, sat down and unzipped my bag.

The contents were irresistible, even to the most difficult of children.

"Fine by me." I dug through the tote, shoving aside the jigsaw puzzle, the Lego set and the teacups. I went straight for my favorite treasure at the bottom.

Violet spotted it as I tugged it free. She gasped.

Victory. Sweet, sweet victory.

"Hello? Anyone in here?" Maddox called as his knuckles rapped on the doorway to Violet's room.

I glanced up from the book we were reading as Maddox flipped open the flap of our tent and bent to look inside.

"Hey, Daddy." Violet smiled. "We built a tent."

"Hey, beautiful. It looks great."

"We'd better get started cleaning it up." I closed the book and set it aside. Then nudged Violet. "Ready?"

She nodded and crawled out first.

I collected the other books we'd been reading, or having Violet read to me for practice, then joined her and Maddox outside the tent.

"Are you done working?" Violet asked him.

He nodded, his gaze skeptical as he looked between the two of us. "Uh . . . yeah. I'm done."

"Can we do something fun?"

"Sure." He kept looking between us, the crease between his

eyebrows deepening. Even I was a little shocked at how quickly Violet's attitude had changed.

I'd won our war using the oldest trick in the book.

Good, old-fashioned bribery.

"Let's clean up first," I told Violet. "Then I'll get out of here."

"Okay." She immediately went to work, dismantling the blankets we'd hauled out of the closet.

Hannah had come in mid-construction and given us extra sheets. That had been after a delightful lunch of grilled cheese and tomato bisque made by the chef.

As Violet and I had sat at the dining room table, eating in comfortable silence, both Hannah and Keith had joined us. Not long after, Heath and Tobias had arrived for a meal. The only Holiday missing had been Maddox.

The looks of sheer amazement at Violet's behavior had been a balm to my soul.

Had I worked a Holiday miracle? *Yes. Yes, I had.*

The satisfaction of taming Violet was nearly worth as much as I was being paid for this job.

Maddox joined to help tear apart the tent, folding a blanket beside me. He leaned in close to whisper, "There are no missing limbs. And no blood. I was expecting blood."

I grinned and picked up one of the pillows we'd been using as our tent floor. "Not today."

Assembling the tent had taken an hour. Dismantling less than ten minutes.

When it was done, Maddox bent to kiss his daughter's hair. "How was your day?"

"Fun." She looked up to me, and I gave her a wink. "Can we go in the hot tub?"

"Yes, but not until after dinner."

Violet frowned. "But—"

I cleared my throat and that frown disappeared.

She shot me a look, then muttered, "Okay."

Maddox's mouth fell open.

"Thanks for a fun day, Violet. I'll see you after Christmas."

"With your bag."

I nodded. "With my bag."

"Okay, good. Daddy, can I have some screen time?"

"Go ahead. Your iPad is in the theater room."

Violet raced away without a backward glance.

"What did you do with my real daughter and can we keep the imposter for the night?"

I laughed and walked to the bed to pick up my bag. With it slung over my shoulder, I patted its side. "Bribery works nine out of ten times."

"What's in there?"

"I'll never tell." I zipped my lips shut, then headed for the door.

"You're really not going to tell me?" Maddox asked, catching up to me in the hallway.

"Nope." I smirked. "That's between Violet and me."

"Today seemed to go better."

"Second days usually do. She's a good kid. The feisty ones are always the most fun."

Maddox stopped, his jaw slackened.

"What?" I slowed.

He swallowed hard. "You're the first nanny to ever tell me she was a good kid."

"Seriously?" My heart squeezed. That was, well . . . awful.

"Seriously." He pressed a hand to his heart and the smile he gave me was blinding.

"Oh." A blush crept into my cheeks. "Well, she is. But can I give you some unsolicited advice? You can say no."

"Please."

I didn't want to overstep, but today had been surprisingly easy. Wrangling Violet hadn't been the challenge I'd expected. Yes, I'd bribed her all morning, but along with each reward had come some firm and unwavering rules. She'd followed them without fail. Not only was she spirited, but that girl was incredibly smart.

"She has so much potential. She's funny and witty and thoughtful. She notices more than most kids her age. And she has these sweet moments when she just melts your heart."

Maddox beamed under his daughter's praise.

"But . . ."

Off went the light.

"She wants attention. She needs boundaries. And she's maybe a little . . . spoiled."

He raked a hand through his hair. "That's my fault. I don't spend enough time with her, and so during the time we do have, I can't seem to tell her no."

"I get it. I've worked for a lot of parents with demanding careers."

"What did they do?"

"Hired me, of course," I teased. "I don't have the answer. One of the moms I worked for would cook dinner with her kids every Friday night. Another family had game night on Tuesdays. It doesn't have to be all day, every day. Just something special that you stick to. Find out what works for you and Violet."

"I will." He nodded. "Thanks. For today and for the advice."

We walked down the hallway toward the staircase. As soon as we reached the balcony, the scent of fresh pine from the Christmas tree filled my nose. Mixed with Maddox's spicy cologne, the combination was intoxicating. My fingers glided over the smooth handrail, and for just a moment, I let myself pretend that he remembered me.

"I was hoping to ask you for a favor," Maddox said as he escorted me to the door.

"What favor?" I plucked my coat from a hook and pulled it on. Unless he asked me to give up sugar in December, whatever favor he asked for—sexual or not—would likely be met with a resounding yes.

"Tomorrow night is my family's annual Christmas party downtown. Mom and Dad invite a ton of their friends. They normally host it the week before Christmas, but the place was booked for a wedding, so the timing worked out that this year it falls on Christmas Eve. I guess enough of their friends didn't mind so they went ahead and scheduled it. I haven't been home for the party in years, but it means a lot to them. And I'd really like it to go off without a hitch."

"You need someone to watch Violet."

"Please." Oh, God, he was giving me the *save-me-Natalie* eyes. How was I supposed to say no to that look?

"I know you're under no obligation to help, but I don't know anyone else. There will be a lot of people who want my attention at the party, and I heard you a few minutes ago. Violet needs my attention too. But this party . . . I'll be swarmed. Everyone will want to know about why I'm moving home and what I'll be doing with my business. I don't want Violet to have to hang by my side, bored to tears the whole time. She's never been to this party either and I'd like her to have a good time. And, uh . . . there was an incident."

"Uh-oh."

"Full disclosure. Last year, I took Violet to a New Year's Eve party in LA. It was the same situation. I was bombarded and she snuck away to the kitchen. She pulled over an entire rack filled with three hundred crème brûlées."

"Eek."

"Ask me if we were invited back this year."

I giggled. "Your kid has style, I'll give her that."

"Just a few hours."

Christmas Eve was my least favorite non-holiday, holiday. Usually I'd spend time with my family, but Christmas Eve typically involved a last-minute trip to the mall and I'd spend hours being bumped into by husbands who'd forgotten to buy their wives gifts.

So many people loved the anticipation that came with Christmas Eve. Me? Not so much.

I was patient in many ways, but when it came to gifts and orgasms, I preferred instant gratification.

As tempting as Dad's famous Cheez Whiz charcuterie board was not, a fancy downtown soiree might make Christmas Eve bearable. I'd heard about the Holiday Christmas party for years but had never been invited. And this year, Maddox Holiday himself was asking me to attend.

Yeah, it was as the hired help but fourteen-year-old me didn't give a crap about that detail.

For her, this would practically be a prom date.

"Do I get to wear a fancy dress?"

"If that makes you happy, then yes. If that makes you lean toward a no, then wear pajamas and slippers."

"I like fancy dresses." It wasn't uncommon for clients to ask me to attend special events. I happened to have a few dresses that I'd bought for those rare occasions and each was collecting dust in my closet.

The corner of his mouth turned up. "Seven o'clock. The Baxter."

"I'll see you there." I reached for the doorknob, but Maddox beat me to it, brushing my knuckles with his fingertips. Sparks flew beneath my skin. The air crackled between us.

He stilled, his eyes finding mine. Then they dropped, tracing the line of my nose before landing on my mouth. His Adam's apple bobbed.

We stood there, too close for a moment too long, until he cleared his throat, and I pulled my hand away, ducking my chin to hide my smile.

Maddox Holiday had just stared at my lips, and unless my radar was broken—it might be—he'd felt the sparks too.

Teenage Natalie did a fist pump.

Adult Natalie smacked teenage Natalie's hand.

You're his employee. Sort-of employee. There were boundaries I wouldn't cross. Not again.

The cool air from outside was welcome on my overheated cheeks as he opened the door. I expected him to wave from the porch, but instead he fell into step beside me as we walked to my car. He even opened the back door for me to stow my bag.

"See you tomorrow, Nat. Everyone used to call you Nat, right?"

"They did. Your mom said you guys went through old yearbooks last night. Did your brothers tell you that?"

"No." He tapped his temple and smiled that sexy smile. His dimple appeared and my heart did a cartwheel in the snow. "Tomorrow."

Tomorrow.

One word and I was already starting to like this Christmas Eve.

CHAPTER 4
MADDOX

"Which tie, princess?" I held up a black one and a red one.

Violet immediately pointed to the red—no surprise.

"Red it is." I laid it on my bed beside the suit she'd picked out, then checked the clock. I needed to get in the shower but I wanted to make sure Violet was ready for tonight first. "Let's do your hair. Then I'll get ready too."

"Are there going to be any other kids there tonight?" she asked as I steered her down the hallway toward her bedroom.

"I think so. And Natalie will be there with us. Nana and Papa. Uncle Heath and Uncle Tobias. It's usually a lot of fun."

"Can I stay up late?"

"Definitely. And you can have extra dessert."

"Yessss." She clapped and skipped ahead to her room.

She was wearing a red dress with roses on the wide collar. The front hem was cut higher than the back, and she'd chosen her gold glitter shoes in place of her favorite red.

She looked beautiful.

She looked grown up.

While I'd been working my ass off, my daughter had become this young person. This incredible, smart young person. No longer a baby. No longer a toddler. She was simply . . . my Violet.

We'd spent the day together today and the realization that I'd missed out on too much had hit me like a freight train. A change was overdue.

When I reached the bathroom, I found her standing by the vanity, running a brush through her hair. She didn't need me to comb out the strands anymore. She didn't need me to prop her on the counter so she could see in the mirror. She didn't need me to help her brush her teeth.

I choked on the lump in my throat that had been there since breakfast. "I had fun with you today."

"Me too." She smiled. I'd seen more of those smiles in the past twelve hours than I'd seen in twelve months.

Natalie had been right. Violet needed my attention, and I needed, well . . . Violet.

My daughter wasn't the only one who'd smiled more today.

We'd gone out to breakfast at a diner on Main. We'd ventured to a few shops, braving the Christmas Eve crowds to shop for some last-minute gifts. Then we'd spent the rest of the day doing whatever Violet had wanted.

She'd showed me some of her favorite YouTube videos on the iPad. We'd devoured a dozen Christmas cookies—next week I'd have to add thirty minutes to my daily workouts to burn them off. We'd played checkers. We'd started a jigsaw puzzle. We'd hit the hot tub and played pool in the game room.

"What are we doing with your hair?" I took the brush from her hand and ran it through her tresses.

Cece had always done Violet's hair. She'd also picked out our daughter's clothes. Violet's appearance was the one thing that Cece had seemed interested in when it came to our child. It was the reason Violet loved red so much. Cece had always found Violet red clothes. Even now, the rare gifts she'd send were typically red. Though the last two dresses had been in the wrong size.

But Violet hadn't cared that they'd been too small. And every time I brought home an outfit in blue or green or pink, I'd earn a scowl and a glare.

Fucking Cece.

She hadn't called once in the past week. I doubted she remembered that tomorrow was Christmas. There'd be no gift for Violet waiting under the tree from her mother.

For the past couple of years, I'd wrapped a present and had labeled it from Cece. I'd made sure the paper and bow were different than anything my assistant had put on the gifts I'd bought.

This year . . . I hadn't had the energy.

I wasn't going to keep pretending that Cece gave a shit, because in the end, I was only delaying the inevitable. Sooner than later, Violet would realize that her mother wasn't interested in her life. I could probably put it off for a few more years, but the hurt was coming, one way or another.

Now that we were moving to Montana, it was time to stop pretending.

Cece wasn't here to do Violet's hair. But I was. And damn it, I'd do everything in my power to be enough.

"I could dig the curling iron out of the suitcases," I said.

Violet's eyes widened in the mirror.

"Okay, no curling iron." The last time I'd tried, there'd been a near-burn incident. "How about a twist?"

In the past couple of years, I'd watched countless videos on how to do braids and twists. While curling-iron skills evaded me, I could wield a bobby pin like a pro.

"Nana bought me a tiara. Can I wear it with a twist?" she asked.

"Sure."

Off she raced into her bedroom, coming back moments later with a smile as bright as the crystals on the tiara. I got to work with the pins, taking strands of her thick, dark hair—my hair—and twisting them up onto the crown of her head. Then when all of the pieces were secure, I placed the tiara.

"Well?"

She turned her face, looking at both sides, then gave me the nod of approval. "I like it."

"Good." If that hairdo lasted all night, I'd be shocked. "So before we go to the party, I have a question for you."

"What?"

"Will you make me a deal?"

"What kind of deal?"

I picked her up and set her on the bathroom counter. "No trouble tonight. This is something Nana and Papa do every year and it means a lot to them. Please be good and listen to Natalie."

"Okay," she muttered.

"Thank you." I kissed her forehead.

"Is Natalie going to be my new nanny when we move here?"

"No." Though I'd already contemplated asking the agency if she was available. Violet had dropped her name a few times today as we'd played, which had never happened with another nanny. Violet seemed to forget them the minute they walked out the door. "She's just hanging out with us for Christmas."

"Oh." She dropped her gaze to her lap.

"Do you want her to be your new nanny?"

Violet shrugged.

That shrug was the equivalent to a five-star review. Natalie had clearly made an impression. On us both.

She'd been on my mind nearly all day. The softness in her blue eyes. The sweet smile. Her musical laugh. Foolish as it was, I couldn't wait to see her tonight.

"Daddy?" Violet peeked up at me from beneath her lashes.

"Violet."

"Is Mommy moving here with us?"

Hell. I hated Cece for making me answer this question. "No, honey. She's not moving here. It will just be us."

"Hmm." She looked to the brush on the countertop, staring at her own hairs stuck in its teeth.

"Do you like it here?" In all the months I'd been planning this, I hadn't asked my daughter if she enjoyed Montana. Here she was, screaming for attention, and I was so busy planning a relocation that I hadn't noticed.

"It's okay."

"We'll be closer to Nana and Papa."

She nodded. "I like their hot tub."

"What if we didn't have a nanny when we moved here? What if we had more days like today?"

Her eyes flew to mine and the hope in them nearly broke my heart. "Really?"

"You might have to have babysitters if I get super busy. And you might have to spend some days with Nana and Papa because they get lonely for you. But most days, it will just be me and you. What do you think?"

"Do I have to go to school?"

I chuckled. "Yes, you have to go to school."

"I don't have any friends here."

"I know." I touched a fingertip to her nose. "But you'll make new friends. Great friends."

"Maddox?" My mother's voice carried from the hallway.

47

"In here, Mom." I lifted Violet off the counter, then we headed out to meet my mom.

"Oh, look at you." Mom clutched her hands to her heart when she saw Violet. "You look beautiful, darling."

"Thanks, Nana." Violet beamed and touched her tiara.

"You look gorgeous, Mom." I leaned in to kiss her cheek. She was wearing a pretty green dress with a matching jacket, embroidered with a shimmery thread of the same color. Her hair was pinned back, much like Violet's, and her makeup flawless.

"Thank you." Mom cupped my cheek, then she realized I was wearing jeans and a long-sleeved T-shirt. "You're not dressed. Why are you not dressed? We're leaving in thirty minutes."

"Don't worry, I'll be ready." I winked at Violet, then left her with Mom while I rushed to my bathroom for a quick shower and a shave. Dressed in my black suit, I knotted my tie and made it downstairs with five minutes to spare.

"We'll drive separately," I told Mom and Dad.

"See you there." Dad nodded and headed for the garage. Violet and I were close behind him, going to the Audi SUV I'd rented for this trip.

"Wait for me." Heath appeared in the doorway, a beer in hand. He dropped the bottle in the trash can, then rounded the Audi's hood for the passenger side. "You're my DD tonight."

"What's a DD?" Violet asked from her booster seat in the back.

"Something I'll teach you about when you're older," I answered.

Heath twisted in his seat, giving Violet a grin and fist bump. "Excited for tonight?"

"Yes," she answered.

"How about you, brother?"

"I am." This was the first time in years I was truly looking forward to a party. My family was one reason. Natalie was another.

"Heard you took a day off," Heath said. "How'd that treat you?"

"Not bad. Thinking of making a habit of it."

"Yeah?"

"It's time. And someone told me about this new thing. They call it vacation."

He chuckled. "Good advice. I bet that someone is ridiculously smart. And handsome. And hung like a—"

I smacked his shoulder. "Young ears."

"Sorry. In all seriousness. Are you really going to step back?"

"Yeah. I am." I'd made billions of dollars in my short career. My team was talented and capable, but even if the wheels came off the bus, if it crashed and burned, it didn't really matter.

My financial future was locked in. So was Violet's.

"I can't keep working like this," I confessed, glancing to the rearview mirror. "It's not fair to her."

"Listen, I think it's great you're coming home. We've all missed you these past seven years, especially Mom and Dad. They think *you know who* is Satan's mistress for trapping you in California."

"They're not wrong," I muttered.

While we'd been married, Cece hadn't enjoyed visiting Bozeman. Even after the divorce, my infrequent visits to Montana hadn't been enough, and with Mom and Dad's busy careers, it was hard for them to get to LA more than two or three times a year.

"But . . ." Heath said, his tone growing serious. "Before you come up here, I need to ask you an important question."

"Okay," I drawled.

49

"Can you get me early access to the last season of *State of Ruin*?"

I chuckled. "It's really good. I watched the final episode on the flight here."

"I need it." Heath groaned. "Please? I have not once played the brother card. But I'm calling it in."

"Consider it your Christmas present. But don't tell anyone."

"Yes." He grinned. "I'm binging tomorrow unless I'm too hungover to function."

My company, Madcast, produced and distributed *State of Ruin*. We were the fastest growing streaming video service in the world.

My lucky break had come my senior year in college when I'd been out at a bar, drinking at some run down joint and bull-shitting with the guy on a stool beside mine. He'd turned out to be one of the most famous directors in Hollywood.

He'd told me about a screenplay that he'd drafted, but no matter who he'd pitched it to, the major media companies weren't buying. They'd wanted him as a director, not a writer, but screenwriting had been his passion.

When I'd gotten a full-ride academic scholarship to UCLA, Mom and Dad had gifted me my college tuition. Responsible kid that I'd been, I'd saved most of it.

A magazine reporter who'd interviewed me a few years ago had written that it had been divine intervention that I hadn't spent that money. Because instead of blowing it on a car and spring-break vacations, I'd used it to buy that screenplay and the rights to the show. I'd also partnered with the director to make a low-budget version of season one.

It had gone viral and been picked up by one of my current competitors. They'd done well on it. The director and I had both made money from the sale. He'd gone on to other projects while I'd taken that money and used it as the seed for Madcast.

Fast-forward seven years from that conversation in the bar, and we'd had countless hits in all the major genres—drama, documentaries, comedy, children, romance. *State of Ruin*, a worldwide phenomenon, was poised to be our biggest show yet. If you wanted the best of the best film and television entertainment, you paid Madcast eleven ninety-nine a month for a subscription.

We'd become a publicly traded company three years ago and our stock price was at its highest value yet. I was the majority shareholder and CEO.

Some people said I had a gift for choosing projects. Mostly, I selected the ones that sounded like something I'd watch. I'd read books and buy the film rights because even though I loved TV, books were almost always better. That, and there was an endless supply of incredible stories waiting for the screen. My team helped fill in the gaps as they had damn good taste too.

Moving away from California was a risk. I'd miss the day-to-day happenings at headquarters, but I'd regret missing Violet's life even more. If the board had a problem with me in this new satellite office, I'd step down as CEO and let someone else run the show.

There were countless opportunities for a man with my wealth. Leaving Madcast would be hard as hell, but I'd start something new in Bozeman if I had to.

"So, Violet." Heath twisted in his seat to talk over his shoulder. "Nana told me that Natalie brought you a bag of secrets yesterday. Want to tell me what was in the bag?"

"No." She stared out her window.

"Come on. Tell me," Heath begged.

She zipped her lips closed, just like Natalie had done.

"It's no use." I laughed at Heath's frown. Whatever Natalie

had done to get Violet's silence and loyalty had been ironclad. "Trust me. I asked her no less than fifty times today and she's not talking."

"Natalie's a magician," Heath said, dropping his voice.

"You're not wrong."

He rubbed his hands together as we approached Main Street. "I love this party."

Glittering garlands were strung over the street. Trees glowed with their strings of white lights. Stores were decked out for the season. There was truly nothing like a Christmas in Bozeman. With any luck, we wouldn't be missing any more.

"I wonder who will cause the drama this year," Heath said.

"Maybe there won't be drama."

"There'd better be." He scoffed. "That's the best part of the party."

I shook my head, smiling, and pulled into a parking lot. Then we all piled out and, with Violet's hand in mine, headed toward the hotel.

"Excited?" I asked her.

She nodded, her eyes wide and full of wonder as she took it all in. As we walked through the hotel's gold and glass doors, she squeezed my hand tighter.

The lobby of The Baxter was bustling with people, some going into the adjoining restaurants. Others stood at the small bar, laughing and talking with a festive cocktail in their hands.

I shrugged off my coat and helped Violet out of hers. With them draped over my arm, I stood straight, ready to head upstairs where the party was held. But when I looked up, the sight that greeted me sent my jaw to the marble floor.

Natalie was descending the grand staircase that led to the second-floor ballroom.

She was definitely not in pajamas. Her strappy heels sank into the plush maroon carpet covering each step. Her decadent body was wrapped in a fitted black gown that hugged her slight curves. A slit ran up the gown's side, showcasing one toned leg with miles of smooth skin.

Other than that slit, the dress was simple, with long sleeves and a high neckline. On any other woman, it would have been demure.

On Natalie, it was pure sin.

My mouth went dry.

It had been a long, long time since the mere sight of a woman rendered me speechless.

"I should have paid more attention to Nat in school," Heath whispered at my side, his eyes locked on her bare thigh. He took one step, ready to pounce, but my hand shot out and grabbed his elbow.

"Don't even think about it. She's mine." The claim blurted from my mouth before my brain could engage.

A slow grin spread across his face. "Gotcha. I wondered if you might have a thing for her."

"There's no thing." *Shit.* "She's . . . my nanny."

"Right. Whatever you say, brother." He'd heard the possession in my voice. The claim. Backtracking was pointless.

"Good luck." Heath clapped me on the shoulder, then jogged up the stairs, giving Natalie a smile and nod as he passed.

She reached the bottom step and walked toward us. It took considerable effort not to drool over the silhouette of her body and that damn leg that peeked through with every other one of her graceful strides.

The blood rushed to my cock and I shifted, holding the coats over my groin in an attempt to hide the growing bulge behind my pants. *Christ.*

She was the nanny. This was a business relationship only, and for my daughter's sake, one I couldn't afford to fuck up.

The moment we got up the stairs, I'd let her take Violet and I'd get a strong drink. Just one so I could drive us home later. Or fuck it, maybe I'd get smashed and we'd catch a ride with my parents.

Natalie smiled as she came closer, which only made my arousal grow.

Drunk. Definitely drunk. Maybe that would help me control this urge to sink my lips onto hers.

"Hello." She waved at me, then gave her undivided attention to my daughter. "You look beautiful, Violet."

"Thanks." Violet did a half twirl, twisting so her skirt would sway. She looked up to me and nodded toward the enormous tree in the corner and the bowl of candy canes being pilfered by the other kids in the lobby. "Can I go look at the tree?"

"Sure. Come right back."

Violet nodded, then darted away.

Natalie stood and took me in. Her gaze stopped on my throat, like she could see my heart stuck there.

When her hand came out to straighten the knot on my tie, I lost the battle with my will. "You look magnificent."

"Thank you." Her cheeks flushed. "It's fun to get dressed up."

"Fun is not the word I'd use for that dress." Sexy. Stunning. Maybe fun if I was the man stripping it from her body.

Natalie tucked a lock of hair behind her ear, pulling her lips in to hide a smile. "You're looking pretty sharp yourself, Mr. Holiday."

Mr. Holiday. My last name had never sounded so good. "Maddox."

"Maddox."

God, this woman. How had she not called me by my name? Now I wanted to hear her say it over and over, preferably while she was naked in my bed.

Fuck my life. I'd just broken my own damn rule. Never in my life had I flirted with a nanny. There'd never been a desire. But Natalie didn't fit the typical mold.

She was sassy. Smart. Sexy. And she liked my kid.

Maybe I should have felt guilty for this attraction.

I didn't.

Instead, I waited for Violet to come back from the tree, then offered Natalie my arm. "Shall we?"

CHAPTER 5

NATALIE

This was so surreal. It wasn't a date. *It's not a date.* The hours spent repeating that sentence while getting dressed up for the party had worked. When I'd showed up at The Baxter, I'd been ready for an evening shift with Violet.

But then Maddox had strolled through the doors with that confident, sexy swagger. One glance at him in that tailored suit and I'd skyrocketed to fantasyland. The man was so hot he could turn the lobby's Christmas tree into kindling with a single sultry look.

This was not a date.

But what if it was? I was giving myself the climb to the second floor to pretend.

The heat from his arm radiated through his jacket as we ascended the staircase. Never in my life had I thought I'd be walking into a party on Maddox's arm.

With every step, I felt the pressure of eyes aimed our way. Maddox was a billionaire, and even though he didn't live in

Bozeman, his success made him a local celebrity in his small hometown.

A quick glance over my shoulder and I saw more than one gaze aimed at his face. To be fair, it was a fantastic face. We reached the ballroom and the conversation inside it died. For a split second, the only sound was the holiday-themed background music.

Maddox commanded attention and all eyes swung his way.

My way.

"Daddy, there's punch." Violet let go of his hand to point to a table with various carafes and pitchers. She was totally unfazed by the people staring. Then again, she was part of Maddox's orbit and probably used to the spotlight. "Can I get a drink?"

"Sure. You need to stay in this ballroom or with Natalie. All night, got it?"

"Got it." Then she was gone, her dress a red streak across the space.

"Thanks for the escort." I slid my arm free of his.

"My pleasure." Maddox grinned as he looked down. His blue eyes sparkled. They were almost . . . flirty?

No. No way. Maybe?

Filling my lungs was a challenge. My imagination had hitched a ride on Santa's sleigh and was soaring to new levels. Just the notion that Maddox might find me attractive was insane.

The crowd came to my rescue, bringing my feet to earth. As Maddox had suspected, people began moving our way. In moments, he'd be inundated.

"I'd better catch up with Violet."

"Save me a dance later?"

"Um . . ." What. The. Christmas Fudge. "Sure?"

His grin widened, then he was swallowed up by guests. He stood taller than most until Keith came over to shake his hand.

I tore my eyes away and spotted Violet. In both hands, she clutched a plastic cup nearly overflowing with cherry liquid. At least if she spilled, it would blend with her dress.

She put it to her lips and the smile she gave after the first swallow was so sweet, I found myself smiling too.

"Nat!" A wave caught the corner of my eye and some of the nerves from the party vanished at seeing a familiar face coming my way.

I waved back and crossed the room. "Hey, Stella."

"It's so good to see you." She pulled me into a hug.

Stella and I had been friends since high school. She'd been a freshman on the swim team my junior year. No sweeter soul had ever graced the pool. All these years later and we'd stayed in touch, meeting for a drink now and then to catch up. I'd tell her about the kids I was watching, and she'd entertain me with her older brother's latest antics.

"I had no idea you'd be here," she said.

"It was a last-minute invite. I'm actually here to work."

At that moment, Violet appeared at my side, her punch cup empty. "Can I have more?"

I laughed. "Let's pace ourselves. We have all night."

"How are you?" Stella asked. "It's been forever."

Before I could answer, Heath appeared at her side along with Stella's brother.

Guy was midsentence when he noticed me and did a double take. "Natalie?"

"Hey. Good to see you, Guy."

"Been a while."

We'd graduated together but it had been a while since we'd bumped into one another. Guy had always been a source of entertainment. He'd been our class clown. The boy who'd try anything, no matter how reckless. Wherever Heath and Tobias had gone, Guy had been close to follow. Our lockers had been beside each other's, and he'd always had an extra piece of his spearmint gum to share.

He was chewing some tonight, his jaw working as he checked out my ass.

"Guy." I waited until he looked at my face, then I gave him a headshake.

"You sure?"

I giggled. "Quite. But thanks anyway."

He chuckled. "Are you here alone?"

"Nope." I looked down to Violet, holding out my hand to take hers. "Violet's my date tonight. And we're raiding the dessert table before any of the good stuff disappears."

"Natalie's the coolest of the cool," Stella told her. "You're going to have a blast tonight."

"But not as cool as Uncle Heath, right?" Heath held out his hand for Violet to smack it.

She ignored him.

"Ouch." Heath feigned a wound to the heart.

Stella laughed, a blush coloring her cheeks as she looked to him. She'd had a tiny crush on him in high school. Clearly it hadn't gone away.

Heath glanced at her, his gaze drifting down the low-cut V of her dress. He tore his eyes away, too quickly, when Guy nudged his arm and jerked his chin to the door.

A cute brunette and a petite blonde had just walked into the ballroom.

"Be my wingman," Guy said. "Hit on the blonde."

"Um . . ." Heath rubbed the back of his neck, looking to Stella.

She was studying her heels.

Guy clapped Heath on the shoulder, steering him away and leaving Stella crestfallen.

"You okay?" I bumped elbows with Stella.

"Great!" She winced at her own volume.

"I didn't know you'd be here tonight."

"I just started working at Holiday Homes." She shrugged. "Keith invites the whole office. I was actually going to skip and go to church with my parents, then hang out at home, but Guy talked me into coming. He promised to hang out with me because his girlfriend just dumped him. He's kind of broken up about it, even though he won't admit it. I felt bad for him, so I told him I'd be his date. But . . . he just ditched me."

"Want to hang with us?"

"I think I'm going to grab a drink." She smiled at us both, then nodded toward the bar.

The bar where Heath was now standing alone. Sans the blonde. I guess he'd already shirked his wingman duties.

"Have fun." I winked, then tugged on Violet's hand. "Sugar time?"

"How many desserts can I have before dinner?"

"One."

"Four," she countered.

"One."

"Three."

I arched an eyebrow. "One."

Her eye roll was spectacular. By the time she hit sixteen, she'd be able to teach a masterclass on attitude. "Fine. One."

"Glad we could agree."

She got two, which I blamed on her father. While we were at the dessert table, eyeing the assortments of mini cakes and cookies and candies, I'd caught sight of Maddox.

From across the room I'd felt his pull. His allure.

He'd been surrounded by men, all wearing suits and ties

with cocktails in their grips. Each one of them hanging on Maddox's every word. When he spoke, you listened to that deep, soothing voice. I'd been too far away to hear whatever it was he'd been saying, yet still, I'd been glued to the sight of his mouth moving, his lips forming words.

Violet had snuck a second cookie while I'd been drooling over the way he'd combed his hair tonight. Dark and stylish, pulled artfully away from a part over his left eyebrow. He'd kept one hand in his pocket while the other had held a tumbler with a gin and tonic. Whenever he'd smiled, that sexy dimple would pop on his clean-shaven face.

Violet reached for a caramel, thinking I wasn't watching, but I caught her fingers. "Let's get away from this table."

The band's lead singer took the microphone and welcomed the growing crowd. As the caterers swept into the room carrying trays of heavy hors d'oeuvres, he crooned the beginning of a sultry jazz number that enticed couples to the dance floor.

The space was a simple square with a row of windows on the exterior walls to overlook Main Street. Cocktail tables had been staged with white tablecloths. The ballroom's crystal chandelier cast a golden glow over the guests. The bar in the corner would be a popular spot.

"What do you think of the party?" I asked Violet as we lapped the room.

"It's nice. Some of the parties Daddy took me to at home are way bigger though. But they were *so* boring."

"Every single one? Come on. I bet one of them was fun, wasn't it?"

"Well, this one time, we got to go to a pool party. There was a waterslide and noodles and a lot of other kids to play with."

"Oooh. Now you're talking. I love pool parties and swimming is my favorite thing ever."

"Really?"

I nodded. "We have a couple of days together after Christmas. Maybe I'll see if I can convince your dad to let me take you swimming. What do you say?"

"Yessss." Her smile widened, then dropped in a flash. "Daddy didn't pack my floaties. They're still at home. I can stand up in Nana and Papa's hot tub but he doesn't let me swim in a pool without my floaties."

"Don't worry. I won't let you sink. I teach kids how to swim."

"You do?" She cocked her head to the side, staring at me like I was this entirely different person.

"Yes." I giggled. "Want me to teach you how to swim?"

"Okay." She nodded so wildly that her tiara came loose.

I fixed her crown, then we wandered around the ballroom, stopping at every window to peer outside. We ate food, hunting down different trays when something caught our eye. We refilled our punch cups twice. And when she got bored watching the adults, we escaped the ballroom and ventured downstairs for a change of scenery and closer inspection of the tree.

Once I found a topic Violet liked, she became this animated, wonderful storyteller. From her favorite books to cartoons to games, she was pure entertainment. Minute by minute, she was letting her guard down.

The party was in full swing by the time we returned to the second floor, the noise having doubled.

Keith spotted us as we walked through the doors and his whole face lit up when he looked at his granddaughter. "Violet, there you are. I was hoping you'd be my first dance. Wanna boogie?"

"A boogie? Eww." She giggled and took his hand, letting him lead her to the floor.

I hovered by the wall, watching as he twirled her around and made her laugh. She really was a beautiful child, inside and out. She was shy at times. Incredibly sweet at others, like how there'd only been one double chocolate cookie left, and when we'd both reached for it, she'd insisted I take it. The more she talked, the more her personality came alive. Her spirit was enchanting.

The naughty girl I'd met just days ago was nowhere in sight, which only confirmed my suspicions. That attitude of hers was an act to attract Maddox's attention. That, or her mother's. Not that Violet had mentioned her mom, not even once.

"So this is where you've been hiding." Maddox's rugged voice snapped me out of my trance. He stepped beside me, his suit jacket brushing against the sleeve of my dress. "Dance with me."

God, it was sexy that he didn't ask. "Don't feel obligated to entertain me. I'm fine."

"Actually, you're the only one in the room who I *want* to talk to. So I thought maybe you could entertain me." He held out his hand and maybe a different woman would have had the power to resist, but the moment my palm slid against his, any notion of objecting vanished.

Wide and warm with long fingers, his hand enveloped mine as he whisked me to the dance floor and swept me into his arms, holding me closer than was professional.

The scent of his spicy cologne filled my nose. The strength of his arm banded around my hip. The temptation of those lips was heady. Fuck professionalism. This was my only chance to dance with Maddox Holiday.

My prom dreams were coming true.

"I'm not a great dancer," he confessed as his fingertips pressed in deeper to the small of my back.

"Oh, I'd say you're doing fine." I followed his lead, savoring the feel of his body pressed to mine.

"Having fun tonight?"

I nodded. "I am."

"How is Violet doing?"

"Good. She is wholly entertaining. And I mean that as a compliment."

He chuckled and turned us, both searching out his daughter. She was still dancing with Keith. "Thanks for hanging with her."

"You are paying me."

"This is true. I can still say thank you."

Boy, he was something. Genuine. Nice. Sexy. My cheeks flushed and I dropped my gaze to his sinful red tie. Visions of undoing that Windsor knot and flipping the buttons free on his starched white shirt flooded my mind and I glanced at the couples around us, looking anywhere but at Maddox.

"Are you having fun?" I asked, trying to put a little space between us. Anything to ease the bloom of desire spreading in my lower belly.

Maddox wouldn't have it. He pulled me closer, flush against his hard planes. "I am now."

Oh, sweet baby Jesus in the manger. "Are you flirting with me?"

"I am. Do you mind?"

"No," I confessed, looking up to meet his gaze. What single woman in her right mind would object to Maddox Holiday flirting with her?

"Excellent." He spun us in a circle, the smile on his face widening. "But to answer your question, it's been . . . what I expected. I think I've told every business associate of Dad's in attendance that yes, business is good. Yes, I'm moving here at some point. And no, I'm not interested in investing in their next great idea. For the rest of the night, I'm ignoring anyone in a suit unless they have the last name Holiday."

"Good thing I'm in a dress."

He chuckled. "And a very nice dress it is."

"There you go, flirting with me again."

"I haven't flirted with anyone in a long, long time. I forgot how much fun it could be."

"Who's the last woman you flirted with?"

His smile faded a bit. "My ex-wife."

"Ah." Whoops. "Sorry."

"Don't be."

"So . . ." Time to change the subject. "You should know that I promised Violet I'd teach her how to swim. I hope you don't mind."

"Fine by me." His grip on my hand tightened as we moved the other direction. The song had changed but we'd just kept on dancing. "I should have gotten her into private lessons ages ago. We've got a pool at our place in LA and she loves to swim. She's got the basics and safety techniques down, but I guess I'm paranoid and overprotective. I don't let her swim without water wings unless I'm in the pool with her."

"I promise I'm qualified. And if she's comfortable in the water, it won't take her long to feel confident."

"I trust you."

Those words warmed my heart.

"What was in the bag?" he asked. "Your magic tote."

"Violet didn't tell you?"

He shook his head. "No."

"Good for her." A lot of children would have spilled our secret. "It was a family-sized bag of M&M's. Swedish Fish. Skittles. I had toys and games too, but I decided to go straight for the candy."

"I should have guessed." He laughed. "She's got a mouth

65

full of sweet teeth. That was part of the reason for the crème brûlée fiasco at that party last year. When I asked her why she'd climbed up that rack, she told me it was because she wanted the biggest one and they probably kept the big ones on top."

"I believe it." I laughed. "When I pulled that bag of M&M's out and started eating them, her entire attitude changed. It was just something to loosen her up. Something to bribe her with until she let down her guard and realized I wasn't her enemy."

"Smart."

I shrugged. "I've spent a lot of time with kids, working as a nanny and working with kids at the pool. They aren't all that complicated."

"What do you do with kids at the pool? Swimming lessons?"

"Sometimes. Mostly, I assist a physical therapist in town. He does pediatric aquatic therapy. That's what I want to do someday. Maybe. When I save enough to go to school and work up the courage to enroll. The idea of studying is . . ." I grimaced.

"You'd do great."

"Eeek. School? Granted, I always liked school but I haven't had to study in a long time. And I'm comfortable where I am."

"But it's not your dream."

I sighed. "No. It's not. I love kids but I have more to offer."

"Then it's time to step outside of your comfort zone."

Damn, but he was right. And motivating. One conversation and I was ready to dash to the admissions office at Montana State and hand them my application. If I wanted to become a physical therapist, I couldn't be a nanny forever. Maybe it was time to get serious.

Maddox let me go to twirl me beneath his arm, then hauled me back against his body, holding me close again.

"This is very surreal," I admitted.

"How so?"

"You're Maddox Holiday." *Duh.* "You had to know that every girl at Bozeman High was in love with you, including me."

Oh, hell. What was wrong with my mouth? Why couldn't it keep words on the inside?

The corner of his mouth turned up. "You were in love with me?"

"Maybe?" *Damn.* But now that it was out there, I might as well own it. "I was in love with you the way that awkward teenage girls love the smart, handsome boys who will never know they exist. Writing our names together in a heart. Naming our future children. Following you after class and home from school. Lurking outside your bedroom window, watching you sleep."

Maddox's feet ground to a halt.

I winked. "Kidding."

He threw his head back and laughed, a sound so warm and rich, it was worth whatever embarrassment from admitting my adolescent crush. He shook his head, the sparkle in his eye breathtaking as he smiled. "Well, you've got one thing wrong. I knew you existed."

"Did not."

"Did so. I saw you once at the pool, and I remember having to take a long, cold shower afterward."

I leaned back to study his face. "Seriously?"

"Swim caps. They get me every time."

I burst out laughing, relaxing as we moved together, dancing until the end of the song.

He kept my arm as he escorted me off the floor. "Should we join Violet at the dessert table?"

"Lead the way."

Violet stood beside Keith, each shoving cakes in their mouths. My watchful eye, even distracted by Maddox, hadn't strayed far from his daughter.

He'd had a pulse on her too. With every other turn, he'd searched for her. His love for her was written all over his face. And *my, my mistletoe* it was attractive.

"She's going to be up all night with the amount of sugar she's had," he said.

"Probably." I laughed. "I need to tell you something."

"What's that?"

I took in Violet as she plucked a cookie from a tray and handed it to Keith. I made out the words *the best ever* on her little lips before she took a cookie of her own. "You have a cool kid. She's almost impossible not to love."

Maddox stopped walking, forcing me to stop too. The expression on his face was almost . . . pained.

"What?" Had I said something wrong?

"You're killing me here."

"Why?"

He shook his head and let out a groan. "I have a policy. A firm policy. And I've never once wanted to break it until you."

"What policy?"

He leaned in close to whisper in my ear. The faint stubble from his cheek tickled mine as his breath caressed the shell of my ear. "Never kiss the nanny."

CHAPTER 6

MADDOX

There was a very real chance that Natalie Buchanan was going to shatter my self-control.

Thirty-two nannies, and number thirty-three was going to be my ruin.

The scent of her hair wrapped around me, sweet like the most decadent dessert in the room. Her touch, warm and light, was the perfect caress on my arm. She was beautiful. Graceful. Enchanting.

But it was her intelligence and wit that would be my undoing. That, and her praise of my daughter.

No woman, besides my mother, had ever said they loved Violet. No other nannies. No friends. Not even Cece. I couldn't remember a time when I'd heard her tell Violet *I love you*.

But Natalie had said it—had meant it. After just days of knowing Violet.

I was putty in her delicate hands. One dance and I was in trouble.

"Sorry." I leaned away. "That was inappropriate."

Everything I'd done with her tonight had been inappropriate. The dancing. The flirting. Yet here I was, practically glued to her side.

"No apologies," she said, with a pretty flush in her cheeks. "The teenage girl inside me is doing backflips into the pool at the moment because of that comment. You just made her dreams come true."

"Glad I could help." I chuckled. Though it was time to remember that Nat wasn't my date, so I slipped my arm from hers and glanced around the room. "Who do you think it will be this year?"

"Who and what?"

"This party has become infamous. There's always someone who has too much to drink and gives the rest of us something to talk about for the year to come."

"Really? Everyone here seems so . . . snobby isn't the right word. Classy. Composed."

I laughed. "See the woman in the gray dress over by the tree in the corner?"

Natalie followed my gaze. "Yeah."

"The last time I was at this party, ages ago on a rare trip home from LA, she started stripping on the dance floor."

"Are you talking about the woman who looks like my grandmother? Short gray hair. Pearl earrings. Probably in her early sixties."

"That's the one. She got all the way down to her slip before her husband realized what was happening and rushed over from the bar and took her home."

Natalie's eyes widened. "And she comes back here? I would have moved out of Bozeman by New Year's."

"I don't think she remembers and no one has the heart to tell her. That's sort of the unspoken rule at this party. What happens here, stays here."

"Ahh." She nodded. "Good to know."

"I missed it, but last year, Tobias told me that one of Dad's friends went around propositioning women to join him and his wife in a three-way. The wife didn't realize it was happening until he found a winner and introduced the two."

Natalie giggled. "I wonder how that conversation went."

"That's the three of them right there." I pointed to the trio at a cocktail table. Their heads were bent together, the women whispering a secret. The man kept eyeing them both, looking rather pleased with himself.

"Oh my God." Her eyes widened. "They totally hooked up, didn't they?"

"Definitely. Whatever keeps the magic alive, I guess. Though I'm not one for sharing, even if it is with another woman."

If I had Natalie in my bed, it would only be the two of us.

The flush in her cheeks deepened. "So, um . . . what else has happened?"

I spent the next ten minutes entertaining her with tales from past parties. I'd missed most of the embarrassing moments firsthand, but Tobias and Heath never failed to give me the play-by-play each year. And I knew my parents' friends well enough to place stories with faces. Some years hadn't been as exciting as others, but with Natalie's rapt attention and the smile on her face, I kept talking just because I didn't want her to walk away.

"I would not expect any of that from this crowd." Natalie laughed after my last story about the man who'd gotten drunk three years ago and convinced half the party to do tequila body shots.

"Every year. People let loose. Have a little fun."

"But body shots? A threesome? I'd expect that at a fraternity party, not your mom and dad's Christmas function. I mean . . . that's the mayor. And I recognized Principal Hammer from the high school."

"I think this is a pretty safe space. My parents keep the invite list to those they know and who don't run their mouths. Too much." Bozeman was expanding fast but the small-town roots grew deep.

"Really? That's actually amazing."

"Oh, don't get me wrong. They all talk amongst themselves, like we're doing. But it usually doesn't go further than this room." I scanned the crowd, loving that even though I'd been gone for so many years, it felt like coming home. "I missed this party. I missed Christmas in Montana."

"Violet told me you guys are moving home. Are you excited?"

"I am. It will be nice to be around my family. I'll be even more excited when Violet and I can get our own place. I just bought some property this week."

"When are you moving?"

"I haven't nailed down a date. I was hoping before the school year starts next fall. I need to get the satellite office up and running. Build a house. It would actually be easier to do all of that if I was here. Trying to do it from LA just makes it all harder and takes longer."

"You can't live with your parents for a while?"

I opened my mouth to tell her no but . . . why couldn't I live with my parents for six months? Their house was enormous. Violet and I had our own space, and they'd love having us under their roof. "Huh."

"Huh, what?"

"I'm wondering why I didn't think of moving here now."

She laughed. "Probably because it's the middle of the school year. Parents usually think about doing everything in the summer."

"True." Except why wait? It wouldn't take more than a phone call and some paperwork to enroll Violet in the Bozeman school district. She wouldn't be excited about leaving her friends, but that feeling wouldn't change between now and next fall.

"Do you need to be in LA for work if your satellite office isn't ready?" Natalie asked.

"No, I can work from Bozeman. My team won't move until the office is ready, but if I was here, I could expedite that process. And I would like to be here during construction of the house."

"I assume your dad is building it for you."

I nodded. "That's the plan. Heath will run lead on it."

"And you can be here to help with the details. Violet can switch schools. You can work remotely. And both of you can enjoy Bozeman in the winter."

I stared at her, blinking twice. She made it seem so simple. I wanted to live here. So I should live here. "Then I guess . . . I guess I live here."

"You live here." She smiled. "Welcome home."

There wasn't a smile in the world as welcoming as Natalie's.

"I live here," I repeated. Saying it out loud made it all click. I lived here. This wasn't a trip to visit family for the holidays. We lived here. It was time for us to live here.

The to-do list in my head exploded.

First, I needed to get Violet enrolled in school. Then I'd need to arrange for some of our things to be sent up here next week. Clothes. Toys. Books. I'd probably need to take a quick trip to LA to make arrangements at the office. My assistant could organize the actual move and getting the rest of our belongings packed. The nanny I had hired for after the holidays

73

would need to be notified. Our home in LA needed to be put on the market.

I fought the urge to send my assistant an email tonight, knowing he'd drop everything, including his holiday plans, to dive in. Then I'd have to call Cece and tell her about the new timeline.

I swallowed a groan.

"Are you okay?" Natalie put her hand on my forearm. "Your smile disappeared."

"I was just thinking about Cece, my ex. She knows we're moving here but I haven't told her the details. It won't be a pleasant conversation telling her it's happening and happening immediately."

"Ah." Natalie nodded. "Will she fight you on it?"

"Exactly the opposite." I looked to my daughter, still standing beside Dad. Mom had joined them, and they were pointing out the best desserts. "Cece won't care. That's hard on Violet."

"Oh." Natalie cringed. "I'm sorry. For you and Violet."

"Cece was in Hawaii when we left to come here. I don't know if she's back or even remembers that it's Christmas. I haven't spoken to her in weeks and neither has Violet. Part of the reason we haven't come home for the holidays in recent years was because it was easier in LA. Easier for me to hunt down Cece and remind her to acknowledge Violet. But this year . . . I just needed to come home."

Montana was home.

"I can understand that."

"Before the divorce, we didn't come here often either. Cece doesn't like Montana. She gets bored."

"Bored? In Bozeman?"

"Not enough shopping or friends to entertain her," I explained. "She never got along well with my parents. The first couple of years after Violet was born, I was swamped with work and it was easier to stay at home. We came here one year and all Cece did was complain that it was too cold. In hindsight, I should have just come without her."

In hindsight, there were a lot of things I should have done differently where Cece was concerned.

"That put a damper on the conversation." I sighed. "Sorry. I don't talk about Cece much. Mostly because I know how she'll look at the end of the conversation."

"Like a spoiled bitch?"

"Pretty much." I chuckled. "I don't ever want people to run her down and risk the chance that Violet will overhear."

"My lips are sealed."

And what beautiful lips they were.

A waiter passed us with a tray of champagne flutes. I snagged two and held one out for Natalie.

"I'd better not." She waved it off. "I'm on the clock. And speaking of such, I'd better get back to your daughter."

"She's fine with my parents."

"You're paying me to watch her."

"Would you feel better if I didn't pay you?"

"Actually, yes. It feels strange to be paid when I'm enjoying myself so much."

I held out the champagne again. "Done."

She took it and smirked. "You're still going to pay me, aren't you?"

"Yes." I tipped my flute to my lips and smiled. After a sip— my parents didn't skimp on the champagne and it was as delicious as it was expensive—I caught Mom's eye and motioned to Violet.

Mom waved, then nodded to Violet, mouthing, "I've got her."

"Thank you," I mouthed back, then took Natalie's elbow and steered her toward the door. "Consider this your break."

"I just had a break."

I grinned. "An extended break."

She sipped her champagne as I led her down the stairs to the lobby. Some of the crowd from earlier had cleared out and there wasn't as much bustle and noise. One of the tables beside a large window was open.

I walked over and pulled out a seat for her, then took my own. "I forgot how pretty this building is."

"I rarely make it here." She turned her blue eyes up to the star on the massive tree.

I traced the long column of her throat with my gaze, wishing I could trace it with my tongue instead. Wishing I could latch my mouth over her pulse and suck.

Christ. My cock swelled behind my zipper—again—and I drew in a long breath. There hadn't been a woman who'd stirred my blood in years. I hadn't even cared about women, and my fist had served me fine since my divorce. But Natalie . . .

I was fully under her spell.

"I don't want you to think that I do this," I told her.

Her gaze shifted to mine. "Do what?"

"Chase Violet's caretakers."

The corner of her mouth turned up. "Is that what you're doing? Chasing me?"

"I'd like to."

Her smile widened. "I think maybe we should table this conversation until my gig working for you is up."

"That would probably be the prudent decision. I can wait a week."

She lifted a shoulder. "We'll see."

"We'll see?" That wasn't the enthusiastic agreement I'd

76

expected. She'd told me that she'd been into me in high school. That she'd had a crush. Was that where it had ended? I could have sworn she was into me but . . . "Did I read this wrong?"

"Maddox, you just decided to move here thirty minutes ago. When you do, Violet will need your attention. And it sounds like there are a lot of lingering feelings where your ex-wife is concerned. So . . . we'll see."

Damn. Taking on a relationship at this point would be hard. I didn't have much extra to give. But for Natalie, it was tempting to find a way.

"You're right about Violet. She does need my attention. But where Cece is concerned, there are no lingering feelings. I fell out of love with her three years ago when we got divorced. Probably longer than that, if I'm being honest. The way she treated Violet . . . well, I couldn't love a woman like that."

"Can I ask you a very personal question that you have every right to ignore and tell me to mind my own business?"

"Of course." I grinned, doubting there was much I wouldn't tell her. Even tonight, after sharing a single dance, it was like my filter had disappeared.

"Cece sounds awful." Natalie made a sour face. "Why did you marry her?"

"Now you sound like my mother."

"Sorry. We don't have to talk about this."

"No, it's fine." I sighed and took a sip of my champagne. Talking about Cece was never easy but Natalie deserved the details. "She wasn't always awful. Or, I didn't see it. Cece is beautiful and vivacious. We met in college and she was that girl who everyone gravitated toward. She is always up for a party. Her laugh is infectious. And I was a young guy who had a lot happening and she made my life . . . lighter."

Natalie shifted, leaning her elbows on the table. She listened, intently. During the party. On the dance floor. Even in a room full of people, she listened. It was addictive, having Natalie's focus.

Cece had always kept one ear on the activity, sparing the bare minimum to conversation unless it was about her. And she would have never let me steer her away from the party.

"When we got together, I was just starting Madcast," I said. "I was working my ass off to graduate and get the company off the ground. Cece would haul me out of my house and take me to a bar and we'd have a blast for a few hours. At the time, I needed that. I asked her to marry me before graduation. We got married not long after. And things were good. Until . . ."

"Violet," she whispered and a little of the heartache I felt for my daughter was written on Natalie's face.

"Yeah." I nodded. "Cece was on birth control. She let a little too much time go between shots and got pregnant. Everything changed after that. Gone was the fun woman who'd added some levity to my life. She hated that I worked so much. Looking back, she had that right. As Madcast took off, I worked all the time. I only went to one of her doctor's appointments, and when she started having contractions, I was in a meeting and missed her calls, so she went to the hospital alone."

Natalie winced. "Ooof."

"Not my proudest moment."

"My dad always said it takes two to make a relationship work. Or not to work."

"He's right about that. I let Cece down. I won't blame the demise of our marriage entirely on her. But I will hold her responsible for how she's treated Violet. Our daughter is innocent. She's just a little girl. Cece might not have wanted to be a mother, but she *is* a mother."

"That's fair."

"One day, Cece decided we weren't what she wanted anymore. She didn't want to settle down. She'd been having an affair and fallen in love with a guy she'd met at the gym. Some model. That was the end. I can't even say I was upset. We'd been over for a long time before that. The divorce just made it official."

"And you fought for Violet."

"I always will." I nodded. "I've stayed in LA hoping that Cece will suddenly change, but I'm just fooling myself and making it harder on Violet. Cece travels. She's with the same guy. They hop all over the world, posting pictures of her glamorous life paid for by the money she made from giving me custody of Violet."

Natalie's eyes softened. "While you post pictures of Violet because she is the glamour in your life."

"Yes. I posted one yesterday of her blowing bubbles—"

"In the hot tub. I saw. It was so cute."

"You looked me up?"

"Absolutely. I stalked your Instagram earlier today. It's how grown women research handsome men these days. You really should make your account private."

I chuckled. "So noted."

"For the record, I think you're doing the right thing. Moving here. Creating a new life for Violet."

"Thank you." I saluted her with my champagne, then drained the rest of my glass.

Natalie did the same, and when she set her flute down, she gave me another one of those dangerous smiles.

"It's taking all of my willpower not to kiss you, just to see what it would feel like." The confession came out without any restraint or regret.

"Oh, it would be fantastic." She leaned in a little closer as she teased. "I'm really good at kissing."

"Of that, I have no doubt."

"But . . ." She shook her head. "I'm still your employee."

79

"I'm contemplating firing you."

She laughed, the sweet sound ringing through the lobby.

When was the last time I'd just talked to someone this openly? The only people who really knew what had happened with Cece were my parents and brothers. Sharing it with Natalie came as naturally as breathing. She was alluring and real and honest. With her, things seemed . . . easy.

I could use a little easy in my life.

A strand of hair fell across her cheek. I reached out and tucked it behind her ear, earning a small gasp as my fingertips brushed her skin.

Now that she'd caught my attention, I struggled to look away, even as a flash of red caught the corner of my eye.

Natalie was the most beautiful female I'd ever laid eyes on.

Except for the very pretty and very angry little girl marching our way.

CHAPTER 7
NATALIE

"Hi. How was dancing?" I gave Violet a smile, expecting one in return. Instead, I got the death glare. The same one she'd sent me when I'd wrung my wet sweater out over her head on our first day together.

"What's wrong?" Maddox slid from his seat and took a step toward her.

Violet sent her glare his way, then spun around on a gold slipper and ran away.

What the hell? I stood, my mouth falling open.

"Violet!" Maddox called but she was already gone. "Shit."

He jogged in the direction she'd gone, toward one of the restaurants, and even though the crowd had thinned from earlier, there were still enough people that they swallowed her up.

I scurried in my heels to catch Maddox who was blocked and slowed by a family coming out of the restaurant.

"What's going on?" I asked as I reached his side. I pressed in close to his arm, keeping pace as he squeezed by people and kept pushing forward.

"I don't know. I thought she was having fun." His head swept back and forth, searching for his daughter. "Violet!"

I inspected every piece of red I spotted, hoping it was her dress, but wherever she'd gone, she'd done it with the intention of disappearing. Why? What was wrong?

Maddox kept walking, down a hallway that led to an exit door. He tested the handle. Locked. "Damn it."

"She must have gone into the restaurant and we passed her." I turned and hurried back that direction, bypassing the hostess as I searched between tables. I weaved through them, seeing Maddox the next row over doing the same.

When we reached the wall of windows that overlooked Main Street, I found Maddox already backtracking.

Where would she go? Why would she run away from us? Had something bad happened at the party? Was it because I'd been sitting with her dad?

He didn't wait for me as he ran out of the restaurant, headed to the other across the lobby. I did one more sweep of the hostess station, checking beneath the counter, then rushed out, meeting Maddox at the base of the staircase.

"Anything?" he asked.

"No. What's going on?"

He raked a hand through his hair. "She does this."

"Does what? Run away?"

He sighed and nodded. "She gets mad at me or her feelings get hurt, and she'll run off and hide. But it's always at home. She's never done it in public before."

"Why? Was it because we were sitting together?"

"It has to be." The worry on his face cracked my heart. "Fuck."

"We'll find her. Where does she normally hide at home?"

"I don't know. I've never found her. She hides and comes out when she's ready. One night, she hid for six hours."

"Oh, hell," I muttered and looked around the lobby. We did not need Violet hiding here for six hours.

If she had backtracked and snuck away from us, she probably would have gone upstairs. She might be mad, but she'd likely stay close to the party where there were familiar faces mixed in with the strangers.

"We'll find her." If we had to interrupt the party and enlist the guests to help, then so be it. "We'd better divide and conquer."

Maddox nodded. "You go upstairs and start searching there. I'll talk to the managers of the restaurants and see if they'll let me into the kitchens. It wouldn't shock me if she snuck in with the waitstaff."

"Good idea." I spun and hurried up the staircase toward the party.

There were so many people in the ballroom it was nearly impossible to see if she'd gone in there, but I did a lap around the outer edge of the space, looking between legs and under tables. When I saw no sign of her or her red dress, I hit the dessert table and loaded up a plate with the biggest piece of chocolate cake I could find.

So far, sugar and bribery had been key with Violet. There was no point in changing tactics now.

My stomach twisted as I walked out of the ballroom, glancing down the staircase. Maddox stood beside the last step, talking to a woman in a pantsuit. There was so much fear and anxiety written on his face that it hurt to look at him as he spoke.

"Violet, where are you?" I headed for the hallway across from the ballroom. Thankfully, The Baxter wasn't a huge hotel. The top floors were only accessible with an elevator keycard, meaning she couldn't have gone too far.

Unless she'd snuck in with someone who had a card.

"She wouldn't do that." *Would she?*

Violet and I had been doing so well. Then I'd screwed up by flirting with Maddox. And I knew better, damn it.

I knew better.

How many women had Cathy fired over the years for this very thing? Three or four? There was a professional line I should never have crossed, no matter who the man was.

The first door down the hallway opened to a sitting room. When Violet and I had explored earlier, she'd peeked inside. Maybe she'd crawled under one of the couches. I pushed the door open, glancing inside, but instead of seeing Violet, I found Stella.

And her bare breasts.

"Oh my God." I tore my eyes away. "Sorry."

Stella gasped and pushed at the broad-shouldered man whose mouth was latched on to a nipple. Then she scrambled to right her dress as the man glanced over his shoulder.

"Natalie?"

"Heath?"

I looked between the two of them, my mouth hanging loose. "I wasn't here. I didn't see anything. You two, um . . . have fun."

My face was aflame as I closed the door. Better me walk in on them than Violet.

I moved to the next room—the men's restroom. I eased the door open and carefully peeked inside. The urinals were empty but I checked the toilet stalls too.

The bathroom's door swung open as I was checking the last stall, and I spun around, nearly spilling the cake in my hand.

"Uh . . ." The man coming in had already unzipped. His entire body froze when he spotted me.

"Sorry." I avoided any and all eye contact as I walked past him, keeping my gaze on the floor and not the organ peeking out from a pair of green silk boxers. "Wrong bathroom."

The women's restroom was my next stop. There were no ladies at the sink and the first three stalls were empty, but the last one's door was closed.

I crouched, looking for a pair of shoes. There were no feet dangling from the toilet, so I shifted, peering through the small gap by the door's lock.

And there it was.

Red.

Thank God.

I sighed and walked to the counter, hopping up on its edge. If it took more than two minutes to flush Violet out, I'd drag her out of here if necessary. Somewhere in the hotel, Maddox was worrying. But I'd rather avoid a scene and the chance of completely alienating this little girl.

So I took the fork I'd put on the plate with my cake and dove in, refusing to think about eating in a public bathroom. At least this one was clean.

"Yuuuuum," I moaned and chewed. "This is the best cake I've ever had in my life. It's new. They just put it out on the dessert table. Want to come out here and have a bite?"

Silence.

"Suit yourself. I'll eat it. It's so good, I doubt there will be any left when we go back to the party. It's got fudge frosting."

Silence.

Wow, this girl was stubborn.

I forked another huge bite and let out another moan. "So. So. Good."

The rustle of a skirt and the click of shoes on floor tiles before the door squeaked open.

"You're gross." She harrumphed and crossed her arms over her chest.

"Gross? Why am I gross?"

The tiara had come loose somewhere during her escape

and was askew on her updo. She'd never looked more adorable. And sad. My heart ached for the sad. "You're just like all of the other nannies. All you want to do is kiss my dad. That's *gross*."

So she'd stormed off because I'd been talking with Maddox. And because I did want him to kiss me. *Shit*.

I set the plate aside and jumped off the counter. "Do a lot of nannies have crushes on your dad?"

"All of them," she muttered.

"Want to know a secret?"

She didn't answer but there was a flicker of interest in her expression.

I waved her over, then gave her the cake as a peace offering.

She took it and went to the counter, trying to climb up between the sinks to sit like I'd been. But with the height and her dress, she couldn't boost herself up.

"Let me help." I hoisted her up, and when I had her seated with the cake on her lap and a bite in her mouth, I resumed my own perch, hooking my ankles together and letting my feet swing.

The room had been designed so that as the door opened, anyone passing down the hall couldn't peer inside and see anything but a tiled partition. It wasn't the most elegant of places to talk, but with just the two of us in there, it was at least private and quieter than taking her to the ballroom.

"What's your secret?" she asked, her cheeks bulging and a chocolate crumb on her lip.

"I had a major crush on your dad when he was just a kid. All of the girls did."

"You knew Daddy as a kid?"

"In high school. When we were teenagers. I went to school with him and your uncles. Did you know that?"

She shook her head.

"Your dad was a nice boy. And now he's a nice man. Girls usually get crushes on the nice ones."

"Boys are weird."

"Yes, they can be weird." I laughed. "But someday you'll meet a nice one and maybe have a crush on him."

Her face twisted and she looked at me like I'd cracked.

"I do have a crush on your dad, Violet. That doesn't have to be a bad thing. And it doesn't have to mean anything. I'm still your nanny and your friend."

"He loves my mom." There was no confidence in her voice as she spoke the words, only the heartache of a girl who hadn't quite come to terms with her parents' split.

My chest ached because once upon a time, I'd been that little girl too. "I don't know how your dad feels about your mom, honey. Have you asked him?"

She shook her head, using the fork to poke at the cake. "She didn't send me a Christmas present. I checked under the tree and all of my presents are from Dad and Nana and Papa."

Ouch. Yeah, Cece was a bitch. No wonder Maddox was so frustrated with her. "Do you miss her?"

Violet shrugged. "She didn't come and see me at Christmas last year either. She promised to take me ice skating and lied."

I'd been around enough seven year olds to know that a broken promise was equivalent to a lie. And they delivered the biggest hurt. "Does she lie a lot?"

"All the time." Her chin started to quiver. "Now we're moving here and she's never going to see me."

I was off the counter and in front of her before her first tear fell. Taking the plate and setting it aside, I wrapped my arms around her and pulled her close as she cried.

"I'm sorry," I whispered when her breathing evened out except for the occasional hiccup. "Can I tell you another secret?"

"Yeah." She leaned away and the sadness on her face was familiar agony. This girl was breaking my heart.

"I only had a dad when I was your age."

"What happened to your mom?"

I swiped my thumb across her cheek. "I think maybe she was like your mom."

"Oh." Her chin fell.

My mother had left Bozeman when I was five, moving to North Carolina with the man she'd been sleeping with behind my father's back. Of course, I hadn't realized that at the time. Not until Dad had told me the truth on my fifteenth birthday.

When Mom had left Montana, she'd taken everything important with her except a little girl.

And an old 1969 mint-green Volkswagen bus.

Magdalena.

That bus was all I had left of my mother. Maybe it was foolish to cherish it like I did, but it was more mine now than it had ever been hers.

"There are moms like ours in the world," I told Violet. "I'm sorry you got one of them. But girls like us are lucky too."

"How?"

"Because even though we don't have the best moms, we have the very best of the best of the best dads. Don't you think?"

"I guess," she murmured.

She'd see, later in her life. She'd realize that Maddox adored her and would do anything to ease some of the pain.

"Want to know something else cool?" I asked, earning a nod. "I have a mom now. And she's the best of the best of the best. Her name is Judy. She became my mom when I was twenty."

"Twenty?" Ancient to a little girl.

"Yep. I was twenty. She met my dad at a restaurant in town.

Dad and Judy started talking and then they started dating. And kissing."

"Kissing is gross."

I giggled. "Judy and my dad kiss *all* the time."

"Eww."

I pushed a lock of hair off her forehead. "I'm okay with the kissing because she married Dad and asked if she could be my mom. I love her a lot. Do you know why I love her so much?"

"Why?"

"She makes the most amazing chocolate cake. Better than this one." I tapped her plate. "She always remembers Christmas presents. And because she loves my dad with her *whole* heart."

Judy had never married or had children before she'd met Dad. She'd told me once that she'd come to terms with her life as a *spinster*—Judy loved her Regency romance. But it just hadn't been her time. She'd been waiting for Dad to find her. She was younger than him by a decade, but because of their love, I believed in soul mates.

"Judy makes my dad happy, and since all he ever wants is for me to be happy, I feel the same way about him. Like a circle. We want what is good for each other. Does that make sense?"

"Yeah." Violet nodded.

"I think that's all your dad wants for you. Just to make sure you're happy. Maybe someday, you'll be okay if he finds his own Judy."

She thought on it for a long minute, her forehead furrowed. "Are you a Judy?"

"No, I'm a Natalie. And though your dad is nice and I still have a teensy, tiny crush on him, right now I think we should not worry about Judys and go find him. He was freaked out when you ran away."

"Very freaked out." A deep, soft voice came from the doorway. Maddox strolled inside, and whatever fear he'd worn in the lobby was nearly gone, probably because he'd been listening at the door for a while.

"Sorry, Daddy." Violet flew across the bathroom, a streak of red, shooting into her father's arms.

He picked her up and held her tight, letting out a long breath and closing his eyes. "Never again, Violet. Don't you ever run away from me again. You scared me. If something happened to you . . . never again. Promise."

"I promise." She nodded and buried her face into his shoulder. "Sorry."

He held her tight, then let her go and set her on the floor. "Want to dance with me? You haven't danced with me tonight."

She nodded and took his hand, letting him escort her out of the bathroom.

I picked up the plate of decimated cake and followed, giving Maddox a wink when he glanced over his shoulder.

"Thank you," he mouthed.

"You're welcome," I mouthed back.

The party guests were none the wiser to our drama. Music blared and people laughed, enjoying their Christmas Eve.

Maddox took Violet straight to the dance floor, twirling her twice before picking her up and touching his nose to hers. Then he danced with her through the crush of couples, not once letting her feet touch the floor.

He was a good dad. The best of the best of the best.

And he needed her more than I wanted him.

The decision to stay away was the right one. Timing was not on our side. So with that resolution in mind, I went to my happy place.

The dessert table.

Eating one last piece of chocolate cake, making tonight the

most sugar-filled night of the year—not even on Halloween when I ate one piece of candy for every twenty that I handed out could top this.

Judy was on a health kick at the moment, even through the holidays, and she'd warned me there'd be no chocolate cake after our Christmas dinner tomorrow. So tonight I indulged, in the sweets and in Maddox, watching from my spot against the wall as he danced with his daughter.

Hours later, midnight chimed on the grandfather clock in the hallway and people slowly began to drift out of the ballroom.

Maddox hadn't let go of Violet the rest of the night. The fright from earlier had rendered me useless. When I'd offered to take over, he'd told me he had her. When I'd told him I'd leave, he'd asked me to stay close.

Violet seemed to have forgiven me. She'd even held my hand while people had come to talk to her father. Maybe she'd scared herself a bit too with that stunt.

Around one o'clock, she began to yawn. Maddox picked her up, holding her like she weighed nothing while he continued visiting. And with the deep murmur of his voice, she drifted off against his shoulder.

"She's out," I told him, yawning too. "I don't blame her. I'm an early bird, not a night owl. I think I'll take off, unless you need me to stay."

"No, we'll get out of here too."

I followed them out of the ballroom, smiling at Hannah and Keith who stood sentry by the doors, bidding farewell to their friends.

Maddox kissed his mother's cheek. "See you at home."

I collected my coat from the check room where I'd left it earlier, and shrugged it on, pulling my car keys from my pocket.

"Brr," he said, wrapping his jacket around Violet as we stepped outside.

Fresh snowflakes fell from the dark sky. They quieted the street and blanketed the sidewalk.

It was magical. The perfect scene for a farewell.

"Thank you for inviting me tonight."

"Can we give you a ride home?" he asked.

I jingled my keys. "I'll be fine."

The white specks of snow clung to his dark hair. The faint streetlights made his features stronger. More handsome. His blue eyes were like sapphires, glowing bright as he stepped closer.

Foolish as it was, I hoped for a kiss. Just one before I walked away.

His breath tangled with mine in white wisps in the frozen air. He leaned in and my heart leapt. Then his lips were there, the faintest brush against mine before he was gone. "Merry Christmas."

"Merry Christmas."

I smiled at him, then looked to Violet, sleeping happily in her father's arms.

I wouldn't fall for a client. Not again.

And for her, I'd walk away.

So I took one step backward, then another and whispered, "Goodbye, Maddox."

CHAPTER 8

MADDOX

I checked the time on my phone for the hundredth time. Where was Natalie? She should have been here by now. I'd hoped that maybe she'd come early since we hadn't seen her yesterday. She'd been on my mind constantly since the party, even with the flurry of Christmas activity—Violet's toys and gifts and meals—and I was anxious to see Nat's smile.

"What are you looking at?" Mom asked, coming to stand by my side at the front window.

"The snow," I lied.

She laughed. "Sure, son. If snow is how you think of Natalie."

"If you knew, why ask?"

"Because I'm your mother and forcing you to squirm is one of my job descriptions."

I chuckled and put my arm around her shoulders. "Are you working today?"

"I've got a few things to hammer through in the office, but no. I'm going to try and take most of the day off. Your brother said something about watching the last season of *State of Ruin* already."

"He was supposed to keep that a secret."

"You have met Heath, haven't you? Despite what he thinks, he's never been able to keep a secret."

"I'll email you the link and login."

She smiled. "It's so good to have you home."

Home. "It's good to be here."

"Are you sure you're okay with us staying here?"

"I wouldn't have it any other way."

When I'd pulled Mom and Dad aside yesterday after breakfast and asked if they'd be okay with my accelerated move date, both had been ecstatic. When I'd offered to move into a condo in town, they'd both scoffed and insisted Violet and I stay right where we were. And since I was going to attempt life without a nanny, Mom had promised to help with Violet.

But first, we had a few days left with Natalie. If she'd get here already. I hadn't been this excited to see a woman in years. She made me smile effortlessly. She made me hang on her every word. And she was a miracle worker with my daughter.

When I'd eavesdropped on their conversation in the bathroom at the hotel during the party, I'd had a hard time breathing as Natalie had spoken. Not because of the story about her own mom, but because no woman had ever spoken to Violet that way.

Like a mother.

Not Cece. Not Mom—who'd always tried her best but she would always be a grandmother, prone to saying *yes.*

The crunch of tires on snow sounded outside, and I let Mom go, leaning closer to the window.

"Oh, Maddox." Mom laughed. "Don't lick the glass."

I shot her a scowl, then narrowed my eyes at the unfamiliar car coming down the lane.

94

That wasn't Natalie's Subaru. And it wasn't Natalie behind the wheel.

"Expecting someone?" I asked Mom.

"No." She shook her head and went to open the door.

We stood together, watching as an older woman stepped out of a gray sedan and walked our way.

"Good morning." She smiled brightly, extending her hand my way. "I'm Cathy Caron."

The owner of the agency where Natalie worked.

"Hi . . . Cathy." I shook her hand and waved her inside out of the cold. Then we stared at each other, that awkward silence hanging over our heads until Mom cleared her throat and excused herself.

"Should we start with an introduction to Violet?" Cathy asked.

I blinked and rubbed my jaw. "I'm sorry, Cathy. Forgive me for the confusion. What are you doing here?"

"Oh, sorry." Her smile dropped. "You must not have received my email."

"No." I hadn't logged in this morning, and over breakfast, while I normally checked email, I'd played a rock, paper, scissors tournament with Violet instead. "I apologize."

"That's my fault." Her façade cracked as her shoulders slumped and she smoothed the hair from her face. "It's been a hectic morning."

"Where is Natalie?"

"She's not coming. And I didn't have anyone else available over Christmas, so I came instead."

I didn't hear much of her explanation other than Natalie wasn't coming. "Is Natalie sick?"

"No, she's . . . unavailable."

Oh, shit. Had she gotten fired? Because of me?

I opened my mouth but nothing came out. What the hell

did I say? Did Cathy know about my feelings for Natalie? How? I wasn't even sure exactly how I felt. "I, um . . ."

The last time I'd been this speechless had been when Violet had run away from one of her nannies in LA, locked herself in my bedroom and proceeded to remove the laces from my shoes and tie them together in one long string.

When I'd asked her why, she'd told me that she'd been planning to tie one end to the bed post and use the other to climb out a window. Granted, the laces combined had only been about eight feet long and my bedroom had been on the first floor, but her plan had been insane, albeit fairly well-thought-out.

"Yes?" Cathy asked.

"Nothing." I swallowed my disappointment and waved her deeper into the house. "Welcome. Thanks for coming. Violet was just in her room. Please, make yourself at home and I'll get her."

Cathy nodded and unzipped her coat.

I took the stairs two at a time and strode down the hallway to Violet's room, finding her on the bed with the Nintendo. I'd bought her a new game for Christmas and she was on a mission to dominate within the first forty-eight hours.

Maybe it would distract her today, so we didn't have a wreck with a new nanny.

"Hey, princess. Can you come to the living room? I'd like to introduce you to someone."

"Who?" She didn't look up from her Nintendo.

"There's a new nanny here to play with you today while I'm working."

Her fingers stopped moving. Her eyes lifted to mine. "Where's Natalie?"

"She's not coming today."

"Why?"

Because I fucked up. "I don't know," I lied. "I'm sorry."

Violet stared at me for a long moment, then huffed and put her game aside.

The introduction to Cathy went about as well as expected. I showed her around the house while Violet begrudgingly followed. But she didn't throw a fit. Maybe that was because Cathy was in her fifties.

Violet's outburst at the party had been eye-opening. How was it that I could run a multi-billion-dollar business, but I didn't have a clue how to read my own child?

The nannies we'd had over the years had always been younger women. I assumed that was typical—my colleagues in California had caretakers around the same age. Sure, there'd been times when a former nanny had stood too close. Had laughed or blushed too often. I hadn't thought much about it because I hadn't considered any of them attractive. Who cared if they had a crush? I hadn't thought twice about a single one in that way.

Until Natalie.

But Violet had seen it all along while I'd been oblivious to just how much she noticed. And just how much it had bothered her.

"Do you have any special instructions?" Cathy asked as we ended the house tour.

"No. My parents have a chef here for the week, so he'll have lunch and snacks prepared. I have a meeting outside the house this morning but please call if you have any questions. My mother and father are around here somewhere. Violet can track them down if needed." I smiled at my daughter, earning a pout.

That pout actually made me happy. That pout meant she wanted Natalie here as much as I did.

So why the hell wasn't she here? I'd come on strong at the

party but she hadn't seemed to mind. She'd put her boundary in place too, one I'd respected.

Damn it.

I knelt and took Violet's hand. "Have fun today. I love you."

"Love you too," she mumbled.

"Thanks, Cathy."

She smiled and nodded. "My pleasure."

Leaving her with Violet, I retreated to the office for my first call with the office in LA. I broke the news to my assistant about my expedited move first. As expected, he immediately got to work and promised to do whatever necessary to make it a seamless transition.

After that call, I spoke with my general counsel and the head of human resources who informed me that one of our employees had been leaking content to Russian piracy sites.

Then I spoke to my CFO who reported that our actual revenue numbers as we approached year-end would be higher than the projections. But even with that good news, I was stuck on Natalie's absence.

Where was she? It had been a while since I'd flirted with a woman, but she'd flirted back, hadn't she? Why wasn't she here? Why hadn't she called?

By the time my conference calls for the morning were finished, I was late getting out of the house for my meeting with Tobias.

Holiday Homes was closed the week between Christmas and New Year's, so when I pulled into the parking lot ten minutes late, my Audi and Tobias's GMC were the only vehicles around.

Tobias was leaning against the empty reception desk, staring off into space, when I walked through the door.

"Hey." The scent of strong coffee and sawdust clung to the air. "Smells like Dad's old office in here."

Tobias nodded. "Brand-new building and it smells like the old one. But I like that."

"Me too." I shook his hand. "Thanks for meeting today."

The rest of my week was slammed, and this was the only free spot I had to talk construction plans. The second that property was officially mine, I wanted the permits approved and the crew ready to break ground.

Tobias would be designing my home because I wanted the best architect in town.

"Want some coffee?" he asked, leading me toward the break room.

"Sure." I followed, taking in the office. Dad had built it three years ago and today was only my second visit. "This is nice."

"You know Mom and Dad."

They'd declared a few years ago that they were going to spend some money. They'd worked their asses off their entire lives, teaching us boys how to do the same. And now they were reaping the benefits.

A custom home. New office buildings. Travel. Dad had bought Mom a three-carat Tiffany diamond ring for Christmas because the jewel in her original wedding ring was beginning to dull. Mom had bought Dad a five-thousand-dollar Bremont watch because he was always letting his phone run out of power and never knew what time it was.

The watch was almost identical to one Cece had bought me our last year together. She'd always been one to splurge on the holidays. For me. For Violet. For herself.

At the base of our tree, she'd have a mountain of gifts. After the divorce, I'd gotten rid of the gaudy watches and cufflinks she'd bought me over the years because none of them had meant a thing.

What I wanted was a woman who bought me a gift because

she knew how much I'd love it, not simply because the price tag was five digits. I wanted gifts to make me smile. To make me laugh.

I could use more laughter in my life.

And from the look on Tobias's face, he could too.

"You okay?" I asked as he walked into his office and took a seat behind his desk. He'd been quiet yesterday through the Christmas festivities. I'd thought it was just because there was so much activity, but even now when we were alone, he seemed just as distant.

"Yeah." He rubbed his bearded jaw. "Great."

Not great. "Missed you at the party at The Baxter."

"Yeah. Had something come up." His eyes were unfocused as he stared at his desk.

"Tobias."

He swallowed hard.

"What happened?"

"Nothing."

"Talk to me."

Between Tobias and Heath, it was Tobias who I'd lost touch with the most. He'd been busy in college and working afterward. And I hadn't made time to keep in touch with my brothers.

With Heath, it hadn't mattered. He'd made up for my shortcomings over the years. Not a week had gone by since I'd moved away from Montana where he hadn't texted me at least once.

But Tobias and I had begun to drift apart. I hoped to make up for that now that I was home.

"I've been a shit older brother as of late. Give me the chance to make up for it."

The color drained from his face as he turned to stare blankly at the wall. "Do you remember Eva?"

"I never met her, but yeah." Eva had been Tobias's girlfriend through college. I wasn't sure exactly why they'd broken up, but according to Heath, it had wrecked him for a time.

Mom had always loved Eva, and during one of her regular phone calls—the ones where she'd gossip about my brothers—she'd told me how much she wished they'd get back together.

"She came over the other morning," Tobias said. "Christmas Eve."

"Okay," I drawled. "Are you getting back together or something?"

"No." He rubbed his hands over his face, then dropped the bomb. "She's pregnant."

"Oh." *Shit.*

"We hooked up a while back. The condom broke. She's pregnant. And she's moving to London."

Four statements, delivered with no inflection. Like he didn't have a clue how to deal with a single one. Before I could think of something to say, Tobias shook his head and picked up a pencil from his desk. "Let's go through what you want for your house."

"We can do this another day."

"No, today's good." He slid a notebook under the graphite tip and waited.

"Tob—"

"Five bedrooms? Or would you like six?"

I sighed, not wanting to push. "Six. And one in the guesthouse."

"Bathrooms?"

We spent the next hour discussing the house. Tobias asked questions and I answered. When he was done, before I could bring up Eva again, he stood from his desk. Meeting adjourned. "I'll get a preliminary draft sketched and bring it over soon."

"Thank you." I nodded, taking the hint that it was time to go.

I'd give Tobias some time to adjust to the pregnancy news, then talk to him again. I wasn't going anywhere, not this time.

The minute I was in my Audi, I pulled out my phone, hoping to see a missed call from Natalie. The screen was blank. Where was she? Why hadn't she come today? My curiosity was driving me insane.

Fuck it. I sent a quick email to my assistant that something had come up and I needed him to reschedule my next two meetings. Then I dialed Heath's number.

"Hello?" he answered, his voice muffled.

"Are you still in bed?" It was after eleven.

"Maybe."

"I need a favor."

"What?" he yawned.

"Do you happen to know Natalie's phone number? Or her address?"

"Why do you need it? Isn't she working for you today?"

"Heath," I grumbled. "Do you have her number?"

"Hold on." There was a rustling sound, then I was put on mute.

"Christ, what am I doing?" If Natalie wanted to see me, she would have showed up at the house this morning. The right thing to do would be respect her privacy and leave her alone. But did I hang up the phone? No. Because damn it, there was something different about her.

Maybe not different but . . . familiar. She wasn't fake like many women in the entertainment world—my world. She didn't seem interested in status. She was grounded and real. Being around her was like being blasted to the past, before Madcast. Before the money.

Before I'd left Montana.

I wanted to taste her lips. I wanted to feel her curves beneath my palms. I wanted to thread my fingers through her soft hair and devour her whole.

I wanted her more than I'd ever desired a woman.

The silence on the other end of the phone ended abruptly. "Maddox?"

"Still here."

"I guess Natalie lives in the house where she grew up."

"With her father?"

"No, I think she bought it from him. Or something. I'm not sure. But do you remember where it is?"

"Vaguely, but a specific address would be good."

"I don't have one. It's in our old neighborhood. Dark green house two blocks over."

"Which direction?" I clenched my teeth.

"Uh . . . toward the elementary school?"

"You're killing me."

"Dark green isn't that popular of a color. You'll find it. How many could there be?"

Two. There were two dark green homes on the street that was two blocks away from my childhood home.

The first of the two dark green homes was occupied by a *lovely* older woman—Christine—who'd threatened to sic her Pomeranian—Roxy—on me if I didn't *get my soliciting ass off her front porch.*

Apparently in faded jeans and a black sweater, I resembled a door-to-door solicitor.

At the second dark green house, I figured I was in the right spot when I read the welcome mat.

The Neighbors Have Better Stuff.

I chuckled as I stood outside Natalie's home, uninvited. Before I could knock or ring the bell, the door whipped open and there she was with a houseplant tucked into the crook of one arm.

"Hi."

She blinked those beautiful blue eyes. Twice. "H-hi."

"You didn't show up today."

Her shoulders fell and she held out the plant. "I'm sorry. This is my apology aloe. I was leaving to bring it over and say goodbye."

"Apology aloe." I took the pot from her hands. "Never heard of it."

"It doubles as a Christmas present and a housewarming gift. They're very useful if you have kids who are accident prone. Or kids who might attempt to melt their Barbies into zombies with a blowtorch."

She'd bought me a gift. An aloe plant. For my daughter who might very well melt her Barbies into zombies with a blowtorch.

I threw my head back and laughed, the sound carrying down the block. God, it felt good to laugh. It felt good to know that she'd been on her way over. Yes, she'd come over to say goodbye, but we'd deal with that word later.

"What are you doing here?" she asked.

I answered by stepping forward, forcing her inside. With the aloe plant set on the floor, I closed the door behind me and moved into her space. Before she could retreat out of my grasp, I framed her face with my palms. "I met Cathy."

Her shoulders slumped. "Yeah."

"You're not my nanny anymore."

"No, not anymore." Her mouth turned down. "Sorry."

"I'm not."

Then I kissed the sad look off her face.

CHAPTER 9
NATALIE

Best. Kiss. Of. My. Life.

Of course Maddox Holiday could kiss. He'd barely kissed me after the party and I'd thought about it all day yesterday. That had been nothing more than a touch. Whatever expectations I'd had were destroyed with one sweep of his tongue across my bottom lip.

Maddox's hands stayed firm on my face, holding me against his mouth as I melted into a puddle.

My knees weakened. A moan escaped my throat.

He took advantage and slid inside, his taste exploding on my tongue. The heat from his mouth was heady. A dizziness washed over me as his mouth slanted over mine. So lost in the feel of him, I just stood there. Motionless. Stupefied. A woman on the verge of becoming goo.

Was this a dream? Maybe I was dreaming. *Kiss him back.* Why wasn't I kissing him back?

Before I had the chance to tangle my tongue with his, he pulled away, dropping his forehead to mine.

No, I was just getting ready to kiss him back.

"Natalie, I—"

"Kiss me again," I blurted, then rose up on my toes and tossed my arms around his shoulders, holding on tight.

He didn't miss a beat. He slammed his mouth down on mine and whatever sweetness had been in that first kiss morphed into sinful, delicious lust. Maddox devoured me, his tongue dueling with mine.

My fingers dove into the thick strands of his hair, tugging and toying while I poured everything I had into this kiss.

If this was all I'd have of Maddox Holiday, damn it, I was going to make an impression. For us both.

Maddox's arms banded around my back and he picked me up off my feet, carrying me to the nearest wall.

My legs wrapped around his narrow hips as he pressed my spine against the surface. I clung to him, my mouth never leaving his. We kissed for what felt like hours, until my core throbbed and I ached for more.

He arched his hips, digging his arousal into my center for one blissful second before he tore his mouth away. "Fuck."

"Yes, please."

Maddox shook his head. "I wanted to kiss you on Saturday. But this . . . damn, you can kiss, Nat."

Oh, thank God. If the only thing I achieved in this life was Maddox thinking I was a good kisser, I'd die a happy woman. "I used to practice on my arm when I was a teenager."

He grinned and set me down on unsteady legs. "What else did you practice when you were a teenager?"

"That's for me to know and you to find out. Though let's just say it involved a banana."

"Natalie," he groaned. "You're killing me here."

"What? I make excellent banana bread. Someone told me once that men loved banana bread."

He threw his head back and laughed.

106

What a sight he was when he laughed. It transformed his face from the stoic businessman to this blindingly beautiful man.

When he looked at me again, he was still laughing, the dimple on full display. Because I might not have another chance, I reached up and touched it with a fingertip.

Maddox's fingers threaded through the hair at my temples. "Why didn't you come today?"

"Because as much as you wanted to kiss me on Saturday, I wanted it ten times over. I couldn't do that to Violet. She needs you. And . . ."

The truth was so freaking embarrassing. I didn't really want to tell Maddox about the past, but I didn't want him to find out from any other person.

"And what?"

"I've made this mistake before," I admitted with a cringe. "I can't do it again."

"Again?" His forehead furrowed. "With a father?"

I sighed and walked past him, leading the way to the living room couch.

He followed, sitting beside me.

"When I was eighteen, I started working for a single dad. Deacon," I said, keeping my eyes trained forward on the coffee table. Not many knew this story because it was humiliating. "He had twin boys who were seven. His divorce was new, or so I'd thought. Deacon's ex-wife wasn't around much but the boys talked about her all the time. I didn't think a thing of it because I never saw her at the house. I assumed she just lived in town."

When it came to the twins, I'd only ever dealt with Deacon. He'd been at the house to greet me each morning before leaving for work, and he'd been home every night at five-thirty so I could go home before dinner.

"It was just for the summer. It was more like babysitting

and my first full-time job before I'd gone to work for Cathy. I was watching the twins while school was on break."

"He wasn't divorced, was he?"

I shook my head. "No, he wasn't. His wife was a journalist and she'd been given an assignment in Italy for the summer. I didn't know."

Maddox put his hand on my shoulder. "Nat, this isn't on you."

"I know." I gave him a sad smile. It had taken me years to realize that I'd been Deacon's prey. He'd been a handsome, older man who'd known exactly what to say to lure me into his bed. I'd slept with that man three times before learning that his wife had been out of town but very much still his wife.

I'd kept the affair a secret for a few years, finally admitting it to Judy after she'd married Dad. Cathy knew too because I'd wanted to be completely up front with her when I'd applied to work for her agency.

Otherwise, no one knew and I was certain that Deacon wasn't gossiping. Last I heard he was still married.

"When I found out about his wife, I quit immediately. The worst part was knowing that I'd betrayed those boys. They'd trusted me, and I'd gotten wrapped up in their father. He was a bastard for lying to me, but I should have known better. And that's on me. I can't go there again. Certainly not with you."

"With me?"

"I like you, Maddox. I've always liked you. I don't know if you want to explore this or not—"

"I do."

Relief coursed through my veins. "Then I can't be the nanny. Violet needs someone who's only about her. She deserves that."

"Agreed." He took one of my hands. "You're fired."

I laughed. "I already quit. And I have an apology aloe to prove it."

"Go on a date with me."

"But what about Violet?"

"She can find her own date."

I swatted his arm. "You know that's not what I mean."

"I know." Maddox shifted, inching closer. "But hear me out."

"Okay."

"Violet is and will always be my priority. Everything you just said about her needing someone that's only about her is right. And it's sexy as hell that you care enough about my daughter to walk away. But . . ."

He straightened, sitting taller. His gaze locked with mine and sheer determination was written on his face. This was the Maddox who led a billion-dollar company. This was the man in charge, ready to make his case.

Talk about sexy as hell.

"Violet doesn't have a lot of positive female relationships. She's had some great teachers. My mom. But thanks to Cece and her other nannies, she's seen a lot of women walk out of her life."

My hand pressed against my heart, aching for his girl. "I hate that for her."

"I hate that for her too." He gave me a sad smile. "I want her to know there are kind, caring women in this world. That you're one of them. So go on a date with me and spend time with Violet. It doesn't have to be one or the other."

"You are extremely convincing." A smile tugged at my mouth. "Do you always get your way?"

"Usually." He chuckled. "Is that a yes?"

"Yes." A date with Maddox. My heart skipped. "When?"

"Is tonight too soon?"

"Not really."

"Good. I'll pick you up at six."

"Actually, what if I came over? I feel awful for ditching Violet today and I have a present for her too." It was candy and a coloring book.

"Whatever you want." Maddox brought my hand to his mouth, kissing my knuckles. Then he stood. "I'd better get back. Make sure Violet hasn't chased Cathy out of the house. See you tonight?"

"Yes." I escorted him to the door with a smile so wide it pinched my cheeks.

"One more." He pulled me into his arms, kissing me again and giving me one more taste before leaving to go home.

I waited, watching from the threshold until his Audi was out of sight. Then I closed the door and screamed. "Ahh!"

Maddox had kissed me.

Maddox Holiday, the hottest man I'd ever known, had freaking kissed me.

I ran around the house screaming with my hands waving above my head. I was in the middle of a happy dance on the couch when the front door opened. My heart dropped to my feet as I shoved the hair out of my face, hoping above all hope that Maddox hadn't forgotten something and had decided to come back.

No, it was just my father. He didn't believe in knocking.

"What are you doing?" Dad gave me a sideways look. In his arms was the potted houseplant I'd left at his place yesterday.

"He kissed me." I hopped down from the couch. "I had to celebrate."

"Judy!" Dad bellowed over his shoulder.

"I'm right here, Garrett." She scowled at him as she shoved past him and stepped inside. "Do you always have to shout?"

Dad had two volumes. Loud and super loud. But his deep, boisterous voice always made me smile.

"She's talking about kissing," he said. "That's not my department."

I rolled my eyes. "You pretend like you didn't give me the sex talk when I was twelve."

"And I still have nightmares about that, so if we're celebrating you kissing someone, I'm out." Without another word, Dad set the plant on the tiled entryway beside my potted aloe, then backed out of the door, closing it behind him.

"We're celebrating a kiss?" Judy asked, taking off her coat.

"Yes." I jumped back up on the couch and did another shimmy. "Maddox kissed me."

I spent the next thirty minutes telling Judy everything, from my crush in high school, to being hired as Violet's nanny, to the party, to the kiss. When I was done, she texted Dad and told him it was safe to come inside—he'd been hanging out in the car, listening to a true crime podcast.

"So is he the reason you were in a bad mood yesterday?" Judy asked.

"I wasn't in a bad mood."

"Okay, not exactly bad. But you weren't yourself."

We'd spent Christmas together yesterday, per our tradition, eating and watching movies. I'd lazed the entire day away on Judy and Dad's couch. Maybe there'd been a little sulking too over Maddox and the phone call I'd had to make to Cathy to quit.

When I'd finally peeled myself off their couch at midnight, I'd trudged home, leaving my gifts behind—the snake plant Dad had brought over and a personalized recipe binder Judy had filled with her favorites. She was still holding out hope that one day I'd become a fantastic cook, like she was. She failed to forget that I'd once exploded a hot dog in the microwave.

"What are you wearing on your date?" Judy asked.

"I don't know yet."

"Do I know this guy?" Dad asked.

"Maddox Holiday."

He raised his eyebrows. "As in Madcast, Maddox Holiday?"

"The one and only." This was a fantasy. This was a dream.

"What's he like?" Judy asked.

"Nice. Smart. Sofreakinghot."

"Do I need to leave again?" Dad asked, hooking a thumb over his shoulder toward the door.

I smiled. "Maddox has a seven-year-old daughter and she's a spitfire. I sort of love that she isn't an angel."

Judy put a hand on Dad's leg, looking up to him with a smile. "I sort of love that your daughter isn't an angel either."

"What are you talking about? I'm an angel."

She scoffed as Dad studied a speck on his jeans.

"I've always been a good girl."

"Sweetheart, do you not remember how we met?" she asked.

"We met at dinner. In this house."

"Technically, yes. We had dinner. But the first time I saw you was when you were toilet papering the neighbor's yard."

"Whoa. Whoa. Whoa." I held up a hand. "You can't prove that was me."

Dad pulled his lips in to hide a smile.

In all the years since Judy had been a part of Dad's life, I had yet to, and would never, admit guilt of that night. Besides, it wasn't like I'd actually toilet papered Mrs. Henderson's yard. I'd simply ensured that she'd had an adequate TP supply since she'd kept sending her puppy over to poop on Dad's front lawn.

I'd been living at home at the time, saving money for when I decided to quit nannying and enroll at Montana State. Dad had brought Judy home after one of their early dates, wanting to introduce the two of us. An hour before they'd showed up, I'd come home and walked to the front door, texting and not paying attention. It had been dark and I'd been in my favorite pair of tennis shoes. My foot had splattered in a huge pile of fresh puppy shit.

That had been the final straw.

So I'd gone inside and decked myself out in head-to-toe black. Then I'd waited for the Hendersons' light to go off before staging my attack. It hadn't been your typical toilet papering. No, I'd scooped up every pile of puppy poo and made a little mountain of it in Mrs. Henderson's yard. Then I'd built a pyramid out of toilet paper beside it.

Because I *was* an angel.

The only actually toilet papering had been done to a shrub. The smallest shrub in her yard because I was nice like that. I'd been winding down that single roll when Dad and Judy had pulled into the driveway.

Dad had been talking about Judy nonstop for days, and the moment she'd stepped out of the car, laughing at something Dad had said, I'd panicked and raced down the block. I'd killed two hours in the elementary school playground waiting to make sure she'd gone home.

Two days later, when Dad had arranged a do-over introduction, Judy had showed up with a pack of Charmin Ultra-Soft.

The next day, she'd come back, this time bearing home-made chocolate cake and I'd instantly given Dad my approval.

He'd married her four days later and they'd moved into Judy's house. Instead of selling this home to a stranger, he'd rented it to me so I wouldn't have to move.

Mrs. Henderson still lived next door. As far as I knew, she had no idea it was me who'd left the toilet paper. I'd cleaned it up the next day because I'd felt bad. Her dog still pooped in my yard. And I still piled it in hers.

"Any word on Magdalena?" Dad asked. He didn't love the bus, because it had been Mom's, but he also hadn't sold it because after Mom had abandoned me, I'd used Magdalena as my childhood fort. Then when I'd been old enough to drive, we'd gotten her working.

"No." I sighed and collapsed on the couch by his side. "I'm worried, Dad. What if they can't resuscitate her?"

"She's a car, kiddo."

I gasped and shot him a glare. "How dare you talk that way about Magdalena?"

"Do you need money for *Magdalena*?"

Yes. "No."

I'd planned to use the money made from watching Violet for the mechanic. But now that would have to wait. I could dip into my school savings, but I'd made myself a promise years ago when I'd started saving never to raid the college stash.

"I've been thinking about school."

Judy sat straighter, looking past Dad to my face. "And?"

"I think it's time. As much as I like watching kids, it's not the long-term goal." And maybe telling my dreams to Maddox, a man who was wildly successful, made me want to finally start chasing them.

To afford it all, I might need to sell Magdalena. An older-model Subaru like Dad's would be less expensive to maintain and more dependable in the winter.

Dependable. *Blech.*

"We're here for you." Dad smiled. "Whatever you need."

"Thanks." I rested my head on his shoulder.

"What time is your date?" Judy asked.

"Six."

114

"We're going to Costco," Dad said. "Want to come with us?"

"No, I'd better stay and get ready."

He checked his watch. "You have hours."

"There's a lot that needs to happen before a first date. I'll need to take another shower and wash my hair. Exfoliate. Shave my legs in case—"

"Come on, Judy." Dad bolted off the couch and strode for the door.

"You torture him." Judy laughed, standing to follow.

I giggled. "He makes it too easy."

We hugged goodbye, and then I did another victory lap around the house, dancing and cheering, before I spent the rest of the day on my laptop, going through the application for school.

When I had an hour left, I took my second shower for the day so I could wash my hair and shave my legs. Then I collected the aloe plant, Violet's bag of jellybeans and her book to take with me as I headed across town to meet Maddox.

The honeybees in my stomach swarmed when I pulled into the driveway. "I can't believe this is happening."

This was happening.

I was going on a date with Maddox.

I smiled as I walked to the stoop, reaching for the bell only to have the door yanked open before I could touch the button.

"Hey." Maddox was a vision, his dark hair finger-combed. He was dressed like he had been earlier in a pair of jeans and a black sweater. The dark color made the piercing blue of his eyes pop.

"Hi." I handed over the plant and came inside, shedding my coat. I'd opted for jeans too and high-heeled boots with a caramel sweater.

"You look beautiful." He kissed my cheek, lingering for a moment with his lips by my ear.

"Thanks." I leaned into him, dragging in the spicy scent of his cologne.

"Hi, Nat."

I pulled away from Maddox as Heath came striding through the entryway. "Hi."

"How's it going?"

"Good." I studied his face, wondering if he remembered that I'd caught him sucking Stella's nipples at the party.

If he did, we weren't going to talk about it, which was fine by me. "So are you here for game night?"

"Uh . . ."

"Slight change in plan." Maddox gave me a pained look. "Mom and Dad declared tonight family game night."

"*Mandatory* family game night," Heath said, raising a half-full tumbler. "But there is alcohol."

"You don't have to stay." Maddox's hand dragged along the back of my arm. His featherlight touch left a trail of tingles in its wake. "But if you're up for it . . ."

"I'm very competitive. And I show no mercy."

He grinned. "Bring it on, Buchanan."

An hour later, I was officially dominating the Holiday game night.

"Who invited you again?" Heath asked as he shuffled the cards.

"Me," Maddox grumbled, rearranging his short stack of chips. It was clear he was just as competitive as I was, and the fact that I'd just won a huge poker hand was grating on him.

After surveying the massive collection of board games, we'd all decided on a Texas Hold'em tournament so we could all play the same game. Hannah and Keith. Maddox. Heath.

Violet. Tobias was nowhere in sight but I hadn't wanted to ask why he'd shirked the attendance mandate.

"How are we doing?" I asked Violet. She'd declared herself my teammate early on in the game. According to Maddox, she'd had a nice day with Cathy. Though she'd told me I was *funner*.

"Seventeen, eighteen"—the clay chips clinked together as she stacked them—"nineteen blue ones."

Blue chips were worth one hundred fake dollars and there were only thirty in play.

"Excellent." I sent Maddox a malicious grin.

He glowered as Heath dealt the next hand.

Hannah had lost out early and was perfectly content to be the cheerleader for Violet and me. Judging by chips stacks, Keith was in second place. Heath had a similar stack to his father's. And then there was Maddox, dead last.

"Where did you learn to play poker, Natalie?" Hannah asked.

"My dad and I love playing card games. He taught me how to play when I was a kid."

"He did a good job." Keith picked up his cards, then tossed them back to the table. "I fold."

I showed my cards—a two and a seven—to Violet. She shook her head and I tossed them down. "We fold too."

"Why are we even playing?" Heath asked. "We should just declare Natalie the winner and move on to something else."

"Agreed." Maddox tossed his cards down. "I vote for any other game besides poker."

"Can I pick, Nana?" Violet asked.

"Sure." Hannah took her hand and the two of them went to the cupboard, browsing the massive collection of board games.

Maddox stood from his chair and nodded for me to follow him into the kitchen.

I hurried after him, checking over my shoulder that we were alone.

He walked without hesitation to the pantry. Hannah had brought out an enormous spread for us to graze on during the games, so I had no idea how he could be hungry after all of that but I followed.

"What are you—"

He snatched my hand and tugged me into the tiny room, gripping the back of my neck with one hand while the other pulled the door shut. Then his mouth was on mine, his lips greedy. His hands threaded into my hair while mine roamed his chest, my palms dragging against the hard lines of his body.

A groan escaped his lips.

A mewl came from mine.

He pressed me against the pantry's shelves, his arousal digging into my hip. "Fuck, I've wanted to do that all night."

"Good, then do it again."

He obeyed, wrapping me in his arms as his tongue twisted and tangled with mine. I was practically climbing him when he tore his mouth away just as the door whipped open.

Please don't be Violet.

"There's someone here for you," Heath said quickly, then slammed the door shut.

"Damn." Maddox sighed. "This was not how I wanted our first date to go. Sneaking around in my parents' house. Sorry."

I laughed and stood on my toes to press a kiss to the corner of his mouth. "Don't be. I'm having a blast."

"I'm glad you're here. But tomorrow, let's try this again. Dinner. Just the two of us."

"It's a date." I smiled as he dragged his thumb across my mouth before stalking out of the pantry.

I followed behind him, almost through the kitchen when a

laugh carried through the house. A laugh that made Maddox freeze midstride.

"What?" I asked, nearly colliding with his back.

He closed his eyes and his jaw clenched.

"Maddox."

The carefree, fluid grace in his body disappeared. When he took off for the living room, his shoulders were bunched, and his hands fisted by his sides.

I followed, not sure what the problem was until I heard a word that made my heart stop.

"Mommy!"

No. My stomach plummeted.

We walked into the living room to see Hannah and Keith glaring at their newest guest—their anger barely contained—as Violet threw her arms around a beautiful brunette.

The woman straightened when she spotted Maddox, keeping one hand on Violet's shoulder. "Hey, Mad."

Mad.

Yes. Yes, he was.

"Cece," he clipped.

"Merry Christmas."

"Christmas was yesterday."

She smiled, oblivious or purposefully ignorant to the tension in the room. But when her gaze drifted past Maddox to me, the smile vanished. "Who are you?"

I opened my mouth to answer, but Violet beat me to it. "That's Natalie. She's my nanny."

Cece huffed. "You always loved the nannies, didn't you, Maddox?"

Ouch. Well played, Cece.

So much for game night.

CHAPTER 10

MADDOX

"What are you doing here, Cece?" I shut the office door behind us. Violet had a tendency to listen in, and I didn't want her hearing if we got into a fight.

Cece walked to the desk and perched on its edge. "It's Christmas. I wanted to see Violet."

"And you couldn't have called first?"

She crossed her arms over her chest. "Would you have hidden the nanny if I had? Seriously, Mad. Another nanny? Could you be more of a cliché?"

"No." I held up a finger. "We're not discussing Natalie."

Who I dated was none of Cece's business. She'd lost the right to explanations when she'd abandoned our daughter. Besides, she'd had her mind made up for years. This wasn't the first time she'd falsely accused me of sleeping with the nanny.

It wouldn't matter to her that Natalie had known our family for years. That she'd graduated with Heath and Tobias. Or that her tenure as Violet's caretaker had totaled two days and a party. Cece would never accept Natalie.

"Answer my question," I ordered. "What are you doing here?"

"I wanted to see Violet."

"And?"

"And nothing." She pursed her mouth into a firm line.

I waited, my hands fisted on my hips. There was more behind this visit than her wanting to see Violet. If that was the case, she would have gotten here in time for Christmas.

Cece's hazel eyes flickered to mine as I waited. We'd had this standoff many, many times, during our marriage and after. She was as transparent as the office's windows.

So I waited, the clock on the wall ticking as the seconds passed. I'd do this all night if I had to. Though the longest Cece had ever gone in one of our stare-downs had been three minutes.

She huffed and flung out a wrist. "God, I hate it when you just stare at me. Fine. I had to cut my holiday vacation short, okay? Rip and I broke up and the last place I wanted to be was California while he flaunts his new girlfriend all over Instagram."

Rip. The model. The moron.

Now this visit made sense. Cece had always come rushing to Violet when there wasn't someone she'd deemed a better companion for her time.

I pinched the bridge of my nose. "You can't just show up whenever you feel it's convenient. You have to call first, like a guest."

"A guest?"

"Yes, you are in fact a guest."

"I'm her mother."

"Then fucking act like it," I barked.

She flinched.

121

Shit. I cringed, hoping like hell our daughter wasn't listening beyond the door.

Mom had pulled Violet aside when I'd told Cece to follow me to the office. With any luck, they were still in the living room. Natalie was probably home by now. A few snide comments from Cece and she'd all but bolted for the door.

It had physically hurt me to let Natalie leave tonight, but I wouldn't force her to endure what promised to be a disaster. Cece had claws, and though I suspected Natalie had enough bite of her own, I'd save the drama for another date. If there was another date.

Goddamn, I hoped she'd give me another date.

"We're not going to do this." I raked a hand through my hair. "Not again. You don't have the right to show up uninvited. You don't have the right to barge into my family's home. You can stay here tonight because it's late, but tomorrow you're in a hotel."

"A hotel?" Her jaw dropped. "You're kidding."

"No, I'm not kidding. I won't do this to Violet."

"You have no right—"

"I have every right!" I bellowed. "I have every right. The judge granted them to me, and if you'd bothered showing up at the hearing, you would have heard it too. Except money was more important than our child."

Cece stared at me, her eyes wide. Violet had inherited Cece's nose and the shape of her face. But otherwise, Violet was mine with blue eyes and dark hair. She was mine. And it was time to set new boundaries.

"We're moving here."

"You said it was a possibility after school was done for the year."

"It's happening. Now. We're not waiting for school to be out. I want to get Violet into the Bozeman school system as soon as possible. The move is effective immediately. We'll stay here with Mom and Dad until my own house is ready."

"You can't move—"

"I can. How many times do I have to tell you that? I can. You let her go for twenty-five million dollars."

Her face paled. "Maddox."

I'd never been this blunt and harsh with Cece before. Instead of brutal honesty, I'd pandered to her, hoping if I didn't make waves, she'd show up for Violet. Hoping that if I walked on eggshells, she'd keep at least one promise.

No more. Natalie had showed Violet more genuine affection and attention in days than Cece had in years.

"Did you bring her a Christmas present?" I asked.

The guilt on her face was enough of an answer but she launched into an excuse, typical Cece style. "I was in a rush to make my flight. I got home from Hawaii, swapped out some clothes and went straight to the airport. There was no time to shop."

In a rush to make her flight. I scoffed. It wasn't like she had to make it through security lines in time. She had a private fucking plane and a pilot who'd wait for her to swing into a store and buy a last-minute gift.

"Please don't be mad." She pushed off the desk and crossed the room. That famous pout of hers, the one that hadn't worked on me in years, was fixed on her face. "I'm sorry I didn't get a gift. I'll take Violet shopping tomorrow for whatever she wants. Hopefully I can find something other than a dollar store. Tell me there's at least a mall or something."

"Don't do that."

"Do what?"

"Turn up your nose at Montana. Bozeman is a fantastic town. You've been here before and you know there are some upscale shops downtown. And a mall. I won't have you tainting this place for Violet by being a snob. This is going to be her home."

She snarled. "Why are you being such an asshole tonight?"

"Do you really need me to answer that question?"

"Come on, Mad." Cece sighed, placing her hands on my chest. "I don't want to fight."

My hands clamped over her wrists and I pried her away. "No."

It wasn't the first time she'd made a pass at me since the divorce. Sex was her way of getting out of trouble, and during our marriage, it had worked. But never after we'd split.

"This is about that woman, the nanny, isn't it?" she sneered and stepped away.

"Natalie. Her name is Natalie. And you can get used to her being around." Because if I had my way, Natalie was going to be a familiar face in everyone's lives, Cece's included.

"How long have you and *Natalie* been fucking?"

"That's none of your business. And I'm done with this conversation. You can stay here tonight and tomorrow I'll expect you to find a hotel. You're welcome to visit Violet while you're here but you need to call first. If you take her anywhere, you need to tell me where you're going and how long you'll be gone."

She tossed her hands in the air. "You act like I'm a criminal."

"No, I'm acting like a parent. I've been the one to pick up Violet after you leave. I'm the one left holding her while she cries and deals with the fact that her mother doesn't give a shit about her life. So things are going to change. My daughter, my rules. You can either conform or get the fuck out. Understand?"

Her mouth fell open.

"Do. You. Understand?"

She blinked.

124

"I'll take that as a yes." Without another word, I walked to the door, whipping it open and holding it for her as she marched out of the office and down the hallway to find our daughter.

Thankfully, her irritation with me didn't bleed into her time with Violet. Cece managed to stow her frustration and act perfectly happy to shower Violet with hugs and kisses.

I spent the rest of the night hovering, watching as Violet showed her mother all of the Christmas presents she'd received. While Violet took her shower, I hauled up Cece's three suitcases to Violet's room because they'd decided to sleep in the same bed. Then after Violet was dressed in her pajamas and had brushed out her hair, I tucked her into bed.

"Good night, princess." I bent to kiss Violet's forehead and give her a hug. "I love you."

"Love you too, Daddy." She snuggled into her pillow.

I stood and glanced at Cece who was propped up on a bunch of pillows beside our daughter.

"Night, Mad."

"Night." I nodded, my heart twisting at the smile on my daughter's face.

Cece could be a good mother. When she tried, when she put her own selfishness aside, she could be a good mother. Violet adored her and craved her attention.

But Cece wasn't there enough. She never had been.

I walked out of the room, easing the door closed save for a small crack. Then I leaned in to listen.

"Did you know that we're moving here?" Violet asked Cece.

"That's what Daddy said. You like it here, don't you?"

"Yeah. It's pretty fun."

Yesterday, after the presents and Christmas meal, I'd sat Violet down and asked her if she'd be okay moving to Montana sooner than later. Though she'd been bummed to leave her friends, I'd promised she'd make new ones. And I'd promised that every Saturday, we'd go sledding.

Natalie had suggested we find a special activity. Sledding and swimming in the hot tub and whatever else we fit into our Saturdays would be our special activities.

"Can you move here too, Mommy?"

I held my breath, leaning in closer.

"I don't know if I can. Sorry."

"Oh," Violet murmured.

I rolled my eyes. It wasn't like there was a job keeping Cece in California.

"Should we go shopping tomorrow?" Cece asked.

"Sure." There was a rustle of covers as Violet shifted. Then an audible yawn—it was three hours past Violet's normal bedtime.

I inched away from the door, walking downstairs to where Mom was waiting in the living room with a full glass of wine.

"Where's Dad?" I asked.

"He went out to the hot tub."

I nodded and took a seat on the couch beside her, blowing out a long breath. "If she just tried . . . why can't she be like this every time?"

"I don't know, son."

"It breaks my heart. Because when she wants to be a mother, Violet adores her." I hadn't seen Violet this happy in weeks. Her smile. Her laugh. It was almost painful to witness because I knew it would all vanish when Cece did. "What do I do?"

"What you're doing." Mom put her hand on my knee. "Be there for Violet when she leaves."

"Christ, this is hard." I ran a hand over the stubble on my jaw. "How pissed is Dad?"

"Oh, he's pretty pissed. I expect him to disappear first thing in the morning like your brother did tonight. He's worried that if he is around Cece, he won't be able to keep his mouth shut."

Dad was the steady in the house. When Mom was angry, she let it blow. But not Dad. My family hated Cece and rightly so. Mom might be one to lose it, but Dad would simply steer clear and keep it to himself. On the rare occasion he did lose his temper, it was best to be out of the county.

"That would actually be fairly entertaining to see Dad lose it."

Mom laughed. "He rarely does, but I wouldn't want to be in her Jimmy Choos if he does."

"We were having such a good night."

"Yes, we were."

"I screwed up with Natalie. I shouldn't have let her leave." Maybe I should have kicked Cece out instead and made my choice crystal clear.

"No, it was right to talk with Cece alone."

Maybe. But I couldn't leave things with Natalie like this all night. She had to know that she was important too.

"Mom, I need to get some air." I stood from the couch. "Would you mind being here in case Violet needs anything?"

"I've got her. You go. And say hi to Natalie."

I grinned. "How'd you know I'm going to see Natalie?"

"Because I have three very smart sons. It's not easy to fit into the Holiday mix but Natalie does. Like she's always belonged."

Good to know I wasn't the only one who'd felt it.

Maybe it should have unsettled me, diving headfirst into a new relationship. After the disaster with Cece, I'd been hesitant to date. But not with Natalie. Every bone in my body vibrated with the need to be around her. To hold her close and see just where this was headed.

I bent down and kissed Mom's cheek. "Thanks."

"See you in the morning."

I hurried toward the garage, grabbing one of Dad's coats from the hook beside the door. Then I stepped into my shoes and hopped in the car, speeding across town for the dark green house and a woman who was quickly stealing my heart.

The lights were off except for a flicker of blue and white flashes through the front window from the TV. I knocked on the door, waiting in the cold as my breath billowed around me. Then the lock clicked open and there she stood, wearing a pair of Santa-print pajamas. Her hair was piled on top of her head in a messy bun. The makeup she'd had on earlier was gone.

She'd never looked more beautiful.

"Maddox?"

"I'm sorry."

"You drove across town to apologize?" She waved me inside. "You could have just called."

"No, I wanted to do this in person. I'm sorry that we didn't get our date. I'm sorry that the date we had was interrupted."

Her gaze softened. "I had fun."

"Still, that's not what I wanted. But what if we pretended?"

"Pretended what?"

"What if we pretended it was exactly as I'd planned? We went to dinner. I flattered you with my charm and kissed you good night at this door."

"Hmm." She hummed, a smile at the corner of her mouth. "You know, I'm not good with pretend. Maybe show me what you mean."

"Like this." I took her face in my hands and dropped my lips to hers, inhaling her sweet scent and savoring the softness of her lips.

She sank into my arms, opening her mouth for my tongue.

Just one taste, then I let her go. "About what Cece said.

The nanny comment. It's not true. I've never been with one of Violet's nannies. Until you."

"I know."

"You do?"

"I trust you, Maddox. I believe *you*."

I'd been lucky in my life. With my family. My daughter. My career. Certain days stood apart from the others. Like the day last week when I'd opened the door to Natalie.

"I'm going to kiss you again."

"Hold that thought." She laced her fingers through mine and pulled me through the house, stopping at the living room to flip off the television. Then she tugged me down a hallway to her bedroom.

"Natalie." I stopped inside the doorway.

"I thought you were going to kiss me."

Oh, I was. Everywhere. "Before I do, I want you to know that I want this. You and me. I don't want to take it slow. I don't want to wait to be with you. But if you need time—"

"I don't." She walked over and slid her hands up my coat and to my shoulders. Then she shoved it off, the jacket landing with a thud by my feet.

I dove for her as she came at me, our lips smashing together. There was no hesitancy in this kiss, no reservation. I kissed her like I'd wanted to kiss her since that first time. A kiss that was just a prelude to what was to come.

She fumbled with the hem of my sweater, shoving it up my stomach. Then her hands came to my abs and she yanked her lips away.

"What?" I glanced down to where her hands were frozen on my skin.

She blushed and reached past me for the light switch, flooding the room in color. "No way we're doing this in the dark."

I chuckled and grabbed a fistful of my sweater and the T-shirt underneath, yanking them over my head.

Natalie's eyes went wide as they raked down my chest and to where my jeans sat low on my hips. "Hello, Maddox Holiday."

Every hour spent with my personal trainer in LA letting him torture me paid off with the flare in her eyes.

"Your turn." I unclasped the buttons of her pajama shirt one at a time, taking my time as I popped them apart. When I reached the last one, her breath was coming in short pants. My fingers grazed the creamy skin of her stomach and the small jewel that adorned her belly button. Then like she'd done with my coat, I shoved the top off those pretty shoulders.

My arms flew around her, hauling her into my chest. Those rosy, pebbled nipples grazed my skin as I shoved at the waistband of her bottoms.

Her fingers worked the zipper on my jeans but I kept them on, even though my cock ached to slide inside her tight, delicious body. If she wanted an orgasm with the lights on, I was all for it. I could stare at her long, toned legs and sexy curves for days and not have my fill.

I dropped my lips to her neck, sucking below her ear, then I fell to my knees.

Her fingers threaded through my hair as I took in her bare mound.

"Nat." I placed a kiss below her navel.

"Maddox." My name on her lips was the best gift I'd had in years.

I leaned in and dragged my tongue across her folds, her sweetness exploding in my mouth.

Natalie's hands tightened in my hair, the sting in my scalp all the encouragement I needed to do it again.

Sliding one hand up the inside of her leg, I found her wet

center and plunged a finger inside. She shuddered as I sucked and licked and fucked her with my tongue until she shouted my name and nearly collapsed as the first orgasm washed over her.

Her limbs trembled with the aftershocks of her release as I picked her up and carried her to the bed, whipping back the covers and settling her on the cool sheets. Then I went back to the light switch, bathing the room in darkness.

It was going to kill me to walk out of here.

I went to her side and kissed her forehead. "Good night."

"Ni—wait. What?" She shoved up on her elbows. "Where are you going?"

"I don't have a condom." So I was going home for a cold, cold shower. Maybe I'd just jump in a snowbank.

"Oh." The disappointment on her face made the sting of blue balls pinch a little less. "I haven't been with anyone in over a year. And I'm on birth control."

"It's been longer for me."

She shoved the covers aside and smiled, her hands drifting up her flat stomach to her nipples where she pinched them between her fingers.

I groaned and stripped out of my jeans, my cock, aching and hard, springing free. I wrapped a hand around the shaft and stroked before climbing into her bed and settling into the cradle of her hips.

She kissed me, not caring that her taste was still on my lips.

And when I slid inside, my eyes locked with hers, I knew this was the Christmas that was going to change everything.

CHAPTER 11

NATALIE

"That was . . ." I panted, trying to regain my breath. Two orgasms and I was wrecked.

Maddox had collapsed beside me, his chest rising and falling as my heart thundered. "Fuck, I'm never leaving this bed."

"Good plan." I smiled as he yanked me into his side, holding me tight. I draped an arm over his abs, drawing circles in the dusting of hair on his chest as we both regained our breath. "So what happened with your ex?"

He shifted, propping his head up with an arm as the other kept me pinned to his side. "Probably something that should have happened years ago. I wasn't nice."

"Eeek."

"She needed to hear it. Cece can step up or step out. But I'm done pandering to her."

"Good. And how is Violet?"

"I love that you ask about my daughter." He kissed my hair. "She's good. She loves Cece, despite it all."

"And she will. Until she's older."

"I'm sorry that you had to go through that with your mother."

I leaned up and put my chin on his chest so I could see his face. "It used to bother me. I'd get so mad, especially when I was a teenager, but every year I think about her less and less. The anger fades. The resentment. And I have Judy. I wouldn't trade her for anything in the world."

Judy was ten times the mother that my real mother had been. And even though not having a mom for most of my life had been difficult at times, Dad had been enough.

The two of us had simply been waiting for Judy.

Maddox leaned forward, brushing a kiss to my lips. "We need to talk."

"Uh-oh."

"A good talk." He twisted fast, forcing me to my back. Then he hovered over me, his hands tangling in my hair. "What do you say we lean into this? Lean hard."

"What do you mean?"

"It seems crazy that we've only known each other for days. It feels like longer."

"I was thinking that tonight too when we were playing games." Like I'd always been there. Maybe the Holiday crew was simply welcoming, but we'd all clicked so effortlessly that there hadn't been a single awkward moment.

"Good. Because I have an idea and I need you to hear me out."

"Okay," I drawled.

"I don't want to hire another nanny. Violet needs me around, and I'm willing to admit that when I have a nanny, I rely too much on someone else's help. That said, I have to work. It's her legacy I'm building. She'll have every opportunity in the world because of my company, and selfishly, I don't want to give up Madcast. It's my dream. We've got a long way to grow and I want to be there."

"You shouldn't give it up." He'd built it and he should have the chance to see it flourish.

"My job isn't a nine-to-five," he said. "I need some help with Violet and as much as I love my parents, they've already raised their kids. I'm not putting this on them either. I hope you won't be mad, but earlier tonight before Cathy left, I asked her what you have coming."

"You did?"

He nodded. "She said you're going to work for another family starting in January."

"That was the plan. Until today."

"What do you mean? What happened today?"

I blew out a long breath. "I've been thinking of making some changes too. It's time to stop stalling. I don't want to be a nanny my entire life. I want to get my degree and become a therapist. It might take me twenty years because I'll probably need to work part-time too. But it's time."

"Then this could work." The excitement on his face was contagious and I smiled before he even pitched this idea. "Be ours. Or friend. Or girlfriend. Whatever you want to call us. Just be ours. Mine. Violet's. We'll work everything around your school schedule. But I want to see you every day. And I want Violet to see you every day."

Maybe it was crazy to jump this far into a commitment with a man I didn't know very well. Or maybe it would be crazy to push him away.

Dad had met Judy, and in only two weeks, he'd married her. When I'd asked him why he hadn't dated her longer, he'd told me it was because he already knew. They'd both known instantly. And neither had wanted to delay the start of their life together.

Things were different with Maddox and me. Violet wasn't a twenty-year-old woman with a job. She was much younger, and for her, we'd have to take it slower.

But this idea . . .

"Girlfriend," I said. "I don't want to be the nanny. I don't want to be paid. I don't want anything but to see you every day. Violet too."

Maddox moved so fast I'd barely finished my sentence when his mouth crushed mine.

I ran my hands down his spine until my palms squeezed into the curve of his ass. The honed muscle might as well have been carved from stone.

He pressed into my side, his cock hardening between us as his spicy, heady, dizzying scent surrounded me. "I want you. Not just for tonight."

"I want you too." This was happening so fast but I didn't want to slow down. I was diving into Maddox, stroke after stroke, swimming toward the deep end of the ocean.

"Natalie," he whispered into my ear as he shifted, dragging his erection through my center before rocking inside.

I wrapped my arms around his strong back, feeling the muscles bunch beneath my hands. I spread my legs wider, circling his hips as my body stretched around him. My God, he was addicting. It shouldn't be this good so soon. It felt as if we'd been lovers for years, decades, not an hour.

"You feel so good, Nat." He pulled out only to slide inside again. Maddox's hands drifted down my ribs, his touch dragging sparks across my skin. He skimmed my hips and my thighs. He gripped the backs of my knees, pressing me apart as he came up onto his knees, staring down at me.

Our gazes locked as he thrust forward, hitting that place inside that made my toes curl. Move after move, he worked us together, his hips like pistons, until my legs were shaking and I writhed beneath him, a slave to his stamina.

"Maddox, I'm—" The words died on my tongue as the orgasm raced through my body, consuming every inch. Stars broke in my eyes and I cried out, surrendering to the man who was turning my life inside out.

"Fuck," Maddox hissed as I pulsed around his length.

My orgasm loosened its hold enough that I managed to crack my eyes open in time to see Maddox squeeze his shut and surrender to his own release on a groan.

I could watch this every freaking day and twice on Sunday. His muscles glistened with sweat as he poured himself inside of me. His handsome face barely illuminated from the window's muted light.

But he was mine.

Tonight, Maddox Holiday was mine.

Maybe this was fast. Maybe it was reckless and a little crazy. But there was something here. Something powerful and something worth holding on to.

Something to chase.

Maddox collapsed onto the bed, wrapping me in his arms. His heartbeat hammered against my own, his breaths a short staccato against the skin of my neck.

And I clung to him, not wanting him to let go. Not yet.

"Maddox." My voice shook as I breathed his name. From the orgasm. From the wave of emotion crashing over us both.

He leaned back, our bodies still connected, and met my gaze. His fingertips brushed the hair from my face. "What?"

"Do you feel this?"

"Yeah, Nat. I feel it."

I smiled, swallowing the lump in my throat. Shoving aside tears of joy as I leaned up and kissed him.

Maddox Holiday.

The boy who'd been my crush.

The man who'd win my love.

"I'll see you later." Maddox dropped a kiss to my lips. "Give me until nine."

"Are you sure this is a good idea?" Dealing with Cece was inevitable but I was hoping to avoid it for a while longer.

"She'll be gone." He kissed me again.

"Okay. Bye." I stood in the doorway, the cold seeping through my pajamas, but I wanted to watch him drive away. So I clutched my coffee mug, shivering, and waiting until he waved from the driver's seat of his SUV and pulled away from the curb.

It was still dark outside at four in the morning, but Maddox had wanted to leave early so that Violet wouldn't catch him coming home and wonder where he'd slept last night.

The moment his taillights disappeared around the block, I retreated to the warmth of my house. I settled on my couch and turned on the TV. I went straight for the Madcast app to re-watch the most recent season of *State of Ruin*.

Five minutes into my episode, I went in search of my phone. I doubted he was home yet, but I texted Maddox anyway.

What are the chances I can get early access to State of Ruin's last season?

He didn't type a reply but, a second later, my phone vibrated in my hand.

"Is this why you're sleeping with me?" he asked.

"Who slept?" He'd woken me twice for sex and we'd done it again this morning before he'd climbed out of bed and dressed in yesterday's clothes.

137

"Good point." He chuckled. "I'll send you the login info if you keep it a secret."

"Yes." I fist-pumped. "Are you home?"

"Just about."

"Okay. See you in a bit."

"Bye, babe."

I smiled, hung up and snuggled under a blanket as I waited for the sun to rise so I could make my next phone call.

Actually, two phone calls.

My stomach was in a knot, the dread making me sick, but at promptly eight o'clock, I dialed Cathy's number.

"Tell me that you've changed your mind and you'll be going to watch Violet Holiday today."

"I'm going to go watch Violet Holiday today."

"Phew." She blew out a long breath. "She's a sweet girl but it's been a long time since I've had to entertain a seven-year-old. It was exhausting."

I smiled, loving that Violet had taken it easy on Cathy yesterday.

"What made you change your mind?" she asked.

"Do you want the good news or the bad news first?"

"No. Oh, Natalie. No."

"I'll finish out my week with Violet, but please consider this my resignation. I'm going to go to school."

The other end of the line was quiet for a long moment. Then she sighed. "I knew this call was coming. You're too smart and too driven to do this job forever. But I just hate to lose you."

My eyes flooded. I always cried at endings. "I'm sorry for the short notice."

"No, it's fine. You're in between families and this gives me time to juggle before you were supposed to start with the new family in January."

"Thank you, Cathy. For everything."

"Same to you, Natalie. Let's meet for coffee soon."

"I'd like that."

I hung up the phone, wishing I felt lighter. But quitting a job I'd had for years to start school was a fear of its own. What if I hated it? What if I failed?

What if I didn't?

The physical therapist I worked with in town had always encouraged me to consider school. He knew I loved being in the pool. Swimming had become a hobby as a kid, my dad taking me whenever he'd had a free minute in the summers. Then I'd become a lifeguard in high school and captained the swim team.

It would take me years to get my undergraduate degree, and that was only the beginning.

But today felt like the right first step.

It was time to say goodbye to nannying. Time to pursue a dream.

Time to let go of the past.

Which brought me to my next phone call.

"Hi, this is Natalie Buchanan," I said to the receptionist at the garage where Magdalena was being fixed. "This is going to seem strange since I was so anxious to get her fixed, but . . . I need to sell my bus."

CHAPTER 12

MADDOX

Violet shuffled into my bathroom, her hair mussed and her eyelids heavy.

"Morning, sweetie."

She yawned as I picked her up and set her beside my sink. Then I went back to shaving, half of my face still covered in shaving cream.

There were two scratches on my shoulder from Natalie's nails. Having just come from the shower, I was only wearing a towel around my waist so I pivoted, not wanting Violet to ask how I'd gotten the marks.

"Why were you whistling?" she asked.

"Oh." I hadn't realized I'd been whistling. "I don't know. I guess I'm just in a good mood."

A damn good mood.

Last night with Natalie had been the best night I'd had in years. Sex, phenomenal sex, was part of it. But the other part of my good mood was just . . . Natalie. She made me happy.

"I like it when you whistle." Violet yawned again and gave me a sleepy smile.

"Me too." I finished shaving, rinsed my face and patted it dry. Then I left Violet, content on the counter, and went to the closet to get dressed.

In a pair of jeans and a simple gray sweater, I collected my daughter, taking her to the bedroom where the bed was still made from yesterday.

After I'd gotten home from Natalie's, I'd spent an hour in the office, not wanting to wash her scent off my body quite yet. Then when I'd suspected Violet would be waking up soon, I'd hurried through a shower.

"I need to talk to you about something," I said, sitting beside her.

Her shoulders stiffened. "What?"

"It's about Natalie. She's going to come back and hang out with you today."

"Okay." She relaxed. "What about Mommy? She said we could go shopping."

"And you can." When—if—Cece followed through, I'd have a little alone time with Natalie. "But Natalie is going to be around a lot more."

"As my nanny?"

I shook my head. "No. As my girlfriend."

Violet dropped her eyes to her lap, her fingers tugging at her cotton pajamas.

"How do you feel about that?"

She lifted a shoulder. "What about Mommy?"

"Your mom will always be your mom." There was an unspoken message there, one that Violet didn't miss. Cece wouldn't change, something Violet was beginning to understand.

My daughter was too smart for her own good at times.

"Mom doesn't make you whistle."

"No, she doesn't." I took one of Violet's hands and pressed

it between mine.

"I like Natalie," she whispered.

"Me too. Want to take her on a date tonight?"

"I can go too?"

I nodded. "Just the three of us."

"What if Mommy is still here?"

"She can hang out with you for a while today. But she's going to be sleeping at a hotel tonight. And while I'm working, Natalie will be here. Then we'll go to dinner."

If Cece surprised me and entertained Violet all day, I'd be shocked. Hence why Natalie was coming over because I was betting that we'd need backup.

"Okay. Can I have breakfast?"

"Sure." I kissed her hair and led her to the hall. We passed her room and I glanced inside, not seeing Cece. Her suitcase was open on the floor and the bed was unmade. "Where is your mom?"

"She was getting some coffee."

I was surprised that Cece had let Violet out of her sight. Not because she'd missed her, but because Cece was in enemy territory. I'd assumed she would have used Violet as a shield around my parents.

The house was quiet as we made our way to the kitchen. The door was closed to Mom's office. I'd heard the garage door open and close earlier. That had probably been Dad disappearing to Holiday Homes.

I'd send them both an all-clear text later once Cece was gone.

Violet and I found Cece in the kitchen, sitting at the island with a steaming mug of coffee. She was dressed in a pair of jeans and a turtleneck. Her hair was perfectly styled and her makeup artfully applied.

"Morning," I said.

"Hi." She barely looked at me, but smiled at Violet.

"Would you like breakfast?"

"No, thanks."

"Suit yourself." I went to the pantry, smirking that I'd kissed Natalie here last night.

Violet chose cereal and I set her up beside Cece at the island.

Other than Violet's crunching, silence consumed the kitchen, awkward and tense. Cece refused to make eye contact. I poured my own cup of coffee and watched my daughter eat, the occasional dribble of milk dripping down her chin.

When she was finished, I took her bowl and put it in the dishwasher. "Can you go get dressed? I need to talk to your mom for a few minutes. Grown-ups only."

Violet frowned but obeyed, trudging from the room. Her footsteps paused past the first wall.

"Violet," I warned.

"Fine." She huffed and this time she actually obeyed.

"How was your night?" Cece's teeth ground together when she finally looked at me.

"Good."

"Is it really appropriate for you to leave Violet in the middle of the night to visit your nanny?"

"Natalie," I corrected, keeping my voice even. "And I don't think you get to talk to me about what is and is not appropriate, considering you used to fuck Rip in my bed."

Her eyes narrowed.

"I didn't notice a car outside. Would you like me to order you an Uber to take you to a hotel?"

"If you're going to be disappearing every night, then maybe Violet should stay with me there."

"Absolutely not. You can take her shopping today if you'd like, but I expect her back by five. We have plans tonight."

"You made plans? I rarely get to see her. You're taking her away from California. I fly all the way up here and you make plans?"

There was so much I could tackle in her statement. So much to throw in her face. But I'd said it all before and it hadn't mattered. It wouldn't now. "Yes, we have plans."

"Unbelievable. I'll be back for Violet before lunch." She huffed and slid off her seat, marching out of the kitchen, but before she could disappear, I called her name.

"Cece."

"What?" She spun around and crossed her arms.

"Natalie will be here today. She's important to me. She's important to Violet. I expect you to show her the same respect I've shown your boyfriend, and by that, I mean you need to keep your mouth shut."

"Seriously?"

"I'm glad we understand each other."

With a hair flip and an eye roll, she disappeared, leaving me in the empty room.

I shook my head, rubbing at the ache forming behind a temple. It was never easy with her. But I was giving Cece a day and then I suspected she'd be gone. She'd throw her temper tantrum and fly home.

My phone vibrated in my pocket like it had been all morning and I was sure that a string of emails and voicemails would greet me when I got to my desk. But all of that was going to have to wait until Cece was gone and Natalie was here. Where she belonged.

Last night had been the turning point. Like I'd warned her, I wasn't going to wait. I wasn't taking this slow.

Maybe it was foolish, given my history with Cece, but my gut screamed that Natalie was the one. It was the same feeling

I'd had when I'd started Madcast. It was the same feeling I had when someone pitched a hit show.

I knew.

Soul deep.

I took out my phone and pulled up her name, hitting the screen.

"Hi," she answered with a sniffle that made me stand straighter.

"What's wrong?"

"Nothing," she said, too brightly. "Still want me to come over and hang out with Violet?"

"If you're up for it."

"Of course." Another sniffle.

"Nat, what's wrong?"

She blew out a long breath. "I quit my job. And I gave up Magdalena."

"Magdalena?"

"My 1969 mint-green Volkswagen bus. She's been at the mechanic, and I realized this morning if I'm going to pay for school, I need a vehicle that doesn't require specialty parts when she's broken down."

"You named your car Magdalena."

"Um . . . yes. Don't you name your cars?"

"No." But it didn't surprise me in the least that she did. "Do you want to stay home today?"

"I'll be fine. A lot is changing."

"For the better?"

"For the best," she whispered. "Don't worry about me. I'm good. See you soon."

"Bye." I refilled my coffee, then lingered outside of Violet's room as Cece packed her luggage. I hauled her suitcases to the front door and waited for her Uber to arrive. She promised to be back by eleven, which meant noon.

145

Not ten minutes after Cece left, Natalie pulled up in her Subaru.

"So who is that?" I asked, motioning to the car as she came inside the foyer.

"My dad's. He loaned it to me. He doesn't name his cars either, but I'm considering calling him Barney."

I chuckled and pulled her into my arms. "Hi."

"Hi." She melted into me, rising on her toes as I brought my lips down to hers. The kiss wasn't long enough, and if Cece showed up like she'd promised, I'd ignore whatever was on my calendar and take Natalie to my bedroom.

We tore ourselves apart, both turning to freeze at the blue eyes waiting.

Violet had definitely been watching as I'd kissed Natalie.

My daughter studied us, her eyes darting back and forth, then she smiled at Natalie. "Can we play with my Christmas presents?"

"Absolutely." Natalie whipped off her coat, winked at me and let my daughter steal her away.

I went to my office with a smile on my face.

It only lasted through the morning.

Because by noon, when Cece was supposed to be back for Violet, I received a text that her plans had changed and she'd already hopped on a plane for California.

"Fuck." My curse echoed through my office.

I shouldn't have been surprised. With my attitude yesterday and today, I'd pissed her off. Add in Natalie, and it wasn't a shock that Cece had chosen to leave rather than deal with circumstances like an adult in order to spend time with her child.

But it had never been about Violet. Cece was uncomfortable and therefore she was gone.

And I'd be the one to deliver the news to my girl.

I found Natalie and Violet in the kitchen, raiding the fridge. The chef had his earbuds in, chopping herbs on the opposite end, as far from Violet as possible. He kept one eye on her, another on his knife.

"Hi, Daddy." Violet looked past me as I strode into the room, probably wondering if Cece was here.

"We were just going to make sandwiches for lunch, keep it simple." The smile on Natalie's face faded when she noted my expression. "What happened?"

I nodded to Violet, my heart breaking.

Natalie's shoulders fell.

"Violet, I need to talk to you, princess."

"Why?" She studied my face for a long moment. Then her chin began to quiver. "Mom left, didn't she?"

Fucking Cece. I wouldn't forgive her for this. For any of it. How could she not take one look at Violet and see an amazing little girl who just wanted to be loved?

"Yeah. She left."

The first tear fell down Violet's cheek and I opened my arms.

But she didn't turn to me. She turned to Natalie.

"I'm sorry, Violet." Natalie closed the fridge and knelt beside my daughter.

The first sob escaped Violet's mouth and then she flew into Natalie's arms, clinging to her as she cried. "I hate her. I hate her! She didn't even bring me a Christmas present."

Natalie wrapped her up tight and closed her eyes, stroking Violet's hair. "I'm sorry."

Hearing Violet cry was too much, so I walked over, dropped down, and held them both.

It took Violet a while to stop, but when she did, we let her go and I wiped the tears off her cheeks. "I love you."

"I love you too," she whispered, her tiny mouth turned down.

"Let's have some lunch. Then we'll have fun the rest of the day." I'd call my assistant and tell him to cancel my meetings for the rest of the week. I needed to spend time with my daughter. And I wanted Natalie with us.

"What kind of fun?" Violet asked.

"I thought we could drive out and look at the place where we're going to build our house. Then maybe we could go sledding. Or to a movie."

"Sledding," Natalie and Violet said in unison.

So we went sledding. Afterward, we drove past our new property and Violet squealed when she saw the pond. Then we went to a movie, just the three of us.

In a way, it felt like the first day of our new life.

"Who's hungry?" I asked as we left the theater.

"Me." Violet and Natalie both raised their hands. They'd eaten an entire tub of popcorn and a bag of M&M's.

"Okay, we need to make one more stop, then we can go to dinner."

"Where are we going?" Violet asked.

"You'll see." I winked, taking her hand.

Violet grabbed Natalie with her other and we swung her between us while Natalie looked over with those beautiful blue eyes and breathtaking smile.

"Thank you," I mouthed.

If not for her, I don't think Violet would have recovered so quickly from Cece's disappointment today. As we'd driven around town, bouncing between activities, Violet had asked Natalie questions about her own mother. How old she'd been when she'd left. How many Christmas presents Natalie's mom had forgotten to give her.

For Violet, knowing that she wasn't alone in this seemed to help her cope.

Natalie had mentioned Judy a few times throughout the day, and each time Violet would look to me and smile.

Mom had said last night that Natalie fit.

I knew it.

So did my daughter.

Natalie was Violet's Judy.

We piled into the car and drove away from the theater, heading across town.

"Where are we going?" Natalie asked.

"I was going to buy you some flowers for our first date."

"Aww." She smiled. "That's sweet."

I grinned and kept on driving.

During the movie, I'd excused myself under the ruse of refilling the popcorn and using the bathroom. Really, I'd swiped Natalie's phone so I could call her father.

After a quick introduction, I'd asked him if he knew about Magdalena.

Garrett had told me everything, about how the bus had been Natalie's mother's, and despite his hatred of that vehicle, Nat had always loved it. His voice had been so loud and deep that I'd had to listen with the phone an inch from my ear.

He'd given me the mechanic's name and number, and I'd told Garrett we'd meet soon. Then I'd made another call.

"Where are we going?" Natalie sat straighter in her seat, recognizing the street I turned down. This part of Bozeman was made up of industrial buildings and a lumberyard.

Not a flower shop in sight.

"Like I said, I was going to buy you flowers but I had a better idea." I slowed and pulled into the garage's small lot, parking in front of the first bay door. When I'd spoken to the owner, he'd promised to stick around until we arrived. "We're going to rescue Magdalena."

"Maddox." Natalie pressed her hands to her cheeks. "This is too much."

I shook my head. "Let me do this."

"Maddox—"

"Consider it your Christmas present. From Violet and me."

"No. It's too much. Way too much."

"Do you love Magdalena?"

"Who's Magdalena?" Violet asked from the backseat.

"My car," Natalie answered.

"Your car is named Magdalena? Daddy, why doesn't our car have a name?"

"Well, this is a rental. I don't know if you name rental cars."

"You can," Natalie said.

"Okay, then we'll just have to come up with one. You can pick."

"James," Violet declared with a nod.

"I like it." Natalie reached back for a fist bump. "What about a middle name?"

Before Violet could answer, I held up a hand. "How about you introduce us to Magdalena, I'll pay for whatever repairs she needs, then you two can discuss a middle name for James over dinner?"

Natalie sighed. "You can't pay for Magdalena to get fixed."

"It's happening, babe." Eventually she'd get used to lavish gifts because there were many in her future. "Come on."

She opened her door and moved to the back to help Violet out, and then we met with the shop owner. And met Magdalena.

The bus screamed Natalie. The moment I spotted it, I knew I'd do whatever was necessary so she could drive that bus for as long as she wanted.

I thanked the mechanic, who assured me that he'd have the new parts installed soon, and Magdalena would be as good as new in a couple of weeks.

With that settled, I loaded Violet and Natalie into *James* and drove us to dinner. We talked about everything over a large supreme pizza. Natalie's favorite foods. Violet's favorite movies. My favorite part of the day.

This.

Our first date.

The best first date of my life.

With any luck, the last first date.

"Thank you for coming in," the waitress said as she delivered our check to the booth.

Behind her, another waitress walked by carrying a skillet heaped with ice cream.

Natalie and Violet shared a look.

Kindred sweet tooths.

I held up a hand before the waitress could set down the bill, then pointed to the dessert. "We're going to need one of those."

Natalie cleared her throat.

"Make that two."

EPILOGUE
NATALIE

O *ne year later* . . .

"Dance with me." Maddox took my hand, rescuing me from the group of ladies who'd surrounded me and dragged me into a conversation about water births.

"Yes, please." I followed him through the crowd, squeezing past clusters of partygoers.

This year's Holiday Christmas party was packed. If I'd thought last year's party had been busy, the ballroom was practically bursting at its seams. Probably because it wasn't on Christmas Eve.

Most of the faces in the crowd were unfamiliar, even though there were plenty of friends and family here too.

Dad and Judy were at the bar. Judy's cheeks were red and her smile bright. Dad was the designated driver tonight and Judy was into the champagne.

She spotted me and waved just as Violet raced up to them, taking Dad's hand and pulling him toward the dance floor.

Maddox swung me into his arms, holding me close.

"Who called you?" I asked. He'd stepped away a few minutes ago to answer his phone.

"Cece," he muttered.

I stiffened. "What did she want?"

"She wants to come up on Monday to see Violet. We'll see if she actually shows up."

"I don't think we should tell Violet."

"Yeah, I was thinking that too. If Cece shows, it will be a surprise. If she doesn't, Violet will never know."

We'd learned our lesson the last time Cece had called and announced she was coming to Montana for a visit.

Our beautiful girl had sat by the front window, watching the driveway for hours and waiting for her mother to show. Finally, worried that something had happened, Maddox had called Cece only to find out she'd changed her plans last minute. She'd given him some excuse about the weather and flying conditions.

I suspected it was because before her flight, Cece had called Violet who'd slipped and told her that I was pregnant.

Maybe ditching Violet was her way of punishing us. Whatever her reasons, Cece hadn't changed and I doubted she ever would. She came and went whenever it suited her, which wasn't often. And when she broke Violet's heart, Maddox and I were there to pick up the pieces.

I leaned into his broad chest, smiling as his hand drifted to the small of my back. The song was a fast one, but the two of us danced to our own rhythm.

There was barely any space to move anyway. This close to midnight, the floor was full of happy, drunken adults.

"Violet's having fun," I said, finding her and Dad in the crowd. "And she looks so pretty tonight."

When we'd gone to a small shop downtown to pick out a dress, I'd let her choose. I'd assumed she'd go with her standard red, but as we'd perused the racks, she'd chosen a velvet green dress that swished at her knees.

Like last year, Hannah had bought her a tiara.

"She does." Maddox glanced over at his daughter, then bent and kissed my neck. "You look beautiful."

He'd told me the same countless times tonight. My fitted gray dress molded to my baby bump. The diamond earrings he'd bought me as an early Christmas gift were my only adornment, except for my wedding rings.

Just like we'd decided last year, Maddox and I hadn't waited.

We'd started this life together without delay and not a day had passed when I'd regretted a single moment.

After Christmas last year, I'd enrolled at Montana State, adjusting my class schedule so I could pick Violet up from school every day. Maddox had given his father and brothers the green light to build his house and the day it was finished, we'd all moved in together.

We'd been dating for six months at that point. The week after we'd moved in, Maddox and I had gotten married. The ceremony had been simple. I'd worn a fitted white gown. He'd opted for a black suit. And with Violet as our flower girl, we'd stood beside the pond in our yard and exchanged vows with our family and close friends watching on.

One week later, I'd realized that the reason my stomach had been in a constant state of tornado hadn't been because of wedding stress. But because I was pregnant.

When I'd showed him the positive test, Maddox had let out a whoop so loud the ducks in the pond had flown away. We'd talked about a baby—it was just happening sooner than planned.

But we both wanted Violet to have a sibling. I loved being her stepmom, and though a baby might delay my education for a while, I didn't mind. Someday, I'd be a therapist. In the meantime, I was going to enjoy time with my family.

"Are you having fun?" I asked my husband as we danced.

"Yeah. You?"

I hummed my agreement just as someone bumped into my butt. "Yes, but your parents are going to have to find a bigger venue."

Maddox chuckled. "Mom said the same thing earlier."

"I love you," I said, yawning and leaning on Maddox's shoulder.

"I love you too."

He moved us around the dance floor, holding me tight. He did the same when we were at home. He'd come up behind me and twirl me into his arms, dancing me around the bedroom while he stripped me out of my clothes.

Maddox had a way of balancing naughty and nice, and I thanked the universe every day that I'd been called to be his nanny.

THREE BELLS, TWO BOWS AND ONE BROTHER'S BEST FRIEND

CHAPTER 1

STELLA

J itters danced through my fingertips as I smoothed the fabric of my sweater. "How do I look?"

"Cute." My best friend, Wendy, inspected me head to toe. "But you can't wear those pants."

"Why not?" I spun sideways, checking out my butt in the mirror.

Wendy stood from my bed and handed me the green smoothie she'd brought over. "Drink this."

I took a sip from the straw and grimaced. "Blech. How can you stand this every day?"

"It's good for you. There's kale in it. Drink up," she ordered, disappearing into my walk-in closet.

"Eww." I took the smoothie to the trash can in the kitchen and tossed it in. It landed beside the smoothie she'd brought yesterday. Then I grabbed a red licorice stick from the open bag on the counter.

"Are you eating candy?" Wendy's eyes bugged out as she came out of my bedroom, a pair of distressed skinny jeans in her hand.

"Yes. I had an egg white omelet this morning for my health." I waved the licorice in the air. "This is for my happiness."

She frowned and thrust the jeans in my face. "Wear these."

"I'm not wearing jeans on my first day. My trousers are fine."

"They're too baggy."

"They're wide leg."

"They don't showcase your ass."

I rolled my eyes. "I'm trying to showcase my brain. Not my ass."

"But Heath is going to be there."

Heath. Just his name made my heart flutter. "It doesn't matter."

"Sure," she deadpanned.

"It doesn't. Not anymore. He's about to be my coworker and nothing more." That sounded so convincing I almost believed it myself. "I'm over it. I'm ready to meet a guy who actually notices me."

"Really?" Wendy asked.

"Yes. It was just a silly crush." A silly, fifteen-year-long crush.

Ever since my twelfth birthday when I'd stopped believing that boys had cooties, I'd had a crush on Heath Holiday. My brother's best friend.

Of all my childhood fantasies, winning Heath was the only one that had lasted into my twenties—I'd given up hope of winning a Grammy because I was tone deaf and winning an Olympic medal because I had no athletic talent.

My crush on Heath had experienced its peaks and valleys. The occasional boyfriend would steal Heath's thunder from time to time. But the crush had endured.

Until now.

Two weeks ago, his father, Keith, had hired me as a project manager for his construction company. Heath and I were about to be coworkers at Holiday Homes, and it was time to smother my crush for good.

Fifteen years was long enough.

Once upon a time, I'd have worn tight pants in the desperate hope that he'd appreciate my ass and maybe, just maybe, see me as more than Guy's little sister. Those days were over.

"So does this mean you'll go out with Jake?" Wendy asked.

"No."

"Come on. He's so hot."

"Then you date him."

"We work together," she said. "That would be weird."

Jake, like Wendy, was a personal trainer at the biggest gym in town. He was hot, she wasn't wrong. Except Jake knew exactly how hot he was and I had no desire to date a man who spent more than three hours a day staring in the mirror.

I finished my piece of licorice, and despite the scowl on her face, grabbed another.

"Okay, I'd better head to the gym. I've got a client at eight." She walked to the couch and swiped up her parka, pulling it on. "Good luck on your first day. I expect a full report."

"Aye, aye, Sheriff."

"That's not even close." She giggled. "Captain. Aye, aye, Captain."

"I'd much rather be a sheriff than a captain. I get seasick."

She laughed again and came over to give me a hug. "Consider pants that actually flatter your figure."

"I won't." I walked her to the front door, waving goodbye as she hurried through the crowded parking lot in my apartment complex. Then I rushed to my bathroom for one last check of my makeup and hair.

My blond locks were pulled away from my face in a tasteful—boring, professional—bun. My lips were stained a light pink, a classic but cute shade. My gray sweater was soft and fuzzy. Though I preferred bright, bold colors, today I was the epitome of plain. The only thing wild about my outfit was its appropriateness. Trousers and all.

Okay, maybe Wendy had a point. The pants were just a tiny bit . . . slouchy.

I stood in front of the mirror, turning sideways to glance over my shoulder at my butt. It looked . . . huge.

"This is why I don't wear these pants." I worried my bottom lip between my teeth, wiggling my rear in the mirror. No matter the angle, it looked twice its actual width and flat as a pancake.

So what? My coworkers wouldn't be looking at my ass. Impressing Heath wasn't the goal here, not that he'd notice.

A year ago, my brother had arranged a ski-slash-party weekend at Big Sky. Heath and I had both been there, and I'd paraded around that condo in my skimpiest bikini before taking a dip in the hot tub. Had he noticed me practically naked? *No.* A pair of tighter pants wouldn't make a difference.

Besides, I didn't care if he noticed me at work today, right? *Right.*

The reason I undid the clasp on the waistband and shoved the pants to the floor was not for Heath. It was for me. Because on your first day of work, you should love your outfit. That's why I was changing. Not for Heath. Not at all. Not even a little bit.

Kicking off my shoes, I raced through the house to the laundry room. My favorite black pants were in the dryer so I rifled through the heap, finding the right ones. I shoved my legs in, zipping them up as I hustled for the bedroom. With my heels on, I did one last check in the mirror. In these pants, I had an ass. A great ass.

"Much better."

Coat in hand, I headed outside. Snow blanketed the parking lot and streets around Bozeman, Montana. The shining sun made the drive across town to Holiday Homes blinding white.

My hometown was decked out for the holidays and had been since Thanksgiving. Evergreens were strung with colored lights. The old-fashioned lampposts along Main were adorned with garlands and bows. Window displays were teeming with fake snowdrifts and candy canes. This was my favorite time of year, the perfect day to start a new adventure.

Bozeman had changed during my twenty-seven years. The once sprawling farm fields on the outskirts of town were now filled with homes and businesses. Most of the faces at the grocery store were unfamiliar, though the smiles remained. Our small-town roots grew deep. I liked to believe that Bozeman's friendly culture was partly because of the families who'd lived here for generations, like my own. And the Holidays.

It was exciting to see the community grow and to be a part of this boom. Since graduating from college with a degree in business, I'd worked for a local construction company as a project manager. The homes they built were nice, albeit predictable. Spec houses and cookie-cutter blocks weren't overly appealing, so when I'd heard that Holiday Homes, the valley's premier custom home builder, was looking for someone to join their team, I'd tossed my name into the hat.

I had years of relevant experience and was damn good at my job. But if the reason they'd picked me out of all the other candidates was because Guy and Heath were best friends, well . . . this was my chance to prove myself.

Starting today.

My stomach did a somersault as I eased my SUV into the Holiday Homes parking lot. My hands shook as I parked and shut off the engine. But I couldn't seem to force myself out. I sat there and stared at the beautiful wood-sided building with enormous windows that gleamed beneath the blue sky.

The pay was nearly double what I'd been earning. With this salary, I might actually be able to afford a home in the next year so I could stop renting my apartment.

"Here we go." I sucked in a deep breath, then straightened my shoulders, grabbed my handbag and walked inside.

It smelled like coffee and sawdust, exactly as it had the day of my interview.

"Good morning," the receptionist greeted. Her long, gray hair was streaked with white. "Nice to see you again, Stella."

"Hi." My voice shook. "Nice to see you too."

"Excited for your first day?"

"And a little nervous."

"I've seen your résumé. You'll do great. I was actually just going through your new employee paperwork." She stood and rounded the corner of her desk in the lobby, holding out a hand. "Gretchen."

"Of course. I remember you from the interview." I shook her hand, excitement radiating through my fingers.

Gretchen seemed like a no-nonsense person because we skipped the get-to-know-you small talk and she led me straight to my office. She spent twenty minutes getting me oriented with a phone, laptop and company email. Then she handed me a pile of paperwork that needed my signatures.

"Let's do an office tour," she said. "Then I'll let you go through this paperwork. Keith is at a customer meeting this morning but he should be in the office by ten."

"Sounds good." I nodded too wildly. My voice was still

rattling with nerves. And damn it, when were my hands going to stop trembling?

"Keith's a great boss. I've worked here for fifteen years. You won't find a better family."

I opened my mouth to tell her I'd known the Holidays nearly my entire life, but clamped it shut and gave her another overly enthusiastic nod.

Maybe Gretchen knew that the Holidays had known me since my pigtail days. That I'd spent my childhood chasing Heath and his twin brother, Tobias, around the playground. Maybe she knew that I'd gone to their high school and college, and that our personal connection was likely the reason I was sitting at this desk.

But I didn't need to announce it to anyone. I was here to show this company, this team, that I was an asset. There was a chance favoritism had gotten me through the door. But I'd show every employee I could do this job.

Gretchen's office tour was a whirlwind of names and titles. Holiday Homes had grown from its start in Keith's garage thirty years ago to a twenty-person office staff and triple that on the labor crew.

The office building was two floors, the upstairs having most of the offices, including mine. On the first floor, there were three conference rooms with large, wood-paned windows. Next to them was a break room with a stainless-steel refrigerator, an espresso machine and two coffee pots.

Keith's corner office was dark and empty. The room beside it was also empty, though the lights were on. I didn't have to ask whose office it was. I caught a whiff of Heath's woodsy cologne.

I didn't let myself hold in that incredible smell. Not today. Because as of now, Heath was my coworker. My boss-type figure. A friend of my family. Nothing more.

"Heath must have snuck in while we were upstairs," Gretchen said. "I'm sure we'll find him."

I'd spent most of my life finding Heath. "Okay."

"He takes the lead on our larger builds, and the construction staff all report to him. You'll get to know the foremen and the crews with each project. They mostly come and go from the shop. We hold an all-staff meeting there once a month. And you'll see the guys on project sites."

"Can't wait to see it." Again.

The shop was on the other side of town, located in an industrial area of Bozeman and not far from a prominent lumber yard. It was completely out of my way from anything, work or home, but in high school, when I'd been at Bozeman High and Heath had been attending college at Montana State, I'd drive by the shop almost daily just in the hopes that I'd catch a glimpse of him.

During summer breaks from college, he'd be the guy at the shop reloading trailers with supplies. I'd spot him occasionally, sweating and gorgeous, loading boards onto a flatbed truck.

"Tobias?" Gretchen poked her head into the next office over.

"Come on in, Gretchen." A familiar face greeted me with a wide, white smile. Tobias stood from his desk and rounded the corner to sit on its edge. "Hey, Stella. Welcome aboard."

"Thanks." I smiled at Tobias, my nerves taking on a whole new edge.

Yep, this is weird.

This was Tobias, my childhood friend. The kid who'd chased Guy and me around my living room when we'd played tag. The boy who had once accidentally walked in on me in the bathroom while I was peeing.

Now he was basically my superior. As the architect at

Holiday Homes, he'd be giving me orders and making sure I followed through.

If he felt any of the same awkwardness, he didn't let it show. "How's it going so far?"

"Great. Gretchen has been showing me around. I'm sure she'll be sick of answering my questions before the day is over."

"Pfft." She waved it off. "I'm here to help. Whatever you need."

"Gretchen, you remember our friend Guy Marten, right?" Tobias asked her. "Stella is his sister."

"Oh, I hadn't put that together," Gretchen said. "But now that you mention it, I can see the resemblance."

Guy and I both had blond hair, though his was a shade darker than mine. We had the same hazel eyes and narrow noses. But where he was always goofing off, content only if he was earning laughs and standing in the center of attention, I'd been the girl who loved the quiet moments most. The girl who swam or hiked or lost herself in a book. My Friday nights were typically spent in flannel pajamas with a bowl of popcorn and the latest hit show.

"Since you know Heath, I guess we don't need to track him down," Gretchen said, then checked her watch. "Okay, we've got a little time before Keith gets in. I'll let you chat and then settle into your office. Would you like some coffee?"

"I can find it. Thanks, Gretchen."

"Like Tobias said, welcome aboard. We're a family here at Holiday and are so excited to have you here. Keith was so impressed by your interview. He's probably going to dump a bunch of stuff on you today."

"She can handle it." A deep, rugged voice came from the doorway.

I glanced over and my stupid heart tumbled.

Heath leaned against the threshold, his hands tucked into his jeans pockets. "Hey, Stell."

"Hey, Heath." *Don't blush. Don't blush. Please, don't blush.*

My cheeks felt hot, despite my silent commands. I'd been fighting that damn blush for what felt like my whole life.

Why couldn't I see Heath the way I saw Tobias? A friend, nothing more. They had the same dark hair. The same piercing blue eyes. The same soft lips and straight nose. Hell, Tobias had even grown a beard and I'd always thought beards were sexy.

But did my face flame for *that* Holiday brother? No. Never. Not once.

There was something different about Heath.

Maybe it was how whenever he wore a button-down shirt, he'd roll the sleeves up his sculpted forearms. Maybe it was the way his smile was a little crooked on the right side. Maybe it was the way he laughed often and believed cookies were a major food group.

Heath was . . . Heath. A cute boy who'd grown into a ridiculously handsome man. He was the dream.

The dream I needed to banish. Effective immediately.

He pushed off the door's frame to stride into Tobias's office, standing close, but not too close. His cologne wrapped around me like a warm hug. His six-foot-two frame dwarfed my five-four, and I had to tilt up my chin as his blue eyes drew me in. "How's the first day going?"

"Good." My voice was breathy. Though considering it was always breathy when he was in the same room, he probably thought it was normal. Gretchen and Tobias would not. I cleared my throat, dropping it a bit. "How are you?"

Too low. Damn it. Now I sounded like I was impersonating a man.

Gretchen was staring.

I simply smiled. *Nothing strange here, Gretch. Everything is normal. Totally normal.*

"Busy," Heath answered. Right, I'd asked a question. "Thursdays are always hectic."

Thursday was a strange day to start a new job, but when I'd given my former employer my two weeks' notice, he'd asked for a few more days to wrap up the project I'd been working on.

"Did you get an office?" he asked.

"Yep. Gretchen got me all settled."

"Good deal." He nudged my elbow with his. And there went my cheeks again. *Shit.* "I'm getting some coffee. I'll come up and visit later. Guy told me something about a clogged toilet. You'll have to tell me how that all turned out."

My mouth fell open.

Why, of all the things that Guy and Heath could discuss, was the fact that I'd clogged my toilet something conversation-worthy?

I hated my brother. I actually *hated* my brother.

Guy wouldn't even have known about the toilet incident had he not come over while I'd been mopping the bathroom floor with towels.

"It was nothing." I looked to Tobias and Gretchen, my new coworkers who didn't need to think I had plumbing issues—with my house or my bowels. "I was cleaning and the top of my toilet wand, the disposable ones, didn't go down like it should have. My dad came over and snaked it clear for me. All fixed now. And from now on I'll only be flushing the number ones and twos."

Oh. My. God.

Why, Stella? Why?

The room was silent for a beat, then Gretchen smiled and excused herself. Tobias chuckled and went back to his chair. And I slid past Heath, slinking away for the break room.

I swallowed a groan. So it wasn't the best way to start this off. Not the worst, but not the best. But considering my history of embarrassing moments with Heath, I'd settle for a strange toilet discussion.

It was better than the time I'd gotten my period at the park when I was fourteen. Heath and Guy had been out tossing a football and I'd decided to go out there with a book and a blanket, hoping Heath would talk to me. I'd had on my cutest pair of white shorts.

Guy had spotted—literally—it first. He'd declared, right in front of Heath, that I needed to go home and get a tampon.

It was arguably the worst of my embarrassing moments.

Though a close second runner-up was the time in seventh grade when Heath had been over to play video games with Guy. I'd stopped by the living room to watch. Mom had made eggs that morning and eggs always made my stomach rumble. I'd been sitting there, hanging on Heath's every word. He'd said something funny. I'd laughed. And farted. The noise and smell had chased them from the room.

Clogged toilet? No sweat. I'd survived much, much worse. The rest of my day would be nothing but normal. I'd get some coffee, then breeze through the paperwork in my new office before my meeting with Keith.

"Mugs . . ." I opened the cupboards above the coffee pots in the break room, finding them all empty. "Okay, maybe I don't need coffee."

"Mugs are over here." Heath strode in, going for the cabinet beside the fridge. "I told Dad that this was not the logical place to keep them but he likes them beside the dishwasher."

"Ah. Well, for the record, I agree with you."

"Thanks." He grinned and handed me a white, ceramic mug. "Glad you're here. We've been swamped and it will be great to have someone with experience."

"I'm excited to be here too." I filled my mug and smiled. "I liked my other job, but I think this will fit my interests more. I really do love the homes you guys build."

Holiday Homes was known for its meticulous attention to detail. For the past five years, each of their showcases in the annual Parade of Homes had been my favorite.

"We've got some fun projects coming up too," Heath said.

"Good." I raised my mug in a salute. "I'd better get going on my new employee paperwork. See you later."

He nodded. "Have a good day."

I walked away, entirely impressed with myself that I'd made it through that exchange without flushed cheeks or rambling nonsense.

Obviously, I'd spoken to Heath many, many times. But usually, Guy was there to tease me or goof around. Now that we were working together, maybe Heath would see me as an adult if we spent some time away from my brother.

I was a step away from the door when Heath called my name.

"Stella."

"Yeah?" I turned.

He walked over, coming straight into my space.

My breath hitched as he stopped so close that the heat from his chest radiated against my body.

He bent, his large, strong body dropping to a crouch. His fingers brushed my calf.

I watched stunned, speechless, as he stood tall and held out a small scrap of black lace.

A thong.

My thong.

My thong that had been stuck to my pants all. Freaking. Morning. During my time with Gretchen. During the tour to meet my new coworkers. During my break room conversation with Heath.

There wasn't a word for this level of mortification.

"Um . . ." He held out my thong.

I swiped it from his hand, utterly stunned. If I hadn't changed my pants, if I'd just worn the trousers, static cling wouldn't have been an issue. Yet here I was, wearing tight pants with a pair of panties in my fist.

The period and fart incidents paled in comparison.

Heath gave me a small smile, then slipped past me and strode down the hallway to his office.

"Oh. My. God." I set my coffee aside and buried my flaming-red face in my hands.

When it came to Heath Holiday, I was doomed.

CHAPTER 2
HEATH

"Any chance you could get me the Winthrop bid by tomorrow?" Dad asked.

"Ha." I chuckled. "No."

He frowned. "Why not?"

"Because it's third on my list." I tapped my pen on the notepad in front of me. "You told me that the Grant and Freeman bids were priority."

"Damn," he muttered. "We have too many priorities."

"You're not joking."

"Hopefully if Stella gets up to speed quickly, we can shift some of these projects from your plate to hers."

"That would be great." At this point, I couldn't keep up with the estimates let alone tracking every build, because I was being pulled in seven different directions.

Even in December, a month when business should have been slower than average, our crews were struggling to keep up with demand. It was too cold to pour foundations for new builds, but we had enough homes in progress that every construction team was assigned to a jobsite. Most were putting in overtime on framing or flooring or one of many other tasks that didn't start with the letter *f* but my brain was so fried I'd forgotten them at the moment.

"I'm late for dinner and your mom's going to be mad. I'd better head home." Dad stood from his chair across from my desk. "See you tomorrow."

"Yep. Bye, Dad."

He waved and walked out, swinging by his corner office to grab his laptop and coat before the lights flickered off.

"Bye, Dad," Tobias said from his office. Five minutes later, after the shuffle of paperwork and closing of desk drawers, he hollered down the hallway, "I'm leaving too."

"See ya," I called back.

"Want me to lock up?"

"I'll do it."

"Don't stay too late." His footsteps echoed on the hickory floors as he made his way through the lobby and out the front door.

If there was any chance of me taking off the week between Christmas and New Year's, I'd definitely be staying late.

The quiet settled in the building, and I sank deeper into my chair, facing the mountain of work on my desk. It was daunting. Good thing I didn't mind a challenge.

Dad wanted the Winthrop job estimated so I reached for the Winthrop file. I fished out the notes I'd made during our last meeting and found the rough sketch that Tobias had put together after his initial consult.

He was our only architect at the moment. His predecessor had retired this spring and Tobias had stepped in to fill his shoes. My brother was just as busy as I was after New Year's. We'd talked about finding another architect to join the team.

While Tobias loved the planning, the measurements and the tiny details, I simply liked to get shit done. I liked to watch a

174

bare patch of dirt be transformed into a home. As long as the construction was quality and our clients were happy, I didn't care if the roof style was gable, hip or mansard.

For Dad's succession plan, our varied interests had worked out perfectly. He didn't have to choose a son to take over management because Tobias had no interest in replacing him as the general manager. That position would fall to me while my brother would happily spend his days at a drafting desk.

Dad was nowhere near ready to retire, and at twenty-nine, I was nowhere near ready to take over. I had too much to learn from Dad. I had too much respect for him to step on his shoes.

So for now, I managed the foremen and their staff while putting together estimates for our largest and most pretentious jobs. Dad supervised the project managers who acted as the liaisons with the foremen to make sure the customers were happy and that schedules and budgets were on track. In the past year, we'd hired three new project managers, and still, we couldn't keep up.

Holiday Homes was growing. And with it, so were my hours.

I pushed away from my desk, hitting the break room for a glass of water. Then I came back to my office and got to work. I was about halfway through my notes on the Winthrop project when a noise echoed from the ceiling. My fingers froze above the keyboard. "What the hell?"

Another noise had me standing and hustling to the stairs. Everyone should have gone home already. The lights in the hallway were off. Every office was dark.

Except one.

Stella's.

What was she still doing here? It was her first day. If anyone should have headed home by now, it was her.

Stella's feet were bare, her heels discarded by the window.

The sleeves of her sweater were bunched at her elbows as she scrambled to pick up ice cubes off the floor.

"What are you doing?"

"Ah!" she screamed, her face whipping to the door. "Oh my God, you scared me."

"Sorry." I held up my hands, stepping into the office. "I thought I was the only one left, then I heard a noise."

"I bumped my glass over. It was empty except for the ice." She plucked up three more cubes, dropping them into the glass before standing to her feet.

Her hair was coming out of its knot, a few long, blond tendrils framing her face.

Stella Marten was one of the most beautiful women I'd ever seen.

And my best friend's sister.

I don't get to think she's beautiful. I'd been reminding myself that for years.

I didn't get to drown in those hazel eyes or think about kissing her soft lips. I didn't get to fantasize about her toned legs wrapped around my hips or the fact that I'd had her panties in my hand this morning.

Off-limits. Stella had always been off-limits.

"How was your first day?" I asked, walking into the room and taking the single empty chair opposite hers at the desk.

"Good." She sank into her chair, swiveling it back and forth. There was more paperwork on the desk than I'd expected to see. "Your dad believes in drinking from a fire hose, doesn't he?"

"Two fire hoses." I laughed. "What did he give you?"

"The Jensen remodel."

I cringed.

"That bad?"

"It's over budget and behind schedule."

I expected a groan. Maybe a string of expletives. But Stella sat straighter and nodded. "I'll fix it."

"I believe you can."

Stella, like me, didn't back down from many challenges. Even though she was two years younger, as kids, she'd always kept up with Guy, Tobias and me. On our bikes, no matter how hard she'd had to pedal, she'd kept pace. At the swimming pool, when we'd dared her to try the high dive, she'd plugged her nose and jumped. And at the ski hill, when we'd all attempted our first black diamond, she'd followed us down the mountain.

"Thanks." Her cheeks colored.

That blush of hers was as pretty as her eyes. I'd seen it countless times in my life and it never got old.

"So what can you tell me about the Jensen project?" she asked.

"Well . . . it's been a disaster from the start, partly because we didn't have the time to take it on and should have turned it down. But Dad is friends with Joe Jensen and didn't want to say no. Then, because we didn't turn it down and no one had time, it hasn't really had a primary resource. We've all chipped in, here and there, but what it needs is a driver to see it through."

"I can do that." She nodded at the mess of papers on her desk. "As soon as I make sense of this."

"I did the original estimate. I think they've had a few change orders since, but I can go through the details with you if you'd like."

"Really? That would be great."

"How about now?"

"If you don't mind."

"Not at all." I had other work to do, but in the past year, I'd found it harder and harder to stay away from Stella.

I blamed it on that damn party Guy had organized last

year at Big Sky. Stella had come along to ski, then party at the condo. She'd taken a dip in the hot tub every night and the image of her in that orange bikini was burned into my brain.

It was like a lightbulb had turned on. Stella wasn't Stella, my friend's little sister and the tagalong. Stella was *Stella*.

Beautiful. Smart. Charming. Sexy.

I liked Stella.

Despite the reasons I shouldn't.

I carried my chair around to her side of the desk as she slid over a file folder. Then we dove in, spending the next hour going through the drawings, schedule and progress update notes.

"Tomorrow, let's find an hour, and I'll take you out to the jobsite."

"Thanks, Heath."

"You're welcome."

Her eyes met mine, and for a moment, I almost leaned in. For a year, I'd been tempted to cross the line. To taste the lips I'd wanted to taste for months. But Guy's voice rang in my head.

Off-limits.

"This project seems to be costing a hand and a foot, doesn't it?" she asked.

"Huh?" I blinked. "A hand and . . . oh. You mean it costs an arm and a leg. That's the saying."

"A hand and a foot seem less extreme than an arm and a leg." She waved it off. "You know how sayings go. Potato, tomato."

"Also not a saying."

"Po-tah-toe, toe-mah-toe."

I fought a smile. "Still not right."

"It makes sense to me." She shrugged. "Disagree to agree."

178

"That's . . ." I lost the battle and laughed. God, she was funny. In the way that she never tried to be funny.

She was just . . . Stella.

"It's late." I relaxed into my chair. "I was planning on ordering in some dinner. Want to stick around and eat? Or are you ready to get out of here?"

"I could eat."

"What do you feel like?"

"Whatever you want. Surprise me."

I pulled my phone from my pocket and opened the Door Dash app. I'd had enough meals at the Marten house to know that Stella loved pepperoni pizza. With it ordered, I nodded to the papers on her desk. "Besides the Jensen project, what else did my dad give you?"

"That's the only project for now, but he mentioned some general organization stuff. During my interview, I told him how I'd researched this new project management software for my old company. I put this entire pitch together about how it worked and how it could improve efficiency and customer communication, but my boss didn't want to show it to the owner. He said our processes worked fine, so why change them?"

"Ah. Is that why you left?"

"Partly. I also really like the homes you guys build."

"They're the best." Pride laced my voice.

Dad had established Holiday Homes with his two hands, blood, sweat and back-breaking hours. His standards had been passed down to our craftsmen, and he never settled for less than exceptional. He might not wield a hammer these days, but he hired men who shared his craftsmanship. They built homes that they'd all be proud to live in themselves.

"What's the software?" I asked.

"It's just a client interface. The customers can log in to see

179

their schedules and invoices. It's where you'd process change orders. The crew takes pictures of their progress each day so we can upload the photos into a dashboard. It makes the entire process more transparent. Which is probably why my old boss didn't want to do it. It would be harder to hide missed dates."

"Dad's a big advocate for being upfront about the schedule. I bet he started salivating about this."

She smiled. "He was pretty excited."

"Dad's all about organization these days. He feels like we've got a solid crew, but we're short-staffed on the business side of things." Considering Stella and I were both here after dark, he wasn't wrong.

"What do you think?" she asked.

It was the first time anyone had asked me that question in a while. "I think sometimes Dad wants to make this business perfect so that when he retires, it's smooth sailing for me and Tobias. Except he forgets that neither of us mind some rough waters."

"You'd get bored if it was perfect."

"Yeah, I would." A familiar feeling settled in my chest. A feeling I usually got around Stella. Talking to her was like talking to my oldest friend. She knew me, understood me, arguably better than anyone else, including her brother.

Stella was more insightful. Maybe it was just a female thing, but she asked the questions guys didn't often ask.

My comfort with her was just another reason that she'd been tempting me for a year. The bikini incident had opened my eyes, but if I was being honest with myself, I'd been drawn to Stella for a lot longer. Which was why I tore my gaze away from her beautiful face and stood, returning the chair to the other side of the desk.

"I'm keeping you from your work," she said. "Sorry."

"Don't apologize. I'm going to head downstairs." I needed

to put a staircase between us before I did something dumb. "I'll holler when dinner gets here."

"Okay. Thanks again."

"Always." I smiled and disappeared.

My office was cold compared to hers and didn't smell half as good without her sweet perfume, but small interactions with Stella were necessary. Otherwise, my body would get ideas about doing things to hers. Dirty, delicious things.

The delivery guy was prompt, and before I'd resecured the boundaries with Stella, he came into the building. I traded him a seven-dollar tip for a pepperoni pizza, then set it up in the break room before taking the stairs two at a time.

Stella was focused on the Jensen file when I reached her office, a pen in her hand and a pencil between her lips.

To be that pencil.

I swallowed hard. "Dinner's here."

Her eyes flew to the door and her mouth fell open, the pencil dropping. "Be right there."

Damn, but she was pretty with her hair falling out and her guard down.

I forced myself away, dragging a hand over my face. What the hell was wrong with me tonight? As of today, we were coworkers. Another reason to keep our relationship strictly platonic.

When Dad had hired her, I'd told him it was a great decision. Stella would be an asset to our team. Except maybe shoving my attraction aside might be harder than I'd realized. We'd be spending time together. I'd see her daily.

Off-limits.

Whatever was going on with me, I needed to get my shit together and fast because Stella wasn't going anywhere. We worked together now, and Guy would cut off my balls if I dared touch his sister.

What would he say if he knew I'd had her panties in my hand today?

Poor Stella. I chuckled to myself as I took out plates and forks and napkins in the break room. I doubted anyone else had seen her thong. Gretchen would have told her if she'd noticed. The only reason I'd spotted it was because I'd been checking Stella out, drinking in those long legs and those perfectly fitted black pants. Not too loose. Not too tight. Just sexy as fuck.

The thong had been clinging to her hemline, almost dropping to her heels. The image of her wearing only those stilettos and that thong popped into my head and my cock jerked behind the zipper of my jeans.

Don't think about Stella naked. Don't think about Stella naked.

"Fuck my life," I muttered.

"What?"

I turned to see Stella behind me. "Oh, nothing. Just thinking about a job."

A blow job.

Goddamn it, Holiday. I gestured to the table, taking the chair in the corner.

Stella sat opposite me and flipped open the pizza box, closing her eyes as she dragged in the scent of garlic and cheese. "I love pepperoni pizza."

"I know."

She opened her eyes and took a slice, moaning at the first bite. "I was starving."

I watched her chew, the way her lips moved and the satisfaction on her face as she closed her eyes again, her entire focus on tasting her food. That was how Stella did most things. With intent. She'd always had this way of savoring the tastes, smells and sounds that the rest of us took for granted.

In my world of endless distraction, Stella made me stop and take pause.

A drop of sauce leaked off the slice and landed on her sweater, right at the upper swell of her left breast.

I stared, my mouth watering to lick it away.

"Seriously?" She set her pizza down and dove for the napkins. "I swear you are cursed."

"You're not curs—wait. Did you say *I'm* cursed?"

"Well, yeah." She blotted at the sauce but all it did was make the orange stain grow. Finally she gave up, balling the napkins and tossing them aside. "Damn it. This was a new sweater."

"I'm sure it will come out. But you didn't answer my question. Why am I cursed?"

"Because my most embarrassing moments all happen when you're around." She gestured to her sweater. "Example one. Example two is the thong in my purse."

I grinned. "So that makes me cursed."

"Absolutely. The list goes on and on. Remember that time Guy bought a Slip 'N Slide my sophomore year? You and Tobias came over to try it out and dared me to do it too. Which I did."

"And your top came off." The image of her bare breasts as she'd streaked into the house was crystal clear, even all these years later.

That pretty pink flush crept into her cheeks. "See? You're cursed. That was horrific."

"I didn't mind," I teased. "That Slip 'N Slide incident was one of my favorite memories from high school."

"Cursed." She reached for her pizza and took a bite.

I took my own piece, turning my attention to eating so I wouldn't think more about Stella's breasts. But that orange stain was like a beacon to her chest, and after my tenth glance, I knew it was time to call this day quits. Before I made a mistake.

"Want any more?" I asked, and when she shook her head, I flipped the lid on the box closed, taking it to the fridge. "Are you about done tonight?"

"Yeah. Thanks for dinner."

"You're welcome." I nodded to the door. "It's dark. Grab your stuff and I'll walk you out."

"Okay." She collected the trash and put it in the garbage can, then slipped out of the room.

"Hell." I rubbed a hand over my face.

This had to stop. For good.

I'd made a promise years ago and had kept it for too long to break it now.

Guy had always been protective of Stella, in his own way. He teased her mercilessly. But behind her back, he'd been a pit bull since high school, barking at any male who'd so much as glanced in her direction.

The day she'd walked into Bozeman High as a freshman, a shy, beautiful girl, Stella had turned a lot of heads. Guy had made me promise that if anyone made a move on his sister, I'd help kick their ass. He'd spread that word and no one had been stupid enough to cross him and ignite his infamous temper.

Guy was right to watch out for Stella. Sweet, sweet Stella.

I went to my office and grabbed my coat and keys, then walked to the lobby and waited for her. When the click of her heels sounded on the stairs, I looked up and my mouth went dry.

She'd taken her hair out. The blond strands draped around her face and hung down nearly to her waist. That hair had been a part of many adult fantasies.

"Ready?" she asked.

"Yeah. Let's get out of here." Fast. I strode to the door,

holding it open for her. Then I locked up the office and fell into step beside her as we crossed the parking lot to her SUV.

"See you tomorrow, Heath."

"Bye, Stell." I walked to my truck, climbing in and waiting until she reversed out of her spot and pulled onto the street. Then I let out a frustrated groan.

She was off-limits.

Why did that make me want her even more?

Of all the women in the world, why was Stella the one who tempted me? Maybe she was right.

I was cursed.

CHAPTER 3

STELLA

"This is fantastic," Keith said.

I beamed under his praise. "Thank you."

"I vote we buy it." He rapped his knuckles on the conference room table. "Everyone good with this?"

Heath, Tobias and the other two project managers who'd watched my presentation all agreed.

"I'm excited to try out this software," Tobias said, glancing at his phone, then pushing his chair away from the table. "Great suggestion, Stella. I've got to duck out for a call."

"And I've got a date with my lovely wife so I'm taking off too," Keith said. "I'll be out most of next week. Maddox is coming home so I'll be sticking close to the house. But I'm a phone call away if you need anything."

Keith stood and made his way to the door with the project managers shuffling out close behind.

Leaving Heath and me alone.

I breathed for what felt like the first time in an hour.

"Good job, Stell."

"Did I do okay? Be honest."

"You did awesome." His smile was contagious.

I'd found Heath's gaze often as I'd given my pitch today. Not only because his blue eyes were the most alluring in any room, but because over the past two weeks, something had shifted between us.

The nerves that normally came with seeing him had subsided. Maybe because we saw each other every day, either in the break room or when we crossed paths in the hallways. Maybe I was getting over my crush—*probably not*. Whatever the reason, the swarm of yellowjackets in my stomach that usually accompanied Heath's smile had moved on and found a new hive.

Butterflies had taken up their place. Delicate and lovely butterflies that had fluttered each time he'd given me a sure nod while I'd demoed the software I'd told him about on my first day.

"I thought it would take longer." I glanced at the clock on the wall. "Is it bad that there weren't many questions?"

"Your presentation was solid." He leaned his elbows on the table. "I had questions but you answered them all."

"Okay, good." I shut the lid on my laptop. "Then I'm calling it a win."

"A big win." He shoved out of his chair. "We should celebrate. Want to head downtown for a drink?"

Ooh . . . bad idea. In the past two weeks I'd managed to avoid any other embarrassing moments with Heath, but it was only a matter of time before the curse returned. Adding alcohol to the mix would surely accelerate the inevitable.

Say no. "Sure."

"Grab your stuff. Meet you in the lobby in five." He strode out of the conference room, and I smacked a hand to my forehead.

Weak. So weak. But it was too late to take it back—that and

I didn't want to take it back because this was Heath—so I scrambled to collect the materials from my presentation and head upstairs to my office where I put everything away. With my camel wool coat pulled on and a gray blanket scarf wrapped around my shoulders, I grabbed my purse and slung it over a shoulder.

Flipping the lights off in my office, I moved toward the staircase, hearing a familiar voice echo from the lobby.

"Guy, you'd better stop flirting with me," Gretchen warned. "I'm old enough to be your mother."

"You say that every time I come in here."

"And you never listen."

"Nope." My brother chuckled, and with his laugh, my spirits sank. So much for a celebratory drink with Heath. Guy would hijack the night and steal his best friend.

Damn.

The clomp of my heels as I trudged down the stairs drew his attention and he smiled when he spotted me. "Hey, Stella Bells."

"Hi. What are you up to?"

"Thought I'd see if Heath wanted to head downtown. Grab a drink."

"Oh. Great," I lied.

"Hey." Heath came down the hallway from his office, shrugging on his black coat. Combined with his dark hair and rugged voice, that coat was sexier than it should have been. Oh, what I wouldn't do to shove it off those broad shoulders.

Yeah, my crush wasn't entirely dead.

"You up for a drink?" Guy asked him.

"Actually, we were just heading downtown. Celebrating Stella's successful presentation today."

"We don't need to." I waved it off. "You guys go without me."

"Come on, Stell." Heath nudged my elbow with his. "One drink."

"Or three," Guy teased. "For me. You can be my designated driver."

Being the third or fourth wheel hadn't bothered me as a kid. But now it felt . . . pathetic. And I had no desire to be Guy's chauffeur.

"Or . . ." Heath shot him a flat look. "You can call a cab."

"I'm just kidding." Guy shrugged. "Mostly I like it when Stella drives because she's the safest drive in Gallatin County."

Yes, I typically drove five miles per hour below the speed limit, but I'd never had a ticket or gotten into an accident.

"Come with us, Stella," Guy pleaded. "Don't be boring."

"Fine," I muttered. I loved my brother. I adored Heath. But the two of them together weren't always easy to be around. Not because of Heath but because of Guy.

He had no filter and loved to tease. Most of the time he'd forget I wasn't one of the guys. The last time we'd gone out, a bunch of his college fraternity brothers had been in town for the homecoming football game. He'd coerced me into going out with them, and the group had traded stories for hours about the women they'd screwed.

As the drinks had flowed, the stories had become more and more far-fetched, and finally, after three hours, I'd told Guy he could find a different ride home. The only good thing about that night was that Heath hadn't been there. I don't think I would have been able to handle hearing him describe his sexual escapades with other women.

Though I doubted he would have shared anyway. Heath had never been that sort of man.

At least, not around me.

But Guy had a way of bringing out the crude, and whenever he and Heath were drinking together, I'd made it a point to stay away. One glass of wine and then I'd go home to trade my jeans for a pair of pajama pants.

We drove separately downtown. Parking was a nightmare because Main was a popular place for holiday work functions and parties, but I managed to find a spot two blocks away from the bar where we were meeting. I left my car in the snow-covered lot, then headed for the bar.

I'd just rounded the corner of the sidewalk when a rumbling voice called my name.

"Stella."

I glanced over my shoulder to see Heath rushing to catch up.

His long legs ate up the distance between us. Under the faint streetlamps, he looked unbelievably sexy. His jaw chiseled. His hair finger-combed off his forehead. His lips soft and supple.

I used the moments it took for him to reach my side to stop my heart from doing cartwheels. There would be no acrobatics. We were coworkers. Friends, maybe? Nothing more.

"Hey." Damn. My breathy voice was back after a two-week hiatus in the office. I hadn't missed it.

"Ready?"

"Is anyone really ready to go drinking with Guy?"

"True." He laughed. "You might think you're ready. But you never are."

I smiled and fell into step beside him, turning my face to the decorations strung across the street. "I love that they still string the same garland that they did when I was little."

"Same here. Mom and Dad used to bring us down here for the Christmas Stroll each year. So much around Bozeman has changed, but I love that this is the same."

The green, gold and ruby garland draped over Main in thick, glittering strands. Wreaths had been hung on the doors of most businesses. Golden twinkle lights illuminated the trees, making them sparkle against the background of the black, winter sky.

The temperature was creeping toward zero, but downtown, it felt warmer with the scent of apple cinnamon and pine clinging to the air.

So busy glancing around, I missed a patch of ice on the sidewalk and my heel caught it, nearly sending me crashing to my knees. Except a strong arm wrapped around my waist, pinning me to an equally strong body.

"Whoa." Heath stopped, holding me up until my legs were steady.

"See? You're cursed. I haven't slipped on ice in years."

He chuckled, loosening his grip. "Yes. It was my fault that you weren't paying attention."

"Exactly."

"To be safe." He took my forearm and tucked it beside his ribs, holding my arm as he started down the sidewalk again.

I caught our reflection in a shop window and my breath hitched. We looked like a couple. A hot couple. I bit my lip to hide a smile and kept walking. There was no harm in pretending for a block, right?

Our journey ended too soon, and when we reached the bar, Heath let go of my arm to open the door.

Guy was waiting at a table with three shots already lined up. Knowing my brother, they were all for himself.

"This is going to be interesting," I muttered.

"Your brother is nothing if not entertaining." Heath touched my elbow. "Think you can make it to the table on your own or do you suspect I'll twist your ankle?"

"Har har," I deadpanned, then joined my brother. After we took our coats off, he surprised me by sliding a shot to Heath and me.

"Cheers." He raised his glass, waiting just long enough for ours to clink his before he tossed the tequila back. "So Mel and I broke up today."

"Oh, Guy." I pressed a hand to my heart. "I'm sorry."

He shrugged. "No big deal."

Liar. It was a big deal. He and Mel had dated on and off in high school, but had broken up for the final time before heading to college. They'd kept in touch over the years, and when she'd moved back to Bozeman a few months ago, they'd started dating again.

Guy had talked about Mel all the time. He'd even told me that this time around, it might be the real deal.

"What happened?" Heath asked.

"She wanted to be done, so now we're done." He slid off his stool. "You guys want another shot? Because I do."

Without waiting for us to answer, he stalked toward the bar and flagged down the bartender. This time, his three shots were just for him. He threw them down his throat in quick succession, then clapped and forced a too-wide smile.

"Check her out." My brother jerked his chin over my shoulder.

I shifted, following his gaze to a brunette standing at the bar wearing a tight yellow dress and over-the-knee boots. Not exactly winter apparel but she did make a statement. A redhead in a similar dress, this one pink, joined her friend, the two of them scanning the bar.

Hunting. They were hunting.

And Guy would gladly become their prey.

Technically, I'd had my drink. Could I leave now?

I should have known this would happen when Guy had suggested the Rocking R Bar. It was his favorite bar and where I suspected he picked up most of his women. It was typically a college hangout, but this close to Christmas, most students were into finals and the bar was mostly people our age, adults in their twenties and thirties.

"That brunette's eye-fucking you, Holiday." Guy grinned. "Get over there."

Annnnnd it was time for me to go.

"Nah." Heath didn't so much as look toward the women. "We're here to celebrate Stella's successful first two weeks at work."

"Don't be lame," Guy said.

Heath's jaw clenched. "Don't be an asshole."

"Whatever. So work's been good?" Guy asked me.

"Yeah, I like it."

"She's doing a hell of a job." Heath gave me a little smile.

"Of course she is." Guy clapped his hand on my shoulder. "You guys were lucky to steal her. Stella's a rock star."

"Thanks." Yes, Guy could be a huge, blunt idiot. But he also had so much confidence in me that it gave me confidence in myself. Whenever I was unsure, he'd tell me I could do anything I set my mind to.

"Welcome." My brother nodded, then glanced around the bar. "Hey, look. It's that guy you had a crush on, Stella."

"W-what?"

The only guy who I'd crushed on was Heath. But there was no way Guy would call me out here, now, would he? No way. Guy was a jerk sometimes but that would be cruel.

"Joel? Isn't that his name?" Guy pointed to the other side of the bar.

I spotted who he was talking about and my heart climbed out of my throat. "Yes, his name is Joel. But no, I never had a crush on him."

"Yes, you did."

"Pretty sure I didn't." Joel and I had gone to college

193

together, and this crush Guy was thinking of had been the other way around. "He liked me. I wasn't interested."

"That's right. Because you were too busy drooling over Heath." Guy laughed, oblivious to what he'd just said.

Meanwhile, my heart splattered on the table. *Ouch.* Tonight, the humiliation was courtesy of my brother.

"Jesus, Guy," Heath clipped. "What the hell?"

My brother scoffed. "It's not like we all don't know she was into you for like a decade. Who cares?"

Heath's jaw clenched. "Shut up, Guy."

"What's wrong with you two tonight?" My brother scoffed. "I thought we were here to have some fun."

"I think I'm all *funned* out." I stood from my stool, grabbed my coat, scarf and purse, then headed for the door, not even bothering to bundle up for the cold.

Tears pricked at the corners of my eyes as I flew out the door. I huffed it down one block, pulling on my coat as I walked, and by the time I made it down the second, the sting in my nose and the burn in my throat made it hard to breathe.

Why would he say that? Now, of all times. Heath and I weren't just acquaintances anymore but coworkers. Why was my brother such a dickhead? Guy had always teased me, but he'd never teased me about my crush on Heath. Never, not once. Why tonight? Was it because of his breakup with Mel? He was hurting, so what, he'd spread the pain? I was his sister, for fuck's sake.

"Asshole," I muttered, refusing to cry.

Heath was never going to be into me. I *knew* Heath was never going to be into me. I'd known for fifteen years. There was no need for Guy to rub it in my face.

Normally after an embarrassing incident, I could avoid Heath for weeks. Months. Not this time. I had to see him on Monday morning. There would be no avoiding this, and now, thanks to Guy's non-existent filter, it would be awkward in the office.

Heath would stare at me with his sparkling gaze and pity me for a silly crush. I didn't want Heath's pity.

"Damn it." A tear dripped free, leaking down my cheek. I brushed it away, walking faster around the corner that would lead me to the parking lot.

"Stella."

I kept my eyes down, my focus on the sidewalk, even though Heath's voice bounced off the downtown buildings.

"Stella, wait."

My legs moved faster.

"Stella." Damn those long legs of his. Heath caught me just before I could open my car door, gripping my elbow and forcing me to stop.

"What?" My voice cracked as I dropped my chin.

"I'm sorry."

"Why?" I shrugged. "It's fine. Just Guy being Guy."

"It's not fine."

No, it wasn't. "Let's forget about it, okay?"

"Stella." That voice. He was making it hard for me not to cry. Because there was pity in his voice. "Look at me."

I shook my head.

He released my elbow, but before I could bolt, he hooked a finger under my chin, tipping my face up to meet his. "Did you really have a crush on me?"

"You know I did," I whispered.

He had to have known. Subtlety had never been one of my talents, especially as a teenager.

"I did know. But I want you to tell me."

"Why? To prolong the humiliation? Can we not talk about this? Please."

"Yeah." He let me go and I spun, reaching for the car, but

then he stopped me again by placing a hand beside the window, trapping me between the door and his towering body. "Stella."

"You keep saying my name."

"I love your name."

"I—what?" The tequila had to be messing with me because there was no way I'd heard that right. I twisted to stare up at him and the expression on his face stole my breath.

Not an ounce of pity clouded those blue eyes.

"I think Guy's a prick because it's his way of saying he knows."

"Knows what?"

His eyes searched mine. "That I have a crush on you too."

My mouth fell open.

Which seemed to suit Heath just fine. Because one second he was standing there, staring at my open mouth. The next, his lips covered mine and his tongue slid between my teeth.

CHAPTER 4

HEATH

Kissing Stella was not the smartest decision I'd ever made. I mean . . . it was a great fucking move because her lips were the sweetest I'd ever tasted.

But this was Stella.

I'd spent the weekend bouncing from elation to regret and still hadn't decided what to do about it. Pretend it hadn't happened? Tell her it was a mistake? Ask her on a date?

Call in sick so I didn't have to face her today?

"Goddamn it." I rubbed a hand over my jaw, staring at the office building through the windshield of my truck.

Stella was inside already. Her car was parked five down from mine. She'd probably gotten here early, hoping to avoid an awkward encounter in the break room. Or maybe she was packing her things.

Dad was going to kick my ass if I chased away Stella. He'd bragged daily about stealing her from her former company. How she was going to be our new superstar. He wasn't wrong.

And I'd placed her in an uncomfortable situation.

Somehow, I had to make it right. I owed her an apology except I wasn't sorry. Not even a little.

Another truck eased into the space beside mine, and I glanced over to see my brother park and climb out. Time was up. There'd be no more stalling. So I joined him on the snow-dusted sidewalk. "Morning."

"Morning. How was your weekend?"

"Uneventful." Technically, it wasn't a lie since I'd kissed Stella on Friday. My Saturday and Sunday had been spent mostly staring at my living room wall, agonizing over a woman. Questioning the kiss. Fretting about how much I wanted to do it again. "You?"

"I spent most of it here, unburying. I don't want to work all week, especially once Maddox gets here tomorrow."

"I'm hoping to take some vacation too. We should see if he can take a day to ski. It's been a while since the three of us did anything together." Years, actually.

Maddox had moved to California for college and had ended up staying after he'd started his mega-successful streaming network. His company Madcast—and a bitch of an ex-wife—had kept him close to LA in recent years. But he was coming home for the holidays with his daughter, and the last time we'd talked, he'd announced that he was moving home. Finally.

He'd gotten sole custody of his daughter, Violet, after his divorce, and Maddox wanted to raise her closer to family, in the same town where we'd grown up. He wasn't sure of his timeline yet, but it would be good to have him home.

"I could ski," Tobias said, stomping his shoes on the mat inside the door. "Morning, Gretchen."

"Good morning, boys."

With Gretchen, we'd always been *boys*. We always would

198

be boys considering she'd chased us around as toddlers. Gretchen was a staple of Holiday Homes, having worked here longer than any other staff member, except for Dad.

"Morning, Gretchen," I said, keeping my eyes trained forward as I strode down the hallway. I didn't let myself glance upstairs toward Stella's office.

Tobias disappeared into his office and I closed my door.

I'd keep it closed today. I'd stay in my chair, bust out a lot of work so I didn't have to work while Maddox was home. And in doing so, I'd stay on my floor while Stella worked on hers.

I cast my eyes to the ceiling after shrugging off my coat and hanging it on the hook beside the door.

Stella had gasped when I'd kissed her. But she hadn't kissed me back. She'd stood there, frozen, either from shock or December's cold temperatures. When I'd pulled away from her delicious mouth, her eyes had been wide and her cheeks flushed. Then before I could say anything, she gave me a tiny shove away, spun for her car and disappeared.

Why hadn't she kissed me back?

That question had been a plague on my mind. It was what bothered me the most. She'd had a crush on me when we'd been younger, but maybe she'd grown out of it. Maybe I was too damn late.

I sat at my desk. I opened my computer. I stared at the ceiling.

"Stella." I truly loved her name—not something I'd planned on admitting like I had Friday.

Where was her head at? Had she liked the kiss? Hated it?

"Hell." There'd be no work today. Not until I cleared the air. So I blew out a long breath and marched to the second floor.

She was at her desk, one elbow propped on her desk and

199

her chin in her hand. The other was unmoving on her mouse. She stared at the computer screen, unblinking. So lost in thought she hadn't heard me walk down the hall.

"Knock, knock."

She jumped at my voice, the mouse flying out of her hand and across her desk. "H-hi."

"May I come in?"

"Of course." She swallowed hard, stood and wiped her palms on her jeans. Her long blond hair was down today, the locks curled in loose waves. She was in a chunky sweater that dwarfed her slender form. "What's up?"

I closed the door behind me, then walked to a chair. "May I?"

"Please." She sat too, sitting so straight I was worried she might fall off the edge of her chair.

"About Friday."

"We don't have to talk about it."

"I owe you an apology." The words tasted bitter.

"Okay." She bit her lower lip, worrying it between her teeth as her gaze dropped to her desk.

"I crossed a line. We work together, and I don't want you to think that I'm taking advantage."

She shook her head, a crease forming between her eyebrows. "I don't."

"It won't happen again." Even if I wanted to kiss her again with every cell in my being.

"Yeah, it's, um . . . better to keep things professional."

"Right." Fucking professionalism. "Um . . . how was your weekend?"

Small talk? Really, Holiday? I hated small talk nearly as much as I hated talking about the weather.

"Good." She shrugged. "Boring. You?"

"Same."

Silence settled, heavy and thick. She looked everywhere but at me. The wall. Her keyboard. A coffee mug with a rainbow as the handle.

My apology was out there. I'd done what I'd needed to do. So why was I still in this chair? "Sure is cold out today."

Goddamn it.

"It is." Stella's gaze darted to mine, then flickered away. "Super cold."

Leave. Stand up. Get the hell out of this room. "Are you going to the party?"

"I hadn't planned on it. I was going to go to the Christmas Eve church service with my parents, but then Guy came over yesterday and begged me to be his date."

"Ah." I hadn't spoken to Guy since Friday.

He'd called once on Saturday but I'd ignored him. Mostly because I was pissed that he'd embarrassed Stella. And partly because I wasn't sure if I could face him, knowing that I'd crossed a line.

I loved my best friend, but he could be a bastard. What the fuck had he been thinking, saying that shit to Stell?

She was incredible, and yeah, she'd had a crush. Big deal. A lot of girls in high school had crushed on me.

I'd deal with Guy later. He'd be at my parents' annual Holiday Christmas party on Saturday.

That gave me the week to figure this out.

"You've forgiven him for acting like an ass on Friday?" I asked.

"No. Sort of." Stella lifted a shoulder. "He didn't think it would bother me."

That was bullshit. Guy had said it because he had no filter. Usually his direct declarations would earn a laugh, but this time, he'd gone too far.

"He's pretty upset about his breakup with Mel," she said.

"That doesn't give him an excuse to be a prick."

"I know." She sighed. "I shouldn't defend him, but he's my brother. It's almost Christmas, and I'm picking my battles. I don't want to fight with him, and you know how stubborn he is."

Yes, I did. If Guy didn't see that what he'd done was wrong, he'd hold a grudge and throw a tantrum. It was . . . exhausting. I'd learned to pick my battles too.

"Do you think there will be a good turnout at the party since it's on Christmas Eve?" Stella asked.

"According to Mom's latest RSVP count, most people are coming." Mom and Dad's annual soiree was always a hit with their friends.

"Why is it on Christmas Eve?" Stella asked.

"The Baxter booked out the room for their normal weekend for a wedding. The bride booked it two years ago, but still, Mom was livid. She threatened to move the venue for the rest of time, so the hotel cut her a pretty sweet deal to have it on Christmas Eve."

"I'm glad it worked out."

"Me too."

The silence returned, and I bit my tongue to kill the small talk. Then I forced myself out of the chair. "I'll let you get back to work."

"Have a good day."

"You too." I lifted a hand to wave, then left her office.

One step into the hallway and I missed the scent of her perfume. But I continued on, returning to my desk and willing Stella from my mind. But did I work? No. I sat in my chair and thought about the beauty on the second floor.

She wanted to keep this professional. Did that mean she regretted the kiss? Did that mean she hadn't kissed me back because of her job? Or because she wasn't attracted to me any longer?

Damn it, I wanted answers. Except this was not the place to discuss it. In the name of *professionalism*, I wouldn't let myself go upstairs again.

My concentration was shot. Maybe I should just pack up my laptop and leave. I could work from home for the week. Or I could work from Mom and Dad's place. Or . . . take vacation time. There was plenty of work to do, but Dad had always encouraged us to take a break when needed.

Today, a break seemed necessary.

"Vacation," I declared and shut my laptop. I'd spend some time away from Stella. Get my head right.

Decision made, I packed what I'd need and grabbed my coat.

"Do you even know what the hell you're doing?" A man's voice carried down the hallway before I'd stepped out of my office.

I set my stuff aside and rushed out, thinking I was about to see Gretchen put someone in their place. But the question hadn't been aimed at Gretchen. It had been snapped at Stella.

"Mr. Jensen, I apologize." Stella's voice stayed calm and collected. "I understand this is frustrating, but if you want zebrawood for the floors, we will have significant delays in finishing your project."

"Just order it. Express ship it. I don't care. I see no reason why it should take longer. You haven't ordered the white oak yet, right? So just swap it out."

I reached the lobby and caught Gretchen's eye. She nodded to where Stella and Mr. Jensen stood on the opposite side of the space.

Stella had a coffee mug in her hand. Joe Jensen was still

wearing his coat. My guess was that Stella had come down for a refill and Joe had caught her in the hall.

"Unfortunately, I can't simply swap it out, Mr. Jensen," Stella said. "Zebrawood is an exotic species and to get the quantity needed will take longer than white oak. The local yard keeps white oak stocked. They don't have any zebrawood."

"Are you sure? Have you asked them?" He leaned forward, bending to talk in her face.

That move right there pissed me right the fuck off. Yes, he was a client, but there was no reason for him to attempt to intimidate her.

Not that his attempt worked.

Stella stood taller and plastered on a fake smile. "No, you're right. I haven't asked them. But I'll make a call right now. If you're sure that's what you want, I'll get a change order and new project schedule to you by this afternoon."

"Yes, that's what I want." He backed away, his lips pursed. Then Joe spotted me and walked right past Stella, nearly bumping his shoulder against hers. He was all smiles as he crossed the lobby, his hand extended. "Heath. How's it going? Do you have a minute?"

"Hi, Joe. Happy holidays. And for you, sure." I nodded toward the nearest conference room. "Have a seat. I'll meet you in there."

"Fantastic." He unzipped his coat as he passed me by.

Joe was going to ask me to take on his project. I didn't have to set foot in the conference room to know exactly what this conversation would entail. But Joe was about to be disappointed.

Stella's shoulders fell as she turned and walked for the stairs, her gaze glued to the floor. She knew what Joe was about to ask me too.

An hour later, I escorted Joe from the conference room. He

wasn't entirely happy that I'd refused to take his build on myself, but after a lengthy discussion, he understood that if he wanted the project done right, he needed Stella.

"Thanks, Heath."

"Sure." I nodded, escorting him to the lobby. "See you at the party Saturday?"

"Wouldn't miss it." He waved at Gretchen, then pushed out the door.

Gretchen watched him leave, tracking his steps until he was in his Cadillac, then she shook her head. "I've never liked Joe. Today just reinforced my opinion. The way he marched in here and practically jumped on Stella. He didn't even tell her hello."

"He's . . . difficult."

"Understatement," Gretchen muttered.

My plan to leave and avoid Stella had been shattered, so I headed for the stairs.

She sat behind her desk, her fingers moving furiously over the keyboard as she glared at her monitor. The *click, click, click* was so loud that I didn't bother knocking.

"Hey."

"Hi." Her eyes darted to mine, but her fingers never stopped. "Zebrawood will take an additional six months to arrive. It's back-ordered and has been for months. For an order this size, and with the lumberyard's specialty wood stocking fee, I hope Joe's got his checkbook ready because this is going to cost him."

I rounded the corner of her desk, propping up on the edge as her fingers continued their assault on the keys. "Hey."

She typed a few more words, then paused, glancing up. "Did he ask for someone else to run his project?"

"Yes."

Her hands dropped to her lap, her chin to her chest. "I figured as much. The first assignment from your dad too."

"I told him no."

Her face whirled to mine. "You did?"

"He's abrasive and arrogant."

"Don't forget condescending."

"He's all those things, Stell. But he's also logical. He wants this job done and he realizes that to make that happen, he's got to make certain decisions. You told him *no*, which is not something he's heard yet with this project. But you stood up for yourself. He respects that. He told me the same just before he left."

"Your dad is testing me with this one, isn't he?"

I chuckled. "Yep."

"Thank you for not pulling me off it. Joe and I might not end this as friends, but I'll do a good job."

"I know you will."

"Just keep rolling with the kicks, right?"

"Um . . . what?" I replayed that sentence in my head. Roll with the kicks? "You mean roll with the punches. That's the saying."

"Maybe but it's a dumb saying. If someone kicks me, guaranteed I'm dropping to the floor. And then if they keep trying to kick me, I'll just roll away."

I blinked. "Rolling with the punches is an expression from boxing. You roll with a punch to lessen the impact."

"But I'm not a boxer. So rolling with the kicks makes more sense."

"Does it?"

"Yes."

I studied her beautiful face. "No."

"Well . . ." She shrugged. "Disagree to agree."

This woman. Somehow, her nonsense made sense.

As her hazel eyes locked with mine, I realized just how close we were. Almost as close as we'd been on Friday before I'd kissed her.

All I had to do was lean down. All she had to do was shift six inches.

Stella Marten was as tempting as a wrapped gift under the Christmas tree.

But she hadn't kissed me back.

So I moved, standing from her desk and putting it between us. "I'm sorry. About Joe. And Friday."

She nodded, her shoulders turning in on themselves. "It's fine."

It wasn't okay. Because all I could think about was doing it again. "I, um . . . I'd better get going."

I had a vacation to start. A very necessary vacation. "Bye, Stell."

With my feet aimed for the door, I was just about to the safety of the hallway when she called my name.

"Heath?"

I turned, putting a hand on the door's frame. Maybe if I held on tight enough, it would keep me on this side of the room. "Yeah?"

"Why did you kiss me?"

I answered her question with one of my own. "Do you still have a crush on me?"

Because if it was over, if it was something she'd let go along with her adolescence, then I'd stop this. Somehow, I'd stop thinking about her.

"We work together." Her answer was like a knife to the heart. "You're Guy's best friend."

"Right." I swallowed my disappointment. "We should keep this professional."

"We should." She nodded. "That's a good—smart—idea."

207

It was a fucking horrible idea. But I'd respect her wishes. "I'll see you at the party."

"Oh, you're not working this week?"

"Maddox is coming home. I'm taking a vacation."

A Stella vacation.

And maybe by Saturday, I'd have forgotten the taste of her on my tongue.

CHAPTER 5
STELLA

"Y ou look hot." Wendy whistled. "Smoking hot."

"That's a lot of eye shadow." I picked up a blending brush, but Wendy slapped it from my hand.

"Don't even think about ruining my masterpiece."

My shoulders slumped as I stared at myself in the mirror. "I don't want to go."

"Why not? I thought you were excited."

"Headache," I lied.

The truth was mine and mine alone. Wendy was my best friend, but I was taking Heath's kiss to the grave. Well . . . maybe not the grave. Keeping secrets was not my forte and the only reason I'd managed so far was that Wendy and I had both been busy.

Tonight was the first time I'd seen her all week, and from the moment she'd walked through the door, we'd focused solely on getting me ready for this party.

A party I didn't want to attend. Not with my brother. And not with Heath.

I still wasn't sure what to think about that kiss. Mostly, I tried not to think about it because the shame that came with that memory—a memory I should have cherished—made me want to curl up in a ball and hide under my bed for the next twenty years.

My only saving grace had been Heath's absence from the office. Never in my life had I looked forward to *not* seeing Heath, but his vacation had been my reprieve.

A reprieve that ended tonight.

"After a couple drinks, I bet you'll feel better." Wendy gave me a soft smile in the mirror.

"Yeah." I smiled back. "Thanks for helping me get ready."

"What are best friends for? I have to live vicariously through you. I can't remember the last time I had an excuse to get dolled up and wear a sexy dress."

"But you get to wear leggings every day. I'd trade leggings for a sexy dress any time."

"This is true." She laughed. "Okay, what shoes?"

"Nude heels?"

"Agreed. I'll grab them."

As she rushed from the bathroom, I twirled the skirt of my dress, feeling the swish of the fabric over my legs.

The top had a plunging neckline that dipped low enough to be sexy but not too low to be scandalous. This was technically a work function. The flowing skirt hit me midcalf with a slit on one end that ran to my thigh. The dress was black with a deep plum overlay adorned with sparkles. My hair was curled. My hazel eyes were lined with black and shadowed in gray.

Wendy was right. I did look hot. A year ago, I would have done all this and more, just in the hope of snagging Heath's attention. Tonight, I wanted to wash it all away simply to blend in with the crowd.

He'd kissed me. Heath Holiday had kissed me.

And he'd regretted it.

I squeezed my eyes shut, willing the pained look on his face from Monday out of my head.

Heath's lips had been so soft. So delicious. One sweep of his tongue across mine and I'd about fainted. How long had I wanted a kiss? How long had I hoped for Heath's?

My one chance and I'd blown it.

He'd kissed me and I'd stood there like a dumbstruck fool. Mouth hanging open. Drool pooling.

That kiss had been a sheer disaster. The equivalent of a Christmas tree catching fire. Suggesting we keep things professional had been my last-ditch attempt to save face.

The worst part? I was a good kisser. I was a really good kisser. I'd had boyfriends who'd told me the same. So why, when presented the one and only opportunity to kiss Heath Holiday, had I failed so epically?

"Damn you, stage fright."

"What?" Wendy came into the bathroom carrying my strappy nude heels.

"Oh. Nothing." I took the shoes, bending to put them on and secure the strap at my ankles. They weren't exactly practical for a December night, but fashion required sacrifice. And frostbite risk. "Thanks."

"Do me a favor. Try to have fun tonight. I know it's always interesting with your brother around, but ditch him and enjoy the party. It's your Christmas Eve too."

"Okay." I pulled her into a hug. "Merry Christmas."

"Merry Christmas."

The doorbell chimed, sending us out of the bedroom in a flurry. Wendy rushed to collect the makeup she'd brought over while I grabbed my coat and clutch.

"Hi, Guy," she said, opening the door before pushing past him. "Bye, Guy."

His lip curled. "Wendy."

My brother and my best friend had never gotten along. Guy thought Wendy was a snob because she never laughed at his jokes. Wendy thought he was self-absorbed and crass— hence the reason she didn't laugh with Guy.

I'd stopped playing mediator years ago.

"You look very pretty, Stella Bells." He took my coat and held it out. "You'll be the most beautiful girl at the party."

"Thanks." I slid my arms in. "You look nice too. New suit?"

"It is. I thought it was time for an upgrade." He offered me his arm. "Ready for this?"

No. I blew out a long breath. "Ready."

"Thanks for coming with me tonight."

"You're welcome." I bumped my shoulder to his. "Sorry about Mel."

"Me too." He gave me a sad smile. "I liked her."

"Want to talk about it?"

"Not tonight. Let's just have fun. Me and you. I get all your dances."

I nodded. "Deal."

The cold night air was brittle on the bare skin of my calves as we hurried to his truck. But he'd left the engine running and the seat warmers on.

"How was work this week?" he asked as he eased out of the parking lot.

"Good. Great, actually. I feel like I'm settling in and I like it so far."

"They're lucky to have you."

"Thanks."

"So what have you been working on?"

I spent the drive downtown telling him about my projects. Guy had spent a lot of years tuning me out—little sisters were probably annoying at times. I'd spent a lot of years ignoring my big brother too. But he listened as he drove and asked a few questions, engaged in what I had to say.

I'd been dreading tonight, not only because of Heath but because Guy had the habit of ditching me. He'd get around his friends and I'd become an afterthought. But maybe tonight would be different. Maybe he'd stick with me and we could have a good time.

Guy could be my savior. The buffer between Heath and me. There was no way Heath would mention that kiss while my brother was around. And I really, really didn't want to hear another apology.

"Want me to drop you off at the door?" Guy asked as we reached The Baxter.

"No, that's okay. I can walk."

"But you're in sandals. Your toes are going to get cold."

"It's fine." I wanted to know where the car was in case he had a few too many cocktails and I needed to drive us home.

"Suit yourself." He shrugged and circled the block, finding the closest spot available.

Guy lent me his arm as we hurried down the sidewalk, the streetlights on Main glowing brighter as we reached the hotel.

The Baxter, like the other buildings downtown, was magical over the holidays. Through the golden and glass doors, the lobby was the picture of holiday festivities. Even on Christmas Eve, the space was bustling with people. Some were here to dine at a restaurant on the main floor. Some were here for drinking. A group was clustered around the bar in the corner, each holding a fancy cocktail.

A couple stood beneath a sprig of mistletoe and shared a kiss. In the corner was a massive tree, its bows adorned with lights and ornaments. A few kids were hovering over a bowl of candy canes.

Guy led us straight for the grand, sweeping staircase that

led to the ballroom on the second floor. "Can I put the keys in your purse?"

"Sure." I opened it for him as we ascended the stairs, stopping by the coat check. Then, with my jacket and clutch tagged and stowed, we walked into the ballroom.

Conversation floated above the background music. Caterers swept through the room, passing from person to person with trays of hors d'oeuvres. Two bartenders, each wearing white shirts and black satin vests, mixed drinks at the bar.

Keith stood next to his wife, Hannah, both welcoming us as we came into the room. I tried my very hardest, but my eyes scanned the crowd, searching for Heath. Old habits.

He wasn't here yet.

"Drink?" Guy asked.

"Please." I nodded, smiling at a few familiar faces as we walked toward the bar.

Gretchen waved from her spot at a cocktail table. A few others from the office were huddled together with their spouses.

Joe Jensen stood at another table, nodding when I met his gaze. I smiled too wide at the asshole. Last week after our encounter in the office, I'd emailed him the updated flooring estimates.

He had yet to respond.

The ballroom was decked out for the party. An empty stage was prepped and waiting for a live band. The tall tables were covered with pressed white linens and each had a tiny bouquet of red roses in its center. The room's crystal chandelier cast a twinkling glow over the empty dance floor.

"What do you want?" Guy asked as we waited in line at the bar.

"Champagne." I'd have a headache tomorrow, not ideal for

Christmas Day, but this party and this room demanded a drink with bubbles.

With my flute in hand, Guy and I headed for a table.

"Cheers." He clinked his vodka tonic with my glass.

"Cheers." I took a sip and scanned the room again, my gaze landing on the doorway just as Heath walked in.

My heart skipped. Wow, he looked good.

His black suit accentuated his broad shoulders. His dark hair was parted on one side and styled with a swoop above his eyebrow. The tie he wore was a blue nearly as bright as the color of his eyes.

No man was as handsome as Heath. Movie stars. Professional athletes. Models. I'd let other women drool over them because Heath outshone them all, inside and out.

Maybe that was why it was so hard to let go of this crush. Because the man himself was unforgettable. He was good and kind and charming. He stood apart from every other face in the crowd, demanding attention. That chiseled jaw. The straight nose. The full lips. My mouth went dry so I took another drink.

Heath spotted us and smiled. A smile so dazzling, I choked.

Coughing and snorting, I somehow managed to swallow and not spew champagne over the table.

"Jesus." Guy patted my back. "Are you okay?"

I waved him off. "Fine. Wrong pipe."

He gave me a sideways look, but when he spotted his best friend walking our way, my near-death incident was forgotten. "Finally. Heath's coming over. Now the party can start."

"Gee, thanks," I muttered.

"You know what I mean."

"Do I?"

Guy shrugged and reached into his suit jacket pocket for a piece of spearmint gum. He almost always chewed gum

215

because he never wanted bad breath if there was—in his words —*a hot chick around who wanted to suck face.*

A poet, my brother.

"About time you got here." Guy clapped Heath on the shoulder as he joined us.

"Hey." Heath shook my brother's hand. "Hi, Stell."

"Hi." I raised my champagne flute to my lips, drinking more carefully this time, and doing everything in my power not to stare. The flowers on the table really were beautiful.

"So, what's the plan of attack?" Guy asked Heath. "Maybe have a few drinks. Dance. Then find a woman to entertain. I do love seeing a sexy dress on my bedroom floor."

I scrunched up my nose. "Please stop talking."

"Kidding." Guy laughed, but we all knew he wasn't joking. I had no doubt that it was rare for either Guy or Heath to leave this party alone. The image of Heath with another woman made my skin crawl.

"Let's just enjoy the party," Heath said, giving me a strained smile.

Awkward. I swallowed a groan.

This wasn't even my fault. I'd been the catalyst for plenty of embarrassing moments, but this one was all Heath. *He'd* kissed *me.* Yes, I could have done a much better job at kissing him, but this wasn't my fault. I did not instigate the kissing.

Why was it that a man could kiss a woman and completely forget it, but a woman would analyze every single second? Or maybe that was just me? I'd likely analyze Heath's kiss for the rest of my life. That really, truly, horrendously amazing kiss.

"Surprised you didn't beat us here," Guy told him.

"I rode with Maddox and Violet." Heath hooked his thumb over his shoulder to where his brother strolled into the room with an adorable little girl at his side and a stunning woman trailing behind them.

I did a double take. Not at Maddox, but at the woman and her friendly face.

"Excuse me." I set my flute down and made my way to my friend. "Nat!"

Her face lit up when she spotted me. "Hey, Stella."

"It's so good to see you." I hugged her, wishing we saw each other more.

Natalie was two years older, the same age as Guy and Heath. She'd been a junior when I'd joined the high school swim team as a freshman. Even though I'd been younger and possessed only a fraction of her talent in the pool, she'd always cheered for me. She'd never treated me like I was beneath her.

Unlike Guy and Heath, Natalie hadn't been in the popular crowd at Bozeman High, and I'd always looked up to her because of her kind heart.

We'd stayed in touch over the years since neither of us had left Bozeman after graduation. She'd started working as a nanny while I'd gone straight to Montana State for my bachelor's degree.

"I had no idea you'd be here," I said. But her presence settled some nerves. Wait. Was she here with Maddox? Were they dating?

"It was a last-minute invite. I'm actually here to work."

The young girl she'd come in with appeared at her side. This had to be Maddox's daughter. She had his dark hair and blue eyes. Without so much as a glance my way, she held up an empty punch cup to Natalie. "Can I have more?"

"Let's pace ourselves. We have all night." Natalie laughed, looking back at me.

"How are you?" I asked. "It's been forever."

She opened her mouth to answer, but Guy appeared at my side along with Heath.

Guy was talking, but the moment he spotted Natalie he did his own double take. "Natalie?"

"Hey. Good to see you, Guy."

"Been a while." My brother's jaw worked as he chewed that gum. And checked out her ass.

I rolled my eyes. Seriously, he'd just gone through a breakup. *Men.*

"Guy." Natalie shook her head when he looked up and met her gaze.

"You sure?"

She giggled. "Quite. But thanks anyway."

He chuckled. "Are you here alone?"

"Nope." She waved to the girl. "Violet's my date tonight. And we're raiding the dessert table before any of the good stuff disappears."

"Natalie's the coolest of the cool," I told Violet. "You're going to have a blast tonight."

"But not as cool as Uncle Heath, right?" Heath held out his hand for Violet to smack it.

She blinked and ignored him.

"Ouch." Heath feigned a wound to the heart.

I giggled. I should have ignored him, but I couldn't help it. I'd spent years laughing whenever Heath made a joke. Another old habit that refused to die, along with the blush that crept up my cheeks when he made eye contact.

His gaze dipped to the low-cut neckline of my dress and for a moment, my heart fluttered. But then he tore his eyes away, guilt creeping into his expression.

Ugh. I really should have stayed home in my sweatpants.

"Be my wingman." Guy nudged Heath's arm, jerking his chin to the door. I followed my brother's gaze to where a petite blonde and pretty brunette had just entered the room. "Hit on the blonde."

Oh, God. I dropped my face to my nude heels. I was going to have to stay here and watch while Heath picked up another woman. He'd said before the kiss that he'd had a crush on me. But I guess my non-kiss had squashed it.

Champagne. What I needed right now was more champagne.

"Um . . ." Heath trailed off as Guy hauled him away.

Unlike me, I bet that blonde would kiss him back if given the chance.

It shouldn't hurt. I was over my crush, right? So why did it hurt so much? How many hurts would it take to finally give this up?

"You okay?" Natalie bumped her elbow with mine.

"Great!" *Too loud.* I cringed at the volume of my voice.

"I didn't know you'd be here tonight," she said.

"I just started working at Holiday Homes. Keith invites the whole office. I was actually going to skip and go to church with my parents, then hang out at home, but Guy talked me into coming."

I should have known better. We'd been here for minutes and I was already getting left behind.

"He promised to hang out with me because his girlfriend just dumped him," I said. "He's kind of broken up about it, even though he won't admit it. I felt bad for him, so I told him I'd be his date. But . . . he just ditched me."

"Want to hang with us?"

"I think I'm going to grab a drink." Drinks, to be accurate. Multiple drinks. And after drinking the multiple drinks, I'd call an Uber or Wendy to drive me home.

Natalie waved, taking Violet to the dessert table, while I headed toward the bar. I didn't want to see him talking and laughing with another woman, so I kept my chin down, eyes on the floor.

So focused on *not* watching for Heath, I nearly stumbled when I lifted my gaze and there he was. My footsteps stuttered. "H-hi."

"Hi. Can I buy you a drink?" he asked, nodding to the bar.

"Oh, um . . . you're not getting one for the, uh . . ." My fingers flittered over my shoulder in the direction of the door.

"No. Guy's on his own tonight."

I glanced behind me to where my brother was talking to the brunette. The blonde was nowhere in sight.

"What do you say, Stell? How about a drink?" There was pleading in his eyes. Maybe if this was just us at the office, him in jeans and a button-down, I would have had the strength to say no. But damn it, he looked so sexy in that suit. It was his fault that my resolve crumbled.

"Sure," I breathed.

His hypnotic eyes sparkled as we shuffled into the line at the bar.

"Do you still keep in touch with Natalie?" he asked.

A man beside me moved too close, accidentally bumping my shoulder with his.

Heath's hand drifted to the small of my back to steady me. Except when the man apologized and inched away, Heath's hand stayed. What the hell? What was happening?

I swallowed hard, trying to remember the question he'd asked. Nope. Nothing. My mind was blank. "Huh?"

"Natalie." He chuckled. "Do you keep in touch with her?"

"Oh. Yes." I nodded. "We meet for drinks two or three times a year. We gossip about people we knew from high school and she tells me about the kids she's watching."

"Then your next meetup should be entertaining since she's nannying Violet." He laughed. "That kid is a handful. Earlier this week, Maddox found her with a butcher's knife in the kitchen. She was going to cut herself a piece of apple pie."

"Seriously?" I giggled.

"It gets better." As we inched forward, he told me story after story about Violet's antics, some from this week and others he'd heard secondhand from his mom.

"She sounds . . . entertaining."

"I think we should put Violet and Guy together. We'd be guaranteed a show."

"Probably not tonight," I said. "There are a lot of breakables in this room."

"Good call." He winked as we finally reached the bar. With a whiskey tumbler in his hand and another champagne flute in mine, we turned to leave.

Heath's hand went to the small of my back again, but as we stepped out of the line, Gretchen appeared. His hand dropped and he slid away. "Gretchen."

"Hi, handsome." She gave him a hug. "Say, I need a few. There's a client who wanted to have a quick chat."

"Tonight?" He groaned.

"No such thing as a day off," she said.

"Right." Heath sighed. "See you later, Stella."

"Bye." I raised my flute.

I stared as Gretchen weaved through the crowd with Heath not far behind. Then I glanced around and realized I was alone.

My brother had vanished. Typical. Natalie was with Violet by the dessert table, and though I was sure she wouldn't care if I hung out with her tonight, I didn't want to intrude since she was working.

So I inched closer to the wall, wishing I could blend in with the wallpaper.

The lead singer of the live band took the microphone, welcoming the guests. Then with his band in position, they kicked off their show with a sultry jazz number that drew couples to the dance floor.

I listened to them perform, drinking my champagne. The bubbly went down too smoothly, and before the band's first set was over, I was three flutes in. My head was beautifully buzzed. My bruised heart coated in delicious bubbles. One more glass, then I'd find a quick bite to eat before sneaking out the door.

With my empty flute in hand, I left the safety of the wall to get in line at the bar. I'd just joined the queue when a man appeared at my side.

His dirty-blond hair was short and neatly combed. His charcoal suit was stylish and tailored to his lean frame. He was cute too. Really cute. Not Heath handsome, but no one was Heath handsome, not even Tobias.

"Hi." He held out his hand.

"Hi."

"I'm Seth."

"Stella," I said, sliding my palm against his.

"Beautiful name."

I smiled. "Thank you."

"Forgive me if this is too forward." He nodded to the dance floor. "But would you like to dance?"

"Um . . ." Why the hell not? "I'd love to."

He offered me his arm and together we navigated the crowd, settling at the edge of the dance floor. His cologne wafted to my nose as he spun me into his arms, one hand taking mine as the other settled on the curve of my hip.

Seth pulled us together, not too close, not too distant. And then we danced, stepping and turning in our own little square. "I'm not the best dancer in the world."

"You're doing great." A new blush crept into my face at the interest in his gaze.

He had dark brown eyes. Attractive, though not Heath's mesmerizing color. Seth's shoulders weren't as broad and his frame wasn't as tall.

What the hell was wrong with me? Here I was dancing with a handsome man who actually wanted me, and I kept comparing him to Heath. This had to stop. Right now. *Stop it, Stella.*

"So how do you know the Holidays?" Seth asked.

"I work at Holiday Homes. You?"

"I'm a realtor at Hannah's firm."

"Ah." I nodded.

"Maybe we'll get to work together on a project one of these days."

"Maybe."

Since Keith was the premier builder in the valley and Hannah owned one of the largest brokerages, often her realtors would meet with buyers who couldn't find a home on the market and instead, they'd decide to build. We'd collaborate on the property and the handoff to get the customer their dream home.

Or so I'd been told. I hadn't had the chance to do one of those projects yet.

"Are you from Bozeman?" he asked.

"I am. Born and raised. You?"

Before Seth could answer, a towering figure appeared at our side. I looked up to find a pair of very blue, very angry eyes, locked on Seth's hand at my waist.

"Stella." Heath's jaw clenched. "May I speak with you for a minute? Work related. You understand."

"Uh . . ." Seth didn't get the chance to finish that sentence.

Heath's hand wrapped around my elbow and he all but dragged me off the dance floor.

"Heath," I hissed when a few people gave us a sideways look.

He didn't slow.

"Heath." I yanked my arm free, forcing him to stop.

He turned, giving me a warning glare, then his hand was back, this time engulfing mine as he led me through the ballroom. He strode out the doors and down the hallway, shoving through the first door we reached.

We stepped into a sitting room. Couches hugged the far wall. A plush chair sat angled into a corner.

Heath let me go and strode into the center of the space, dragging a hand through his hair.

"What's going on?"

He turned and held up a finger to my nose. "You."

"What about me? What's wrong?"

"You . . ." He tipped his head to the ceiling and blew out a long breath. As his lungs emptied, the tension faded from his face. "You look beautiful."

"I—oh." Okay, not what I was expecting. "Thank you?"

"No." He leveled me with that gaze. "Don't say thank you. Just stop."

"Stop what?"

He stepped close, too close. As close as he'd been that night beside my car. "Stop being beautiful. Stop dancing with other men. Just for tonight. Don't dance with that guy. I'm trying to respect your wishes here, Stella. But tonight, it's a struggle."

"My wishes? What wishes?"

"To keep this professional." He sneered as he spoke the last word.

"That was your idea. Not mine."

"Was it?" He arched an eyebrow. "Because I clearly remember it being your suggestion."

Yes, it had been. I'd only suggested it to salvage a tiny shred of my pride. "You came into my office and apologized for kissing me."

"I apologized because you didn't kiss me back."

"I—" *Oh. My. God.* He thought I didn't want him. "I was just surprised."

He studied my face. "What do you want? Tell me what you want."

I wanted what I'd always wanted. "You. I want—"

He cut me off by slamming his mouth on mine.

It took me a heartbeat. Maybe I'd never truly get over the shock of Heath's lips. But I recovered.

And this time, I kissed him back.

CHAPTER 6

HEATH

J ust one more kiss. Then I'd stop. That had been the plan.

But the moment Stella's tongue slid against mine, I lost any hope of restraint. The truth was, I'd lost it the moment I'd seen her dancing with another man.

"Stella," I moaned, cupping her face in my hands.

She clung to me, her tongue tangling with mine, and goddamn it, she could kiss.

Stella could fucking *kiss*.

No reluctance. No shock or restraint. This was not the same woman who I'd kissed last weekend beside her car.

I devoured her, and she met me beat for beat.

Her lips moved frantically over mine as my hands roamed over her shoulders, following the curve of her spine. Like I'd cupped her face, I fit my palms over her ass. Then I squeezed. But I didn't linger. I traced her hips, then her ribs, wanting to feel every inch of this woman. I wanted to lose myself in her slender curves and sweet taste.

My tongue dueled with hers as I banded my arms around her, pulling her flush against my chest. When my growing arousal dug into her hip, she gasped, and that adorable little hitch in her breath only made me want her more.

I tore my mouth away from hers, wanting to taste her skin. As my lips trailed down the long column of her throat, Stella's fingers dove into my hair, threading through the strands. One tug and I was hard as a rock.

She arched her back and I dropped lower, pulling aside the fabric of her dress to reveal a perfect breast. No bra. *Thank fuck.*

A rosy nipple popped free and I didn't hesitate to suck it into my mouth.

"Heath," she whimpered.

I nipped and lapped at the bud until Stella moaned my name again. Her skin was so smooth. Her breast was the perfect swell to fit the cup of my hand. I was just about to move to the other side when the door to the sitting room swung open.

"Oh my God," a woman squeaked. "I'm sorry."

Stella gasped, shoving at my shoulders.

I glanced over my shoulder as Stella scrambled to right her dress. "Natalie?"

"Heath?"

Natalie glanced between the two of us, her eyes wide. "I wasn't here. I didn't see anything. You two, um, have fun."

There was a smirk on Nat's lips as she slipped out of the room, leaving Stella and me alone.

My breath came in labored pants. Stella's face was beautifully flushed and her pink mouth swollen. God, I could kiss her for years if it meant that color was mine and mine alone.

I dragged a hand through my hair and inspected the door. No lock. Damn it. I was teetering on the edge of control, but I didn't need another person walking in on us—like her brother—so I took a step away.

Stella cleared her throat and smoothed down the skirt of her dress.

This was wrong. So, so wrong. My reasons for not chasing Stella hadn't changed in the last week. Nothing had changed. Yet everything had changed.

Seeing her with that guy on the dance floor had felt like a lightning rod piercing my heart. No woman had ever made me feel so jealous. The only man she'd be dancing with tonight was me.

"Heath, I . . ." She put her hands on her cheeks. "What are we doing?"

I stepped closer, pulling her hands away. "Don't hide from me."

She looked up to me and those expressive eyes were so full of uncertainty it made my chest ache. "I don't know what you want. That's fairly terrifying for me because the one thing I've always wanted was you."

Stella spoke like those words had been waiting a week, a year, to make their way free. The vulnerability in her voice was humbling.

"I meant what I said the other night. Stell, I've wanted you for a long time."

"Really?"

"Longer than I would let myself admit."

She pulled her lower lip between her teeth to hide a shy smile.

I put my thumb on that lip to tug it free. "We should stop."

"No." She shook her head. "We should leave."

"Together?"

She nodded and let out a rushed breath. "But you should know I used it up."

"Used what up?"

"My champagne bravery." She tucked a lock of hair behind her ear. "I just told you that I've always wanted you. That used up all of my bravery. So now you have to take charge because I'm too busy having a mental freak-out that you just kissed me and sucked one of my nipples and said that you want me too, and oh my God, you want me too? How is this even happ—"

"Breathe, baby."

She obeyed, nodding as she dragged in some air.

"Better?"

"Yes."

"Good." I leaned forward and kissed her forehead, then took her hand in mine and dragged her out of the sitting room.

Our first stop was at the coat check. After we got her jacket and clutch, she checked Guy's keys under his name while I ordered us an Uber. As soon as we had her belongings, I rushed her down the staircase and into the winter night.

Snow was falling lightly as we slid into the backseat of a black sedan. The icy flakes melted instantly on the car's windshield. Even over the smell of air freshener and leather, Stella's sweet scent filled my nose.

The driver confirmed my address and that was the last shred of attention he earned. I focused entirely on Stella, drawing in her perfume, holding it for a heartbeat, before leaning in close for a deeper inhale.

We were only blocks away from The Baxter when I buried my nose in her curled tresses, pulling her hair away from her shoulder so I could duck down to kiss her throat.

The moment my lips hit her pulse, her breath hitched. Shy. Sexy. The sound shot straight to my cock. I'd earn a hundred of those tonight if she had them to give.

"Stella," I whispered against her skin.

Her hand came up, cupping the back of my head and holding me in place.

I grinned and peppered the delicate spot beneath her ear with open-mouthed kisses until her fingers dug into my scalp.

Other than my mouth, I didn't dare touch her. I didn't trust myself not to take her in the back of this car, damn the driver watching through the rearview mirror.

Traffic was light and by the time we stopped in front of my house, my dick was aching. Stella unbuckled her seat belt first, practically shoving me out of the car. Then we raced up the sidewalk to my front door.

The moment I had the key in the lock, Stella reached beneath the hem of my suit coat and slid her hands up the plane of my back. I leaned into the touch, forgetting for a second that we were outside. That the snow was falling and catching the white glow of the Christmas lights I'd strung on the eaves.

"Are we going inside?" she asked.

I answered by twisting the lock and stepping inside with Stella on my heels. Then I kicked the door shut before sealing my lips over hers.

She rose on her toes, twisted her tongue against mine as I banded my arms around her and hauled her to my chest. When I shuffled toward the nearest wall of the entryway and hoisted her up, she wrapped her legs around my waist, pressing her center into my erection.

Stella might have told me to take control, but I was following her lead. She nipped and I sucked, tasting every corner of her mouth. One of her hands slipped between us, her fingers searching for my belt buckle.

I tore my mouth away, gritting my teeth. I ached for her, but when we crossed this line, there was no going back. "Stella, be sure."

She lifted her hand free and brought it to my forehead, pushing the hair away. "I'm sure."

"This changes everything."

"I think that we've already changed everything, don't you?"

"Yeah," I whispered, drowning in her gaze. "I guess we have."

She leaned in, pressing her lips to the corner of my mouth as she tilted her hips forward, urging me on.

Maybe she hadn't used all that bravery. Or maybe she had more courage than she let herself believe, champagne or not. Timid or bold, I'd take her in every way.

Her fingers found the clasp on my belt and began to tug.

"Wait." I pulled away, panting. "We're not doing this against the wall."

"No?"

I shook my head. "No."

She moved to let her legs down but I swept her away, earning a little laugh as I carried her out of the entryway. Every room was dark, the only light coming from the Christmas tree in the corner. Its multicolored bulbs cast their red, blue, green and yellow light over the living room.

If Stella was curious about my home, she didn't let on. She didn't look away from my face or loosen her hold on my shoulders as I strode down the long hallway to my bedroom.

Like the living room, I'd put a small tree in a corner. Maybe other men wouldn't bother with decorations, considering there were no family gatherings planned for my place, but I loved Christmas and falling asleep to the glow of the lighted tree.

Stella unwrapped her legs as I set her on the foot of the bed. She reached for me but I shook my head and dropped to my knees. My hands were trembling.

When was the last time I'd been anxious with a woman? Maybe my first time? That had been in high school, after prom.

Even then, we'd each had enough cheap liquor to chase away the nerves.

This was Stella.

My fingers fumbled with the straps on her shoes. I willed my heart to stop racing. When her hands came to my hair again, I leaned into her touch and closed my eyes.

"I can't believe this is happening." Her confession was barely audible. The honesty in her voice, the heart shining through those dazzling eyes, was my undoing. There was no woman as beautiful as Stella Marten.

And I'd been a coward for too long. A fool for not acting sooner.

Now she was fucking mine.

When I went back to her heels, the shaking in my fingers was gone. If all I did tonight was make this good for her, I'd call it a win. I plucked her shoes from her feet, tossing them aside, then trailed my fingers across the smooth skin on her ankle, working my way toward the inside of her knee.

My fingertips moved in slow, torturous swirls, never leaving her skin as I inched along her legs. A shiver shook her shoulders as I brushed the skirt of her dress across her thighs, pushing it higher and higher. Her breath hitched again, that sexy-as-fuck gasp, when I skimmed her hips and along the lace of her panties.

Her eyes were hooded when I met her gaze, her bottom lip between her teeth again.

I gave her a smirk as I balled her dress in my fists and dragged it up her torso. She raised her arms as I whipped it free.

"You are . . ." My mouth went dry at the image of her on my bed, naked but for those panties. "Perfect. My Stella. So fucking perfect."

Even in the muted light, I saw the pink blush of her cheeks.

I took her face in my hands, pulling her to my mouth. Then I stood, not loosening my hold, as I laid her on the mattress.

The ministrations I'd done with my hands I now did with my mouth, trailing open-mouthed kisses across her neck and down her chest, stopping to pay her nipples more attention. Then I moved lower, dragging my tongue around her navel.

She whimpered, a sound I was beginning to love as much as that gasp.

I lingered above the hem of her panties, dragging in her sweet scent as I tucked my fingers into the lace and dragged them away from her bare mound.

"Heath." Stella gulped the moment the fabric was free, pooled on the floor beside her dress and heels. "I've, um, no one has ever . . . I mean, I'm not a virgin but, uh, you know."

Oh. Fuck. Me.

I'd be the first to taste her. The only. My mouth watered. "Do you trust me?"

She nodded.

"Good." I pressed at her knees, spreading them apart.

Her folds glistened, her pussy as pretty a pink as her lips. Her muscles tightened, her legs tense. It would be fun to tease her one of these days. To kiss everywhere but where she needed it. But for our first time, I didn't delay.

I dragged my tongue through her slit, moaning at her taste.

Stella let out a little cry, slapping a hand over her mouth.

I chuckled, licking her again.

"Oh my God." It was muffled from beneath her hand, but I was taking it as approval to devour.

I lapped at her, sucking her clit into my mouth, taking her to the edge, over and over. When her legs were shaking, her body writhing, I'd back off.

By the fifth time, the hand on her mouth was gone, and her

hands fisted the charcoal comforter. By the tenth, she was growling in frustration.

"Want to come, baby?" I asked.

"Yes."

"Your wish, Stell." This time, I didn't back off. I kept at her until her back arched off the bed, her entire body spasming as she let out a string of moans. Only when her toes uncurled did I stop.

Her chest was rosy, her body limp.

I licked my lips and stood, shrugging off my suit coat as I memorized the image of a naked Stella on my bed. My cock was painfully hard, the bulge straining at the zipper on my slacks. I made short work of undressing, and when my clothes were strewn beside hers, I gripped my shaft and gave it a hard stroke.

"I haven't been with anyone for a while," I said. "And I had a checkup last month."

Stella nodded frantically. "Me neither. And I'm on the pill."

This night just kept getting better. I planted a knee on the bed, picking her up and hauling her into the pillows. She parted her legs for me, making space in the cradle of her hips.

I kissed her, letting her taste herself on my tongue. I kissed her until she was writhing again, begging for more.

In one long stroke, I thrust inside her tight body. One long stroke, her walls fluttering around my length, and I nearly came undone.

"Fuck, Stell." It took every fiber of my strength not to come, feeling her heat as she stretched around me. I wrapped her in my arms, burying my face in her hair. "You feel so good."

She wrapped her arms around me, holding me close. "Move."

I kissed her pulse, then leaned away, pulling out to slam inside.

"Heath," she cried, her eyes squeezing shut.

I heard my name three more times from her lips before she came again, pulsing and squeezing me with such force that her orgasm triggered my own. I came on a roar, pulsing inside her as white stars broke behind my eyes.

Boneless and sated, I collapsed onto her arms, rolling so she was draped across my chest. Then I held her tight, feeling her heart beat in an opposite rhythm to my own.

How had I gone this long without her? Why hadn't we been doing this all along? She'd ruined me for other women.

One night, and I was ruined.

This was reckless. She was an employee. She was Guy's sister.

But she was Stella.

My Stella.

She made a move to stand, but I held her tight.

"Stay."

She pushed the hair from her face and gave me a sleepy smile. "Okay."

"Stella?" I called through the house, yawning as I squinted at the bright light streaming through the windows. "Stella."

Silence.

I padded to the front door, peering through a sidelight. There were fresh tire tracks in my driveway, ones that hadn't been left by last night's Uber.

No, they'd likely been from this morning. After Stella had snuck out of the house.

"Damn it."

Why would she leave? Why wouldn't she wake me first? Was she upset?

I rubbed the stubble on my jaw, pissed at myself for not waking up and frustrated with her for sneaking out.

Any normal day, I'd track her down. I'd show up at her doorstep and we'd talk this through. But it wasn't a normal day.

It was Christmas.

Merry Christmas, Stella.

CHAPTER 7
STELLA

op. Pop. Pop.
As the popcorn cooked in my microwave, I tapped my finger to its sound while I stared unblinking at my kitchen cabinets.

I should call him. Should I call him? *Yes. Tomorrow. Maybe.*

The microwave beeped and I took out the bag, shaking it before dumping the white kernels in a glass bowl and retreating to my living room. I plopped onto the couch, shoved a handful of popcorn in my mouth and stared at the blank TV.

I'd been doing a lot of staring since sneaking out of Heath's bed on Christmas morning.

Mom had asked me fifteen times yesterday if I'd been feeling okay. I'd lied, promising that I'd been fine. But no, I was not okay. I was a flipping mess.

Heath had literally scrambled my brain. Any time I tried to think of any other subject—work, gifts, food—I'd get about two seconds down one train of thought only to be yanked back to his bed. I'd picture his broad shoulders pushing my knees apart as he'd licked me into oblivion.

A shiver raced down my spine.

Oral Sex Fan Club, meet your newest member, Stella Marten.

I'd had sex, lots of incredible sex with lots of incredible orgasms, with Heath Holiday. *My* Heath Holiday.

What did this mean? Did he want a relationship? Were coworkers allowed to be couples at Holiday Homes? Why now?

All questions I could have asked had I stuck around his house yesterday morning, but when I'd woken up deliciously sore, panic had taken over, so I'd slid out from beneath his arm and bolted.

Because this was Heath.

Heath.

How long had I dreamed of this? Of him? I'd fantasized about him for so long, I hadn't been prepared for this to ever become a reality. He'd exceeded every expectation, every dream. And in just one night.

It shouldn't have been so good, right? That was crazy. Wasn't it?

Maybe my juvenile delusions from years past were clouding reality. Maybe my teenage crush was bubbling to the surface. Maybe my subconscious was playing tricks on me because he was forbidden.

And terrifying.

One night and I'd screwed everything up. Because now I wanted him more than ever. And if he decided we'd been a mistake, well . . .

"I'll quit." That wasn't the worst thing in the world, right? I'd only been working at Holiday Homes since the beginning of the month. Maybe my old company would take me back if I begged. And took a pay cut.

Or . . . I could move. If Heath dumped me, I could move.

Yes, I would definitely have to move. I'd have to find a new town. A new job. A new house and a new guy.

If Heath didn't want me, there was no other choice.

"Yep. I'll move." I fisted another handful of popcorn, chewing with fury as anxiety raced through my veins.

I was going to have to move and change my entire life because Heath had ruined me.

Another handful went to my mouth, my cheeks bulging like a chipmunk, and I just kept shoving more in as I endured the hundredth mental freak-out in the past thirty-six hours.

Pull it together, Stella.

More popcorn was stuffed into my mouth. Wendy would be proud because usually, my stress eating involved McDonald's, a can of Reddi-wip and a family-sized bag of Funyuns. This popcorn wasn't even buttered.

Any other man and I'd throw myself into work as a distraction. But work meant Heath and luckily, the office was closed until after New Year's so I wouldn't have to face him quite yet.

"I don't want to move." I groaned, ready to toss the popcorn, find my keys and head to the nearest drive-thru when the doorbell rang.

With the bowl tucked in my arm, I shoved another bite into my mouth and went to answer, expecting Wendy or Guy since they were the only two people besides my parents who visited. It was after dark so Mom and Dad would already be glued to the History Channel.

I checked the peephole, finding Guy on the other side. His back was to me because he was looking at something on the street. I unlocked the door, swinging it open, just as he turned.

Not Guy.

Heath.

239

The popcorn in my mouth came shooting out in a stream of white confetti.

A soggy kernel landed on Heath's gray sweatshirt.

My eyes bulged as I watched him flick it off.

"Hi," he said.

I blinked.

He was wearing a Holiday Homes hoodie and a navy ball-cap. Nearly the same navy Montana State ballcap my brother wore all the time. From the back, those hats were identical. But the fronts had different logos.

He'd duped me into opening the door. I should have looked closer at the hair color.

"May I come in?"

I blinked again.

Heath chuckled and stepped close, using his thumb to brush a popcorn piece off my chin.

"I just spit food on you," I whispered, my cheeks flaming.

Other people didn't get this version of me, the one intent on humiliating herself. Why did she only come out when Heath was around?

He lifted a shoulder, reached in to take a handful of popcorn, then came inside, shuffling me backward so he could close the door as he popped a few pieces into his mouth. His chiseled jaw flexed as he chewed.

No man had ever made popcorn so attractive. If he ever asked me on a movie date, I'd probably orgasm in the theater just by watching him eat popcorn.

He swallowed, his Adam's apple bobbing, then stomped his Nikes, clearing off the snow on the rug in my entryway. He took off his hat, only to turn it backward.

Holy. Shit. Why was that so hot? He was the older, rugged version of the boy I'd loved from afar. A man so utterly attrac-

240

tive I forgot to breathe. As I stood there drooling, his gaze raked up and down my body.

"Jesus, Stell. Are those your pajamas?"

I nodded.

He closed his eyes for a moment, his hands fisting like he was praying for restraint.

I glanced at my attire. The set was black satin, the pants wide and drapey. The top was basically a bra, showing my midriff beneath the jacket that went over the top that I hadn't bothered buttoning. "Sorry?"

He opened his eyes and closed the gap between us, fitting his palm against my cheek. "You ran out on me."

"I'm sort of freaking out. Like, a lot of freaking out." My free hand dove automatically into the bowl, but before I could scoop a handful for my mouth, Heath stole the popcorn and set it aside on the console table.

"Why are you freaking out?"

"Because now I have to move."

His eyebrows came together. "What? You're moving?"

I nodded. "I have to."

"Why?"

"Because we had sex. A lot of sex."

"We did? When?"

"Stop." I smacked his arm, relaxing as he laughed, and led him to the living room couch. I plopped down on one end as he took the other.

He looked so at ease, so confident, as he laid an arm over the back and crossed an ankle over his knee. "Be real with me. Are you okay?"

I melted a little at the worry in his voice and concern in those blue eyes. "Yes. Just . . . confused."

"Is that why you snuck out?"

"I don't do well when things are up in the clouds."

"In the clouds. What do you mean?"

"That saying. Up in the air. I say *up in the clouds* because clouds are fluffier, so if I'm going to be in limbo, I might as well be in the fluff."

He studied me, the corner of his mouth turning up. "That shouldn't make sense. But I guess it does."

"Did you have a nice Christmas?"

"I did. We just hung out at Mom and Dad's. Opened gifts. It was more exciting than normal years with Violet there."

"You're warming up to her."

"She's a terror and she'll turn Maddox gray before he hits forty, but yeah. She's a cool kid. I just came from Mom and Dad's. Mom declared a game night. Natalie was there too."

"Really?"

He grinned. "Maddox is crushing on her. Hard."

I loved that for my friend. Natalie deserved a sweet, billionaire hottie.

Maddox had graduated by the time I'd started high school, but his legend had lived on through the girls on the swim team. He'd been a lot like Heath. Handsome. Athletic. Popular. He'd become extremely wealthy since leaving Montana, but given the way Heath seemed to admire his older brother, I suspected Maddox had always kept his small-town roots.

"How was your Christmas?" he asked.

"Uneventful."

"Did Santa bring you anything good?"

"These pajamas."

"Well done, Santa."

My breath caught in my throat as his gaze raked down my chest and the shift in his expression. Heath looked like he was about to pounce, to drag me across the couch and have his way with me.

I would gladly be dragged.

But then he shook his head, shifting to dig something out of his jeans pocket. "I picked up something for you."

"Oh. You didn't need to get me anything."

"I know." He handed over a rectangular, black velvet case. "But I wanted to."

I sat up straighter, taking the box and flipping it open. Inside was a dainty gold bracelet with three jingling bells. The jewelry brought a smile to my lips. "This is beautiful. I used to have one just like it."

"I remember."

"You do? No way. That was ages ago."

"Your grandpa bought it for you, right?"

"Yes. He used to tease me that I walked silently and could be a ninja when I grew up." Grandpa had been a lot like Guy— loud in every way. So loud that he wouldn't hear me walk up. I'd startled him countless times, and each time, he'd let out this huge yelp before slapping a hand to his heart. "That bracelet was the last Christmas present he bought me."

"I was there the day it broke," he said. "You caught it on the swing set in your backyard, and you cried so hard I thought you were hurt."

I'd been devastated. And he'd remembered. He'd bought me a new one. My eyes flooded as I touched the bracelet. "Will you help me put it on?"

"Sure." He slid to the middle cushion, taking the jewelry from the box. Then he fastened it on my left wrist, his fingers warm against my skin.

I jingled it, smiling at the delicate chime. "Thank you."

"You're welcome." Heath's gaze was waiting when I looked up, and because I hadn't gotten him a gift, I rose up, pressing my lips to his.

It was meant to be a quick kiss, but one brush of our mouths and the heat between us ignited.

His arms wrapped me tight before he pressed me deeper into the toss pillows. His tongue swept between my teeth, stroking my own.

We kissed frantically, neither of us getting enough. Then the clothes between us began to disappear, item by item. His hoodie. My pants. His T-shirt. My top.

He settled between my thighs, his arousal hard and thick and long as it pressed into my throbbing core. "God, Stell."

"I can't believe this is happening," I whispered.

He positioned at my entrance, slowly, inch by inch, thrusting inside. "Believe it now?"

I shook my head, savoring the stretch of my body to fit his. "No."

"You will. Give it time."

Time with him was just another fantasy.

But before I could get stuck in my head, I was lost to Heath's body. I succumbed to the ragged breaths. To the rough touches. To the rhythm of his strokes and the thunder of my heart.

We came together, both crying out, as the orgasm stole my sight, blinding me to anything but this man.

My new bracelet jingled as I shoved the hair out of my eyes, coming down from the high. "Wow."

"Fuck, you are incredible." Heath twisted us so he was beneath me on the couch, our bodies slick with sweat. Then he stared at the ceiling. "I wasn't going to do this."

"Do what?"

He let a hand trail down my spine to cup my ass. "You."

I smiled. "Why not?"

"Because I want more than sex from you. But those goddamn pajamas from Santa were irresistible. They look even better on the floor."

I laughed, closing my eyes to memorize every second. His

spicy scent. His hard body. The weight of his hand. The caress of his touch. The sound of his words still ringing in my mind.

Because I want more than sex from you.

There was a giddy laugh in my chest. The moment he was gone, I was going to let it loose to bounce off the apartment walls.

"I can't stay."

"Oh." The disappointment in my voice filled my living room.

"I want to." He kissed my forehead. "But I'd better get going. Tobias was acting strange at Christmas yesterday, so I want to see if I can find out what's going on."

"Okay."

The two of us dressed and then walked to the door. When was he coming back? What would it be like at work? Should we tell Guy? The only men I'd ever slept with—all three of them— had been boyfriends before lovers. I was a woman who loved labels.

I opened my mouth to ask when I'd see him again, but I caught myself and faked a yawn. There was time to figure this out, right? We didn't have to answer all the questions tonight.

"Tired?" he asked.

I nodded. "Yeah. I'm going to hit the straw."

"Hit the hay."

"They don't put hay in stalls for the animals to sleep on. Did you know that? I went to a petting zoo once and asked the owner, and she told me they put straw in the pens and feed them hay. So you hit the straw."

"That's . . ." Heath's broad chest shook as he laughed. "Okay. Hit the straw."

"Thanks again for my bracelet." I twirled my wrist, loving the tiny jingle.

"Welcome." He inched closer, taking my face in his hands. "You're something special, Stella Marten."

And he was a dream.

With one last kiss goodbye, he winked and headed into the winter night. The smile on my face pinched my cheeks as I closed the door behind him.

Wendy. I had to call Wendy.

I hurried to the living room where I'd left my phone earlier, pulling up her name. But before I could call, the doorbell rang again. I skipped down the hall, my toes dancing that Heath had come back. "Hey th—"

Not Heath.

Guy.

"It's cold." He shuddered and stepped inside.

I peered past him, searching for Heath's truck. His taillights were at the edge of the parking lot.

"Are you going to close the door?" Guy asked, shrugging off his coat. He must not have seen Heath's truck in the dark because he would have asked an entirely different question.

"Oh, um . . . yeah." I stepped out of the way to shut away the chill. "What are you doing here?"

"I was bored. Thought I'd come over." He looked me up and down, his face souring. "Are those the pajamas Mom bought you?"

"Yes. What's wrong with them?"

"Aren't you supposed to button the top?"

I rolled my eyes and buttoned the outer shell. "Happy now?"

"I'll be happy if you have a beer."

All I had was wine and a bottle of vodka in the fridge. I'd never much enjoyed the taste of beer. "You came to the wrong house if you wanted beer."

"True." He walked toward the living room and my stomach dropped.

Oh, shit. Would he be able to smell the sex? Or Heath's cologne? *Please don't let there be a wet spot on my couch.*

Guy tipped his nose to the air. "Popcorn?"

I swiped up the bowl that Heath had set aside and carried it to Guy, shoving it toward his face, hoping all he'd smell was the salt. "Here."

"Thanks." He popped a kernel into his mouth. "No butter?"

"I can make a new batch with butter."

"Yes, please. Want to watch a movie?"

"No. Let's sit in the kitchen." I wouldn't be able to stop thinking about Heath if we sat on the couch and my brother would notice if I kept smiling like a fool.

"Why?"

"I was going to make some cookies," I lied.

"Not as good as beer, but I'll eat a cookie." Guy moved to the counter and took a seat on one of the barstools.

I rifled through my pantry, praying I had all of the ingredients. I was out of flour, but I spied a box of brownie mix. "Oh, how about brownies instead? That actually sounds better."

"Fine by me." He shrugged, finishing the bowl of my popcorn. "So what did you do tonight?"

Your best friend.

I pulled in my lips to hide my smile as I gave him my back to retrieve a mixing bowl from the cupboard.

At some point, Heath and I would have to tell Guy. If this was more than sex. But considering I still wasn't sure exactly what our relationship would be like, there was no point telling my brother I'd slept with his best friend.

Twice.

CHAPTER 8

HEATH

Stella's smile as she answered the door made my drive across town on icy roads worth every white-knuckled second. "Hi."

"Hi." I grinned and stepped inside, sweeping her into my arms and dipping her low for a kiss.

She smiled against my mouth, her hands instantly wrapping around my shoulders. When I finally stood her up, she laughed, the light in those hazel eyes dancing. "Trying to sweep me off my feet?"

"Maybe." I chuckled. "Is it working?"

"Yes."

"Good." I kissed her forehead, then kicked off my shoes before following her into the living room and joining her on the couch. "How was your day?"

"Busy. I deep cleaned, did laundry and braved Costco. You?"

"Worked for a while. Let Mom drag me downtown for shopping." I pulled a red square jewelry box out of my jeans pocket and handed it over. "For you."

"Another gift? That's two days in a row." She took the box. "Now I feel like I should have bought you a jumbo-sized box of Cheerios from the store."

"I do love my Cheerios."

"I know." She smiled. "Mom would always make sure to have them whenever you and Guy had sleepovers."

Looking back at our memories together was an unexpected thrill about being with Stella. It was fun to see what details she remembered. The ones I did.

Our history was the reason I'd had a near-constant smile since last night. It was like a piece had clicked into place. A piece I hadn't realized was missing.

Stella filled the gap.

She opened the box and another breathtaking smile stretched across her mouth. "Bows."

"I saw them and had to get them. They made me think of you."

"You thought of me?"

"Nonstop."

She blushed and pulled one of the earrings out of the box, a tiny golden bow adorned with rainbow-colored jewels. Stella put it in her ear, then did the same with the other. "I love rainbow colors."

"I know."

No sooner than the words had left my mouth, she launched herself at me, flattening my back to the couch as she surged. I wrapped her tight, not wasting a second.

As much fun as it had been having sex on the couch, tonight, I wanted some space. So with her still in my arms, our mouths fused, I stood and carried her down the hallway, hoping like hell I found a bed.

My guess was solid.

We emerged from her room an hour later after a couple of orgasms and a shower.

Stella and I returned to the couch, and as I lay down, I tucked her into my side. A natural fit.

How many movies had we watched in the basement of her parents' house? How many nights had I missed doing this? Hell, I wouldn't have realized it even if I'd tried back then. As a teenaged boy, I hadn't been into cuddling with girls. I probably would have broken her heart, and then Guy would have had a good reason to kick my ass.

There was a reason he'd forbidden any of his friends from going near Stella. We'd all been as bad as him, looking for a score and nothing more. Except I'd grown out of that. The closer I got to thirty, the more casual hookups had lost their appeal. My last girlfriend had been months ago. But I liked commitment. I liked being tied to a person.

I wouldn't miss a chance at being tied to Stella.

"I like your place," I told her.

Her apartment was finished in neutrals, like most complexes around town. Beige walls. Taupe carpet. But she'd added pops of color with the furniture, decor and artwork. The TV stand was a bold coral. The toss pillow behind my head was teal. The coffee table was mustard yellow and the rug beneath had flecks of everything, pulling it all together.

Rainbow colors for my bright, beautiful girl.

"Thanks. It's just an apartment." She shrugged. "It's boring. But I'm saving to buy a house. I want a hefty down payment so it's taking me a while."

"Ever think about building? I know a guy who owns a construction company."

She smiled and curled deeper into my side. "Maybe, I, um . . . never mind."

"What?"

"Don't flip out, okay?"

"When a woman tells a man not to flip out, it means he's probably going to flip out."

"Fine." She zipped her lips shut.

I waited, listening to the clock tick on the wall. But the curiosity got the better of me as the second hand lapped the twelve twice. "Okay, fine. No flip-outs. Promise. Tell me what you were going to say."

"I want to get a house in a good school district. I know that marriage and kids are a ways off, and I'm not saying this about you, but it's a consideration because—"

"You're a planner."

"Exactly."

"I'm a planner too, Stell. Why do you think I bought the best lot in the best neighborhood with the best elementary school and built a five-bedroom house with a huge yard?" I wasn't going to live in that house by myself for the rest of my life.

"You're not freaked out by this?"

I shifted so I could get a better look at her face. "Ten years ago? Yeah. I would have been out the door. But I'm not here for a hookup or something casual."

She smiled but there was a wariness in her gaze.

Stella still didn't believe me. But she would.

I was all about exploring this thing with her. I wanted the first dates. I wanted the sleepovers. I wanted the calls when she was at the grocery store to see if I needed anything.

"I guess I'm still expecting you to react like Guy." She dropped her forehead to my chest, her beautiful blond hair draping around us.

"Guy's my best friend." I twisted a lock of her sunshine strands between my fingers. "But we're not the same. We're exploring this. Got it?"

"Got it," she breathed. "Thank you for my earrings."

"You're welcome."

She propped her chin up on her hands. "How was Tobias?"

"I don't know. He wasn't home and he didn't answer when I called." Ten times. I'd left here last night to track him down but wherever he'd been, he hadn't wanted to be found.

"Guy showed up after you left."

Then it was probably a good thing I'd been gone. Having him show up and see us together would not be a good way to tell him I was claiming his sister. "I'll talk to him."

"Maybe I should."

"No, it should be me." If I was in his shoes, I'd want my friend to tell me. I wouldn't put this on Stella.

"Okay." She sighed. "How do you think he'll take it?"

"I don't know," I lied.

Guy was going to rage. He'd probably try and pick a fight. But she was worth a few punches. If that's what it took, I'd let Guy hit me square in the face.

We lay together, just breathing, until she yawned.

"I should let you hit the straw."

She laughed. "Do you want to stay?"

"Yes, but I'd better get home. I am going to swing by Tobias's place again. See if I can catch him."

"Okay." She shifted, standing from the couch. "When . . . never mind."

"Say it."

"When will I see you again?"

I ran my fingers over her cheek. "Was that so hard to ask?"

"I don't want you to think I'm clingy."

"But you are clingy."

She frowned and a cute little crease formed between her eyebrows. "No, I'm not."

"It's not an insult, baby. I know you. Like you know me. I

like that you want to plan when we'll see each other again. I like that you're trying to be chill about this, but Stella, I'm not chill about this. So you don't need to be either."

Never in my life had I thought about a woman as much as I'd thought about Stella since the party. Never had I watched the clock, waiting for the right time to go over. Never had I planned to see a woman day after day after day.

"This is happening so fast." She shook her head. "I'm still catching up."

"You will." I kissed her again. "Get some rest. Tomorrow night I'm staying and there won't be much sleep."

Her face lit up. "Promise? Maybe I should hydrate."

I chuckled. "Definitely hydrate. And make no plans for Thursday morning."

If we were both on vacation, we might as well enjoy it.

With another kiss at the door, I left her for the frigid winter air. I slid behind the wheel of my truck, cranked the heat, intending to hunt down my brother and find out what had crawled up his ass this week. But as I pulled onto the street, I made a last-second decision to search for another brother instead.

The drive to Guy's condo was short. He'd bought a place close to Stella's apartment on purpose, saying he wanted to be around in case she needed help. In reality, it was because he was just as clingy as Stella and craved attention. So on the nights when there wasn't anything else to entertain him, he'd visit his sister.

Their parents still lived in the neighborhood where I'd grown up. That was before both Mom's and Dad's businesses had boomed and they'd decided to build a massive home in the mountain foothills.

My parents, also planners, had added plenty of bedrooms for future grandchildren.

I parked next to Guy's truck and went straight for the door, squaring my shoulders as I rang the bell. There was no time to overthink this. He was going to be pissed so I might as well get it over with.

"Hey." He swung the door open, lifting the beer bottle in his hand. "Good timing. I just opened this. Want one?"

"Sure." I stepped inside. "But do you have any cans?"

He gave me a strange look. "Uh . . . yeah."

"Then I'll have a can."

That bottle was a weapon. I'd wait to tell him about Stella until he'd finished drinking and it was safely stowed in the garbage where it couldn't be broken in half over my skull.

Guy led the way to his fridge, pulling out a Bud Light.

"Thanks." I popped the top and gulped.

"What are you doing tonight?" he asked. "Maybe after we finish these we could head downtown."

"Maybe." I walked to the living room off the kitchen, sitting down in a chair that faced the TV. My knee began bouncing.

Guy sank into his couch and grabbed the remote to mute EPSN. "Can I ask you something?"

Shit. He knew. The fucker already knew. "What's up?"

"Have any guys been visiting Stella at work?"

"Uh, no." I gave him a sideways glance, keeping an eye on that beer bottle. It would hurt like a motherfucker if he threw it at my face. "Why?"

"I think she's dating someone."

I blinked. Was this a trick?

"So?" He raised his eyebrows.

I took a gulp of my beer to clear my throat. "So, what?"

"So have you seen anyone come to work? Take her out to lunch or anything?"

"No."

He frowned. "Huh."

I waited for more. I waited for an attack. But he simply sat there, pondering my answer. "Why do you think she's dating?"

"I went over to her place last night. She was wearing this slutty pajama outfit thing and when she opened the door, it was like she expected me to be someone else."

Me. She'd expected him to be me.

This was the perfect opportunity to spill and get it over with. But did I fess up? Did I tell him that those pajamas weren't slutty and that if he ever used the word *slut* in the same sentence as his sister's name again I'd break his nose? No. I sat there like a coward.

"So what if she's seeing someone?" I took another long drink. "She's an adult."

"I don't like that she's hiding it from me."

Tell him. "Maybe it's new and she doesn't want to introduce the guy to her family yet."

He shook his head. "She should still tell me. After the shit she went through in college, she knows I worry."

"Wait. What?" I set my beer down and leaned forward. "What shit in college?"

He took a drink, draining his bottle dry. "You can't tell her I told you. She made me promise not to tell."

"Of course. What happened?"

"This friend of mine. Former friend. He lived in our dorm freshman year."

"Which friend?"

"Dave."

Dave. I searched my memory, trying to place a Dave with a face. Who the fuck was Dave? The name was growing more familiar, but I couldn't put it with a face. "Did I know him?"

Guy shook his head. "No. He lived on the fourth floor. I'd go up and play video games with him sometimes."

Video games hadn't ever been my thing and I'd spent my

freshman year in class while Guy had barely passed. He'd aced the art of skipping. The days when I'd been taking notes in a lecture hall, he'd been with *Dave*.

"How would Stella know him?" She hadn't come to MSU until long after we'd left the dorms for our apartment off campus.

"I kept in touch with him." Guy's jaw clenched. "We had a couple of core classes together. I'd meet him in the library to study. One day, Stella was there with me. I introduced them. And . . ."

"And?"

His nostrils flared. "He took her out. Didn't tell me about it. She went with him to a frat party, and he slipped something into her drink."

My temperature spiked from normal to boiling in a flash. I was seconds from exploding as my arms began to shake and my hands balled so tight my nails dug into my palms. I didn't trust myself to speak so I sat there, my jaw locked, and waited for him to continue.

"I showed up at the party too. Thank fuck. Showed up right as he was trying to drag her off to a room. She was totally out of it. I've never seen her like that. It scared the hell out of me."

"Tell me you beat the shit out of Dave."

"I beat the shit out of Dave. That's the reason I got banned from every frat house."

Guy had told me about the fight, just not the reason it had started. I'd rolled my eyes at the time because, by our junior year, I'd been more focused on school than I had been on partying. But not Guy.

Now I wish I would have been with him. Now I wish I would have met Dave.

"After that, I made Stella promise to tell me when she started dating anyone," he said.

"Why didn't I know about this?"

"Like I said, she made me promise. It shook her up. She was really embarrassed, and it was hard for her to trust anyone for a while."

For that alone, I wanted to strangle Dave. I dragged a hand through my hair. "I had no idea."

"No one does. She didn't even tell Mom and she tells Mom just about everything."

Damn. This was certainly not what I'd expected to hear coming over tonight.

"I just . . ." He smacked a hand on his leg. "I have a feeling she's seeing someone."

Yeah. Me. "Her freshman year was a long time ago."

"She's my sister, man. I don't want anything to happen to her."

"Maybe the guy she's seeing isn't a Dave. Maybe he's decent."

Guy scoffed. "Or maybe he's a prick."

"Come on." My heart was racing again. The conversation hadn't gone as I'd expected so far, but maybe that would work in my favor. Compared to the fuckwad Dave, I was a saint, right? I would never disrespect Stella, Guy had to know that. "What if she was dating someone like me?"

Or me.

Guy started laughing. "That's my nightmare, man. That's my nightmare."

"What? Why?"

"Dude. You slept with half the cheerleaders our senior year."

"In high school. That was over ten years ago. And you slept with the other half."

"Exactly. The last person I want Stella with is anyone like you and me. She's too good."

I couldn't exactly argue with that. Stella was as pure and perfect as they came. But damn it, I wanted to earn her. I liked to think so far, I was doing a good job.

Guy stood, picking up his beer bottle. He took a step like he was going to head to the kitchen for another, but stopped and glanced over his shoulder. "This is all rhetorical, right? You're joking."

"Uh, yeah." *Heath, you spineless bastard.*

"Good. Because I'd have to kill you if you ever went after my sister."

I tipped the beer can to my lips, using it to hide my disappointment as he left the room.

Guy wanted a decent man for Stella.

Apparently, he didn't think his best friend fit that bill.

Fucking hell. How could he not think I was good enough? I had a great job. A fantastic house. So what if I hadn't dated much? I hadn't met a woman who made me want a long-term commitment. Until Stella.

I shoved out of my seat, taking my beer can to the kitchen. I dumped out the dregs and put the can in the recycling bin beneath the sink. Because decent men recycled and I was a fucking decent man.

"I'm going to take off."

"What?" Guy popped out of the fridge, two fresh beers in his hand. "You just got here."

"I remembered something I needed to do for work," I lied.

"I thought you guys were closed this week."

"Just because the office is closed doesn't mean I don't have work to do."

"Fine," he muttered with a scowl. "You're in a piss mood anyway."

Nice. "Bye." Without another word, I walked to the door, ripped it open with too much force and marched to my truck.

258

The blood roaring in my veins kept me warm as I drove to Stella's apartment and stood at her door, waiting for her to answer.

The deadbolt flipped first, then there she was. Tonight's pajamas were a tie-dyed sleepshirt that hit her at the knees. The arms were so big they draped to her elbows. "Hi."

"Hi." I stepped inside. "So I just left Guy's place."

"W-what?"

"I went over to tell him that I was going to ask you on a date."

"You did?"

I nodded and fisted my hands on my hips. "Yep. It went great," I deadpanned.

Stella cringed. "Is he mad?"

"No, I didn't tell him." But he'd told me plenty.

Plenty that I couldn't bring up, not yet. Someday soon, I wanted to hear Stella's side of the story with Dave. But I was too angry about it tonight. When—if—she wanted to talk, I needed to be there to listen, not fume.

"He was in a shit mood," I lied. "Thought it would be better to wait. You know how he is."

"Yes, I do." Her shoulders fell and she tugged at the collar of her shirt. "What now?"

We didn't have a lot of options. Not until I told Guy.

So I tucked a lock of hair behind her ear. "Can you keep a secret?"

CHAPTER 9

STELLA

T wo days wasn't exactly a long time to keep a secret. Okay, it was nothing. Two days was nothing.

But I really, *really* hated keeping secrets.

After Heath had asked me if I could keep a secret, of course I'd lied and said yes. I mean . . . what was my other option? Kick him out? Deny him sex? Absolutely not.

This secret might be torturing me, but I'd endure it for the orgasms alone.

Last night, Heath had stayed over, exhausting me with his fingers and tongue and cock. But tonight, we were switching beds, and he was cooking me dinner at his house.

I hurried around my bedroom, rushing to pack a bag. It rested on the foot of my bed, overflowing. So far I'd grabbed a change of clothes for tomorrow. A plum, sheer negligee I'd splurged on this afternoon at the mall. My toiletries were stuffed in a travel case along with my hair dryer because my hair wasn't the type that air-dried well. Then there was my makeup and brushes.

I stared at the bag and the curling wand in my hand, debating adding it to the mix.

Or I could get a suitcase. In my suitcase, it would all fit, no problem. I wanted to be comfortable. But Heath had been a saint so far, not getting spooked by my talk of the future. If I showed up with a suitcase, it might be the final straw.

This was the type of dilemma I'd normally run by Wendy. She'd called me four times in the past two days, trying to catch up. I'd avoided her at every call. Because the minute I spoke to her, I'd spill. So calling my best friend wasn't an option.

The suitcase-versus-backpack quandary was one I'd have to solve myself.

I'd avoided Guy just as deliberately as I had Wendy. He'd showed up at lunch today. I'd hidden beneath a blanket on the couch and held my breath until he'd finally stopped ringing the doorbell and left.

I couldn't avoid them forever. We couldn't keep this a secret forever. Didn't Heath want to tell people? Because I was ready to shout it from rooftops.

Heath Holiday was having sex with me.

That sentence would sound great from the top of my lungs.

Heath was the greatest kisser in the world. How did I know this? Because he was kissing me.

Heath was an excellent snuggler. A fact I'd verified after he'd slept in my bed.

Heath. Was. Mine.

Mine.

God, I wanted to tell someone. Anyone. Then maybe I'd actually believe this was happening.

"I'm spending the night at Heath's house."

Saying it to my empty bedroom wasn't quite as therapeutic as I'd hoped. Oh, well. Keeping a secret for a few more days would give us a chance to feel this out. Heath and I could decide together when to bring friends and family into the mix.

A few more days, then we could tell Guy. When we were sure.

Except I hadn't asked Heath how long this would be a secret. He wouldn't want this to go on for too long, right? No way.

And if this didn't work, well . . . it would be best if Guy didn't know.

My stomach churned at the idea of a breakup.

I studied the curling wand again. While I had him, I was at least going to have good hair, so I tossed it into the pile, then worked to stuff everything into the backpack. I had to sit on it to get the zipper closed and it bulged at the seams.

It was dark beyond the windows as I shrugged on my coat, the winter days short. I loaded up, my bag straining my shoulders, and rushed to my car.

The drive across town to Heath's house was slow, the clouds that had been hanging over town all day finally opening up to dump a fresh coat of snow, and my tires crunched on the quiet streets as I navigated Heath's neighborhoods.

This was one of the best areas in Bozeman. Heath had built his house on a large corner lot, giving himself some distance from the house next door. Three blocks from here was an elementary school.

I imagined kids wearing backpacks nearly as heavy as mine walking down these safe sidewalks, meeting up with their friends along the way. That's how it had been in my youth. Guy and I would leave our house first, stopping to collect Heath, Tobias and Maddox on the way to school. The boys would walk ahead, though sometimes, Heath would hang back and walk beside me instead.

All those years ago, from the time I'd been just a little girl, and I'd never stopped hoping he'd walk by my side.

I smiled as I parked, collected my bag and made my way to the door. Before I could knock, he was there, a sexy smile on that handsome face.

"Hi." He reached for my backpack, taking it from my arm. "I figured you would have brought a little suitcase."

My mouth parted. "How did you know?"

He chuckled and waved me inside. "Because you don't carry a purse. You carry a tote. I've never once seen you pack light. Remember that weekend when your parents were going out of town for their anniversary and you guys stayed with us? You brought three bags for one night."

"I don't know how to pack light."

"You don't have to pack light." He tucked a lock of hair behind my ear. "Not for me. Bring whatever you want. I'll haul it inside."

My heart skipped. I wasn't sure what to say so I rose up on my toes to brush my mouth against his, then stepped inside.

The house smelled like Heath, spicy and male and clean.

"Give me your keys." He held out his hand.

I placed them in his palm. "Why?"

"I'm going to park your car inside. Keep it out of the snow."

Or keep it secret? I shook that thought away, irritated at myself that I'd assume his kind gesture was to hide us. "Here you go."

"Be right back." He set my backpack aside, then walked for the door. "Make yourself at home."

"Okay." I waited until he was outside, then wandered into the house.

When I'd been here on Christmas Eve, I'd been too busy kissing Heath to look around. And the morning after, when I'd snuck out, I'd lingered by the door, watching for my Uber.

As expected, Heath's home was as classy as the man himself.

Rich wood pieces and buttery leather furniture filled the living room. Maple cabinets hugged the kitchen's walls, circling a black, granite island. The charcoal walls and coal rugs added to the moody, manly vibe.

I could live here. Definitely.

"Getting ahead of yourself again." I giggled, walking to the kitchen.

On the counter closest to the gas range rested a cutting board and knife along with a tomato and box of baby spinach.

The garage door hummed as it closed on the other end of the house, then Heath strode into the main room. He went straight for my backpack still by the front door, winking at me as he carted it down the hallway toward his bedroom.

When he returned, he walked right to me, taking my face in his hands to kiss me. "Hi."

"Hi."

"Thanks for coming over."

I smiled. "Thanks for dinner."

"Don't thank me yet. I'm not the best cook."

"Want some help?"

"No, you sit." He nodded to the barstools at the island. "Wine?"

"Sure."

Uncorking the bottle and pouring us each a glass was the only thing Heath didn't fumble with in the kitchen.

I bit the inside of my cheek to keep from laughing when he went to slice the tomato and half of it rolled to the floor. I stayed quiet when he read the instructions meticulously on the box of uncooked fettuccini noodles. But when he took out the chicken breasts from the fridge and realized they were still frozen, I couldn't help it anymore and slid off my seat.

"Shit." He shook his head. "I took these out this morning. Guess I should have done it last night. How do you feel about pizza delivery?"

"Or we can improvise." I joined him beside the cutting board, stealing the knife from his hand. "Do you have any mushrooms or broccoli?"

"Both, actually." He retrieved them from the fridge.

"Perfect. Put a pot of water on the stove to boil and add a bit of salt."

"Yes, ma'am." Heath gave me a mock salute, and after I rescued dinner, we returned to the island with bowls of creamy pasta primavera.

He forked a bite and moaned. "This is awesome."

I shrugged. "Mom's a great cook. I always liked helping her."

"You have her talent. This summer I'll wow you with my grilling skills."

"This summer?" Would we be together this summer?

He met my gaze, his locked with mine, and answered my unspoken question. "This summer."

I smiled through the meal and while I watched Heath do the dishes. Then we retreated to the living room, cuddling on the couch.

"Want to watch something?" he asked.

"Sure. You pick."

He reached for the remote, turning on the TV just as a flicker of headlights came through the front window.

We froze, listening for a long moment, but then he shot off the couch.

"Damn," he said, glancing out the windows.

"What?" I stood but didn't follow him toward the glass. "Is it Guy?"

"It's Tobias." He raked a hand through his hair.

265

"Oh."

He turned and gave me a pained look. "I've been trying to talk to him."

"You should. I can go."

"Would you mind just . . . hiding in the bedroom?"

My mouth parted. I had to hide? Of course, I had to hide. I was a secret. "Um, yeah. Okay."

I took a step to head that way, but Heath stopped me. "Don't forget your glass."

"Right." I picked it up from the end table because we couldn't have any evidence I was here. Good thing he'd already stowed my overnight bag.

"Sorry, Stell."

"It's fine," I lied with too much cheer. Then before he could see my face fall, I hurried down the hallway and eased the bedroom door shut.

"Hey." Heath's voice carried from the front door as he opened it for Tobias. "What's going on? I've been calling you."

"Yeah." Tobias stomped his feet, then from the sound of their steps, walked to the kitchen. "Got any more of that wine?"

That was my wine he was drinking.

I frowned and slunk to the bed, sitting on the edge. The plush comforter was the same shade of gray as the walls in the living space. The pillows were fluffed against the headboard made from narrow slats of wood, each stained in different colors like a small-scale version of barnwood.

Another beautiful, masculine room. Though it needed color. The whole house could use more color.

God, I felt like a fool. Sitting in here alone, thinking some ruby-red toss pillows would add some charm to Heath's room.

This secret thing was supposed to be for Guy. Why did we need to hide from Tobias? Why not just tell him we were together? Unless Heath was worried that Tobias would slip.

Guy and Tobias weren't as close as Heath and my brother, but they were all friends. Or maybe it was a work thing. Maybe it was frowned upon for intra-office relationships.

Probably something I should have asked Heath before sleeping with him. *Sorry, not sorry.*

"Okay, what's going on?" Heath asked Tobias.

It was impossible not to eavesdrop. But if Heath didn't want me to listen, he should have sent me to the garage for an escape. There was nothing to do but sip my wine as their voices carried my way.

"You remember Eva?" Tobias asked Heath.

"Yeah."

There was a long pause. "She's pregnant."

I sat up straight.

Heath choked, coughing to clear his throat. "What?"

"She's pregnant. We hooked up a few months ago. I guess the condom broke because she showed up on Christmas Eve to tell me she was pregnant."

"That's why you weren't at the party."

"Yeah," Tobias muttered.

So focused on Heath and my champagne, I hadn't realized Tobias had been missing from the party.

"So what now?" Heath asked. "Is she keeping the baby? Are you guys getting back together?"

"She's moving to London." Tobias's voice was thick like he struggled to speak the words. "She leaves on New Year's."

"Fuck," Heath hissed.

My hand came to my heart, rubbing at the ache. I knew Eva. We'd met in college when she and Tobias had been together. The few parties when Guy had invited me along—I'd always gone in the hopes of seeing Heath—she'd been there too.

Eva was gorgeous and smart. She was one of the most driven women I'd ever met. The two of us had lost touch after she and Tobias had broken up—I wasn't sure why they'd called it quits because they'd always been great together. But shortly after their graduation, I'd heard from Guy that she'd moved away from Montana.

I guess at some point she'd come back.

And now she was having Tobias's baby. *Whoa.*

"I don't know what to do," Tobias confessed. "I just . . . I can't even wrap my head around this."

"You will," Heath promised. "Give it time. Talk to her. You guys will figure this out."

"I'll miss it. I'll miss it all because she'll be halfway around the world."

"Go with her," Heath said.

Tobias scoffed. "My life is here. Mom. Dad. You. Hell, even Maddox is moving home."

"We're your family no matter where you live, brother."

The affection in Heath's voice melted my heart. I wasn't crazy about sitting here, feeling like I was intruding on a personal conversation. But to hear Heath, it reminded me of all the reasons why no one had ever measured up.

He loved his family. He loved his friends.

"What about work?" Tobias asked. "Dad's going to retire before too long. Then it will be ours."

"There's no reason you have to live here to help run the company. You're in your office most days as it is. We'll get Maddox to buy you your own plane as a baby shower gift. God knows he can afford it."

I smiled, hoping that Tobias had one on his face too.

"I don't want to leave Montana," Tobias said. "When I think about having a family, raising a kid. This is where that needs to happen. Eva . . . she travels everywhere. She doesn't even have a permanent address."

Another long pause and I knew where this conversation was going.

My heart twisted again.

If Tobias wanted to stay here, either he'd have to convince Eva to give up her life or . . .

He'd have to fight for their child. He'd have to fight to keep the baby here.

"She'll hate me." Tobias's voice was so quiet I strained to hear. "If I push to keep the baby here, she'll hate me. But I don't want my child living out of temporary homes. Being passed from nanny to nanny. I don't want to see my kid every other weekend and holiday."

"You need to talk to Eva." There was a clap, like Heath had put his hand on Tobias's shoulder. "I know you both will want the best for your kid. You'll figure it out."

"Yeah." Tobias blew out a long breath. "How about a refill?"

The cork plunked out of the bottle and I heard the unmistakable glug of a glass being poured.

"Want to watch a game or something?" Tobias asked. "I'm not quite ready to head home. I need to think of what to say to Eva first."

"Oh, uh . . ." Heath hesitated. "Sure."

I groaned and brought my own glass to my lips, gulping the rest of my wine. As the TV volume turned on, I set the empty glass aside and flopped back on the bed, staring at the white ceiling.

This was dumb. I felt like an idiot hiding in Heath's room. But it was too late to come out now. What would I say?

Oh, hi, Tobias. Sorry to hear about Eva. Congrats on the baby.

Maybe we could have made an excuse for me being here when Tobias had arrived. A work question or something to do with Guy. But it was too late now, so my only choice was to hide here.

And wait.

Thirty minutes passed. Tobias stayed. Then an hour. Then two.

"Stella." A hand on my shoulder shook me awake.

I jolted up, forgetting for a moment where I was. I'd fallen asleep waiting for Tobias to leave. "Is he gone?"

"Yeah. Sorry."

I pushed up on an elbow, glancing at the clock on the nightstand. It was after midnight.

"He wanted to stay for a game. I don't know if you heard or not—"

"I did. Sorry. It was sort of hard not to listen."

"It's fine. Saves me from rehashing it all. Anyway . . . I didn't want to kick him out."

"I get it."

"So much for dinner and a movie, huh? I'm sorry. We should have just told him you were here."

"He probably needed to talk and wouldn't have if I was there." I gave him a sad smile. "Should I go?"

"No. Stay. Please."

"All right."

The guilt on his face eased my stinging pride. "I'm sorry."

"It's okay."

Except it didn't feel okay. Because he might be sorry, but I had this awful feeling that it wouldn't matter.

And that come tomorrow morning, I'd still be his secret.

CHAPTER 10
HEATH

Twenty-nine years old and I'd never given a woman flowers. Not Mom—Dad had always had her covered. Not my prom dates—they hadn't wanted wrist corsages. Not a girlfriend—there hadn't been many.

I guess I'd simply been waiting for the right woman. With a bouquet of twelve red roses clutched in one hand, I held my breath and pressed Stella's doorbell.

She answered moments later wearing a pair of ripped jeans and a red turtleneck the same color as the flowers. Her hair was curled. Her makeup accentuated those pretty eyes and long, sooty lashes. And in her ears, she wore the earrings I'd bought this week.

"Hi." She smiled, lifting a hand to tuck a lock of hair behind her ear and the faint jingle sound confirmed she was also wearing my bracelet.

I'd be adding more gifts to her collection. The jewelry I'd bought simply because I'd thought of her, but seeing her wear it was a rush I hadn't expected. It was almost as thrilling as it had been to wake up to her in my bed this morning.

"Hi." I leaned in to kiss her cheek, then stepped inside and handed over the bouquet.

"Thank you." She pressed them to her nose, humming as she inhaled their fragrance. "These are beautiful."

"I'm hoping they'll buy me a date."

"A date?" She arched an eyebrow. "What kind of date?"

"The real kind. You. Me. A nice restaurant. Good wine."

"Is that, um . . . allowed?"

"Why not?" I shrugged.

Last night had been a train wreck. When Tobias had showed up, I'd panicked. Not just because he was Guy's friend too, but because I wanted to talk to Dad about Stella first. We didn't need awkward tension in the office. After New Year's, I'd sit him down and explain. Until then, we'd keep this quiet.

Having Stella hide in my room was not how I'd planned the night to go, especially leaving her alone for hours. But Tobias had clearly been avoiding his own home—he'd stayed longer than he had after my Super Bowl party last year.

Tonight, I'd make it up to her.

Dinner downtown was a risk, but Guy had texted me earlier inviting me to a poker game at another friend's house. Tobias was home. Maddox was home. My parents were home, soaking up time with Violet.

I'd called them all earlier just to make sure of everyone's plans.

And if we did bump into anyone we knew, we could just pretend it was a work dinner.

"Sounds fun." She smiled and motioned to her outfit. "Should I change?"

"No. You're gorgeous."

Her cheeks flushed as she smelled the roses again. "Let me put these in some water."

While she took care of the flowers and pulled on some

shoes and her coat, I called Bozeman's newest steakhouse and made a last-minute reservation.

"Why am I nervous?" Stella asked as we left her apartment.

"Nerves? Or excitement?" Because the jitters I was feeling were from the latter.

"Both," she breathed, slipping her hand in mine.

I loved how she was honest with me. That she didn't keep her thoughts to herself.

Stella looked perfect in the passenger seat of my truck, her perfume filling the cab. As we walked from the parking space to the restaurant, her arm rested comfortably in mine, like this was how we should have always walked together. The hostess seated us at a table in the corner of the room, handing us our menus to read by the dim light.

"Want me to order for you?" Stella asked.

"Isn't it customary for the man to order for his date?" Not that I would. She could have whatever she wanted.

"You've been proving how well you know me this week. It's my turn to take a stab at it."

"All right." I closed my menu and set it aside.

She smiled, challenge accepted, and scanned the book. Then she set it aside and shot me a smirk as our waitress came over. Stella ordered wine first, a rich cabernet that I would have picked myself.

After bringing over the bottle and filling our glasses, the waitress took out her notepad. "And what are we having this evening?"

"I'm going to have your filet. Medium with a baked potato, please," Stella said, glancing my way. "And he's going to have the rib eye. Medium rare with fries."

I grinned as the waitress scribbled down her notes and left us to our wine.

"So?" Stella asked.

"Nailed it."

"Yes." She fist-pumped and lifted her wineglass to clink with mine.

I laughed, ready to take a sip when my eyes landed on a familiar face walking our way. My smile dropped. "Shit."

Dad crossed the restaurant with Mom on his arm.

"What?" Stella followed my gaze. "Oh."

So much for our date.

"Hey, you two." Dad extended a hand as I stood. "How's it going?"

"Good." I nodded, my mind racing.

As far as I knew, there had never been an office relationship at Holiday Homes. We didn't have an official policy against it, but tonight was not the night to discuss it with my father. Not until Stella and I'd had more time together. Not until we'd told Guy.

And just like last night with Tobias, I panicked.

"Stella and I were at the office." The lie spewed from my lips in a desperate attempt to make this not look exactly as it was. A date. "We were both hungry and I remembered you mentioning this place was good."

"Ah." Dad nodded. "It is good. I didn't realize you were both working today."

"Just catching up on emails," I lied again, hating the way Stella's spine stiffened.

"I was, um . . . running some new numbers for the Jensen remodel." Her eyes flickered to mine for the fastest glare in history.

"Joe cornered me at the party," Dad said. "Told me about the flooring. Sounds like you handled it just right."

"Thanks." Stella gave him a smile, then turned to Mom. "Hi, Mrs. Holiday."

274

"Hannah," Mom corrected. "Please. And we'll let you kids get back to dinner."

"Unless you'd like to join us?" The invitation came so fast I said it before I thought about the words.

Fuck. Me. What was wrong with me?

"Are you sure?" Mom asked, looking between the two of us.

"Why not?" I held out the chair on my other side for her as Dad took the fourth.

The hostess appeared, bringing with her the other two place settings she'd cleared away earlier. Then the waitress hurried over so we could order another bottle of wine before Mom and Dad placed their orders.

Stella sat rigidly, her hands clasped on her lap, and kept her attention on my parents.

Tell them. Just tell them. I opened my mouth but Dad spoke before I had the chance.

"How was your Christmas, Stella?" he asked her.

"It was lovely," she said. "I spent the day at my parents' house and relaxed. You?"

"We did the same. Let Violet entertain us." Dad chuckled. "That girl is going to give Maddox a run for his money when she hits sixteen."

"Good thing he's worth billions," I teased.

Mom laughed. "Isn't that the truth. Stella, how's Guy doing?"

At the mention of Guy, Stella seemed to throw up even more of a guard. On the surface, she wore her beautiful, enchanting smile, but it didn't reach her eyes. "He's good. Still working as a programmer."

"I never quite understood how he got into computers." Mom shook her head. "For a person who thrives around people, I always thought he'd become a teacher or a coach or a used car salesman."

"Can you imagine Guy teaching kids?" Stella groaned. "That's terrifying."

We all laughed because she wasn't wrong.

Tell them.

Every time I opened my mouth, either my mother or father would speak first. And as the minutes passed, as the conversation carried on, it became harder and harder to find an explanation for lying in the first place.

Damn it. When they walked up to the table, I should have just told them. Dad wouldn't care, right? I'd have to wait and find out at work next week. So I sipped my wine and ate my meal while Stella completely charmed my parents.

She gave them her fullest attention, answering their questions and listening to stories. It was me who was ignored. Through the conversation and our meal, her cold shoulder became as frigid as the winter temperatures.

It was only after our plates were cleared, the tab was paid—by Dad, insisting that he'd expense it since this had been a *staff* dinner—and we were all bundled in our coats, did Stella finally glance my direction.

Her expression was flat. Guarded.

God, I was an asshole.

"Where did you park, Stella?" Dad asked as we congregated on the sidewalk outside the restaurant. "It's dark so we'll walk you."

"I got it. We parked in the same lot," I lied. Again.

That was the tenth or maybe the twentieth lie tonight. I'd lost track. Dad had bought them all. Mom, not even a little bit. Probably because I was a shit liar and Mom had always had a nose for when her sons were being devious.

She looked between Stella and me, and if Mom's expression had a name, it would be *You're Not Fooling Me, Son.*

I'd seen it countless times in my life. Usually before she'd grounded me for doing something stupid. Like the time I'd hauled my sled onto the roof so I could *get some air* and instead of hitting the snowbank beneath the eaves, I'd crashed through the neighbor's fence.

"So lovely seeing you, Stella." Mom pulled her into a hug.

Dad shook Stella's hand. "Don't worry about the Jensen project. Enjoy the rest of your vacation. Same to you, Heath."

"Will do."

Dad held out his arm to escort Mom, and with a wave, they headed down the street.

I sighed when they disappeared around a corner. "I'm sorry."

"It's fine." Stella nodded and spun in the other direction, starting down the sidewalk toward where we'd parked.

It was definitely not fine. Her shoes made an angry click as we walked. She kept her hands stuffed into the pockets of her jacket, her shoulders bunched at her ears.

Any time I moved closer, she'd inch away or walk faster. And at the truck, when I moved to open her door, she waved me off for the driver's side.

The trip to her apartment was silent, the tension growing thicker with every turn. When I parked in front of her place, she bolted out the door before I'd even put the truck in park.

"Damn it," I muttered. Then I was rushing after her, jogging to catch up before she could shut me out. "Stella, I'm sorry."

"It's fine." She fit her key into the lock. "We're a *secret*."

The last word was so enunciated that I felt every letter like the whack of a hammer against a nail's head. S-E-C-R-E-T.

"I need to tell Dad. Make sure he's okay with it. I should have just done it tonight but . . . I'm sorry."

Stella looked up over her shoulder. "And if he's not okay with it?"

"He will be." He would be. He had to be. There wasn't another choice. "There's a chance that he'll ask us to be discreet."

She dropped her gaze, her shoulders falling. "More secrets?"

"It's not forever." I put my hands on her shoulders as I leaned in closer. "I panicked tonight. I didn't think we'd see anyone."

One minute she was starting to lean into my touch, the next she was shoving the door open and storming inside. *Shit.* Maybe I shouldn't talk tonight. I hadn't said a damn thing right.

I stayed on the stoop, watching as she stripped off her coat and hung it up on a hook. "Stell. I want to tell people. I want to tell Guy first."

"Then tell him." She tossed up her hands, standing close to the threshold like a blockade. "I don't like being a secret. I don't like lying to people, especially my brother, my boss and my boss's wife."

"You're right." I held up my hands. "I'm sorry."

She dropped her chin, staring at the floor for a long moment. Then she looked up and the shame in her eyes made me feel about three inches tall. "I know it's only been a week. Less than a week. But you're . . . you. I want to tell people about you. Because I like you. I like you a lot."

"I like you too. More than a lot. I'll tell them. My Dad. Mom. Guy. Tobias. I'll tell them all."

She blew out a long breath. "When?"

"Next week. First thing Monday morning, I'll tell Dad."

"And Guy?"

"Sunday night." Which meant that for my meeting with Dad on Monday morning, I'd probably have a black eye. "Once Guy comes back from that party he's going to in Big Sky."

"Okay." Her frame deflated. "Thank you. I know he's going to be as mad as a hater but . . . he'll get over it."

"You're welcome." A smile tugged at the corner of my mouth. This woman and her messed-up sayings. "And it's as mad as a hatter."

"I know. But—"

"You like your version better."

"Yeah. Haters gonna hate."

"You got that one right."

She gave me a small smile. "I guess so."

"I don't like this either, Stell. The secrets. I swear." But we had years, right? What was a few days of hiding when we had years and years to share this with the world? "Tomorrow. Want to try this again? Just you and me?"

And hopefully, date attempt number three wouldn't be a disaster.

"Actually . . . my best friend Wendy invited me out. She works at a gym in town and they're having a party at The Crystal."

"Oh, okay." Damn. I'd hoped to be with her on New Year's Eve.

"Want to come along? As my date?"

The invitation felt a lot like a test.

I wasn't one for failing tests.

"Yes."

She must have thought I'd say no because the smile she sent me was full of relief. "Are you going to come inside?"

"If you'll let me."

She stepped aside and crooked a finger.

CHAPTER 11
STELLA

Wendy's eyes bugged out as Heath and I walked into The Crystal Bar. From across the crowded room, her jaw dropped when she saw his hand on my shoulder. In a blink, the shock disappeared and she sent me a scowl.

I had explaining to do.

"Sorry," I mouthed.

"You're in trouble," she mouthed back.

I reached for Heath's hand, clasping it tight, as I weaved through the crush.

The bar was packed for New Year's Eve. Women were dressed in shimmering tops and shiny dresses. A cluster of men had noisemakers, blowing them after a round of shots. We were hours from midnight and that sound would get old soon. Party hats and tiaras with the upcoming year's number were scattered on the bar. Foil curlicues hung from the bar's dusty rafters.

The Crystal Bar, though fancy in name, was the roughest bar on Main. It was the definition of no frills. It had yet to be renovated and changed to an upscale, trendy bar like so many others downtown.

Rows of old keg taps were hung high on one of the bar's brick walls, joining the beer and liquor signs. One section of the ceiling had been dedicated to confiscated fake IDs, row after row of them covered safe behind a sheet of Plexiglas. The Crystal had a smell of its own, cultivated from too many years of old drunks and rowdy college kids. The number one Yelp review ridiculed the dive bar for the lewd signs, foul language and filthy bathrooms.

"This place reminds me of college," Heath said, leaning close so I could hear him over the noise.

"Me too." I laughed. "Same musty smell. Same cobwebs."

He chuckled. "Pretty much."

We were older than most of the people here tonight by at least five years. But considering Wendy worked with a lot of college students at the gym, it was no surprise they'd chosen this as their party spot.

"What do you want to drink?" Heath asked. "I'll go order. You can talk to Wendy."

"Champagne if they have any."

"Okay, baby." He bent and brushed a kiss to my cheek and the thrill of his lips on my skin raced through my veins.

We were here. In public. No hiding. No pretending.

No secrets.

I practically danced my way to Wendy. She was frowning, but I couldn't help my smile. "Happy New Year."

"All done crushing on Heath Holiday, huh?"

"Not quite." I blushed, finding him at the bar. He stood taller than the other men, his shoulders broader. As he waited for the bartender, he pushed the sleeves of his black sweater up his sinewed forearms.

"Spill. Right now." Wendy smacked me on the shoulder.

"How long has this been going on? And why wasn't I the first person you called?"

"Sorry. It started at the party on Christmas Eve. But we haven't told Guy yet, or my boss. So we've been keeping it quiet."

"You didn't trust me to keep a secret? Like I'd ever talk to Guy. Or your boss."

"I know." I sighed. "Forgive me?"

"Only if you tell me everything."

I smiled. "I'm having sex with Heath Holiday."

She giggled. "Someone should. Look at that man. He's gorgeous."

I glanced over my shoulder, laughing with her. "I still can't believe it. I just want to scream it, like that will help make it real."

"Do it." She nudged my elbow. "It's so loud in here no one will even hear you."

Neil Diamond's "Sweet Caroline" was blaring over the speakers, most of the crowd joining in at the *Da. Da. Da.* line. The men with the noisemakers were going berserk, honking and blowing their horns.

If there was ever a place to scream, this was it.

Screw it. "I'm having sex with Heath Holiday!"

Halfway through my sentence, the music cut out. The noisemakers stopped. All eyes swung my way and Wendy cringed on my behalf.

"Oh my God," I whispered, shrinking into myself.

"Uh . . ." The bartender had stopped the music to grab the microphone. "Good for you, lady. And Heath Holiday."

I dropped my face to my hands as the room laughed. Why? Why me?

"Anyway," the bartender drawled. "Quick announcement.

Draft pints from now until power hour at eleven are two bucks."

The music started again as abruptly as it had stopped.

I didn't move other than to let my hair drape around me, shielding my face. Tonight, I was wearing a cream sweater and a pair of silver, sequined pants. It was my disco-ball outfit. What I wouldn't give to be in all-black so I could slink into a shadow and disappear.

A strong arm banded around my shoulders, pulling me into a rock-solid chest. A chest I'd slept on every night this week.

"This is my fault, isn't it?" Heath bent low to speak in my ear.

"Yes. All of my embarrassing moments are your fault, remember? You're cursed."

"Sorry."

I relaxed and dropped my hands, spinning to face him. "How bad was it?"

Heath set his beer bottle and my champagne on the table closest to us, then he framed my face with his hands before tipping his head up and shouting, "I'm having sex with Stella Marten!"

The room was too loud, and the only people who heard him were close by.

"See?" he asked. "Not that bad."

"Ugh." I groaned and fell forward into his body. "That is not the same."

He wrapped me up tight, kissing my hair. "Hi. I'm Heath."

"Wendy."

I stayed buried in his chest as he shook her hand.

"What are your intentions with my best friend?"

I groaned again. "Wendy."

"That's a good fucking question."

Except Wendy hadn't asked it.

I stiffened at the angry, familiar voice. So did Heath. It came from over his shoulder.

As Heath's arms loosened, I peeled myself away, peering past him to see my brother.

Maybe the entire bar hadn't heard Heath's announcement. But Guy had. He stood fuming, as livid as I'd seen him in years. My brother wore his emotions on his face, and at the moment, he was close to a rage.

Only one time in my life had I seen Guy this angry.

And that had landed an epic asshole in the hospital.

"Oh, shit," Wendy muttered, coming to my side. "He's pissed."

"You think?" I deadpanned, then shifted, trying to squeeze in between Heath and Guy.

But Heath felt me move and cut me off. One of his hands clasped mine as he spoke to Guy. "Let me explain."

"Fuck you," Guy said. "Fuck your explanation."

"Guy," I hissed.

"Don't." He pointed at my nose. "You kept this from me too."

"We were going to tell you," Heath said. "When you got back from skiing at Big Sky."

"Surprise. Mel showed up and one of us had to leave. So I came home early, thinking I'd call my best friend and my sister. See if they wanted to meet up. Then neither of them answered so I came downtown. And here you are."

"I'm sorry," I said.

Guy had already dismissed me, his gaze locked with Heath's.

"Take it easy," Heath said. "Let us explain."

"Calm down, Guy." I reached for his arm but he jerked away, sparing me a brief sneer before narrowing his eyes on Heath.

"After everything I told you the other night." Guy scoffed. "I can't fucking believe you."

"What?" I looked up to Heath. "What did he tell you?"

"This is not the same." Heath's jaw clenched. "Don't you dare compare me to that motherfucker."

Wait. What had Guy told him? There could only be one story. A story that Guy had no right to share, especially with Heath.

No. My head started spinning and I clutched Heath's hand for balance. This wasn't happening. There was a reason I didn't tell people about what happened to me freshman year. It just wasn't an embarrassing story. It had been a nightmare.

Guy had no right.

"You told him." I stepped closer to my brother. "You told him about Dave."

Guy didn't even have the decency to look guilty. "Yeah, I told him. I knew you were seeing someone. Sneaking around. I was worried about you and asked Heath if he knew who you were seeing. And he lied to me. You lied. To. My. Face. Some friend."

Most of those words were swallowed up by the noise in my head.

Heath knew about Dave. He'd known that one of Guy's friends had drugged me and would have raped me. He'd known all week.

He'd known the night he'd come over and asked if I could keep a secret.

My stomach dropped.

"How could you?" Guy asked him. "She's my sister. You were supposed to be my best friend. What happens when you fuck her over? What happens when you break her heart?"

"That's not—"

"Gonna happen?" Guy arched his eyebrows. "Sure it is."

"Stop." My voice was too soft. Neither of them heard me, and Guy was on a roll.

"You're using her. I told you she's had a crush on you and you decided she'd be easy prey, right? An easy lay?"

"Watch your goddamn mouth." Heath inched closer to Guy. "You will not talk about Stella like she's some cheap score."

"You're treating her like one."

"That's not what this is. I care about her. I would never intentionally hurt her."

"Stop." I managed to make my voice a little louder. But it didn't do any good. It was still too loud.

Guy scoffed, still ignoring me. "You've said that about all your women. You never intentionally hurt anyone, but you do. Over and over. I've watched them cry over you when you've moved on."

"And you're so much better?"

"Fuck you," Guy spat. "This isn't about me. It's about you and my sister."

"Stop." I tore my hand from Heath's. "Stop talking about me like I'm not standing here."

"I hate you for this." Guy's jaw ticked and he turned like he was going to leave, but before he took a step, he spun, moving so fast I barely had time to register what was coming.

Heath saw it. He didn't even try to move. He just let Guy's knuckles collide with his jaw.

The smack echoed around us.

Wendy cried out, gripping my arm to pull me away.

But Heath put his hand on my arm, keeping me behind him as he grunted.

The bouncers rushed toward our corner of the bar, shouting and shoving people out of the way.

286

I held my breath, staring between Guy and Heath, unblinking. *Don't fight. Please, don't fight.*

Heath stood tall, glowering at Guy.

And my brother glowered back.

But thankfully, no more punches were thrown.

"You're both out." One of the bouncers took Guy's elbow, attempting to drag him away. Except the bouncers were all smaller than Guy and Heath.

"Let me go." Guy tore his arm free, and this time when he turned, he didn't stop until he was out the front door. A bouncer followed him outside.

"You have to leave," another bouncer told Heath.

"I'm going." Heath held up his hands as the bouncer shoved at his shoulder, pushing him toward the rear exit.

"Oh my God." Wendy's hand found mine.

I gripped it tight, staring at Heath's tall body as he waded past clusters of people. Most of them were oblivious to what had just happened. Even those in Wendy's party hadn't been paying much attention.

"Come on." I hauled Wendy with me as I pushed through the room.

Guy was furious. The only person who'd be able to talk to him right now was me. But I didn't walk toward the front. I chose the back door.

I chose Heath.

He stood in the snow-covered parking lot across the alley. His hand was on his jaw, rubbing the spot where he'd been hit. When he heard me coming, his hand fell away and he strode toward us.

"Are you okay?" he asked.

"Yes." I gulped. "Are you?"

"I'm fine," he grumbled. "I was expecting it."

He seemed so . . . calm. Meanwhile, my heart was galloping

in my chest. My breath came in heavy pants, the cold air turning it into a billowing cloud around us.

"I'm going back in to get my coat." Wendy pried her hand from mine. "Wait for me."

"Okay." I nodded, taking a minute to breathe as she rushed toward the bar. "That was . . ."

"I'm sorry." He dragged a hand through his hair. "Christ."

"The night you went to his house, what did he tell you?"

Heath's eyes darted to mine. "Stell, it doesn't matter."

"What did he tell you?" I gritted my teeth.

He blew out a long breath. "He told me about his friend. The buddy from school. Dave. That he took you out to a frat party. That you guys kept it a secret. And that it, um . . . ended badly."

"He drugged me. He would have raped me."

Heath flinched. "Don't say that."

"Why not? It's true. It's the most humiliating moment of my life. The one *not* your fault."

My joke fell flat.

Heath looked like he was in more pain now than he had been after Guy'd slammed a fist into his face.

"I didn't want you to know," I admitted. "Guy had no right to tell you that story. Is that why you wanted us to be a secret?"

"What?"

"Is this a pity thing?" I asked. "Is that why?"

"You weren't a secret in that bar, Stella." He pointed over my shoulder, the tension rising on his face. "I told you I was going to tell Guy. This has nothing to do with what that fucker did to you in college."

So why couldn't I get this icky feeling out of my stomach?

"This is not how I expected it to be tonight," I whispered and my chin began to quiver.

Heath reached for me, but I stepped out of his grasp. If he

288

touched me, I'd melt. If he held me, I'd cry.

"I have to talk to Guy."

"We can go see him tomorrow. Together."

I shook my head. "No. Now."

"Okay." He took another step but I held up a hand.

"Alone. He's my brother."

When I'd fallen off a swing set or monkey bars, Guy had always been the first to rush to my side. If I'd crashed my bike, he'd been the one to hold my hand while Dad had picked the gravel from my skinned knees. Guy had watched out for me in high school, scaring the creeps away with his threats. He'd tried to do the same in college too.

I suspected that most of Guy's anger and frustration were not because of Heath. But because of me. Because I'd kept a secret. I'd let Heath convince me that he needed to be the one to tell Guy. But that had been a mistake.

I should have told him.

Guy should have heard it from me.

"Stell—"

"Tell Wendy I'll call her." I jogged away, rushing as fast as I could without risking a fall on the snow in my heeled boots.

"Stella!" Heath called, but I didn't slow.

I reached the end of the alley, rounded the corner and raced to the sidewalk on Main, scanning both directions for Guy.

He hadn't gone far. Just outside The Crystal Bar, my brother paced, his hands balled in fists. Maybe he'd expected us to come out the front door too.

"Guy," I hollered, rushing to his side.

He stopped pacing and looked over my shoulder like he was expecting Heath.

"I'm alone," I said, slowing to a stop.

The adrenaline was ebbing and the chill seeped through

my sweater. These pants were cute but not exactly warm. I wrapped my arms around my waist. "I'm sorry."

"You don't know what you're doing, Stella."

"I'm not a kid anymore, Guy. I know what I'm doing."

"He's not who you think he is."

"Guy." I gave him a sad smile. "This is Heath. I know exactly who he is. He's kind. He's gracious. He's smart. He whistles while he shaves and loves his family. He's loyal, so much so that he asked me to keep this a secret because he knew you were going to freak out."

"A secret? He asked you to be a secret? That's suspect, Stell. Not sweet."

"I care about him. I have since I was a little girl."

"Exactly." He threw up his arms. "You've built him into this dream or fantasy. What happens when the illusion falls to shit? What happens when you realize he's a womanizer? That he's using you and you'll be tossed aside when he's done?"

"That's not going to happen." I believed that down to the marrow of my bones. Heath wasn't using me. This was real.

We were real.

"Yes, it is!" Guy dragged a hand through his hair. "He's a player. I know because we're not that different. You know why Mel dumped me? Because I was hitting on another woman. It was stupid. It was a dumb-fuck move. But I was drinking and this girl wanted to flirt. Mel showed and caught me about two seconds from kissing another woman. She broke it off and told me never to call her again."

My heart twisted for my idiot brother. "I'm sorry."

"It's my fault."

"Yeah, it is. But that doesn't mean Heath will do the same to me."

"I've seen him play women, Stell."

"When? In high school? College? You know Heath. You

know him. Do you actually think he'd play me?"

A flicker of doubt crossed his gaze, but he didn't give in. He just raised that stubborn chin.

"Whatever." I tossed up my hands. There was no talking to him tonight. He'd made up his mind, and nothing I could say would change it. "If he plays me, then I'll dump him as Mel dumped you."

"And I'll lose my best friend."

"I'm not asking you to choose."

He blinked. "Seriously? Like I could be friends with a man who hurt my sister."

If only my brother could be as loyal to his girlfriends as he was to me. "I don't know what will happen with Heath. But you can't protect me all the time."

"Break up with him, Stella. End this now before it goes too far."

I huffed. "No."

"Yes."

"This isn't your business, Guy. You don't get to tell me what to do."

"Then don't come crying to me when he breaks your heart. I won't be there to dry your tears. Not this time." With that, he turned and marched down the sidewalk, leaving me standing alone.

My chin was quivering again, not just from the cold.

I was seconds away from crying when a pair of strong, familiar arms and a comforting scent wrapped around me.

Heath hadn't left. Of course, he hadn't left. He'd never leave me like this. Something Guy would know if he pulled his head out of his ass.

Heath had probably hovered around the corner, out of sight, but listening to our entire conversation.

"Come on, baby." Heath held me tighter. "Let's go home."

CHAPTER 12
STELLA

"So much for a fun New Year's Eve, huh?" I dropped my gaze to my lap as Heath drove us across town toward his place.

When I'd been getting ready earlier tonight, taking care with my hair and makeup, I'd been off-the-charts giddy to end one year and kick off another with Heath by my side. Now all I wanted to do was wash the glittery eye shadow from my lids and strip out of these sequined pants.

This disco ball had deflated.

Our entire week of dates had been a disaster. Was that a sign that this relationship was a mistake? Were we doomed?

"Hey." Heath reached across the console and brushed his thumb over my cheek. "Don't give up on the night yet. We've still got an hour until midnight."

I gave him a sad smile. "Maybe you should just take me home. Then we can start fresh tomorrow."

"No. You can start fresh from my place." He nodded to the backseat. "Besides, you already packed."

Actually, he'd packed. My suitcase was on the floor behind

us. I'd had everything stuffed in a backpack when he'd arrived to pick me up tonight. Like the other night, the bag had been stuffed until the seams had strained. Heath had taken one look at it, then marched to my closet to drag out a suitcase.

"Okay." I checked my phone for the hundredth time since we'd climbed in the truck.

Still nothing from Guy.

When we'd returned to the alley, Wendy had been waiting. She'd opted to stay downtown, understanding why I hadn't been in the mood for a party. She probably would have come home with me but Heath hadn't given her the chance to offer. After my argument with Guy, he'd spared me only a moment to hug Wendy before putting me in his truck and cranking on the heat.

In the distance, a golden firework exploded in the sky. Its tendrils faded to nothing as my eyes filled with tears.

"It hurts that he doesn't want me to be happy," I whispered.

"I'm sorry, baby. This is my fault."

"No, it's his." A tear fell. "How can he not want me to have you?"

"Don't cry." His hand came to my shoulder, sliding to my neck. "Or wait until we get home so I can hold you."

I sniffled but the battle was lost. The tears came in a steady stream, and by the time we eased into his garage, I was sure that my glitter shadow and mascara were all over my face.

Heath shut off the truck and climbed out, rounding the hood to open my door.

As he scooped me out, I buried my face in the crook of his neck and let him carry me inside. "Guy sucks."

He chuckled. "Tonight? Yes."

"How's your face?" I lifted up to look at the red spot on his jaw.

"It'll be fine. Not the first time I've been punched."

"Really? Who else has hit you?" And how did I not know about this?

"Tobias and Maddox when we were kids." He shrugged. "Brothers fight."

"Oh." I dropped my head to his shoulder again. "Guy and I don't really fight."

"He'll deal. When he sees that we're serious, he'll come around."

"You're right. But in the meantime, I'm going to give him the silent treatment. The jerk. I mean . . . you're his best friend. How could he even say that stuff about you? Doesn't that piss you off? That he would think you're bad for me? Because it pisses me off."

A surge of anger streaked through my veins. Anger was good. It dried up the tears, and as Heath set me on the end of his bed, I harrumphed and crossed my arms over my chest. "He doesn't get to talk about you like that."

"Defending my honor?" Heath slid off one of my shoes.

"Yes."

"It's sexy as hell." His fingers skimmed my ankle before he moved to the other shoe, taking it off and tossing it aside. Then his hands trailed up my legs, moving for the waistband of my pants.

If anger had beaten out the sadness, lust was going to kick anger's ass.

I lifted a hand to Heath's hair, messing up the strands that he'd combed earlier. "Will you kiss me at midnight?"

"Stupid question, Stell."

I fisted his hair, giving it a yank. "Are you teasing me?"

"Always." He chuckled and shifted closer, walking on his knees before brushing his lips to mine. "All of your midnight kisses are mine. New Year's Eve or not. You're mine."

Mine. That was a word I'd listen to on repeat as long as it came from his deep voice.

I leaned in, wanting another kiss, but he backed away and a look of concern marred his handsome features. "What?"

"About the thing in college. When Guy told me, it shocked the hell out of me. I wasn't sure what to say. I should have brought it up this week, but . . . every time I think about it, I get mad. I'm so sorry that happened to you."

"It's okay." I took his hand off my knee, lacing our fingers together. "It could have been a lot worse, and it's behind me."

"Should we talk about it?"

"I've talked about it. Guy thinks it's a secret, but Mom knows. She encouraged me to go to therapy. It's embarrassing that I put myself in that position. That I trusted someone who I shouldn't have. Those emotions will probably always be there. I learned a hard lesson. But otherwise, it's in the past."

"If you ever want to talk, I'm here."

"Thank you." I leaned in for a kiss, but he denied me again.

He grinned as I frowned. "You'll get what you're after soon enough."

"What are you waiting for?"

"I'm sorry I asked you to be a secret." He cupped my face with his hands. "No more secrets."

Something unlocked in my chest. The feeling of doubt that he really wanted me. I didn't know how much I needed to hear that until the words were out of his mouth.

"You're beautiful," he said. "You're smart. You're hilarious, and your quirks are enchanting."

"I don't have quirks."

"Disagree to agree." He smiled. "I respect you, Stella. I can't say that I've always treated women the right way. I'm not proud of it. I don't know where this thing will go, but I'll always respect you."

"I know you will."

"No more secrets."

I shook my head. "No more secrets."

"I'll talk to Dad on Monday. I'm guessing he won't care but will ask that we don't broadcast it in the office."

"Fine by me." I needed time at Holiday Homes to establish myself. I didn't need my peers or clients thinking I was getting preferential treatment because I was dating Heath.

"Good." This time when I leaned in, he met me in the middle for the kiss I wanted.

The kiss that erased the tension from the night. The kiss that assured me there'd be no more hiding. The kiss that promised it would be okay.

That one kiss led to another and another until we were connected in every way. Breathless, skin against skin, it was at midnight with Heath buried inside of me that I stopped crushing on Heath Holiday.

And fell in love with him instead.

"You know what I don't know about you?" Heath asked as we stood in the kitchen the next morning.

"What?"

"How do you like your coffee? I should know. I've seen you get some at work. But I was too busy staring at your ass to remember if you added cream or sugar."

"Cream and sugar."

"Sweet." He pulled me into his chest. "Like you. I should have guessed."

The coffee pot brewed on the counter beside us.

We'd slept in this morning because he'd kept me up late. I'd woken in his arms and after he'd made love to me again, we'd hopped in the shower before dressing in sweats. Heath had asked me to spend the day here. Just the two of us.

As the start of a new year went, this one was the best I'd ever had.

"What should we have for break—"

The doorbell rang, cutting him off.

He grumbled. "So much for our day alone."

"What if we just ignored it?"

"Good plan." We stood motionless, our gazes aimed in the direction of the door.

The doorbell rang again, not just once, but five times.

"There's only one person who does that." *Guy.* I looked up to Heath's jaw. There was a faint bruise forming but the stubble disguised most of it. "We can ignore him."

"Your call, baby."

My nostrils flared. "I don't want him to wreck our day. But I want to hear what he has to say."

"All right."

"We'll give him five minutes. Either he apologizes in those minutes or we boot him into the snow."

"I'll do the booting."

I laughed. "Piece of chocolate cake."

Heath opened his mouth but instead of correcting me, he simply smiled. "I love chocolate cake."

"Me too. Let's make one later."

"As long as you do the baking."

"You got it."

He let me go and took my hand, walking us to the door. He opened it, but stepped aside so I could take the lead.

Guy stood on the porch.

With Wendy.

"Hi." I smiled at her, then glared at my brother. "What?"

"Can we come inside?" he asked. "It's cold out here."

"Then you should have brought a coat."

"Stella."

I waved Wendy inside. "She can come in. You can't."

"Morning." Wendy pulled her lips together to hide a smile as she crossed the threshold. "Happy New Year."

"Happy New Year." I glanced between her and Guy. She had a green smoothie in her hand. Guy had another. Unlike me, he'd drank half the cup. "How did you two wind up together?"

"After you guys left last night, our party moved to another bar," she said. "I found this idiot there, drunk. And because I'm a better person than he is, I let him sleep it off on my couch."

"Ah." I nodded.

"Stella." Guy's teeth were chattering. "Please."

"No. You're a jerkface, butthole loser."

As kids, that had been the ultimate insult. I had no idea why it had popped into my head, but it did and well . . . it fit.

Heath's chest shook with silent laughter.

Wendy snorted.

"I know," Guy muttered.

"You hurt my feelings. Asshole." *So there.* A grown woman's insult.

"I'm sorry," he said.

"Good." *Victory.* "Now you may come inside. But mostly because I'm cold too, and you're letting all of the heat out."

Guy stepped inside and kicked the snow from his boots. He'd been pretty focused on me, but he risked a glance at Heath. "How's the jaw?"

Heath shrugged. "Stella kissed it better."

Wendy, who'd been sipping her smoothie, choked on her drink, coughing and sputtering. "Oh, God, I love this. I'm so glad neither of you are taking it easy on him."

"I regret getting in your car last night," Guy told her.

298

"Keep groveling, Marten," Wendy ordered. "Get back on your figurative knees so we can leave these two alone to enjoy their day."

He sighed but didn't argue. Then he squared his shoulders and faced Heath. "I love my sister."

"I know."

"I don't want her to get hurt."

"I'm not going to hurt her." There was such conviction in Heath's voice.

Guy heard it. So did Wendy.

She leaned against my arm and swooned.

"Good." Guy nodded, then faced me. "Heath's my best friend."

"I know."

"I don't want him to get hurt either."

I nodded, my heart swelling. For such a pain in my ass, he really had a soft heart.

"I'm sorry about what I said last night." Guy stepped closer, holding his arms out. "Forgive me?"

"Yes." I stepped into his hug. But one sniff and I shoved him away. "You stink like the bar."

"Wendy wouldn't let me shower." His stomach growled. "And all she'd give me for breakfast was this disgusting green goo."

"It's healthy," she and I said in unison.

Heath stepped up and clapped Guy on the shoulder. "We were about to make breakfast. Want to stick around?"

Guy nodded. "As long as Stella's cooking and not you."

"I'm cooking," I said.

"Mind if I hop in the shower?" Guy asked, sniffing his own armpit and grimacing.

"Go for it." Heath jerked his head down the hallway toward the guest bathroom. "I'll grab you some clothes."

299

As Guy disappeared, Wendy sighed. "My work here is done."

"Thank you for taking him home." I hugged her. "And bringing him here."

"You're welcome."

"What are you doing today?"

"Nothing much. Why?"

"Want to stick around?"

She looked between the two of us. "You don't mind?"

"Stay," Heath told her.

I smiled and skipped to the kitchen to make us all breakfast. After our plates were clear and the dishwasher was running, we moved to the living room.

"Should we watch something?" Heath asked.

"I wish the last season of *State of Ruin* was out on Madcast," I told Heath as we snuggled on the couch.

"Maddox gave me early access."

I gasped and sat up straight. "And you're just telling me this now?"

"We've had a busy week. There was no time for TV."

"True." I settled into his arms as he pulled up the wildly popular show and hit play. "It feels longer than a week."

He held me tighter. "Because it was always supposed to be you and me, Stell."

"Would you two shut the fuck up?" Guy barked from the recliner. "I want to watch."

Heath responded by swiping up a toss pillow and throwing it at my brother's face.

"I need to go home," Guy said, swatting the pillow away, but he made no move to leave.

"I never did get into this show." Wendy was curled into the end of a loveseat, her eyes closed as she burrowed beneath a throw blanket. "I'm taking a nap."

"Shh," Guy hissed.

Heath laughed and stretched out behind me, curling an arm around me as I fit my back to his chest as the opening credits played. "Happy New Year."

"Happy New Year."

He leaned in to whisper in my ear. "Do you believe it yet?"

I met his bright eyes. I saw the promise in his gaze. We'd only been together for a week. But this was the week that everything had changed.

Heath Holiday was mine.

"I believe it."

EPILOGUE
HEATH

O ne year later . . .

"Was it this loud last year?" Stella asked as we swayed on the dance floor at my parents' annual Christmas party.

"Yes, but we missed the loud parts."

"Right." She gave me a dreamy smile. "Because you were sucking my nipples in the sitting room."

The couple dancing next to us gave her a sideways look, but Stella was too busy surveying the ballroom to notice.

I pressed a kiss to her temple and spun her in the other direction. She blamed me for her embarrassing moments, and over the past year, I'd taken the fall many times to keep the smile on her face. But the real culprit behind this curse was Stella's verbal filter—or lack thereof.

"These guys are the best." Stella nodded toward the stage. "Good choice."

"Thanks, baby."

The live band was rocking The Baxter. Maybe I was biased

because Mom had put me in charge of music this year, but I saw more people dancing than in years past.

For the first time, my parents had relinquished some control over this annual Holiday event and had enlisted their sons to help.

I'd been in charge of music. Tobias had been assigned decorations. And Maddox had volunteered for food and drinks. His daughter's sweet tooth would not go unsatisfied tonight because the dessert table was twice as long as usual.

"Oh, no," Stella groaned.

"What?"

"Joe Jensen is coming this way." She put on a fake smile, pretending to be glad to see him. "Hey, Joe."

"Hi, Stella." He stopped close enough that it forced us to stop dancing. "Say . . . I was thinking about the kitchen earlier and before I forget, I'd like to change the design."

She tensed but that smile never faltered. "Okay. What are you thinking?"

"Can we make room for a subzero fridge and a professional-grade range?"

Joe had just told her last week that he didn't cook much. But my beautiful wife didn't throw that in his face. She simply nodded. "You got it. I'll work up the numbers for you next week."

"You're the best. Heath, she deserves a raise."

"Noted." I chuckled, waiting for him to disappear into the crowd before I swept her into my arms again. "You're going to win the bet, aren't you?"

"Easily."

"Damn."

This summer, we'd made a bet about Joe Jensen's house and when it would be finished. I'd figured it would be done by New Year's. She'd promised it would take well into spring.

Given his constant change orders and the specialty products he wanted in each room, it was now the longest-running project in Holiday Homes history.

And through it all, Stella had managed it perfectly. Not only had she won Joe over, but she'd won our bet and got to pick our next vacation spot.

"I'm thinking Hawaii," she said.

"Last time you said Alaska."

"I changed my mind. I don't think I'll be up for hiking this summer."

"Why not?"

She took a deep breath, then dropped a hand to splay across her belly.

"Wha—" Holy. Shit. "Does that mean what I think it means?"

"Yeah." The light in her eyes danced.

A rush of fear and anxiety and excitement hit me all at once and I had to stop moving before I tripped over my own damn feet. Was this happening?

"You're pregnant?"

She giggled. "I'm pregnant."

My arms snaked around her and I crushed her to my chest. "I love you. Fuck, but I love you."

"I love you too." She clung to me as I buried my face in her hair, drawing in that smell and letting it steady me.

My beautiful, amazing wife was having our baby.

"When did you find out?"

"Right before we left the house."

"That's why you were in the bathroom so long."

She nodded. "I would have told you then, but I wanted to be alone."

This, us on the crowded dance floor, was as alone as we'd been all night.

Guy and Wendy had been at home with us earlier, the women getting ready together. Then we'd all ridden to the hotel in my truck. Stella had been quiet on the drive, but I'd thought it was just because Guy and Wendy had been arguing.

Or . . . *debating*. They called their arguments debates.

Never in a million years would I have put those two together as a couple. They *debated* all the time, rarely agreeing on anything. But Guy was nuts over her and the way Wendy looked at him, well . . . it was the way I'd catch Stella looking at me.

"Are you happy?" she asked.

I nodded, holding her closer. "So happy."

Next to our wedding day, this was the happiest day of my life.

We'd only been married for a few months, but nothing with Stella had ever felt rushed. She'd always been a part of my life. She'd been that missing piece. When her lease ran out on her apartment this summer, she'd moved in. Two weeks later, I'd proposed. We'd planned a fall wedding and the day she'd walked down the aisle wearing a white lace dress and my diamond on her finger was the day she'd made my whole life.

"You're going to be the best mom."

"Stop." She pinched my ribs. "You're going to make me cry."

I leaned away, framing her face in my hands. Then I kissed her like we were home in our bedroom, not surrounded by family and friends. When I broke away, she had a pretty flush to her cheeks. "This is why you didn't want champagne."

"Yeah."

"Hey, Heath. Hi, Stella." Gretchen danced over with her husband. "How are you guys tonight?"

"Good." I clutched Stella's hand. "Having fun?"

"It's always a fun night."

"We're going to grab some dessert," I lied, taking Stella's hand in mine and leading her off the floor.

There'd be time to tell friends later. There'd be lots of celebrating. But what I really wanted was a minute alone with my woman. We weaved through the crush, nodding and smiling as people said hello. Then we escaped the ballroom and I pulled her to the same place where we'd started a year ago.

The sitting room was empty. It looked the same as it had last year. The second the door swung closed, I had Stella in my arms again, my mouth sealed over hers.

She gave a little laugh, a breath hitch, then kissed me back. When she wrapped one leg around my hip, I pressed my arousal into her center. My hand cupped her breast and my fingers were tugging at the fabric of her dress when the door flew open.

"Oh, hell," Guy muttered. "Get a room."

Stella and I broke apart to see him and Wendy both averting their eyes.

"We did." I dried my lips and made sure Stella's dress was covering her nipple.

"Get a room with a locking door," he said, dragging Wendy out and leaving us alone.

Stella giggled. "We should probably go back."

"Yeah. But we're leaving early."

"We can't. Remember we promised your mom we'd help clean up."

I frowned. "I'll get us out of it."

"No, don't. We'll help. It might even be fun."

I raised an eyebrow. "It will not be fun."

"Cleaning can be fun."

"Baby, I love you, but no. We're not staying."

She smiled. "Disagree to agree."

A PARTRIDGE AND A PREGNANCY

CHAPTER 1
EVA

'm pregnant.

"Nope," I muttered. There was no way I'd be able to say those two words out loud. Not yet.

Maybe tomorrow, but definitely not today.

My insides churned as I stared at the house in front of me. This was not where I wanted to be standing.

The cold was becoming unbearable. My nose was probably as red as Rudolph's by now. There was a very real chance I'd lose my pinky toe to frostbite if I stayed out here much longer. I should go. Back to the car. Up to the door.

Yet here I stood.

Stuck.

I'd planned to spend my Christmas Eve at home, lounging in my flannel pajamas in front of my gas fireplace with a cup of cocoa in one hand and a book in the other. Instead, I was frozen to the sidewalk in front of my one-night stand's house, working up the courage to ring the doorbell and announce I was pregnant.

I'm pregnant. Oh, how I wished those two words would stop bouncing around my head, and instead, bounce out of my mouth.

But first, I had to get unstuck.

My car was parked in the driveway at my back. Driving across town hadn't been an issue. Neither had putting the sedan in park and stepping out from behind the wheel. I'd even managed to walk to the sidewalk. Twenty feet separated me from my destination. But my shoes might as well have been ice blocks in the concrete.

How had it come to this? How was I even here? I'd asked myself the same questions hours ago when I'd been sitting on the bathroom floor with a positive pregnancy test in hand.

One night. One night with Tobias. A farewell.

And now I was pregnant.

Stupid freaking farewells. Though technically, it had been *another* farewell.

Tobias and I had met for a drink to catch up. There'd been a little flirting. A lot of cabernet. When he'd asked me to come home with him, I'd decided it was fate giving me a second chance to say goodbye.

Our first goodbye hadn't gone so well. There'd been crying —me. There'd been angry silence—him. There'd been heartache—us.

Over the years, I'd thought a lot about the night Tobias and I had ended our relationship. I'd replayed it countless times, wondering what I should have done and what I should have said.

Regrets had their way of ambushing you during the quiet moments.

So six weeks ago, I'd seen an evening together as my do-over. We'd spent the night laughing and talking, reminiscing about times past. And in true Tobias style, he hadn't disappointed in the bedroom. It had been a one-night stand to set things right.

Why did one-night stand sound so cheap and sleezy? Tobias was neither. He was handsome and caring. Witty and charismatic. Loyal and steadfast.

Our night had reminded me just how wonderful he was. And maybe he'd remembered too, that once I hadn't been the villain. Once, I'd been the woman he'd loved, not the woman who'd broken his heart.

We'd had our second goodbye. The perfect goodbye. Yet here I was, knocked up and about to say hello.

"Oh, God." My stomach roiled. Was it too soon for morning sickness?

I didn't know shit about pregnancy. I didn't know shit about babies. I didn't know shit about being a mother. How was I supposed to raise a child when I couldn't even traverse a side-walk, ring a doorbell and spit out two words?

This was Tobias. It wasn't like I was telling a stranger. He knew me, possibly too well, which made this terrifying.

There'd be no hiding my fears. No stalling the uncomfort-able conversations. There'd be no raising my chin and pretending this was no sweat.

One step. Just take one little step.

I lifted a foot. And put it right back down in the snow print where it had been.

Maybe I could write him a note? My hands were shaking so badly I doubted I'd be able to hold a pen.

The pregnancy test was in the pocket of my red parka. Maybe I could just drop the pee stick by the door and make a break for it, like that teenage prank where kids put dog poo in a paper bag, lit it on fire, rang the doorbell and ran like their lives depended on it.

Not that I'd ever done that prank.

311

Being the getaway driver and waiting around the block for my friends didn't count.

My chin began to quiver.

Why was this so hard? Why couldn't I move?

Thank God, Tobias didn't have neighbors. They probably would have called the cops on me by now.

Come to think of it . . . it was too bad he didn't have neighbors. Because if the police showed up, I could just give them the pregnancy test and ask them to deliver the news.

Damn Tobias and his country house.

I'm pregnant.

Just two little words. One sentence. *Say it, Eva. Just say it.*

I opened my mouth.

Nothing. Just a puff of white air.

This trip was pointless. I should have stayed home and paced. After I'd missed my period, I'd started to worry, but as a self-proclaimed master-of-avoidance when it came to my personal problems, I'd dismissed it as stress.

Moving was always stressful, no matter how often I'd relocated, and I'd been busy gearing up for London. But avoidance could only last so long, and this week, when another day had passed without my cycle and my boobs felt as tender as my favorite medium-rare filet mignon, it had been time to face reality.

I'd gone to the nearest grocery store, picked up a pregnancy test, rushed through self-checkout and scurried home to pee.

The world had stopped spinning when the word pregnant had appeared in pink letters on that white stick. I'd clutched it to my chest while I'd sat on the bathroom floor for an hour. Then I'd paced.

An apartment void of all furniture gave a girl a lot of room for walking. So much so, that I'd paced for two hours. Then my feet had carried me to my car, which had led me here.

Whatever courage I'd had on the drive over had evaporated. And now I was stuck. I hadn't been this stuck in years.

My hands wouldn't stop shaking. Tears welled in my eyes. How was I supposed to do this? Not just tell Tobias, but what happened next? How was I going to be a mother?

I was seconds away from collapsing in the snow and giving in to a good cry when the door to his house whipped open. And there he was, standing tall and broad, filling the threshold.

"Eva, what are you doing?"

I glanced at my feet.

"You're standing there," he answered for me.

I nodded.

"It's been thirty minutes."

That long, huh? Now it made sense why I was so cold.

"Are you going to knock?" he asked.

"I'm not sure yet." I gave myself a little fist pump for actually verbalizing a thought. Progress. This was good. Words were good.

"It's cold."

"Yeah. You should go inside. I'm good here."

"Eva."

See? This was the problem with Tobias. He could look at me and know I was very, very not good.

"Come inside," he ordered.

"I can't."

"Why not?" He stepped off his stoop and onto the sidewalk. His long strides ate up the distance between us, and when he stopped, he towered over me. "What's going on? Is everything okay?"

I shook my head. "I'm stuck."

He blew out a long breath, then he fished my right hand from my coat pocket, cupping his fingers to mine so our thumbs were opposite. "One. Two. Three. Four. I declare a thumb war."

I closed my eyes so I wouldn't cry, then said the next words. "Five. Six. Seven. Eight. Try to keep your thumb straight."

"I win, you come inside."

"Okay," I whispered.

"Shake." He touched his thumb to mine, wiggling it up and down. Then he pinned my thumb beneath his because I didn't put up a fight.

We both knew I needed him to be victorious.

This was how our thumb wars had usually gone. He'd instigate. I'd surrender.

And as he clasped my hand tighter, giving me one gentle tug, he unstuck my feet.

The warmth in the entryway was like stepping into a sauna after being outside for so long.

Tobias closed the door behind us. "Want me to take your coat?"

"No, thanks." I stuffed my hand into the pocket again and wrapped a fist around the pregnancy test. Later, after I'd dropped the bomb, I'd tell him he'd better wash his hands.

"Would you like to sit?" he asked.

I lifted a shoulder in a noncommittal shrug.

Would he hate me for this? Maybe in the past six weeks, he'd found someone else. A woman he *chose* to have a baby with. That thought made my pulse pound behind my temples so I shoved it away.

"Eva."

My throat had closed again.

He sighed and took my elbow, steering me toward the kitchen where he pulled out a stool for me to sit at the black quartz island. Then he rounded its corner and leaned against the far counter to wait.

He waited.

It was one thing I'd always loved about him. Tobias never rushed me. My sister would have gotten so annoyed by the silence that she would have given up outside in the snow. My father would have asked question after question, badgering me until I talked.

In my youth, I'd needed Dad to push me until I'd confessed how I was feeling. About school. About friends. About Mom. But I wasn't a teenager anymore dealing with an absent parent and adolescent drama.

Tobias knew if he pushed, I'd crumble.

Why was I like this? At the moment, it wasn't the most important question but it seemed to scream the loudest. At work, I never got stuck. Never. I always knew what to say. What to do. Which was possibly the reason I loved to work and dodge anything resembling a personal conversation.

Would our kid be patient like Tobias? That question sent my stomach into a tailspin. We were going to have a baby. Would he be mad if I puked on his fancy wood floors?

I squeezed my eyes shut, willing the nausea to pass. It did after a few deep breaths, and when I cracked my eyelids open, Tobias hadn't moved. He stood stoically beside that farmhouse sink.

The light from the window at his back limned his broad frame. His hair was longer than it had been our night together. The dark strands were slightly damp and finger-combed, like he'd come from the shower not long ago. Tobias's sculpted jaw was covered in a beard that went perfectly with the soft, buffalo-plaid flannel shirt molded to his muscled frame.

He looked like a sexy lumberjack.

"I like your beard."

He nodded. "So you've said."

Right. I'd told him that a few times six weeks ago, specifically when those bearded cheeks had been between my thighs.

That must have been before the condom broke and his sperm had freestyled through my vagina and into my fallopian tubes where one of them had dominated an egg.

Fucking sperm.

But hey, this could be worse. Tobias Holiday was a catch. He laughed often. His smile was as dazzling as the stars on a clear Montana night. Those blue eyes were like jewels, and they always shined especially bright when he was looking at me.

Or . . . they had once.

Now he was looking at me like I'd lost my mind.

Nope, just my menstrual cycle.

Speak, Eva. Say something. Anything. "Merry Christmas Eve."

"Merry Christmas Eve."

"Are you, um . . . doing anything?"

He nodded. "My parents' annual holiday party is tonight."

"On Christmas Eve?" I'd gone to that party many times but it had always been the week before Christmas.

"There was a scheduling conflict for last weekend."

"Ah. Well, that's always fun."

"Should be a good time."

I forced a shaky smile, then looked around the space, twisting to give him my back and hide the terror on my face.

Tobias's home was no doubt something he designed himself. It reminded me of one of the drawings he'd done in college. We'd gone on dates and he'd sketch houses on napkins while we'd waited for our food.

He'd always wanted a place in the country where he didn't have to worry about neighbors peering through his windows or the noise from constant traffic.

After years of bouncing from city to city, I'd probably go crazy out here alone.

"Eva." Tobias's deep voice had a slight rasp that always made my heart flip.

"Yes?" I stiffened.

"Will you turn around and look at me?"

I cringed but obeyed, turning just in time to see him push off the counter and come to the island, bracing his hands on the edge.

"What's wrong?"

"H-how do you know something is wrong?"

He shot me a flat look. "Eva."

It was unfair how well he knew me, even after all these years.

"I—" The sentence lodged in my throat.

"You're scaring me." The concern in his face broke my heart. "Is it your dad?"

I shook my head.

"Your sister?"

"No," I whispered. "It's . . ."

My hand tightened around the pregnancy stick so tightly, I worried it would crack. I closed my eyes again, squared my shoulders and did the first thing that came to mind.

I sang.

"On the third day of Christmas, my true love sent to me."

Tobias had always loved it in college when I'd make up stupid songs in the shower. He'd sneak into the bathroom and sit on the toilet to listen. He'd often scared the hell out of me when I'd pulled back the curtain and there he'd been, those blue eyes dancing at my ridiculous lyrics.

"Eva, what the hell is—"

I held up a finger. "Three French hens. Two turtle doves."

I opened my eyes, slid my hand out of my pocket and threw the stick at him.

Tobias snagged it from the air.

"And a partridge and a pregnancy."

CHAPTER 2

TOBIAS

Think about it.

That's what Eva had told me two days ago after she'd thrown me that positive pregnancy test.

Think about it.

I'd done little else but think about it.

Eva was pregnant. We were having a baby. Holy fucking shit. Maybe we were having a baby. I'd been so stunned that I hadn't asked what she was planning. When we'd hooked up weeks ago, she'd told me her next move was to London. Was she still going?

The questions came like rapid fire. Did she want the baby? Did I?

Yes.

As I stared across the empty lobby at Holiday Homes, looking around the building I'd designed, *yes* might as well have been painted on the wall.

Yes, I wanted this baby. I wasn't prepared for it. I doubted Eva was either. But in my heart, the answer was yes. That was about the only conclusion I'd landed on in the past two days.

That, and I needed to talk to Eva.

I pulled my phone from my pocket, my heart beating like a bass drum in my chest as I found her number. It had been saved in my phone for years, but since our breakup in college, I'd called it only once.

After her father's stroke.

When my finger hit call, I leaned against the lobby's counter, afraid I might fall over if I wasn't propped up against something.

She answered on the third ring. "Hi."

"Hey."

Awkward silence dragged and dragged, but my heart just kept on thumping.

"How was your Christmas?" she asked.

"Fine. Yours?"

"It was nice. Just Dad and me hanging out. My sister and her husband and kids went to her in-laws."

"How is your dad?"

"He's good. The assisted living place he's in is really nice. He's got his own apartment and a bunch of friends."

"That's good."

"I never thanked you for the flowers you sent after his stroke. They were beautiful. Thank you."

"You're welcome." This small talk was as excruciating as the nail I'd once accidentally driven into my hand with a nail gun. "We need to talk."

"Yeah." She sighed. "We do."

Even with the distraction of Christmas yesterday, the unanswered questions were beginning to fester. "Can you come over later?"

"Sure. What time?"

"I've got a meeting now for about an hour or two. Then I'll

be heading home." The office was closed all week until after New Year's Day.

"I'll come over around two."

"See you then." I ended the call, tucked my phone away and some of the tightness in my chest loosened. Two o'clock. I only had to make it until two.

The front door opened and my brother Maddox strode into the building, drawing in a long breath. "Hey. Smells like Dad's old office in here."

"Brand-new building and it smells like the old one. But I like that." Like strong coffee and sawdust. That scent was the reason I'd spent my fair share of time in the office in the past two days. It grounded me. It was a constant when the world felt like it was spinning too fast in the wrong direction.

"Me too." Maddox walked over and shook my hand. "Thanks for meeting today."

It was me who was grateful. It would do me well to work. To pinch my fingers around a pencil and simply draw.

Maddox had decided to move home to Bozeman with his seven-year-old daughter, Violet. He'd been in California for years building his billion-dollar streaming company, Madcast. But his ex was a piece of work and escaping her by coming home held a lot of appeal.

Except he needed a home. Literally. And that's where I came in.

I was the chief architect at Holiday Homes and custom builds were our specialty. Our father had started this company out of the garage of my childhood home. He'd forsaken a parking place so he could store his tools inside. After decades of building quality houses around the Gallatin Valley, his reputation was unmatched.

Maddox had never taken an interest in construction or our mother's real estate company. He'd blazed his own trail. I'd always admired that about him. Maddox took risks. And damn, but they'd paid off.

Meanwhile my twin brother, Heath, and I had both landed here. We'd always loved tagging along with Dad to builds, and helping him organize tools in the garage or construct our own playhouses. Being at Holiday Homes fit, for us both.

Heath preferred management while I simply wanted to design beautiful buildings.

Maddox's house would definitely be in that category. He had the money for something magnificent, and I wouldn't let him down. Dad wasn't the only Holiday with a reputation to uphold. I was making a name for myself too.

"Want some coffee?" I asked, leading him toward the break room.

"Sure." He followed, taking in the office as we walked.

It was only three years old and ranked as one of my favorite projects. The beams I'd found for the vaulted ceilings had come from an old barn on a local ranch. I'd loved the hickory flooring so much I'd picked the same for my home. From the enormous gleaming windows to the wood-sided exterior, there wasn't a thing I'd change about this building.

"This is nice," Maddox said.

"You know Mom and Dad." They knew the value of beautiful buildings and didn't mind spending some money.

They'd worked hard their entire lives to build a legacy for their sons. They'd far exceeded their own expectations and had declared a few years ago that they were going to reap the rewards. They'd earned it.

Mom and Dad's massive home in the mountain foothills was another favorite of my designs. They'd given me free rein to be creative so I'd designed a home that blended and complemented the landscape.

Mom's only request had been bedrooms. Lots and lots of

bedrooms. One was for Violet. And the others for her future grandbabies.

I guess she could earmark another room soon.

For my baby.

The sweater I'd pulled on this morning squeezed around my ribs like a ratchet strap, making it hard to breathe as we each carried steaming coffee mugs to my office.

"You okay?" Maddox asked as I took a seat behind the desk.

"Yeah," I lied, rubbing my beard. "Great."

Maddox didn't buy it. He studied my face, much like he had yesterday during the Christmas festivities at our parents' place. Violet had been the center of attention, entertaining us all as she'd opened her gifts. I'd hoped with her as the focal point, no one would notice that I'd been busy *thinking about it*.

Guess not.

"Missed you at the party at The Baxter," he said.

"Yeah. Had something come up." Impending fatherhood had killed my desire for dancing and drinking.

"Tobias."

I swallowed the lump in my throat.

"What happened?" he asked.

"Nothing."

"Talk to me. I've been a shit older brother as of late. Give me the chance to make up for it."

Maddox and I hadn't talked much lately. He'd been busy in California. I'd been busy here. I was looking forward to connecting with him again. To skiing on the weekends or grabbing a beer downtown.

Maybe he could teach me how to change a diaper.

"Do you remember Eva?" I asked, staring blankly at the wall.

"I never met her, but yeah." He leaned forward in his chair, giving me his undivided attention.

"She came over the other morning. Christmas Eve."

"Okay. Are you getting back together or something?"

"No." I rubbed my hands over my face, then spoke the words I still couldn't believe. "She's pregnant."

"Oh." The absent *shit* in that sentence hung in the air.

"We hooked up a while back. The condom broke. She's pregnant. And she's moving to London." There. The truth was out. Now I wanted to get to work. So I picked up a pencil from the desk. "Let's go through what you want for your house."

"We can do this another day."

I slid a notebook under the graphite tip and waited. "No, today's good."

"Tob—"

"Five bedrooms? Or would you like six?"

Maddox sighed but didn't push. "Six. And one in the guesthouse."

"Bathrooms?"

After an hour discussing his home, me asking questions, Maddox answering, I had what I needed and was ready to get home in case Eva showed up early. "I'll get a preliminary draft sketched and bring it over within the week."

"Thank you." He nodded, and after I showed him to the door, I put on my coat and locked the office behind me.

I drove the familiar streets through town until I reached the country road that wound toward the mountains. My home was in the center of a six-acre plot I'd bought before land prices in the valley had boomed. Mom had seen the listing come through and she'd known how much I wanted to live out of town.

I'd owned the land for two years before I'd broken ground on my own home. Now that it was complete, I couldn't imagine living anywhere else. Not only because this was another favorite build, but because Montana was home.

At least Eva was from here. That gave us one less hurdle to

clear. Her family was here and it was the obvious place for us to raise this kid.

I pulled into the garage, heading inside, where I hovered in the living room, my gaze alternating between the floor and the windows that overlooked the driveway. The clock on the wall ticked too slowly, and every time I glanced up, expecting it to be nearly two, the hands had barely moved.

Its ticking grew louder and louder until I let out a frustrated groan and forced myself away from the living room. I stalked to my room, not for any particular reason just that its windows didn't face the front of the house. My feet stuttered to a stop when my gaze landed on the bed.

For weeks I'd pictured Eva there. Her dark hair spread out on my pillow. Her hazel eyes locked with mine as I'd moved inside her.

I hadn't noticed the condom had broken. Granted, we'd had a bottle of wine downtown and another when we'd come here. By the time I'd given her three orgasms, I'd been spent and hadn't paid much attention.

Or maybe she'd scrambled my brain. Because that night with Eva, well . . . it had been like traveling back in time.

I walked to the dresser against the wall, easing open the top drawer. Buried beneath rows of folded socks, stuffed in the far corner next to my boxer briefs, was a square velvet box. The last time I'd held it in my hand was the day I'd moved in.

The hinges gave a small pop as I pushed open the top. A golden band sat firmly in the white satin enclosure. The marquise-cut solitaire diamond glinted under the bedroom light, like a star caught in this tiny box.

There was no logical reason for me to keep this ring. I'd bought it for Eva, and it wasn't like I was saving it for another woman.

Yet the day I'd taken it to the pawnshop, a brokenhearted

twenty-two-year-old man, I hadn't been able to let it go. I'd walked to the counter, showed the shop's clerk the ring, and before he'd even muttered a price, I'd told him it was a mistake and walked out the door.

No one knew I'd proposed. Not my parents. Not my brothers.

I doubted Eva had told many people either. Maybe her father. Maybe not. I suspected she'd done much like I'd done and had tried to forget that night.

We'd dated through college. Eva and I had met in the dorm's cafeteria our freshman year, and after our first date—dinner at a pizza place and a movie—we'd been inseparable.

She'd mentioned wanting to move to a city and explore the world after graduation, but they'd always been offhand comments. Like dreams you threw into the air like a balloon, knowing it would catch the wind and vanish.

During our last semester, she'd applied at a few places in Bozeman. I hadn't realized those had been her backups, not her first choice.

She'd hidden a lot from me our senior year.

Like her plans to leave Montana. Like her plans to leave me. Like the interviews she'd had with a global construction company that specialized in managing large-scale projects. They helped build enormous, boxy, boring buildings around the world.

She'd kept it all quiet until I'd proposed.

After graduation, I'd taken her to a fancy dinner before bringing her to my apartment where I'd dropped down on one knee and asked her to be my wife. She'd taken one look at that ring and the truth had spilled out.

A life in Bozeman hadn't been her dream.

She'd left my apartment with tears streaming down her face, and seven days later, moved to New York.

We'd gone years without speaking. Mutual friends would give me random updates on her whereabouts. New York. San Francisco. Tokyo. Melbourne. Boston. Eva always seemed to be somewhere new.

Meanwhile, I'd been in Montana, wondering how many years it would take for me to let her go.

I hadn't realized until our night together six weeks ago that the resentment had faded. That instead of feeling angry toward her, I'd just . . . missed her.

Her laugh. Her snark. Her intelligence.

Her quirks. Her smile.

Our hookup had been for closure. Our second chance at a decent goodbye.

Now we were having a baby. Maybe. God, this was messed up.

I stuffed the ring into the drawer, shoving it closed, then crossed the bedroom as the sound of a car door slammed. I quickened my steps through the living room.

Would I find her on the sidewalk again? Or would she actually make it to the door? I'd learned a long time ago that rushing Eva usually meant she'd shut down. She needed a distraction whenever she was stuck, which was why I'd invented our thumb wars.

One of us always let the other win.

Today, I wouldn't give her thirty minutes in the cold. Freakout or no. There'd be no thumb war. If I had to drag her inside, so be it. But when I opened the door, she was making her way up the sidewalk.

My sweater was too tight again, forcing my ribs together so I couldn't fill my lungs.

Eva's rich, chocolate hair was tied in a ponytail with a few tendrils framing her face. Her eyes were hidden behind a pair of mirrored sunglasses that reflected the bright white of the snow on my lawn. Her red parka was the same one she'd worn on Christmas Eve, but her hands weren't stuffed in her pockets this time.

She was beautiful. Always beautiful.

"Hi." I stepped aside, holding the door.

"Hi." She shoved the sunglasses into her hair as she stepped inside. Then she planted a hand against the wall to toe off her snowy boots. "How was work?"

"Fine. I was meeting with Maddox. He's moving home."

"Really? That's good. I'm sure your mom will love having all three of you in town."

"She will." The only thing Mom would have loved more would be for all of us to have wives so she could spoil her daughters-in-law. Especially had one of those been Eva.

I helped Eva from her coat, hanging it on a hook in the entryway, then waved her to the living room instead of the kitchen. Sitting on the couches seemed safer than the island. And considering her long-sleeved tee fit snugly to her body and her leggings left little to the imagination, I doubted she'd throw a stick coated in urine my way today.

"Your house is lovely." She ran her hand over the leather arm of a chair. "The windows. The wood. The vaulted ceilings. The mountains outside to greet you good morning. The trees as neighbors to say good night. It's exactly what I would have expected you to build."

"Thanks."

That compliment seemed to diffuse a fraction of the tension in my spine. Like she knew I needed a millisecond of normal conversation. We might not have spoken in recent years, but she knew me. And if there was a woman to go through this with, I wouldn't want it to be anyone else.

"So . . ." She plopped in the chair.

"You're pregnant."

"I'm pregnant." The words were hoarse and rough, like this was the first time she'd said them. Maybe it was. Eva met my gaze and there was an apology there. "About the other day. I didn't handle it very well."

"It's okay." No one but Eva would have made up fake lyrics to a Christmas carol to announce a pregnancy. Someday in the future, maybe that little jingle would make me laugh. Depending on what she did. "Have you decided what you're going to do?"

"It's not just my decision. We're sort of in this together."

"I appreciate that. But if it were just your decision, what would you want?"

She dropped her gaze to her lap. "I don't know if I'll be a good mother."

She would. Maybe she didn't have confidence in herself, especially given her own mother. But Eva would be a great mom.

Her heart was too full of love.

"You will be," I said.

She looked up to me with tears in her eyes. "I'd like the chance to try."

The air rushed from my lungs. "So would I."

I hadn't let myself hope for this answer but damn, it was good to hear. It didn't really lessen the panic or fear. But it gave us a direction.

A baby. We were having a baby.

"I didn't plan this, Tobias," she whispered. "To trick or trap you."

"The thought never crossed my mind." Maybe it would have if this were another woman, but not Eva.

"There's a lot to figure out. And not much time."

Wait. What? "What do you mean there's not much time? Don't we have eight or nine months?"

"Um . . . no."

It clicked, the conversation from weeks ago. Part of the reason we'd met was that she'd wanted to see me before she left Bozeman again. "Wait. You're still moving to London?"

"Yeah." She nodded. "My next job starts in a week."

A job in London.

Well . . . fuck.

CHAPTER 3
EVA

Tobias. Was. Pissed.

On the outside, he looked exactly the same as he had seconds ago. Crystal-blue eyes. Attractive beard. A charcoal sweater that shouldn't have been sexy but was because it showcased his strong arms and broad shoulders.

It was his hands that gave him away. His hands always matched his mood.

His fingers dug into his thighs and the veins that traced up from his knuckles to his sinewed forearms were pulsing.

"It's only for six to eight months." *Or a year if we hit any delays, but I'd work extra hard to make sure it was done on time.*

"Six. To. Eight. Months?"

Oops. One-word enunciation wasn't a good sign. Clearly explaining my job was not the right thing to say. "It, er . . . goes by fast."

Tobias blinked.

"London's not that far away." *Just a teeny, tiny ocean. And most of the contiguous United States.*

His nostrils flared. Those hands clamped tighter on his legs.

Shut up, Eva. I opened my mouth, but my brain engaged and clamped my lips together before more spewed out and I caused more damage.

"This changes everything." Tobias nodded to my belly. "Do I have a say in this?"

"In where I live? Well, no. I have a job. This is my career."

"How are we going to parent living on opposite sides of the globe?"

"Maybe we could rent Santa's sleigh?" I laughed.

Tobias did not. His hands balled into fists on the tops of his knees.

"I don't know, okay?" I tossed up my hands. "I don't know. I spent the past two days trying to wrap my head around the pregnancy. I haven't gotten to the actual child-rearing yet." I mean seriously, I was growing a human being. Wasn't I entitled to a week or so to process that one first?

"We need a plan," he declared.

Oh, how Tobias loved his plans. They were as dear to him as the first edition Millennium Falcon Lego set he'd had since middle school.

His talent for planning was what made him such a successful architect. His organizational skills and determination had made him a wealthy man, even at twenty-nine. But he clung to his plans like twinkle lights to a tree. Heaven forbid he give spontaneity a try.

Like move to New York with your girlfriend for one year. That was all I'd asked for. One year away from Montana, then we could assess. Make a new plan.

I'd loved him wholeheartedly, but I'd needed to spread my wings and see if they had the strength to fly.

Sure, Tobias had loved me too. Of that, I had no doubt. Maybe I hadn't loved him enough to give up my dreams. But he hadn't loved me enough to change his plans. He hadn't loved me enough to ask me to stay.

Why hadn't he asked me the night of the proposal to stay? I'd waited for it. I'd prepared a speech about the merits of living around other cultures and trying different experiences. Instead, he'd let me walk out the door.

And everything that I'd thought I'd known, everything I'd believed in—him, us—had been untethered. Shattered.

Turns out, I did know how to fly. I'd been flying on my own for years.

Our lives had split down different streams. Now we needed to find a way to merge them together again.

"We have time to figure this out. Months," I said. "Let's work together on a plan."

A statement I was sure would make him relax, but instead, he shot off the couch and began pacing in front of his live-edge coffee table. His hands flexed and unflexed, over and over until I found myself copying the gesture too.

Gah! I tucked both beneath my legs.

"I don't want to miss the pregnancy, Eva."

"You don't?"

He stopped pacing and sent me a glare.

"Okay," I drawled. "Maybe you could fly out for some of the doctor's appointments. And we can FaceTime."

"FaceTime. You want me to be a father through FaceTime."

"I'm just throwing out options."

Tobias started pacing again. Back and forth. Back and forth. That poor, beautiful rug might not survive this pregnancy. "My life is here."

I'd heard that one before. "My job is not."

"This is bigger than your job."

Now it was my turn to get mad. "Then give up yours."

"You know I can't do that."

I opened my mouth but once more my brain engaged and stopped the stream of expletives before they could escape. This would only lead to the same stalemate we'd landed in years ago on the night he'd proposed.

We hadn't solved that puzzle then. I doubted we would today.

"I don't want to fight," I said.

"No, you just want to run away."

Ouch. "That's not fair."

"It's—sorry." His feet stopped. His shoulders fell. His hands relaxed. "I don't want to fight either."

I believed him. But I also believed that if I stayed here for much longer, we'd end up going twelve rounds, and I hated fighting with Tobias. "I'm in town for the whole week. Now that we know we're having this baby, let's think on it. We're intelligent adults. We can figure this out."

There was a lot more confidence in my voice than I felt. *Fake it until you make it.*

"All right." He nodded.

I stood from the couch and skirted the end table, stopping in front of him. Then I took his hands in mine and squeezed the last shreds of tension from his fingers. "I'm scared."

Tobias laced his fingers with mine. "Same."

"But if there's anyone I'd do this with, it's you."

His eyes softened. "Again, same."

"Call me later?"

"I will." He let me go and escorted me to the door, helping me into my coat. Then he stood on the stoop, waiting until I pulled away from his house before going inside.

When his house had disappeared from my rearview, I let out the breath I'd been holding.

Not bad. Not great, but not bad.

He wanted the baby. That was a good thing. A *great* thing.

Kids needed dads, and I couldn't imagine life without my own. And Tobias would be a wonderful father.

We just had to figure out logistics, and luckily, he wasn't the only specialist in that area. Yes, this was a lot different than constructing a building, but we'd manage, especially if we didn't rush a decision.

There was time. I wasn't leaving until New Year's Day.

Traffic picked up as I reached the outskirts of town. Bozeman had grown considerably over the years since I'd been gone. As a kid, Dad would take my sister and me to Bozeman from our little town of Manhattan. The twenty-mile stretch between communities had been mostly prairie.

I'd driven out yesterday for nostalgia's sake, even though a new family lived in the home I'd once called mine. Where open fields of wheat and barley had bloomed a decade ago, housing developments had sprouted instead.

But despite the traffic and influx of residents, this valley was still home. A landing place for the holidays. For the past three months, I'd been fortunate to call it home.

My company had been contracted to oversee the development of a data center. Another project liaison had been tasked with the beginning of the project. I'd already been assigned to a job in Houston, otherwise, I would have vied for it. But the other woman had quit three months ago, and I'd managed to slide in and take her place.

Turnover was fairly constant. Though my job paid well, it was demanding. Sometimes I'd see a project from start to finish. Other times, I'd be pulled to smooth the feathers of a frazzled client.

London was one of those jobs. The client was temperamental and didn't like the current project manager. Enter Eva.

I'd be a fresh face for them to chastise. Or maybe I'd win them over.

Next week, I'd know which way this one was going to go.

But for now, I was savoring my last days in Montana.

Three months here had given me long-overdue time with my dad. I'd been able to spend evenings at Elena's home, getting to know her two daughters.

And Tobias.

During my first month here, I'd worried about seeing him. If I wasn't at the jobsite, Dad's home or Elena's place, I'd basically existed as a recluse. Mostly out of fear that he hated me. But partly at the idea of seeing him with another woman on his arm.

Then I'd bumped into his mom at the grocery store. Hannah had been so happy to see me that she'd pulled me into her arms with tears swimming in her eyes. I'd had them in mine too. Hannah Holiday was arguably the best woman I'd ever known. We'd stood in the frozen foods section for so long that the ice cream in my cart had melted.

She'd hinted that Tobias was single and had encouraged me to reach out. It had taken me days to work up the nerve. But one evening after a bottle of cabernet for bravery, I'd called the same number I'd memorized years ago and invited him to meet for a drink.

When I'd walked into the bar that night six weeks ago, he'd hugged me. And we'd just . . . clicked.

It was the reason I knew we could do this. He could still have his life here. I could have mine, and together, we'd have this baby.

"We can do this." My reassurance rushed over the steering wheel. We could do this.

The condo my company had found for me was next to a golf course, the greens and fairways hidden by a blanket of pristine snow. The bare aspen and cottonwood trees were covered in ice, their branches glittering with crystals that caught the sun in the cloudless blue sky.

Bozeman was sunny, even in winter. I'd miss the constant sunshine when in London. The few times I'd visited, it had rained and rained.

There was a U-Haul moving truck in the driveway to the condo beside mine. As I parked and made my way to the front door, a man came out carrying a box. He waved, pausing like he was going to introduce himself. I simply waved and disappeared inside.

There was no point in introducing myself. I'd be gone before he unpacked.

It was cold inside the condo, or maybe it just seemed cold because it was empty. I dropped my purse and keys on the floor in the living room, then kicked off my shoes before walking to the one piece of furniture that hadn't been shipped to England or sold online.

An air mattress.

It was pushed against the living room wall. The sleeping bag I'd bought was laid neatly on top. I'd decided to sleep here instead of in the bedroom because the gas fireplace kept this room cozy at night.

I plopped down on the mattress and grabbed my laptop from the floor, propping it on my lap as I leaned against the pillow. The data center was done, only waiting on the cleaning crew, and most people had taken this week off for the holidays. My inbox was mostly empty. With nothing to do at night but stare at the place where the TV had been, I'd resorted to working. Which wasn't all that different than when the TV had been here.

My job was my best friend. And I loved her. Most days.

Today, I was a little lonely. This feeling usually came when I was wrapping up one project and gearing up for the next.

The barren rooms didn't help. The movers had already come to clear out this condo. What I hadn't wanted to ship, I'd sold on Facebook and Craigslist. Sure, I could just buy new furniture or lease a furnished home, but I had this thing about my own stuff. Especially my own bed.

My boss indulged the added expense, mostly because I never balked when he asked me to move. So my bed went with me everywhere. At the moment, it was being set up in my London apartment, hence the air mattress.

My suitcase in the bathroom had enough clothes and toiletries to last me the week. I'd pack it up too and board a plane on Sunday. Six days.

Then I wouldn't have time to be lonely.

The London project was a fulfillment center for an online retailer. They were building a new warehouse outside the city, and given the most recent status update, it was proving to be a challenge.

Tobias would probably scoff if I told him that a square building made mostly of steel and concrete could be so complex. It was exactly the type of structure he'd loathe.

He'd already given me a ration of shit for helping on the data center *monstrosity* we'd built outside Bozeman. He wasn't entirely wrong. The blocked walls did contrast sharply with the beautiful mountain landscape.

But aside from its lack of character, the center was done and now it was time for me to move along. I'd harass foremen and argue with suppliers until another ugly building was marring a different landscape.

The nature of my job meant I didn't have a cushy office. I usually had a desk in a dirty construction trailer staged beside the portable toilets. Certainly no place for a baby.

I pressed my hand to my belly.

How was this going to work? My job was demanding.

Twelve hours was a short day. I was usually the first to arrive on site and the last to leave. My boss liked having us hover close to each build, but maybe he'd be okay with me working from home a few days a week.

I'd have to hire a nanny. There was no question. It wasn't like I'd have friends to babysit or pitch in. I never stayed long enough in one city to make reliable friends.

That hadn't bothered me until today.

Who would I call in an emergency? Could I find a nanny who'd be willing to work the nights when I'd have dinner with clients? How often would we be able to get away and visit Tobias?

I couldn't expect him to come to us every month. I took three, maybe four vacation days a year. The London project was behind schedule, and once I started, it would be a dead sprint to the finish line.

Unless . . . oh, God. What if he wanted full custody? What if I was the parent doing the visitation?

No. Tobias would never do that to me. He had to know that would break me apart.

He had to know I'd despise him for trying.

The questions and worries screamed at me in the empty space. The walls began closing in, so I climbed off the mattress and hurried toward the door. The car's seats were still warm as I drove away.

There were two places I went regularly, either my sister's or my dad's, and the sedan seemed to steer itself to my father's assisted living home. I parked in the same place I'd parked yesterday for Christmas, and walked inside the building, waving to the woman stationed at the reception desk. Dad called the receptionists his wardens because they kept track of when he left and when he came home.

Not that he left often. Most of his friends from my youth

still lived in Manhattan. And the friends he'd made since moving here all lived close so he'd simply visit them in their respective apartments.

The home provided grocery deliveries and had a dining room, serving three meals per day. On occasion, my sister would take Dad to her house so he could play with the girls. But mostly, she'd bring her daughters here because Dad preferred it that way.

He'd confessed to me yesterday that he often felt like a burden on Elena.

I'd confessed to him yesterday that I often felt like I'd abandoned them both.

But it was my job that paid for this home. Elena was a stay-at-home mom with two kids, living off her husband's single income. She couldn't afford this facility. Dad hadn't wanted an in-home nurse, and in another one of his confessions, he'd told me that the house reminded him too much of Mom.

He was happy in his apartment. Therefore, I'd happily pay so he had help close by if necessary.

Dad's door was open as I walked down the hallway. The television was blaring.

I smirked before knocking loudly so he'd hear me over the noise.

"It's loud enough, Nancy!" He shuffled out of the kitchen, his bad side leaning heavily into a cane. "Eva?"

"Hi, Daddy."

"What did you say?"

I rolled my eyes and pointed to the television.

"Oh." With his good hand, he reached into his jeans pocket and pulled out the remote, hitting the power button.

Blissful silence flooded the room.

"Eddy, I can't hear it!" Nancy shouted from across the hall.

I pulled in my lips to hide my smile as I closed the door. "I see that Nancy still hasn't gotten her television fixed."

"No." He grumbled something under his breath as he made his way to his recliner. "There's a chance I'll go deaf if she doesn't get it replaced soon."

Nancy had been Dad's neighbor since he'd moved in. She was twenty years his senior and he treated her like a beloved grandparent. Her television wasn't just old and outdated, the volume hadn't worked in weeks. Rather than cross the hallway to watch Dad's TV, Nancy preferred to watch from her own apartment so she could sit in her own chair. For the past month, she'd pick a channel and Dad would crank the volume on his so she could hear.

"What are you up to? Figured you'd be at work." He pulled the lever to raise the footrest on his chair.

"No, today's been quiet." I unzipped my coat and tugged it off before plopping onto his overstuffed loveseat. "How are you feeling?"

He gave me a crooked smile. "Right as rain."

Dad was the youngest resident at this home by decades. Three years ago, he'd suffered a massive, fluke stroke. He struggled with movement and function with the left side of his body. For a few terrifying days, we hadn't known if he'd survive it. But he'd come a long way, thanks to extensive speech, physical and occupational therapies.

His words were still slurred and there were movements that would always cause him trouble, but he was alive. That was all I cared about.

This assisted living facility had been my idea after he'd rejected the idea of an in-home nurse. It was more like apartments than a nursing home and Dad had trained caregivers on hand in case of an emergency.

I hoped every day there wasn't one. Because the guilt from

being halfway across the country when he'd had his stroke plagued me daily.

Guilt was about to become a constant companion again. It always hit hard after a visit home, and having been here for so long this time, I was sure the feeling would linger. Especially when I tossed Tobias and the baby into the mix.

"You okay?" Dad asked.

"Great." I forced a bright smile. "Just wanted to stop in and say hi. It's pretty quiet at my place."

"Want to watch something?" He waved the remote.

"Sure." I tucked my legs under me and relaxed into the couch, as Dad found us a sitcom rerun.

I stayed for two episodes, then kissed Dad's cheek goodbye because he'd fallen asleep.

It was getting dark as I drove home, the winter days short and cold. I shivered behind the wheel, wishing I had more work to do this week. Idle time was dangerous to my mental health. I didn't want to think about how my life mirrored my mother's more than my father's.

Traveling and bouncing from address to address hadn't been a problem a week ago. But then I'd taken that pregnancy test and now . . . everything was different.

My street was quiet. The moving truck was gone—maybe they'd finished unloading. The neighbors' homes were all aglow. Only my condo sat dark and empty.

Except it wasn't exactly empty. There was a truck in the driveway, parked beside my space.

My heart did a little flip.

It always flipped for Tobias.

I wasn't sure why he was here, waiting on my porch. But it was nice to come home and not be alone.

CHAPTER 4
TOBIAS

Eva led the way inside her condo. I'd expected furniture. Maybe a houseplant. Maybe boxes. Instead, the space was empty save for an air mattress in the living room next to the gas fireplace.

"Where's your stuff?" I asked as she flipped on the lights.

"Most of it's in London. The couch and a few other furniture items were sold because the flat I'm renting isn't all that big."

"How long has it all been gone?"

She shrugged and unzipped her coat. "Two weeks?"

I blinked. She'd been sleeping on an air mattress for two weeks with one more to go. "Why didn't your company put you up in a hotel?"

"I didn't ask. And I don't mind the air mattress."

That was a lie. Eva's voice was too bright. This woman loved a comfortable bed. In college, she'd insisted we stay at her place most nights because her pillow-top mattress had been softer than mine.

The idea of her sleeping on the floor, living like a transient, set my teeth on edge. She couldn't stay here. Not like this.

"You should stay in my guest bedroom this week." The offer flew out of my mouth, but I didn't hate it. In fact, it wasn't a horrible idea. "That will give us a chance to talk. And the mattress in my guest bedroom is a good one."

"No, that's okay. I don't want to put you out."

"It's a memory foam."

She glanced at the air mattress and grimaced. "I like memory foam."

"Go pack. I insist."

"I forgot how stubborn you are."

"No, you didn't." I chuckled. "You just forgot that you liked it."

She rolled her eyes. "You have me mistaken for one of your other ex-girlfriends."

Never. There was no mistaking Eva for any other woman. Not that there'd been many. The only woman I'd spent time with lately was Chelsea, and our casual hookups when she was passing through town were far from serious. And I hadn't seen her in months.

"What's it gonna be, Williams? Air mattress or memory foam?"

"Fine. You win. I'll take your guest bed," she said, nodding to her setup on the floor. "But only because that thing has a slow leak and my back is starting to hurt."

"Would you like me to roll that up while you get your stuff?"

"Tonight?"

I shrugged. "Might as well."

"Okay. I'll get its case."

She scurried away and I toed off my shoes so I wouldn't drag snow clumps over the hardwood floors. Then I started with the sleeping bag. The scent of Eva's favorite vanilla bean lotion caught my nose as I folded it into a tight roll.

After our breakup, I'd found a bottle of that lotion in my bathroom. It had taken me a year to toss it out. Then our night together six weeks ago, I'd caught that scent and the next words out of my mouth had been an invitation.

Come home with me.

I hadn't asked. Just another insistence.

And after we'd fucked the first time, against a wall because neither of us had been able to wait, I'd carried her to my bed where I'd let that scent soak into my sheets.

Christ, one whiff and I was hard. A cold shower would be in order when I got home. With a clenched jaw, I tied the straps on the bundled sleeping bag.

Eva came out and tossed me the case for the air mattress, and less than five minutes later, she rolled out a suitcase. "Want some help?"

"No, I've got this." The last of the air was rushing out of the mattress's vent as I folded it into sections. "Just grab the rest of your stuff."

"Oh, this is it."

A single suitcase and a backpack over her shoulder. That grated as hard as the empty apartment. The Eva I'd known hadn't gone anywhere without a bagful of books and a purse so large it could double as a pillowcase.

"Why are you looking at me like that?" she asked.

"Is this what your life has been like? Empty apartment to empty apartment?"

"It's only empty because I'm in transition."

"How often do you transition?"

"Depends." She lifted a shoulder. "Once or twice a year. Sometimes more. Sometimes less."

So she'd spend one or two months a year living with barren

345

walls and a handful of wardrobe pieces. Why did she even bother unpacking? Did this air mattress go with her? Or did she just buy a new one at every transition?

This lifestyle of hers sank into my skin like a rash. This wasn't what I wanted for her. But I guess that didn't matter. This was the life she'd wanted for herself. I'd learned years ago that I had no say.

But where this baby was concerned . . . something had to give.

"I don't mind, Tobias," she said as I began to shove the folded mattress into the case. "I'm not home much while I'm on a project."

"Home?" There was a snark to my voice.

Eva's eyes narrowed. "Home can have different meanings to different people. To me, it's not four walls. It's not a piece of land or a town or a state."

"Then where is home?"

"I guess . . . I've carried it with me." She pressed a hand to her heart. "That's enough for me."

"Except it isn't just you anymore."

Eva raised her chin. "You act like I'm homeless. I'm moving. People move for their jobs. My job means that I can pay for my dad's home. And I *like* my job. Why is that so wrong?"

"It's not. Let's . . . forget it." I sighed, then finished packing up the air mattress, carrying it, her sleeping bag and pillow to the door. "I'm just trying to wrap my head around this, Eva."

"So am I." She gave me a sad smile. "We can figure out the logistics. But maybe me coming to stay is a bad idea. I can get a hotel."

"No." I shook my head. If I actually thought she'd go to a hotel, I might let this go. But she was just as stubborn as I was, and after I left, she'd unroll this air mattress. "Stay with me. Please."

"Only because you have the memory foam."

"And more than one pillow." I laughed and picked up her suitcase. Pillows, she'd once told me, were as important as the mattress.

"Now you're just bragging," she teased.

"Lead the way." I managed to carry everything in one trip to my truck, then waited for her to lock up her condo before we headed across town and down the quiet roads to my house.

Home.

Wasn't a home a place where you could escape? Where you could find peace? Maybe she didn't need four walls to feel at home, but as I pulled into my garage, weight left my shoulders.

It was the reason I'd become an architect. Designing houses wasn't simply making them aesthetically pleasing. It was about creating a sanctuary. It was about giving others the foundation where they could grow roots that ran as deeply as my own.

I hit the button to the second stall and climbed out, waving Eva inside. When her car was parked, I retrieved her suitcase and hauled it inside. "Are you hungry?"

"Sure." She shrugged. "I'm an expert on takeout. Want me to order us something?"

"Or I can cook."

"You're letting me stay. I'll get dinner tonight."

"Okay." I nodded and watched as she scrolled through her phone, her fingers flying over the screen.

She didn't ask what I wanted to eat. She didn't have to.

Eva knew I hated chili. She knew I preferred cooked vegetables to raw. She knew that I drank water with every meal and that I kept homemade buttermilk ranch in the fridge because I always picked it over ketchup.

347

She knew me, better than anyone.

I'd missed the familiarity and how easy it was to be around her.

"Want something to drink?" I asked, opening the fridge.

"Water's fine."

I filled two glasses, mine with ice and hers without because it bothered her teeth. Then we settled in the living room on opposite ends of the couch. "It feels like days, not hours, since you came over."

She laughed, tucking her legs beneath her in the cushion. "I was just thinking that same thing."

Next to her on an end table was a digital frame. Eva picked it up, watching as the photos changed.

"Mom gave me that for Christmas yesterday." I watched past her shoulder, waiting until . . .

Eva gasped. "She put one of us in here?"

It was a photo Mom had taken years ago. One she'd had framed in her office for a few years. I suspected it was still in a drawer, tucked away for safekeeping. Mom had never given up hope that Eva would find her way home.

In the picture, Eva and I were lying on the couch in Mom and Dad's old house. I was asleep on my stomach, wearing only a pair of shorts. Eva was asleep on my naked back. My mouth was open. Her hair was spread over my shoulders and a strand had stuck to her lips.

It shouldn't have been comfortable, but I'd lost track of the times we'd slept like that. Totally content as long as we had each other.

"We look so . . . young." A smile lit up her face, but like the photo, it was gone too soon.

The next shot was of Heath and me on the ski hill a few winters ago. It was a selfie he'd insisted on taking on the chair lift. The next was a picture from last year's Christmas party. I stood beside Dad, each of us with a tumbler of whisky in our hands.

Eva and I watched the pictures rotate the full loop until the one of us returned. She ran her finger across the frame.

A flash of headlights forced us both from the couch. She set down the frame as I went to the door to meet the delivery driver.

"Burritos?" I asked, peeking inside the bag. "You don't like burritos."

"Actually, I do like them." She took a seat at the island, unwrapping the foil from her dinner while I sat beside her and did the same.

"Since when?"

"I lived in San Antonio for about five months. Around the corner from my rental was this burrito place. One night I got home late from work and there was nothing in the fridge. I didn't want to wait for pizza so I decided one burrito wouldn't kill me."

I laughed. "Obviously it didn't."

"I got it with queso. Now . . ." She lifted her burrito and took a huge bite, moaning as she chewed. "I love queso."

It was erotic, watching her eyes fall shut. There was a drop of melted cheese on the corner of her mouth. I lifted a hand, ready to wipe it away, then remembered that she was no longer mine. So I slid a napkin over and focused on my own meal.

When the wrappers were wadded up and tossed in the trash, Eva yawned. "I think I'm going to crash."

"I'll show you to your room." I collected her suitcase from the mudroom, then headed to the opposite end of the house, in the bedroom farthest from my own.

It seemed safer to put the bulk of my four-thousand square feet between us.

"Thanks for this," she said as I set the suitcase down inside the door.

"No problem. Can I get you anything?"

"This looks perfect." She glanced around the room, her eyes landing on the bed.

The comforter was a shade of deep green, much like the flecks in her hazel eyes. The sleigh-style frame was a rich brown close to the color of her hair. And if I stripped her out of those clothes, her skin would be the same alabaster as the walls.

We'd been together so many times it was like second nature to picture her on the bed. I could hear the hitch in her breath when I pushed inside her body. I could taste the sweetness of her tongue. I could feel her orgasm pulsing around my flesh. One inhale of her vanilla scent and my cock twitched.

Shit. I had to get the fuck out of this room and far away from this, or any, bed. "I'll let you get some sleep."

But before I could head to my primary suite for that cold shower, Eva's hand shot out, her fingers wrapping around my elbow. "Tobias?"

"Yeah?" My gaze fixed on her mouth.

"Good night." She stepped closer, wrapping her arms around my waist.

My arms encircled her immediately, pulling her close and burying my nose in her hair. Holding her was another automatic instinct.

I'd missed the way she fit against my frame. I'd missed her long hair threaded through my fingers. I'd missed the softness of her breasts and the tickle of her breath against my neck.

She sighed, sinking into my embrace. Then she leaned away, her eyes traveling up my neck and landing on my lips. Her mouth parted.

And that was the moment my resolve shattered.

I swept in, framed her face with my hands and sealed my

mouth over hers. One sweep of my tongue across her bottom lip and she opened on a whimper.

Eva clung to me, her fingertips digging into my biceps as she rose up on her toes.

I slanted my mouth over hers, our tongues twisting in a kiss that should have been familiar. We'd kissed hundreds of times. Maybe thousands.

But there was desperation to this kiss. Even more desperation than had been there our night weeks ago. Every anxiety about what was to come, every worry and doubt, we poured into the moment.

I ached for her, and when my arousal dug into her hip, she pressed in deeper, the urgency growing. Until I reached between us, intending to flip the button on her jeans, but froze when my knuckles grazed her belly.

Eva tensed, her lips still pressed to mine.

This wasn't a reckless trip down memory lane. This wasn't two former lovers enjoying a night of passion. This wasn't a man and woman giving in to an urge.

This wasn't just about us anymore.

I tore my mouth away and took a step back, dragging a hand over my beard as I worked to regain my breath. "Sorry."

"Me too." She walked to the corner of the bed and put five feet between us.

"Night." I stalked out of the room, pulling the door closed behind me. Then I jogged down the hallway, heading straight for my own bedroom.

My blood was on fire. My heart raced. I closed myself in the bathroom and turned on the shower. "Fuck."

What were we doing? What was I doing?

Those questions ran over and over in my head as I stepped beneath the cold spray. Water streamed down my skin. A trickle ran down the bridge of my nose as my hand found my shaft and stroked. The release was quick and unsatisfying. My body craved hers, not my fist.

I wasn't sure how long I stayed in the shower. Long enough to cool down. Then I toweled off and stepped in front of the mirror.

What am I doing?

Eva wasn't going to give up her job. She'd made that perfectly clear. She'd also admitted today that she didn't have a home.

Kids needed homes. They needed a resting place. They needed roots and routine.

I had all of those in spades.

Which meant if she didn't change her mind, I wouldn't have a choice. Once this baby was born, he or she was coming home to Montana.

I stared at my reflection, hating myself so much that I couldn't hold my own gaze.

If Eva was going to fight for London and the next move and the next move, then I'd fight her for my child. And she'd hate me. She'd fucking hate me.

But my kid was worth the fight.

And I'd just drawn the battle lines with a kiss.

CHAPTER 5

EVA

The scent of sausage links and syrup greeted me when I emerged from the bedroom.

I tiptoed down the hallway, hovering at its mouth, and watched as Tobias moved around his kitchen.

The smell held a memory that transported me straight into the past.

I was eighteen again, walking in a cafeteria with a blue plastic tray in my hands. Surrounded by a mass of other freshmen at Montana State all craving breakfast on a Saturday to chase away their Friday-night hangovers, I met the boy who'd won my heart.

All because of pancake syrup.

Tobias was no longer that boy. I was no longer that girl. But it was still impossible to tear my eyes away.

He shut off the stove, taking his spatula and lifting out the sausage to his plate. His broad shoulders were covered in a long-sleeved thermal, the red color making his hair look darker. I'd always liked it when he wore red, though not as much as blue, which brought out his eyes.

I kept my breaths short and low, not wanting him to catch me spying. A yawn tugged at my mouth but I kept my teeth clamped. Sleep had been elusive last night. Even on one of the most comfortable beds I'd slept on in years, I hadn't been able to shut off my brain.

Instead, I'd replayed that kiss.

That desperate, reckless, incredible kiss.

Staying here under his roof was probably a huge mistake. Temptation was going to run rampant. But at least it was just for a week.

Tobias pulled out a bottle of Log Cabin, squeezing a puddle next to his links.

"Still forgetting your pancakes with that syrup," I said, pushing off the wall.

He chuckled, glancing over his shoulder. "I made scrambled eggs. There's a brand-new bottle of ketchup in the fridge so you can ruin them."

I smiled and strode into the kitchen, taking a seat at the island.

He came and sat down, not at the stool beside mine, but one apart. He kept that boundary, then cut a piece of sausage and swirled it in syrup.

"Whenever I smell syrup, I think of the day we met," I said.

"The day you called me a monster." There was a smirk on his mouth as he chewed.

"Hey, the truth hurts, baby."

I'd come into the cafeteria, still in the sweatpants I'd worn to bed the previous night. My hair had been a wreck. Not a smidge of makeup had been left on my face except for the mascara smudges under my eyes. It had been the second month of freshman year and the first time I'd ever dared leave my dorm room not looking perfect.

But my hangover had been punishing. I'd been desperate

for fluffy carbs to cure my headache. I'd heaped a pile of pancakes on my plate, but when I'd gone to smother them with syrup, Tobias had been at the dispenser, pumping the last few drops onto his sausage links.

"You made up a song," he said, forking another bite. "Remember it?"

I'd made up a bunch of stupid songs over the years, taking popular songs and replacing their lyrics with my own nonsense. Most of them I forgot the moment I was done with my rendition. But that one I remembered.

"Hello, can you hear me?" I sung, crooning Adele's song. "I'm in the cafeteria, dreaming about maple syrup and whipped cream."

Tobias shook his head, a smile on his perfect mouth. "Whenever the real song comes on the radio, I laugh."

"Me too," I lied.

The truth was, that song usually made me sad. Because that song was Tobias's song. There I'd been, hungover and smelly and distraught over my lack of syrup, and Tobias had righted my day. He'd stolen the tray from my hands, taken it to a nearby table and spooned syrup onto my pancakes.

When he'd returned me my tray, I'd let out a pitiful whimper, then told him I loved him.

He'd sat beside me during that breakfast, and after I'd inhaled my pancakes, he'd asked me on a date.

That same night, he'd picked me up from my dorm room. Dinner. Movie. A typical date for two college kids. Then he'd walked me to my door and kissed me good night.

But nothing about that kiss had been typical. Because after that date, we hadn't spent a day apart. Not until the breakup.

We'd been inseparable. Insatiable.

In love.

We'd tackled life together.

Until . . . we hadn't.

"Help yourself." Tobias nodded toward the stove. "Unless you're not feeling well."

"No, I'm okay. No morning sickness so far." I slid from my stool and picked up the empty plate he'd left for me. Then I scooped eggs and sausage onto my plate, stopping at the fridge for ketchup before resuming my seat.

We ate in silence.

We did not mention last night's kiss.

I could still feel his tongue against mine, insistent and firm. That man craved control in every way but especially in the bedroom. When the lights were off and our clothes on the floor, he'd always been the one in charge. He'd never disappointed.

Tobias was better than a vibrator with fresh batteries.

At eighteen, as an unsure girl with zero experience except for a few awkward make-out sessions my senior year in high school, Tobias had been a dream. He'd made me feel wanted. He'd taught me about my body and its desires. He'd given me the freedom to let my inhibitions go and simply feel.

We'd been together countless times, each better than the last. Tobias always seemed to learn new tricks.

Like last night's kiss. He'd fluttered his tongue against mine and I'd nearly come undone.

Maybe it was just the hormones. Maybe it was because it had been a while since I'd had an orgasm—the last courtesy of Tobias. He'd been my one and only.

I refused to think that another woman had taught him that tongue flutter.

Jealousy snaked up my spine as I squirted ketchup on my plate. Irrational, green jealousy.

It had been my choice to walk away. I couldn't exactly fault him for moving on. Still . . . it soured the food on my tongue.

"Is it okay?" he asked.

"Great." I took another bite.

Compartmentalization had become a welcome companion so I shoved away the idea of another woman in Tobias's bed.

This wasn't the time for jealousy. This was the time for eating.

I forked a bite of eggs and dunked it in ketchup. "This is delicious."

"Are you working today?" he asked, taking his plate to the sink while I devoured my meal.

"A little. I'll probably set up camp right here if you don't mind."

"Go for it."

"And you? Are you going into town?" *Say yes.*

"Yes."

I tried not to let my shoulders sag in relief.

If he stayed here, I wasn't sure what would happen. That stool between us would only stay empty for so long before one of us caved. He was just too . . . easy. Too mouthwatering.

"Our office is closed this week," he said. "But I've got more work than I can keep up with so I'll probably head in for a while. Give you some space."

Give *us* some space.

"Okay." I stood and took my empty plate to the kitchen, careful not to get too close as I rinsed it at the sink and put it in the dishwasher.

"Make yourself at home," he said, then plucked a small black remote from a drawer beside the fridge. "Here's a spare garage remote so you can come and go as you need."

"Thank you." I took it, then took one step away.

He did the same, rubbing a hand over his beard. "About last night. Sorry."

"It was just a kiss, Tobias. It's not like we haven't kissed before, right?"

"Yeah." His eyes locked with mine, his expression unreadable. Before I could make any sense of it, he strode from the room. Then the garage door opened and he was gone.

Why had he kissed me? Why did it look like he regretted it?

"Ugh." I wrapped my arms around my waist as my stomach twisted.

Maybe it was the hormones, maybe it was the stress of the unknown, maybe it was my ketchup, but I rushed to the bathroom as the wave of nausea crashed into me like a tsunami.

"So much for my eggs," I groaned as I emerged from a solid thirty minutes of hugging the toilet.

I swiped my phone from the nightstand and retreated to the living room couch, lying on my back as I scrolled through emails. I was typing out a reply to my boss when it rang. My mother's name flashed across the screen.

"Hi, Mom," I answered, forcing cheer into my voice.

"Hi, Eva." There was a bustle of noise behind her and a woman speaking over an intercom. It was the typical soundtrack to Mom's calls.

"Where are you?"

"Atlanta, for about an hour. Then PDX." *Portland.*

Before I was in third grade, I'd been able to name every major city and its three-letter airport abbreviation. We'd had a map at home, and after every one of Mom's calls, I'd run to pinpoint where she was and where she was going, drawing imaginary lines between imaginary places.

Many of those cities weren't so imaginary now.

Mom was living in Miami. At least, she had been the last time we'd spoken. That had been four months ago on my birthday. She'd missed her regular Christmas call this week.

"I'm coming to Bozeman tomorrow. I just talked to Elena and she said you were there until after New Year's."

Shit. Thanks, Elena. "Um . . . yeah."

"We're all having dinner tomorrow." Not a question or an invitation, just a declaration.

"Okay." I'd planned to see Dad but I guess I'd go to his apartment for lunch instead.

"See you then." She hung up before I could say goodbye.

My stomach roiled again and I studied the ceiling until the sickness passed. Leave it to Tobias to have a tongue-and-groove painted ceiling, a shade lighter than the walls. No simple white ceilings here.

My phone rang again and I pressed it to my ear, already knowing it was Elena. "Yes, she called me. Yes, I'll be over for dinner."

"Good." She sighed. "You have to be the buffer."

"'Kay." I'd been the buffer between Elena and Mom my entire life. "Want me to bring anything?"

"Wine."

Wine I wouldn't be drinking. "You got it. Anything else?"

"No. Can you believe she just calls and expects us to drop everything to accommodate her schedule?"

"That's Mom." It didn't annoy me like it annoyed Elena.

"I'm not telling Dad she's here."

"Fine by me." It would only upset him and Mom would be gone on the next flight out.

It was rare that she came to Montana. It was even rarer that she'd stay longer than twenty-four hours.

Mom was a pilot for a commercial airline. She'd earned her wings and nothing would keep her from the sky, not even a husband and two little girls. My entire life she'd traveled, leaving Dad to care for Elena and me.

The times when Mom took a vacation and would be home for an extended period were usually the nights when I'd wake to hear my parents fighting. It was her absence that had made their marriage last as long as it had.

If you could even call it a marriage. They'd made their divorce official after I'd graduated from high school, but they'd written off each other years before the papers had been signed.

Elena harbored a lot of bitterness toward Mom, mostly on Dad's behalf. He'd been a married, single parent. He'd shouldered all the laundry after a ten-hour workday. He'd cooked the meals and packed the lunches. He'd painted our nails and plaited braids into our hair.

Dad had been both father and mother.

Elena had wanted an actual mother, not because he'd failed in any way, but because girls needed moms.

Maybe the reason it hadn't bothered me the way it had her was because I'd known that Mom would have paled in comparison to Dad. He'd made up for her shortcomings ten times over.

And we'd been better, just the three of us.

My hand splayed across my flat belly. "We'll figure this out, won't we?"

There wasn't another choice. When I looked to my parents, the one I aspired to imitate was not my mother.

But her income had meant a mortgage-free home. It had meant college tuitions. On some of her longer stays, after the first day or two of awkwardness, we'd settle into a new routine. Mom would take us shopping and out to a girls' only lunch.

She hadn't been a bad parent. Just . . . absent.

Elena wanted her to change, something that would never happen. Part of the reason I suspected Elena didn't work was because she was so worried about showing any resemblance to Mom.

Elena's daughters would always have a parent at home. They'd have a mother dedicated to each and every aspect of their lives. Mom might be a pilot, but Elena would be the helicopter mother, hovering over the girls until they finally left home.

There had to be a middle ground. I could find a balance, right? Granted, I had no husband to help. That would make it more difficult. But in my heart of hearts, I knew I could find the middle ground. I could be successful like Mom in my career. I could be the mother this baby deserved.

The logistics of that eluded me at the moment, but there was time to plan this out. For now, I'd finish out my week.

I'd be the *buffer*, the peacekeeper, at dinner tomorrow, ensuring Mom and Elena didn't get into an argument. I'd fill the conversation with questions about Mom's recent trips and what her schedule looked like through winter.

Mom had failed at balancing a career and family. But both were attainable, weren't they? I could be a mother and have a career, succeeding at both, right?

Right. I closed my eyes, drawing in a few long, deep breaths.

A hand touched my shoulder and I jumped, nearly falling off the couch. I would have crashed into the floor if not for Tobias standing above me, catching me before I rolled.

"Oh my God. You scared me." I slapped a hand to my racing heart. "I thought you left."

"I did." He glanced at the wall clock. "Three hours ago."

"What?" I shoved up and looked around the room for a clock. Sure enough, the wall clock confirmed his story. Three hours had evaporated while I'd been sleeping on the couch. "Damn. I didn't even realize I'd fallen asleep. I guess I won't be working this morning."

Or this afternoon. My stomach twisted and I curled onto my side. There wasn't much to do, but I'd send my boss an email when I didn't feel like hurling.

"You okay?" Tobias asked.

"I think I jinxed myself saying I didn't get morning sickness."

A frown marred his handsome face as he stood and walked out of the living room, coming back moments later with a glass of water. He set it on the coffee table and moved to the end of the couch. "Lift up."

I raised my legs just enough for him to sit, then he positioned my calves on his lap and began massaging my foot. One touch and my eyes drifted closed, the nausea easing. Tobias's touch was magic.

"I forgot how good you are at that." I hummed.

His long fingers dug into my arch, pressing away the tension in my body. "Drink that water."

I stretched to lift it from the coaster, then sipped it slowly before setting it aside and closing my eyes again, relaxing into his touch. "How was work?"

"Fine. Quiet. I was the only one there."

"What are you working on?"

"I'm designing a house for a couple from St. Louis. They're moving to Bozeman in a year. Pretty standard floor plan except they want a bunker."

I cracked an eye. "A bunker? For what?"

"Doomsday preppers, I think. They didn't explain much, just asked for a twenty-by-twenty bunker."

"Ah." I snuggled deeper into the couch, letting his deep baritone wrap around me like a blanket. "What would you put in a twenty-by-twenty bunker?"

"Food. Water. My hunting rifle. Tools. Toilet paper."

"Tobias Practical Holiday."

He chuckled. "And what would you want in your twenty-by-twenty bunker?"

"Wine. Chocolate. Books." *You.*

If the world was ending, I'd want to be with Tobias. I'd want his arms around me through the scary nights. I'd want his strength to lean on when I felt like collapsing. I'd want his smile to brighten the dark days.

"My mom is coming to town," I said. "She called after you left."

"When?"

"Tomorrow. We're having dinner at Elena's. I get to be the buffer."

"Want me to tag along? Be your buffer?"

"No, that's okay." As tempting as it was, it would only lead to questions, mostly from Elena.

Mom had only met him once. While I'd been in college, her visits to Montana had been infrequent, at best. After the divorce, Mom and Dad hadn't needed to pretend anymore. And I think Mom knew we'd picked Dad's side so she'd stayed away, giving us all space.

But if I showed at dinner with Tobias, Elena would get her hopes up. She'd been on his wavelength, assuming we'd get married after college.

I hadn't told her that he'd proposed. I hadn't told anyone. Did he think about that night? Did he regret proposing? Did he feel like he'd dodged a bullet?

My stomach churned again. Thinking about the ring he'd bought me, the diamond on someone else's finger now, always made me queasy. "Tell me more about your projects. Keep my mind off my tummy."

"Today I was doing some drafting for Maddox's place. He's building a big place out of town. It'll be fun to spend his money."

I laughed. "What are you thinking?"

Tobias shifted, taking my other foot in his hand, and as his fingers moved over my skin, he told me about his ideas for his brother's house. From the layout to the design elements to the state-of-the-art features that would make the home a masterpiece. A theater. A pool. A guesthouse. Everything would be custom.

Excitement radiated off Tobias as he spoke. His energy was contagious, and I turned to see his face. Here was a man who genuinely loved his job. He loved his family.

"It all sounds amazing." Maybe I'd even get the chance to see it.

"I, um . . . when Maddox came into the office yesterday, I told him. About the baby."

"Oh." I wrapped my arms around my stomach. It was only a matter of time. People would need to know. I guess I hadn't planned on telling anyone until I had a better idea of what was happening.

"I can ask him to keep it quiet."

"It's okay." I lifted a shoulder. "It's not going to be a secret for long."

"Will you tell your parents or Elena?"

Dad would be thrilled. Elena would immediately start planning a baby shower. And they'd both expect me to stay.

"Probably not this trip. I'll call and tell them once I get settled in London."

Tobias's hands stopped moving. He stared at me with that same unreadable expression from this morning.

"What?" I whispered.

"Nothing." He slid out from beneath my legs and nodded to the water. "I'll be in the office down the hallway if you need anything."

I blinked and he was gone, leaving me alone. A chill settled in my bones, left by the man striding down the hallway. What was I supposed to say? I had to move. My job started next week. I had responsibilities and I'd made commitments.

He might have been comfortable sharing right away, but I

was still trying to wrap my head around impending motherhood.

I pushed up and stood, ready to retreat to my bedroom and crack open my laptop. But the moment I was on my feet, another wave of nausea hit, and instead of walking, I ran to my bathroom, making it just in time to puke up the remnants of my breakfast and water. I'd thought after round one there hadn't been anything left.

Was this morning sickness? Or anxiety? It wouldn't be the first time I'd worked myself into an emotional mess. My first weeks in New York had been spent in a constant state of ick.

Headaches. Insomnia. Dizziness. Every day had been a struggle. Every day I'd wanted to quit. It was sheer stubbornness I'd gutted it out. I'd missed Tobias and home so much it had been crippling, but I'd kept pushing. Kept going. One day at a time until the heartache had eased. Until the tears had stopped.

I'd survived New York. I'd get through this too.

"Hey." Tobias appeared in the doorway, my water glass in his hand.

"Hi," I muttered.

He set my glass aside, then pulled a washcloth from a drawer, soaking it in warm water in the sink.

"Thanks." I took it from him, expecting him to leave me to my misery. But he walked closer, taking up a seat behind me. Then those wondrous hands began rubbing circles along my spine.

Sooner than later, I'd have to learn to deal with this and all the other pregnancy woes alone. But I loved his touch too much to kick him out. So I hugged the toilet, dry-heaving twice while Tobias held my hair, until finally, my stomach was empty and stopped swirling.

"I'll give you a minute." Tobias stood, easing the door shut behind him.

I washed my face and brushed my teeth, and when I emerged into the kitchen, Tobias had pulled out a box of saltine crackers. "These are for me?"

"I'll run into town and get some ginger ale. Anything else sound good?"

"Apple sauce."

"'Kay. Be back."

"Tobias?" I called as he walked toward the hall.

He stopped and turned. "Yeah?"

"You're going to be a good dad."

He gave me a sad smile, then he disappeared into the garage. His silence rang in the house. I'd expected a *thank you*. Or an *I hope so*. Maybe what I'd really wanted was for him to tell me I'd be a good mom.

But I'd learned a long time ago, Tobias didn't always tell me what I'd wanted to hear.

I guess that hadn't changed.

CHAPTER 6
TOBIAS

Eva was naked in the shower. She'd come home from dinner at her sister's place minutes ago, complaining that the smell of bacon cheeseburgers was stuck in her hair. So she'd retreated to her bathroom for a shower while I sat rigid on the couch, staring unfocused at the TV, because my attention was rapt on the woman occupying the other end of my house.

I glanced at the clock. *Eight seventeen.* In the two days since she'd come to stay here, I'd been watching the minutes pass too quickly.

She was leaving in four days and we had yet to talk about the baby. Or the kiss. The topics might not have earned a voice but lingered in the air, weighing heavy on our shoulders.

I hadn't wanted to bring it up yesterday when she'd been hugging the toilet and retching her damn guts out. Eva hadn't gotten sick today, but before I could broach the baby topic, she'd left for work and to visit her dad over lunch.

We needed to talk. Except I wasn't sure what to say.

Stay? Don't move? I hadn't asked her to stay after the proposal from hell. There hadn't been a point. Her mind had been made up then, as I suspected it was now.

No, our conversation needed to be about custody. Every time that word rang in my head, I cringed. I was going to push for the baby to live here. To be in Montana full-time, surrounded not just by my family, but hers too.

That was the only option. She had to know that was the only option.

"What a clusterfuck," I muttered.

"What?"

I spun around, seeing Eva halfway between the hallway and living room. Her hair was wet and twisted in a knot. Her slender body was covered in a set of baggy gray sweats.

"Nothing." I nodded to the TV where ESPN was playing football highlights. "My team lost," I lied.

"Oh." She sighed and came around the couch, curling up in the same end where she'd napped yesterday.

"How was dinner?"

"Okay." She shrugged. "Elena focused on her girls and cooking. Her husband and I answered Mom's questions. You know how she is. And I guess she moved."

"She did? Where?"

"Salt Lake. Good thing I didn't send a Christmas present to her old place in Florida."

I shook my head. Eddy Williams was a damn good man. Elena was sweet and kind. But I could do without Michelle.

Eva had patience for her mother, more than Michelle deserved. In four years of college, she'd come to see Eva once. We'd gone out to dinner and Michelle had asked so many questions I'd felt like it had been an interrogation. It was like she'd wanted to cram years of missed conversations into a single meal. One dinner, then she'd flown away, off to her life in the sky, and then occasionally sent Eva a text to check in.

From the sounds of it, nothing had changed. Michelle lived her life. Everyone else was ancillary.

"Elena and I decided not to tell Dad she was in town. It bothers him."

"Do they talk?"

"I don't think so. She called him after his stroke, but otherwise . . . not that I know of."

"Do you talk often? You and your dad?"

She nodded. "Almost every day. I usually text Elena a few times a week and FaceTime with her and the girls on Sundays."

Is that why she didn't think living across the country with my baby was going to be a problem? Because she'd made it work with her dad and sister?

This was not the same situation. Eddy might be okay with it because Eva was a grown woman, but I refused to have a relationship with my child via FaceTime. It was on the tip of my tongue to tell her exactly that, but instead, I reached for the remote and changed the channel.

Yeah, we needed to talk.

But I didn't want to.

There was no way this discussion ended happily.

"Feel like a movie?" I asked.

"Sure." She curled her legs into the seat, sinking into a toss pillow. "I might get a snack. I wasn't really hungry at dinner."

"What do you feel like? Chips? Cookies? Carrot sticks?"

"Hey, watch your language."

I blinked. "What did I say?"

"Carrot sticks." Her face soured. "How about popcorn?"

"Popcorn it is. You pick the movie." I tossed her the remote and retreated to the kitchen, needing some distance. That sweet, soft scent was too enticing.

With a bowl of popcorn for us to share, I put it between us and handed her a throw blanket. "Here."

"How'd you know I was cold?"

Because I knew her. Or I had once. "Are you?"

"Yes." She swiped it from my hand, draping it over her legs. Then she grabbed a handful of popcorn and turned up the volume on the TV. "We're watching a Hallmark movie. This one just started."

"Seriously?"

"It's December, Tobias. They only play these once a year."

Which meant she'd watch Hallmark or nothing.

"Fine." We'd have enough to argue about shortly. Tonight, I wasn't going to bicker over *A Cowboy Christmas*.

Eva inhaled the popcorn, eating most of the bowl before she'd realized I hadn't had a kernel. "Do you not want any?"

"Nah. I did my workout already." I'd come home earlier to an empty house that smelled like Eva. I'd needed to burn some energy, so I'd turned around, climbed back in my truck, and headed to the gym.

"Afraid you'll lose the six-pack?" Her gaze dragged down my body, her eyes darkening.

Eva loved my six-pack. She loved the definition at my hips and the strength of my arms. And that look on her face . . . fuck. That was the look that usually landed us in bed.

I scooped a handful of popcorn and shoved it in my mouth, willing myself with every crunch to stay on this side of the couch. Except I wasn't hungry for anything but her.

She squirmed, inching closer to her own armrest. We both faced the TV just in time to see the couple on screen kiss.

Fuck my life.

I hadn't been this sexually frustrated since I'd been sixteen at a friend's house party where all of the senior-year cheerleaders had decided to skinny-dip in the hot tub.

But there was nothing to do but suffer. The movie dragged on and on, and about an hour in, Eva set the empty popcorn bowl aside, then shifted, moving closer to the middle of the couch.

She yawned three times and with each, inched my way. On the fourth, she let out a groan.

"What's wrong?"

"I can't get comfortable."

I threw an arm over the back of the couch. "Come on over."

She didn't hesitate. The space between us vanished and she curled into my side. It took all of sixty seconds until she was asleep.

The remote was too far away for me to reach without waking her up, so I sat and watched the rest of the Hallmark movie, enduring this fictional couple's journey to a happily ever after while Eva's wet hair soaked my shirt.

When the movie was over, I leaned deeper into the couch and stared at the ceiling. What if this was our life? Was it really so bad? Couldn't she be happy here?

No. She'd had her chance at this and had walked away. I wouldn't make the mistake of getting on one knee again only to be kicked in the face.

I blew out a deep breath and shifted, tucking my arms beneath her knees and shoulders. Then in one swoop, I stood from the couch, Eva in my arms, and carried her to the guest bedroom.

"Is the movie over?" she murmured, her eyes still closed.

"Finally."

"Was it good?"

"No."

"Liar," she whispered. "You love Christmas movies."

I chuckled and stepped into the dark room, taking her to the bed. "Sleep tight."

With a quick kiss to her forehead, I moved to step away, but her hand snagged mine.

"Tobias?" Her eyes opened and those hazel pools were my undoing.

She didn't say another word. She didn't have to. We'd done this dance a hundred times.

I swept her into my arms, shifting us both deeper into the bed.

The moment my lips hit hers I fell into the deep end and drowned.

Eva let out a small mewl as my tongue tangled with hers, her sweetness mixed with a hint of salt from the popcorn. I licked and sucked and nipped until she was clawing at my back, tugging at my shirt.

I settled into the cradle of her hips, pressing my arousal into her core and swallowing her gasp before tearing my lips away. "Babe, tell me to stop."

"Don't stop." Her hands trailed lower, her palms molding to the curve of my ass before she gave it a hard squeeze.

I arched into her, earning a moan, then trailed my lips down the long column of her throat. My hands slipped beneath the hem of her sweatshirt and skimmed up her ribs. My knuckles grazed the swell of her breasts. "Eva."

"Tobias."

My name in her voice, laced with heat, and my cock throbbed. "Last warning."

She answered by letting go of my ass to cup my erection through my zipper. "Don't. Stop."

I lifted off of her, working my shirt free. Then I yanked the sweatshirt from her body, sending it sailing to the floor. Her pants and panties came next until every inch of her smooth skin was on display.

Eva lifted and frantically loosened the buttons on my jeans.

She freed me from my boxers, wrapping her hand around my shaft.

"Christ." I savored the feel of her hand for a few strokes before I moved away, standing to strip.

Eva watched my every move, her eyes flaring with lust as they dragged down my stomach. That look right there was worth every minute in the gym and each mile on the treadmill.

I planted a knee on the bed and settled between her thighs before trailing a hand over her thigh and down her calf, taking it in my hand and hooking her leg around my waist. "What do you want?"

"You."

I was one second away from thrusting deep and hard when my gaze landed on her belly. My baby was in there. Ours. In months we'd have a baby.

"What?" Eva propped up on an elbow.

"This. Us." I nodded to her stomach. "You good with this?"

Eva dropped her leg and shoved up to a seat. Then with a fast shove, pushed me over and onto my back until she straddled my hips. One hand stayed planted on my sternum while she positioned me at her entrance with the other, sinking down until I was sheathed.

"Fuck." I thrust my hips up, burying myself in her tight heat.

"Oh, God." She squeezed her eyes closed as her inner walls fluttered.

Every fucking time it was amazing. Like her body had been made to fit mine.

"Move," I ordered, taking her hips and lifting her so she could slam back down.

The worries, the fears, were all shoved aside as she rode me, over and over until her legs began to tremble.

With a twist, I reversed our positions, putting her back to

the mattress so I could work in and out of her pussy, stroke after stroke until she writhed beneath me.

Her hands fisted the bedding. Her teeth held her bottom lip. Her limbs tensed.

"Let go, Eva."

She shook her head. "Not yet."

"Goddamn it, come."

"Together," she breathed.

I growled and thrust faster until the pressure was too much to resist. "Come."

One touch of my thumb to her clit and she detonated. She pulsed around me, her orgasm triggering my own, and I poured into her, long and hard until we were both boneless.

I collapsed on the bed beside her. "Damn."

"Wow." Her chest heaved as she regained her breath.

The stars in my eyes took minutes to clear, and after my heart stopped racing, I jackknifed off the bed and went to the bathroom, getting a cloth to clean her up.

Instead, her footsteps followed. "Take a shower with me."

"We could go to mine. It's twice this size."

She shook her head and turned on the water. It took only seconds to warm since she'd been in here not that long ago, and when she took my hand, I followed her willingly beneath the water.

Her hands slid up and down my body as steam surrounded us. She lifted to her toes, wanting my mouth.

She didn't get it. Instead, I spun her around, gripped her hips and slid inside once more, losing myself in the woman who had me twisted in a knot.

We fucked slow and deep until we both came on a cry. Then I squeezed some soap on the shower puff and scrubbed our bodies clean.

The mirror was fogged when we toweled off. I kept one tied

around my waist as Eva retreated to the bedroom to pull on her clothes.

She climbed into bed, patting the space beside her. "Will you cuddle with me, baby?"

It had been a long damn time since she'd called me baby. Not even during our night six weeks ago had she let that old endearment slip. And that single word sent a jolt of ice through my veins.

"What are we doing?" I whispered.

"Huh?" She yawned.

"Eva, what are we doing? You're calling me *baby*. We're fucking. Cuddling. What are we doing?"

Her shoulders fell. Her gaze dropped to the blankets over her lap. "I don't know. We're in a pickle, aren't we?"

"Pretty much." I huffed. "We have to figure this out."

"Would you move?"

"To where? London?"

She shrugged. "It would be an adventure."

"I don't need an adventure." This baby would be under-taking enough. I opened my mouth to ask her to stay but clamped it shut before the words escaped.

I wouldn't ask. Not when I knew the answer.

Eva stared at me, waiting. Like she could see my restraint. Like the unspoken question floated through the air like the scent of the shower. When she realized I wasn't going to say anything, she dropped her gaze again. "So then I guess it's Face-Time and Santa's sleigh."

My throat felt tight as I moved to sweep up my clothes and stalk out of the room.

FaceTime. Airports. Long-distance. Those were her solutions. What the hell had I been thinking tonight? Sex was complicated and intimate and . . . it made sense.

Why couldn't she see how much sense we made? How good our life could be? How good we were together?

I was a fucking fool. She'd leave me again. Just like she had before.

This time, with my child.

CHAPTER 7

EVA

"I'm sending you my final report as we speak." My fingers flew over my laptop's keyboard as I talked to my boss with my phone sandwiched between my ear and shoulder. "I stopped by the site this morning and everything looks polished. The cleaning crew did a great job. The clients are happy. We should be good to close this project out."

"Thanks, Eva," he said. "You did a fantastic job coming to the rescue, as always. All set for next week?"

"Yes." My insides churned at the lie.

Six days ago, yes. Absolutely, yes. I'd been ready for London. Then that pregnancy test had changed everything and I wasn't sure what to be excited about.

"Fantastic." His keyboard clicked in the background. "Just got your email. I'll reply if I have any questions. Touch base when you get to London."

"Will do. Thanks." I ended the call and set my phone on the island, staring at my empty inbox.

Normally zero emails would mean a happy dance and

takeout dinner to celebrate. So why did I want to curl up in a ball and cry?

This was Tobias's fault. He'd given me two orgasms last night and now I was an emotional mess. Or maybe it was the baby's fault, which was actually his fault because his sperm had escaped the confines of a condom.

"Stupid sperm," I muttered, shooting a glare down the hallway toward his bedroom.

When I'd woken up this morning, the house had been silent. I'd tiptoed toward his office, peeking my head through the door. When I'd found it empty, I'd snuck toward his bedroom, finding it empty as well. Then I'd double-checked the garage and my car had been alone in the last stall.

He hadn't even left a note.

"Isn't the mother of his child and the woman he just had sex with entitled to a note? I bet he left notes for his other girlfriends."

My stomach roiled again. *Don't think about his other girlfriends. Do not think about his other girlfriends.*

Eventually he'd start dating, right? I was going to have to deal with that at some point. Eventually my baby would have to meet the next woman. A stepmother.

"Oh, shit." The bowl of bran flakes I'd scarfed for breakfast began its climb. I barely made it to the bathroom in time to hurl, then lingered on the cool tile floor until I felt steady again. My gaze drifted to the shower.

Okay, so maybe sex with Tobias had been a tad . . . reckless. But the minute he'd kissed me, rational thought had vanished, replaced by an urgent craving for more, more, *more*.

"Damn him and those washboard abs." I shoved to my feet and went to the sink to brush my teeth. Again. Then I retreated to the kitchen to shut down my laptop and sign off for the day. Maybe I'd visit Dad or Elena.

I was filling a glass of water when the doorbell rang. A familiar face peered in through the sidelight.

Hannah Holiday didn't seem at all surprised to see me staring back.

I crossed the space and unlocked the door, smiling as I pulled it open. "Hey, Hannah."

"Eva!" She set her purse on the floor and pulled me into her arms. "Oh, it's so good to see you."

"You too."

She smelled like gardenia and brown sugar, the scent as strong and comforting as her hug.

"I've missed your hugs," she said, finally letting me go.

"I've missed yours too."

Hannah had been like a mother to me during college. My junior year, I'd gotten a nasty cold, and the day Tobias told her I was sick, she'd showed up at my apartment door and had whisked me away to her home where she'd nursed me back to health with homemade chicken noodle soup.

She'd been there for me when my own mother hadn't.

And then I'd lost her too.

That was something no one warned you about when you started dating. That you'd begin to love your boyfriend's family. And that when you lost him, you lost his family too.

"I've brought you something." She held up a finger, then bent to rifle through her purse, coming out with a bag of ginger lollipops. "In case you get sick."

"Thanks." My nose was stinging, but I sniffled it away before I cried. "Tobias told you?"

"No, not exactly. He told Maddox, who let it slip at breakfast this morning. Sorry."

"It's okay." It was bound to come out sometime, but that meant I needed to tell my family before long. The last thing I wanted was for Dad or Elena to hear it through the gossip mill.

Bozeman had changed a lot over the years since I'd moved away, but at its heart, this was still a small town. And the Holidays were one of the most successful families in the valley.

Hannah was a real estate broker, her face on dozens of for-sale signs. Her brokerage was well-known and well-respected because they sold the best properties, including those built from Holiday Homes.

Keith had started his construction company decades ago and had grown it to be one of the most premier companies in the area. With Tobias designing their builds, I had no doubt that Keith's legacy would live long.

"So tell me what's new." Hannah walked into the house, stripping off her coat and tossing it to the back of the couch before she moved to the kitchen, finding the single-brew pods and making herself some coffee.

"Well . . . I'm pregnant." I laughed. "It's strange. I haven't said those words out loud to anyone but Tobias."

"Give it time. Soon you won't have to say a thing." She smiled, opening the fridge to retrieve some cream. With her nearly white coffee, she came and sat at my side. "How are you feeling?"

"Some days are better than others. My morning sickness seems sporadic." If it was even morning sickness. The days when my heart and head were in the most turmoil, seemed to translate to my stomach.

"It'll pass. I didn't have those lollipops when I was pregnant with the boys, but one of my agents just had her third and she swears by them."

"Thank you."

"Hopefully you can find them in London. If not, text me and I'll stick some in the mail."

"Okay." Just the mention of London made my insides twist again.

Was I doing this? Was I really leaving home again? If there was a person in the world to talk about my doubts with, it was Hannah. When I looked at her, she was the mother I wanted to be someday.

She had a flourishing career. She was a fantastic parent. She had found that magical balance. How?

I opened my mouth, ready to ask, but stopped myself. Hannah was Tobias's. She was his mother, not mine. If I dragged her into this mess, it would only put her in a tough position. I didn't want her to be the mediator if he went to her with his own frustrations and fears. I didn't want her feeling responsible to play both sides.

So I stuck to a safe topic. Work. "How is business?"

"Busy." She blew out a long breath. "So busy. But a good kind of busy. Any chance you want to become an agent? I could use a smart cookie like you."

"Oh, um . . ." I scrunched up my nose. Selling homes sounded more like torture. "No, thanks."

"Damn." She winked. "I was secretly hoping that you have been dying for a career in real estate."

"If that changes, you'll be my first phone call." I giggled.

"Oh, it's so good to hear your laugh. Tell me more about what you've been doing. Are you excited for London? How is your dad?"

We spent the next hour catching up. Not once did Hannah ask me about the baby. Not once did she comment about how nice it would be if her grandchild lived in the same country. Not once did she ask how Tobias and I were going to handle the situation.

She simply talked to me the way she'd talked to me years ago. Like a daughter.

Like a friend.

The hum of the garage door halted our conversation.

Tobias walked in and found us both at the island. He went straight to his mom, not sparing me a glance, and kissed her cheek. "Hey."

"Hi." She patted his beard. "Where were you?"

"The office. What's up?"

"Nothing." She stood from her stool and carried her empty coffee mug to the dishwasher. "I just wanted to say hi."

"Hi." He leaned against the counter, his back to me. There was stiffness to his spine, likely caused by me.

"I'll leave you guys alone to visit." I slid off my seat. "It was so good to see you, Hannah."

"You too, honey." She came over and gave me another hug. "And congratulations."

"Thanks." I squeezed my eyes shut so I wouldn't cry.

She was the first to say congratulations. And it struck me right then, with her arms around me, that there was more here to be excited about than to fear.

I was having a baby.

Oh, God. I was having a baby.

Maybe he or she would have my hazel eyes. Maybe Tobias's straight nose and soft lips. The idea of a miniature Tobias Holiday put a small smile on my face.

"Love you," she whispered.

"Love you too."

"See you soon," Hannah said, letting me go.

"Okay." I waved and left the kitchen, feeling Tobias's gaze as I retreated to the guest bedroom where I hovered inside the door, hearing him blow out a long breath.

"So I take it Maddox told you," he said.

"Yeah." Hannah sighed. "You doing okay?"

"No."

That one word, barely audible, hit like a sledgehammer to my sternum.

I eased the door closed behind me, not because I wasn't curious about their conversation, but because I wasn't sure I had the strength to hear Tobias's truths.

"Oof." I plopped onto the edge of the bed and pinched the bridge of my nose.

My phone and laptop were still in the kitchen, so all I could do was sit and wait, letting the minutes pass until finally the front door closed, and from beyond the windows, a car engine started.

It wouldn't always be like this. It would get easier as we had more time to adjust. All major life decisions took time to comprehend. Maybe coming up with a plan—Tobias would do cartwheels when I tossed out that word—would help ease the stress.

I could book an airline ticket to fly back in two months. Or three? Would I have time for a trip home by then? Would Tobias want to come to London? When would we be able to find out the sex of the baby? How often would I go to the doctor?

As the questions raced through my mind, I realized how woefully unprepared I was for a pregnancy. My stomach began another round of dizzying laps, and I shoved to my feet, hoping one of Hannah's lollipops might help. But after one step, I gagged and changed directions for the bathroom.

There wasn't anything in my stomach but I dry-heaved and coughed regardless.

"Oh, this sucks." I groaned. Sweat beaded on my forehead as I shifted to lean against the wall. My entire body felt twisted inside out. My muscles were somehow locked but trembling. My head was spinning and I wanted to cry.

So I did.

I buried my face in my hands and cried. I let the emotions leak down my face. I let the fears sob from my mouth.

There was no reason I should feel so lonely here. I was at home. My dad was ten minutes away. So was Elena. But this bathroom felt like a black hole. Just me and my baby. Just me and the soul-deep fear that I was going to fail. I was going to let this kid down.

How was I going to do this? How was I going to be a good mom? Tobias didn't believe in me. Hell, I didn't believe in myself.

I was crying so hard that I didn't hear the door open.

One moment I was on the cool tile, the next I was against Tobias's chest as he swept me into his arms. "Breathe, babe."

I nodded, too far gone to stop. But instead of crying into my hands alone, I cried into his shoulder as he carried me to the bed and cradled me in his lap. "I hate this."

"It'll get better. Morning sickness doesn't last forever."

"It's not that. At least, I don't think." I pulled away, wiping my face dry and sniffling through the last of the tears.

Except this queasy feeling originated from my heart. The magnitude of what we were facing was breaking me into pieces.

Stress didn't bother me. Hell, I thrived on it. I'd made a career of thriving on it. But the anxiety . . . God, the anxiety was paralyzing.

"I don't know." I moved out of his lap and into the space between his spread legs, hugging my knees to my chest.

He tucked a lock of my hair behind an ear. "When we were younger, I think we took for granted how well we knew each other."

"What do you mean?"

"I mean, we didn't have to talk. You could look at me and, most days, know exactly what I was thinking or how I was feeling. It was always . . . easy."

"I loved that about us." I gave him a small smile. Tobias was the one person who always made it easy.

"Yeah, me too. But it meant we didn't fight."

"You want to fight? Okay, I think the paint color you picked for this room is too gray. It's boring."

He chuckled. "You really want to fight about paint colors?"

"You just asked me to fight with you."

"Woman." He shook his head, a grin on his lips. "My point . . . I think we got used to it being so good. I think we were happy. And then we didn't do anything to fuck it up. Like talk to each other. Or let it get messy."

I sighed. "I should have told you I wanted to move."

"Yeah, you should have." There was a sharpness to his voice, a tone that slashed straight to the bone. Every cell in my body went on edge.

This was exactly the feeling I'd get during the rare times we had argued. It made me want to hurl all over again. *Wow.* How had I not realized that before? He was right. So damn right.

I hated it when Tobias was angry with me. *Hated. It.* So I'd done everything in my power to avoid a fight, including hiding my dreams.

Hiding had only lasted so long. And in the end, the truth had finally come to light.

"Don't hate me," I whispered, my eyes locking with his. "I won't survive it."

"I could never hate you." He caught a new tear with his thumb and brushed it away. "But I can be pissed at you. You can be pissed at me. And we can get to the other side by talking it out. So talk to me. Tell me what's going on in your head."

I sagged, the air rushing from my lungs. "I don't want to give up my job."

Oof. That confession felt like walking down Main Street buck-ass naked.

It shouldn't have been so hard to say. Tobias was just as committed to his career as I was to mine. But I guess, deep down, I was still the woman who'd felt it necessary to hide her dreams. The one woman who'd chosen that job over him. The one who feared he'd never truly forgive me for breaking us apart.

"It's my identity," I told him. "I'm not sure who I am without it anymore. It saved me when I was at my lowest. And it's more than the money, it's my pride."

"Hey." Tobias hooked his finger under my chin, lifting it so I could meet his gaze. Then there it was, the familiar comfort in his eyes. The understanding that he knew what it was like to love a job. To have a career fill a void.

A void that I'd created in his life when I'd left Montana.

The energy seemed to leave my body at once, like a light being turned off with a flick of a switch. I barely had the strength to scoot to the pillows and collapse.

Tobias stretched out beside me, his body on one half of the bed, mine on the other. There was a clear line between us, his pillows, my pillows. Except for one touch. He took my hand, lacing our fingers together, and held it tight until I drifted off to sleep.

A ding woke me up, my head fuzzy as I lifted off the pillow. I shoved the hair out of my face and swung my legs off the bed, taking a few long breaths before getting to my feet.

I braced for a wave of nausea that never came. My stomach felt solid as a rock. Normal. Maybe what I'd needed wasn't lollipops and saltines, but a release. To talk it out with Tobias.

To fight, if that got us to a better place.

I shuffled out of the room and down the hallway, my bare feet quiet on the hardwood floors. The flip of the door's lock gave an audible pop. Then came a woman's voice.

"Hey. I know I should have called first but I thought . . . what the hell? I'd take the chance you were home and had a few hours free."

"Chelsea . . ."

Chelsea? Wait. One of my friends from college was named Chelsea, but I hadn't spoken to her in years.

"I know, you hate surprises. I'll make it up to you in bed."

What. The. Fuck.

Tobias did hate surprises. I wasn't a fan of them myself.

Especially when the surprise was a pretty blonde standing in the entryway with her lips on Tobias's mouth.

CHAPTER 8
TOBIAS

"Chelsea." I pushed her away before she could do more than brush her lips to mine.

"Oh, dang." She deflated. "Bad time?"

"Yeah." I gave her a sad smile. "I think . . . we'd better call it quits. Sorry."

"It's fine. I'll get out of your hair." She waved it off, her car keys rattling in her hand as she spun for the door.

But before she could step out into the bright afternoon sun, I caught her elbow. "Happy New Year."

"Happy New Year, Tobias. Call me if you ever want to start this up again."

I nodded, stood in the cold and waited until her car reversed out of the driveway. "Shit."

Of all the weeks for Chelsea to arrive, this was the one she'd picked. But even if she'd come next week or the next or the next, I would have sent her away.

With Eva . . . everything was different now. There was no going back to cheap hookups and casual flings. Chelsea was a nice woman with a pretty smile and kind heart. She'd kept me company.

But she wasn't Eva.

No one was.

I closed the door, ready to retreat to my office for a few hours of work in the hopes of getting my mind off the shit swirling in my personal life, but as I turned, a pair of angry hazel eyes halted my escape.

"Chelsea?" Eva tapped her foot in rapid succession. *Pat. Pat. Pat.* Yep, she was furious. "Really?"

Fuck. "It's nothing."

She arched an eyebrow.

"It was casual. Just an occasional . . ." *Hookup.* I stopped myself, fear for my testicles if I finished that sentence. "She lives in Billings. Every few months she comes here for work and we go to dinner."

"Like the dinner we went on." She scoffed, then spun and stormed down the hallway.

"Damn it." I hurried to follow, finding her sitting on her bed, legs crossed, arms folded and a death glare on her face. She was the epitome of livid, quivering chin and all. "Eva. It's nothing. It's been months. Before you and I had dinner."

"Don't." She closed her eyes. "I don't want to know."

"Okay." I held up a hand, ready to leave, but her eyes snapped open and that murderous glare found me again.

"Chelsea? How many other friends of mine have there been?"

Here we go. "Just Chelsea."

"I—grr." She huffed. "I can't even be mad."

"Then why are you?"

"Because." She tossed out a hand and leapt off the bed, marching to the bathroom. Drawers were ripped open and slammed, one after another. When I braved the threshold, I found her brushing her hair in a rage.

"Talk to me." Was I always going to have to beg for her to tell me how she felt?

She kept on brushing. "Because it's not fair."

"What's not fair?"

"That you've moved on." The brush went sailing to the counter, clattering as it slid and dropped into the empty sink. "It's not fair. I don't want you to move on. The idea of you with another woman, with a Chelsea or Tiffany or, or, or whoever, makes my skin crawl."

"What do you want me to say?" I raked a hand through my hair. "You left. You left me."

"I know!" Her eyes flooded. "I know I left. And you moved on. But I didn't."

"Wait." I held up a finger. "What are you saying?"

"Never mind." She blew past me through the door, and before I could make sense of what she'd just told me, she was gone.

The garage door opened and closed, followed by the crunch of her tires on the snow as she drove away.

She hadn't moved on. Seriously? So she hadn't been with anyone else? But it had been years. What the fuck did that mean?

"Son of a bitch." I unglued my feet and followed the path she took. Out the door, into my truck and away. Just away.

I'd asked Eva to fight with me. *Stupid fucking idea, Holiday.* I sure as shit didn't feel like doing it again.

So I drove around town for hours until the sun had long set and my tires led me to my brother's house. Heath had been calling me for days. I'd avoided him, mostly because I still wasn't sure what to say.

Or maybe because I suspected what Heath *would* say.

He'd tell me to go with her.

Before I could knock or ring the bell, Heath opened the door. "Hey. What's going on? I've been calling you."

"Yeah." I stomped my feet and walked into the house, straight to the kitchen. It smelled like dinner and my stomach growled. An open bottle of cabernet rested on the counter.

Heath stood behind me, arms crossed and his forehead furrowed. Apparently, Maddox and Mom hadn't told him what was happening with Eva.

Probably a good thing. Maybe if I said it out loud again, I'd find a way to make sense of it all.

So I nodded to the bottle. "Got any more of that wine?"

"Where the hell is she?" I muttered, glancing out the living room window for the hundredth time.

I hadn't seen Eva all day.

Last night, I'd lingered at Heath's place, mostly because I didn't trust myself after dark with Eva under the same roof. Either we'd pick up the argument, sit in awkward silence or fuck.

Every moment with her was laced with an undercurrent of desire. I craved her more and more, and the other night had barely taken the edge off. If she gave me the slightest opening, I'd take it.

So I'd sat on my brother's couch, mindlessly watching a game on TV, and thought about everything he'd had to say.

Talk to her. Go with her.

We're your family no matter where you live.

There's no reason you have to live here to help run the company.

Every time I'd voice a concern, whether it be distance from

391

family or working remotely for Holiday Homes, he'd countered with advice I hadn't wanted to hear.

Could I move? Could I live in London for a year? Then bounce to wherever it was she went next? What the hell kind of life was that?

"Not for me." My hands fisted as I paced the length of the living room. My eyes once more drifted to the windows and black sky beyond.

Her suitcase was still in the guest bedroom so at least she hadn't moved out. She had to come back sometime, right?

It was ten. Twenty more minutes and I was calling. This close to New Year's with ice on the roads, I didn't want her out alone on a Friday night. Would she keep these kinds of hours in London? She needed sleep. Our baby needed her to be well rested.

The seconds ticked by so slowly I was about to lose my shit, until finally the flash of headlights bounced through the glass and the garage door rattled open.

I was at the door before she could get out of the driver's seat of her sedan. "Hi."

"Hi." She walked toward me with her eyes on the floor.

"Are you okay? I was getting worried."

"Fine." Her eyes stayed on my shoulder, not my face, as she slipped past me into the house. "Tired. I'm going to go to bed. Night."

No. We weren't going another night without talking. "Eva."

"Please, Tobias." Her shoulders slumped as she turned. "I can't argue with you."

"I don't want to argue."

"Then what? What do you want?"

You. To stay. The words I couldn't bring myself to say. "I don't want to miss this. I want to be able to tell our kid stories about when you were pregnant. I want to be the nervous dad at the doctor's appointments. I want the ultrasound photo to carry in my wallet. I'd like to figure out a way to make that happen."

"I'm open to ideas."

"I went to Heath's last night. He suggested hitting up Maddox for a jet since he can afford it."

A ghost of a smile crossed her pretty lips. "What else did Heath say?"

"That we both want the best for our kid. So we'll figure it out."

"We will. Maybe not tonight, but we will."

For a man who loved long-term plans and five-year goals, the unknown was unnerving. But the dark circles under her eyes made my chest squeeze. "We've got tomorrow, right?"

She nodded. "I'm going to see Dad. Say goodbye. I'll probably swing by Elena's too."

"Then tomorrow night. You and me. We'll ring in the new year. I'll get some sparkling grape juice, and we'll make a real party of it."

Her eyes dropped to my lips for a split second before she tore them away, looking to her tennis shoes. "Okay. Good night."

God, I hated seeing her walk away. Even if it was just to another bedroom in my own damn house.

"Eva."

She stopped and glanced over her shoulder. "Yeah?"

"Did you find it?"

"Find what?" She turned fully, her head cocking to the side.

"Whatever it was that you were looking for in New York." Whatever dream she'd needed to chase.

"I don't know." She lifted a shoulder. "Living there was an experience. And because of my job, I've had the chance to explore a lot of places I otherwise wouldn't have found."

"Which city was your favorite?"

"Nashville."

"Because you love country music."

She smiled, moving to the island and pulling out a stool. "Any chance I got, I did all the touristy stuff with no shame. It was a blast."

"How long were you there?" I went to sit beside her. Right beside her. There was no stool to keep us apart this time because I couldn't bear the distance.

We'd have plenty of distance soon enough.

"Three months," she said. "Sort of the same assignment as I've had here. I stepped in to help with a project in trouble."

"Ah. What was your least favorite place?"

"New York," she whispered.

I sat up straighter. "What?"

"It was a hard year. I was new to the job and had a lot of learning to do. The hours were brutal. The client was a complete jackass. And I was lonely. I missed you."

Well . . . fuck. That hit me square in the chest. "I missed you too."

"I never wanted to hurt you." She looked up, her hazel eyes full of regret. "To hurt us."

"I know."

"You do?"

I nodded. "Not gonna lie, I was pretty angry at you for a while. And I sort of nursed my anger because it was the only way I could keep a part of you."

A flash of pain crossed her face.

"Then I ran into your dad."

"You did? When?"

"About two years after you left. You were in Florida."

"Tampa. For about eight weeks. I was so busy that I didn't get to visit the beach once."

"Maybe we could go one day. The three of us." Our strange little family unit could take a vacation together.

"I'd like that," she whispered.

"Anyway. Back to your dad. I was downtown, meeting my parents for dinner. They were running late so I was sitting at the restaurant's bar and he came walking over. I guess he was on a date."

"He was?" Her mouth fell open. "I had no idea that he went on dates."

"This one was not a good date." I chuckled. "Probably why you never heard about it. I was his excuse to get away from the table. Apparently, his date picked her nose right as their salads were delivered and the booger was put in the cloth napkin, as green as the lettuce they were about to eat."

Eva laughed. "Eww."

"He was so funny about it. He leaned in close, told me the whole story, and asked if it was rude to dump her before dessert."

"What did you say?"

"I told him to pay the check and scram."

"Did he?"

"He stayed the whole meal, even bought her a piece of chocolate cake." Eddy wasn't the kind of man who cut a date short. He treated women the way he wanted men to treat his daughters.

"That's sweet." She smiled. "I can't believe he never told me about that. Or that he saw you. What else did you talk about?"

"You. He told me you were living in Tampa but traveling all over. That you were kicking ass and taking names at your job. That he was so proud of you for taking a leap of faith."

Eddy was the first one to talk to me about Eva after the breakup. He hadn't pandered to my broken heart like my

395

parents. He hadn't avoided bringing her name into a conversation like my brother. He'd bragged about his daughter, unabashedly.

"It was hard to stay angry at you after that. Mostly I just wanted you to be happy."

"Thank you," she breathed. "I worried for a long time that you hated me."

"Never." Angry, yes. But I'd never hated her. It just wasn't inside me.

My only hope was if I pushed for the baby to live here, she wouldn't be able to hate me either.

"That's good because you're stuck with me now." She forced a too-bright smile, lifting her chin. Then she slid off the stool. "I'd better let you get some sleep. Night."

"Wait," I blurted. "Earlier, when Chelsea was here. You said you weren't with anyone. Why?" I could probably guess, but tonight, I wanted to hear it.

"I just . . . wasn't." She shrugged. "Work was busy. And no one compared to you."

"Eva." My hand reached out and caught hers. A zing raced up my forearm at the touch. "They're always electric, aren't they?"

She nodded, her lips parting. Was that an invitation?

This was only going to get more complicated. The right thing to do would be to let her go. Leave her to her room while I locked myself in my own.

Instead, I leaned down and brushed my lips across hers, the hitch of her breath my reward.

Reward enough for one night.

It took restraint to let her go. It took every ounce of willpower to stand and take a step away.

Maybe I would have made it behind my closed door. But

before I could slip my fingers free from Eva's, she tugged me back.

That string between us was as tight as ever.

This time there was no mistaking her body language as her tongue darted out and licked her bottom lip.

"Fuck it." I slammed my mouth on hers, my tongue sweeping inside. I devoured her, exploring her mouth, memorizing every corner. I held her to me, hoping that if I held tight enough, this might all make sense.

She broke away first, her eyes hooded and her lips swollen.

Fuck, but I wanted her. I wanted her for good. To keep.

But she wasn't mine.

She was her own woman. That was what Eddy had called her that night years ago. Her own woman.

So I took one step away. Then another. And this time, I made it to my bedroom without looking back.

CHAPTER 9

EVA

"Sleep. Go. To. Sleep." I punched my pillow and flopped onto my back. The bedroom was pitch black as I yawned. But did sleep come? Nope. Not even a wink. The last time I'd checked my phone, it had been after midnight.

I should have hit the pillow and crashed. My day had been long and exhausting. Avoiding Tobias had been harder than the boot camp I'd taken a few years ago in Denver. Plus I'd slept like crap last night too, tossing and turning until Tobias had finally come home. Most of my sleepless hours had been spent wondering if he'd been with Chelsea. Freaking Chelsea. That was going to rub me like sandpaper for a long, long time.

Thank God, he'd been at his brother's.

After all that stress, I should have slept straight until eight. Instead, I'd been lying here for hours replaying Tobias's words from earlier.

He just wanted me to be happy.

Was I happy? I hadn't asked myself that question lately. Maybe because I was scared of the answer.

I was *mostly* happy. I was happy in my job. I loved my job, almost every day. Sure, my personal life was a little dull. I moved too often to have best friends. But that was what Elena was for. Okay, so we didn't have nearly enough in common to be *best* friends. Our independent personalities often clashed, but I loved my sister.

The closest I'd ever had to a best friend was Tobias.

And he wanted me to be happy.

"Well, is he happy that I can't sleep and it's all his fault?" I jammed an elbow into the mattress and pushed myself up. "Ugh."

Maybe if he'd stop kissing me, I could get some sleep.

My mind was spinning and my body was strung as tight as a rubber band, about to snap. And damn it, this was all Tobias's fault.

He'd worked me into this turned-on, fidgeting, hormonal mess.

I whipped the covers off my legs and climbed out of bed. The cool air brought goose bumps to my arms and legs as I walked out of the bedroom and down the hall toward the couch. Maybe a Hallmark movie would lull me into dreamland.

But as I reached the kitchen, my path veered toward his bedroom. Toward the soft white glow coming from beneath his door.

I held my breath, creeping closer until I could lean my ear against the frame. The sound of rustled sheets and muted huffs brought a smile to my lips. I guess I wasn't the only one not sleeping.

We could talk. Why wait until tomorrow if we were both awake? So I rapped my knuckles on the door and turned the knob.

Tobias sat up straighter as I stepped inside. His nightstand lamp was on and a book dangled from his fingers. His chest was bare, all of that glorious muscle on display. His hair was sticking up at odd angles.

He looked . . . like my dreamland.

"You kissed me and now I can't sleep."

He tossed the book aside, his gaze tracking my every step as I rounded the foot of his bed.

I went straight for the lamp, flipping the switch to bathe the room in darkness. Then my hand found the center of his chest, the dusting of coarse hair that felt like sin against the steel of his body. With one slight push, his shoulders relaxed into the pillows.

Tobias's hands came to my thighs, skimming the scalloped hem of my sleep shorts. "Eva."

"You kissed me and now I can't sleep," I repeated, straddling his lap. My core rocked against the growing arousal beneath the sheet. "Kiss me again. Please."

He surged to capture my mouth. No questions. No hesitation. No foreplay. Tobias kissed me like I was the air in his lungs, the reason he survived. His tongue fluttering against my own as his hands lifted the sides of my top.

He bunched the cotton in his fists, lifting it higher and higher, tearing his mouth away for only the briefest moment to whip the tank over my head. Then his hands found my breasts, and my God, he was good with his hands.

Cupping. Squeezing. Rolling. My nipples were his personal instruments and he played them like a symphony.

My hips rolled against his, grinding and rubbing. I held his face to mine, his thick beard lightly scraping against my palms. The throb in my core bloomed. "Fuck me, Tobias."

He growled against my lips. Then with one fast move, he flipped me onto my back, pushing my knees apart. His deft fingers slipped beneath my shorts, pulling my panties aside, to stroke my glistening folds.

"Yes," I hissed as he latched on to my pulse and sucked. "More."

He kicked and shoved at the sheets, and as my hand traveled down his spine, I found nothing but skin. Tobias hadn't slept naked in college, but like the beard, I'd gladly take this change.

A finger slid into my core, curling toward the ache. Except it wasn't enough. I needed more. I needed him.

"Inside." I reached between us, fisting his shaft. Velvet and iron. Hot and hard. "Come inside."

"Not yet."

"Tobias—"

"Not. Yet." Each word was accentuated with the plunge of his finger. "I want to feel your pussy like this. Then with my tongue. Then I'll give you my cock."

He made good on his promise, working me into a frenzy with his hand before tearing off my shorts and panties. Then he dragged that glorious beard against the tender flesh of my inner thighs.

I hummed, my eyes falling closed, as a shudder raced through my veins. My hand found his silky, dark hair. My fingertips tangled into the strands as he did that tongue flutter, this time against my clit.

"Tobias." I moaned his name, over and over, as his mouth continued its delicious torture. A lick. A nip. A suck. My breath came in hitched gasps as he feasted until I trembled, head to toe.

My back arched off the bed, writhing as he held my hips in place. I was seconds away from a blinding release, just one more lick, when he disappeared.

He leaned away, looming above me on his knees. Moonlight streamed through the window, casting his body in light and shadow. The cut of his biceps. The peaks and valleys of his chest. The ripples of his abdomen.

Tobias was magnificent. He was mine.

He'd always been mine, even when I'd let him go.

I stretched a hand for his. He took it, lacing our fingers together, and raised it above his head. Then his lips crashed down on mine, and with one swift thrust, he planted deep.

I whimpered down his throat. I trembled beneath his strokes. Thrust after thrust, he held me captive until I had nothing left to do but fall. The orgasm shook my body in waves as I clenched around him.

"Fuck, babe." He gritted his teeth, his rhythm never slowing, as I rode out the aftershocks and let the stars fade from behind my eyes.

The sound of skin slapping, of heavy breaths and racing hearts, echoed in the room. Then he reared up, taking my knees, and holding me to him as he came, pouring inside me on a roar.

He came undone. Entirely. For me.

Tobias panted, taking a few moments to regain his breath. Then he ran a hand over his mouth before bending to kiss my cheek. "Damn. That was . . . it's always better. Every time."

"I know," I whispered, rising to kiss his mouth.

No one would compare to Tobias. Maybe that was why I'd never wanted another man. I didn't need experience to know, in my soul, that I'd already had the best.

He shifted and broke our connection, then curled my back into his chest.

"I can go back to my room," I said, hoping he wouldn't let me go.

Hoping he'd ask me to stay.

But he didn't voice the word. He never had. Instead, he

held me closer and dragged the blankets over our naked bodies. "Good night, Eva."

I closed my eyes. "Good night, Tobias."

"Knock, knock." I tapped on Dad's door and peered into his apartment.

He was in his recliner, asleep as the TV's muted volume did its best to drown out the sound of his snores.

I eased the door closed behind me and tiptoed into the room, taking up a seat on the couch.

Dad deserved to rest. He deserved mid-morning naps on New Year's Eve. And because of my job, he could have them.

So I took out my phone and played a trivia game while I waited. Or I tried to play a trivia game. Mostly I thought about last night with Tobias.

We hadn't spoken much this morning. I'd woken first, slipping out of his bed and heading to the shower. When I'd found him in the kitchen later, he'd been dressed for the day in a pair of jeans and a navy flannel.

He'd had work to do at the office, but he'd promised to be home by dinner. Then we'd celebrate New Year's, assuming I could stay awake until midnight.

I had a feeling that he'd make sure I saw fireworks.

After an hour, Dad's snoring stopped and his eyes fluttered open.

"Hi, Dad." I smiled.

"Eva." He blinked twice, then hit the button on the chair to sit up straighter. "Sorry. I didn't know you were here."

"It's okay. I don't mind hanging out."

He smiled, the crooked smile I'd grown used to these past three years. "Last day?"

"Yep." I nodded. "Last day."

"I'm sure gonna miss you. I've been spoiled having you here so long this time. Did you see Elena?"

"I went over yesterday. And I'll miss you too." I opened my mouth to tell him I had news. That I was having a baby. But the announcement lodged in my throat.

Dad was a practical man. He'd taught us to love schedules and routine. As kids, the kitchen calendar had been marked with all of Mom's travel dates so we'd know where she was going and when she'd be home.

He'd ask questions about the baby. About how Tobias and I were going to handle parenting and if I'd keep doing my job.

If I was going to give him a string of *I don't knows*, we'd better get some food first.

"I was thinking we could go grab lunch," I said.

"Sure." He reached for his cane, pushing to his feet and taking a moment to get his balance.

We decided on a café in town, one I hadn't been to yet. We took our seats in a booth, ordered soup and sandwiches, then sipped our waters as we waited for our meals.

"So you're off again," Dad said, toying with his napkin.

"Yep." It was always difficult to leave Montana, but today, there was more bitter than sweet.

"Any idea when you can take a quick trip home to visit?"

"I'm not sure yet. Maybe in a month or two? Once I get there and get caught up on the build, I'll have a better idea."

"And what are you building this time?"

"A fulfillment center."

"Ah." He nodded. "Big?"

"Not as big as most. The logistics have been tricky. And the clients are, er . . . particular. But I'm up for the challenge."

"Of course you are." He grinned. "My girl never backs away from a challenge."

Was that why I was going? Because I was too stubborn to back away? Or because I genuinely liked the work?

"Can I ask you something about Mom?"

"Yeah. Go ahead." He nodded but there was tension in his shoulders. A tension I'd seen my entire life when Mom was brought into the conversation.

"Do you think I'm like her?" It was the question I'd wanted to ask for years but hadn't had the courage.

"You mean the travel?"

I nodded. "Yeah."

"No." He chuckled. "Not in the slightest."

"R-really?" Because when I looked in the mirror, I saw the similarities.

"Eva, your mom traveled to escape her life. Maybe it was because of me. We were never friends. I think she learned early on that when she came home, it wasn't to her house, but to mine. We didn't talk. We didn't laugh. We just coexisted. And I hate that you girls paid the price for our indifference."

My heart twisted, not for us, but for them. I knew what it was like to be in love with your best friend. Pure magic.

"Probably shouldn't be telling you this, but when you were two, we talked about a divorce," he said. "Michelle was worried that if she couldn't at least come home to you and Elena, you'd forget about her completely. So we worked out our arrangement. We agreed to stick it out until you graduated."

"That couldn't have been easy," I said.

"I've got a lot of pent-up resentment toward your mother. It wasn't easy and I guess . . . I think she could have tried harder to be home. To be a part of your lives. Instead, she took every trip they'd give her. She ran away from anything that resembled being tied down."

"Isn't that what I'm doing?" Guilt crept into my voice.

"Not even close." He stretched his good arm across the

table, his hand covering mine. "You run and run and run. You take every task thrown your way and crush it like an empty pop can, destined for the recycling bin. But when you're ready to stop, you stop."

Was I ready to stop? It was coming. I felt fatigued, more and more each move.

"Mom was here a few days ago," I admitted.

"I know," he muttered. "She came to see me."

"What? She did? I didn't realize you kept in touch."

"Not often. But when she's in town, she stops by. We talk about you. We talk about Elena. She gets the details about you, a lot like she used to when you were younger. Then she goes on her way."

Acquaintances. That was how Mom lived her life, with acquaintances.

He gave me a sad smile. "For a long time, I wished that Michelle would just . . . love us. Love me. But I realized something years ago. She's not built to love deep. It's not in her makeup. But it is in yours."

I swallowed the lump in my throat, trying my best not to cry. "I hope you're right."

"Oh, I'm right." He picked up his spoon. "How's Tobias?"

I shook my head, letting out a dry laugh. *Well played, Dad.* "He's good. I, um, I actually have something important to tell you."

"You two getting back together?" It hurt to see such hope in his face. Dad had always loved Tobias.

"No. We're not. But we are, uh . . . having a baby?"

Dad blinked. Probably because I'd said it like a question. His spoon clattered on the table as it slipped from his hand.

"I'm pregnant." *Eeek.* "Surprise."

By the time I made it back to Tobias's house, I'd felt like I'd run a marathon. As expected, Dad had not been shy about the questions. He also hadn't been shy to tell me that *I'm not sure yet* and *we'll figure it out eventually* weren't real answers when it came to an infant.

I parked in the driveway, not the garage, and slipped the opener from the visor. The car wasn't mine, just a lease. Someone from the relocation company would pick it up from the airport parking lot tomorrow and I didn't want to forget Tobias's garage remote.

The snow was falling like white dust as I made my way inside, stomping my shoes on the doormat. The house smelled like Tobias's cologne. One breath and my shoulders sagged.

I would miss that smell. It was like . . . home.

Until tomorrow.

Like I'd done countless times, I packed my suitcase and readied it for travel. I made sure I had my passport and a book downloaded to my Kindle. I checked in for my flight and made sure I had my visa documentation handy. Then I retreated to the living room, curling up in the chair closest to the window.

The snow was falling heavier now. The yard was a blanket of smooth white bumps. Beyond the leafless trees, on the other side of Tobias's property, there was a hill. Not a big hill, but enough that a kid could go sledding on a day like this.

It was peaceful here. How had I not realized that before today? I didn't miss the city noise. I didn't miss the traffic or public transportation. I didn't miss crowded sidewalks or loud neighbors. Tobias hadn't just built a home, but a sanctuary. His retreat.

Years ago, this house had been a napkin sketch. He probably didn't realize I remembered the night he'd drawn it out.

We'd been in my apartment, just the two of us, eating Chinese takeout. He'd doodled on a box first in blue pen before getting serious and pulling out a napkin. Four bedrooms. An office. Open concept with tall ceilings and a large kitchen. He'd wanted to live outside of town where he'd have an unobstructed view of the mountains. He'd wanted an abundance of windows so he could catch the sunrises and sunsets.

I loved that I'd been the first to hear about his dream home. I loved that he'd made that dream come true.

Snuggling deeper into the chair's cushions, I curled my feet into the seat. I imagined a little girl with dark hair and blue eyes giggling as she made snow angels in the yard. Or maybe a little boy trying his best to build a snowman.

"Why hasn't he asked us to stay?" I whispered, sliding a hand across my belly.

The baby didn't have an answer.

Neither did I.

CHAPTER 10
TOBIAS

found Eva asleep in the chair. Her lips were slightly parted. Her knees were drawn in tight. One hand cradled her cheek while the other was splayed across her belly.

I'd been standing here for minutes, just watching. Hurting. Because goddamn it, I loved her.

I'd always loved her.

I always would.

And tomorrow, I'd watch her walk away. It was like having my heart broken all over again.

I rubbed a hand over my face, then forced myself out of the living room, retreating to my office. I spent the next three hours trying to think about anything but Eva and the baby, while outside the snow continued to fall, weighing heavy on the ground. Weighing heavy like my heart.

"Hey."

I looked up from my desk, finding Eva leaning against the doorframe. "Hey."

"I didn't realize how tired I was." She yawned. "Have you been back long?"

"A few hours."

Her gaze drifted past my shoulder to the windows. The house lights caught the snowflakes as they fell but beyond them it was dark. "It's black and white out there. I hope they don't cancel my flight tomorrow."

I couldn't say the same.

"Hungry?" I shoved out of my chair.

"Sure. I can cook."

"I'll do it. Keep me company." I escorted her to the kitchen, my hand at the small of her back.

If she was leaving, I might as well touch her while I could. The next time we saw each other, she might not want my hands on her. Maybe she never would again.

Eva sat at the island, on her stool, while I got to work making a pasta dish. "So we should talk."

"Yeah." I put a pot of water on the stove to boil. "Probably should."

"I was thinking—" The chime of her phone cut through the room. "Sorry."

She slid off her seat and answered. "Hello?"

I took out some vegetables and sausage from the fridge, working and listening as she spoke.

"Shoot." She sighed. "Well, at least I'll be there soon. First thing Monday morning, I'll meet with them, and see if I can't smooth things out. Forward me their email. I'll review it on my flight."

Eva paced the length of the island as she listened, worrying her bottom lip between her teeth. Then she nodded. "Talk to you then. Bye."

"Trouble?" I asked as she returned to her stool.

"That was my boss. The clients for this project aren't exactly easy to work with. At the moment, they're frustrated that the build isn't moving as quickly as they'd like. They just sent a nasty email threatening to bring in their lawyer if we didn't show some visible progress in the next thirty days. My boss is a great guy, but emails like that send him into a tailspin."

"No build ever happens as quickly as a client wants."

"True. But it will be fine. Once I get there, build a rapport and they see some progress, we'll win them over."

She would win them over. "Of that, I have no doubt."

Eva loved a challenge. One semester in college, she'd signed up for twenty-three credits, adding an extra class than normal. It had been a lot of work, but she'd had this determination not to fail. She'd aced them all.

"What's been your favorite project?" I asked.

"Probably the one in Phoenix."

I focused on making our meal while she told me stories about her favorite assignments. Then I handed her a plate, taking the space beside her and raising my glass of sparkling grape juice for a toast.

"Cheers."

She clinked her glass to mine. "Cheers."

"It's interesting hearing you talk about your buildings," I said as we ate. "You love them because of the clients or the foremen. I love mine because of the actual structure."

"I mean . . . there's not a lot to love about boring, boxy buildings. So yeah, usually the ones that stand out are because I like the people."

"Do you keep in touch with them?"

"Not really. It's hard after I leave. By the time I actually meet friends, it's usually close to the time I'm about to go. We drift apart."

"Sorry."

She shrugged, swirling her fork in her penne. "It can get

lonely. That's my only complaint. There are days when I feel like I'm on an island. But then I call home and talk to Elena or Dad, and remember that I'll always have them."

"And me. You'll have me."

Her eyes softened. "Thank you."

"So . . . before your call, you were going to say something."

"Oh, just that I've been thinking. Maybe we could pick a long weekend for you to come to London. If you can get away. Once I get there, I'll find a doctor. We could time the trip with an appointment."

"Yeah." It was a totally reasonable idea. Totally fucking reasonable. But it set me on edge, and my fingers gripped my fork too tight.

"And then I can come here. I can make a few trips while it's still okay for me to travel."

Until no doctor would let her on an airplane and she'd be half a world away. Who knew when she'd go into labor? Who'd take her to the hospital? Who'd be there to make sure she didn't lift anything too heavy?

I let go of the fork before I bent the metal and fisted my hand on the island. "But you'll be here to have the baby. You said your project would be six to eight months, right?"

"Um, maybe? The project might . . . take longer."

"What?" I clipped. Where the hell had this come from? Why hadn't she mentioned that earlier this week?

"It could take up to a year."

I blinked. "A year?"

What happened when she went into labor? What if it happened too fast and I couldn't make it there in time?

I shoved off my stool, dragging a hand through my hair as I walked around the island. Sitting side by side wasn't working. I needed to look at her face and make sure I had this right. "So you're going to have the baby in London."

"Given the timing, probably. Yes. I doubt my doctor will want me flying to Montana during my third trimester."

"Then what? Maternity leave?"

"Depends on the project. I'll have to talk to my boss. He might want to send someone out to help by that point. But if it's going well, then I might be able to just work from home. Do occasional site visits."

"Is it an option? Finding someone else to do this job?"

She sat up straighter. "Maybe. I'd rather not ask."

"What about finding you a job closer to Montana?"

"Again, I'd rather not ask. I want to do this London project."

"You won't ask your boss to assign you to a job in America. But you'll ask me to fly back and forth, hopefully with enough notice that I can be there for the birth of my child. And then what? You get a new assignment? You pack up and go somewhere else?"

"I don't know." She climbed off her stool, pacing on one side of the island while I did the same on the opposite. "I don't know. Okay? I'm just now wrapping my brain around the fact that I'm growing a human. I haven't exactly figured out how I'm going to raise him or her yet."

"You can't."

She gasped, her feet stopping. "What?"

"This can't be the life you want for our child. Traveling all over. Bouncing from school to school."

"It might not be like that."

"Then you'll quit your job?"

"I don't know." She tossed up her hands. "Do I have to have the answers today?"

"No, but a goddamn direction would be good. I have to know what you're thinking. I have to know what you're going to sacrifice. I have to know that you're not going to be like your mother." I regretted it the moment I spoke. *Fuck.*

Eva gasped. "I can't believe you just said that to me. Why have all our conversations been about my sacrifices? What about you?"

"Me?" I pointed to my chest. "I have a steady job. I am taking over my father's company. I have a house. A fucking address. You really think I'm going to give that up? We both know that the right place for this kid to grow up is here. With me."

Eva's eyes widened. Her mouth fell open. "What?"

"It makes sense. If you keep your job, then the baby should live here."

The air in the room went still. The only sound was my racing heart. Eva stared at me and my biggest fear came to life.

There was nothing but disdain in her eyes. Nothing but resentment.

She hated me.

And if there was a piece of my heart left that she hadn't broken the first time, it shattered in that very moment.

Except I couldn't even blame her. This one . . . this one was on me.

"An ultimatum," she whispered, her eyes flooding. "I can't believe you just gave me an ultimatum. You know what I wished for earlier? That you'd ask me to stay."

My heart stopped.

"But you didn't. Not before. Not now. You've never asked me to stay." And judging by the tone in her voice, now it was too late.

"You broke my fucking heart."

"Then I guess tonight makes us even." She swallowed hard. "Happy New Year, Tobias."

The sound of her slamming door echoed through the house.
I stood frozen, immobilized by the pain.

She hated me.

To be fair, tonight, I sort of hated myself.

CHAPTER 11
EVA

My eyes were puffy and the circles beneath them blue. Splotchy cheeks and pale lips weren't a good look for me. This wasn't exactly how I'd hoped to start my new year, crying through the midnight hours and barely sleeping. But at least I could nap on the plane.

I stretched a hair tie around my wrist, then took one last look in the mirror. Yep, I looked like crap. The last time I'd looked this awful had been years ago. This was the face I'd worn for weeks after moving to New York.

It was like the heartache was so immense that it couldn't stay inside. It blanched my skin. It hollowed my cheeks. It sat like a chimney of bricks upon my shoulders.

Tobias's ultimatum rang through my mind. It made it hard to see straight because the worst part was . . .

He was right.

I was clinging to a foolish hope that my life wouldn't have to change. But nothing about my life was normal. I couldn't drag a baby around with me from city to city. I couldn't keep my job and be a mother.

He was right. I knew he was right. I'd known it for a week.

Yet last night, even after all those words, he hadn't asked me to stay. He wanted the baby. Just not me.

I swiped at my cheeks, sniffling the sting out of my nose. Then I steeled my spine, pulled on my coat and collected my suitcase. No, I couldn't work forever, at least not in the same capacity. But I wasn't quitting today. I wasn't quitting tomorrow.

I'd go to London, give myself time to mourn the loss of my career, then formulate an exit plan. It was time to update my résumé.

With my suitcase dragging behind me, I looped my backpack strap over a shoulder and left Tobias's guest bedroom behind. Would he turn it into the baby's nursery?

I clenched my jaw to keep the emotion from bubbling free as I marched down the hallway.

The scent of coffee greeted me in the kitchen. Tobias stood at the sink, his back to me as he stared out the window overlooking his backyard.

Would he put a swing set out there? Or maybe a playhouse? Would he make this home a child's paradise so that I had no chance of competing?

Tobias turned, his eyes darted to my bags. "I'll help you load up."

"I can do it." I raised my chin. "Thanks for letting me crash here this week. I stripped the bed. Towels are in the hamper."

He nodded. "Appreciate it."

My heart hammered three beats for every step toward the front door. I twisted the knob, but before I could step outside, my suitcase was tugged free from my hand.

Tobias stood there, so close I could smell his cologne. I drew it in, holding it for a long moment, then exhaled.

He followed close behind as I walked into the cold, my

breath billowing in a white cloud as I crossed the clean side-walk. He must have shoveled while I'd been in the shower. He'd also cleaned the snow from my car.

I hit the button for the trunk, stepping aside so he could load my suitcase. Then I tossed in my backpack and met his gaze.

Those blue eyes were like sapphires, glittering in the morning sun. His Adam's apple bobbed as he swallowed. "Call me."

"I will."

He studied me, the dark circles and dull skin, his forehead furrowing. "Eva, I—"

"Don't." My voice trembled. "Please don't. I need to get going."

And I was hanging on by a thread. I couldn't fight with him, not again.

"All right." He moved, shifting out of my way so we wouldn't touch as I brushed past him and hurried for the driver's side door.

I slid inside, the cold from the seat seeping through my jeans.

Tobias braced his hands on the roof, bending as I inserted the key into the ignition. "I'm sorry. For what it's worth, what I said last night, I'm sorry."

The tears threatened, so I simply nodded and turned the key. "Goodbye, Tobias."

His hands fell to his sides and he stepped away. "Goodbye, Eva."

Another miserable farewell.

I didn't let myself look at him as I reversed out of the drive-way. I didn't let myself glance in the rearview mirror as my tires crunched on the fresh snow of his lane. I didn't let myself think that there'd been regret on his face as he'd said goodbye.

This week had been an epic clusterfuck, from that stupid song to last night's fight.

I should have stayed in my empty condo. We should have maintained boundaries. Too much time had passed for us to be jumping into bed together. He might know me better than anyone, but that didn't mean I was the same young woman I'd been in college.

We'd drifted apart. We'd become different people.

And now, we'd have to figure out a way to become parents.

The miles to the airport passed in a blur. My focus was nonexistent, but there was a plus side to moving and traveling so often. I maneuvered the airport with mechanical ease, checking my baggage and navigating security. Most of the chairs outside the gate were full, but I found an empty seat next to a window.

There was an older couple seated across from me. I met the woman's gaze and it was so full of pity that I winced. Okay, maybe I looked worse than crap. The flight attendants would probably ask if I was all right.

I forced a tight smile at the woman, then twisted sideways in the seat, folding my legs toward my chest so I could look outside.

The ground crew was busy loading suitcases onto a conveyor belt. One man in a neon vest was waving two orange wands. Mom had taught us years ago how pilots navigated runway lines and markers.

What airport would she be flying to today? Did she ever feel sad coming to this airport? Because I did. Every single time.

I stared at the workers, keeping my eyes aimed through the glass as the tears began to fall.

This was just so goddamn familiar. This was just like the day I'd left for New York.

I was in a blue, vinyl chair again. I was crying at the

Bozeman airport again. I was staring at a Boeing 737 with a heart torn to confetti.

My hand found my belly. I pressed it close, squeezing shut my eyes.

Was I making a huge mistake? Would I regret this decision?

Before New York, there hadn't been a scrap of hesitation in my mind. Yes, I'd been devastated and broken about Tobias, but when the gate agent had called my row, I'd stood tall, dried my face and walked down the sky bridge.

Today's doubts were paralyzing. They kept me pinned to my chair, even as my name was called. Even as the plane taxied down the runway.

Even as it took flight without me.

CHAPTER 12

TOBIAS

The pencil in my hand snapped in half. That was the third one this morning. The graphite line on my sketch made it unusable so I crumpled it in a fist and tossed it toward the trash.

"Damn it." I shoved out of my chair and stormed from the office. What was the point in working? I couldn't fucking concentrate, and I was so tense that my office supplies were paying the price.

I checked my phone again. Eva had been gone for two hours. She was probably at the airport, about to get on her flight. Was she okay? This morning she'd looked tired and pissed and . . . hurt.

This was why I'd never wanted to fight with her. Because it made me feel like I was crawling out of my skin.

I pulled up her name in my phone, my fingers hovering over the keyboard to send her a text. But what was I supposed to say? I'm sorry? Yeah, I'd tried that this morning.

Travel safe.

I typed it. I deleted it.

Miss you.

Type. Delete.

Stay.

Type.

Delete.

It was too late. After our fight, I'd all but shoved her out the door. Besides, if she was going to stay, it had to be her decision.

Maybe it was a good thing that we wouldn't see each other for a couple of months. Maybe by then our feelings wouldn't be as raw. She'd be settled in London and might have a better idea how long this job would take.

I'd just have to wait.

My hands fisted. Months? No way. I'd turned myself inside out in just an hour. How could I endure months?

The house, my sanctuary, felt empty this morning. Soon, her scent would vanish. I'd forget how it looked when she sat at the island. I'd miss having her next to me on the couch for Hallmark movies.

Was this really a home if my heart was on its way to London?

The stomp of footsteps on the stoop caught my ear, followed by the doorbell. Was it Eva? Had she come back? I flew toward the door and ripped it open.

"Hey." Maddox jerked up his chin.

My shoulders fell. "Hi."

"Hoping I was someone else?"

"Eva." I waved him inside. "She left this morning."

"For London?" he asked, unzipping his coat.

"Yeah." I tucked my hands in my pockets, then pulled them free. I dragged my palm over my cheek, then through my hair. If I didn't move, I felt like I'd explode. "What's up?"

"Just came by to check on you."

I blinked. "Why?"

Maddox chuckled. "Because I'm your brother. And by the looks of it, I came just in time. You keep rubbing your beard like that, you won't have to worry about shaving."

"Huh? Oh." I dropped my hand from my jaw. It went into my pocket and came right back out.

"Talk to me." Maddox clapped a hand on my shoulder, tugging me toward the living room. He steered me to the chair while he sat on the edge of the couch. "You guys talk about the baby?"

"Yeah." I was seated for a whole five seconds before I rose to my feet. "We got in a fight last night. I told her I thought that the baby should live here with me since she travels all over."

Maddox cringed. "How'd that go?"

"Not good."

"What did she say when you asked her if she'd consider staying in Montana?"

"I, uh, didn't ask."

"What? Why not?" He stared at me like I'd grown two heads.

"Because it's complicated."

He leaned deeper into the couch, tossing an arm over the backrest. "I've got time for complicated."

I blew out a long breath. "I don't want her to stay because I asked. I want her to stay because she wants to stay. Because she wants me."

"That's fair."

I paced the length of the fireplace, my heart in my throat. Did she want me? Maybe she would have before yesterday? But after last night . . .

"She's the one," I confessed. "Always has been."

"You don't think she feels the same?"

"I don't know," I whispered. "Once, yes. But then I asked her to marry me, and well . . . we aren't married."

Maddox's mouth fell open. "Wait. You proposed? When?"

"Graduation."

"No one told me that."

"Because I didn't tell anyone. You're the first person I've told. It was, um . . . humiliating."

"I can imagine. But we would have understood. We would have been there."

"I know," I muttered. "I think part of the reason I didn't tell anyone was that I was protecting Eva. I don't want anyone to hate her. Especially Mom."

Maddox leaned forward, bracing his elbows on his knees. "So you didn't ask her to stay because you're worried she'd turn you down again."

I tapped my nose. "It'll be fine. We'll figure this out. I was working on some sketches for your place. Want to see them?"

"No." He scoffed. "I don't give a damn about the house. You're not fine, Tobias."

No, I wasn't.

My chest felt too tight. My limbs weak. "I don't know what to do. I want to be there for her. For the baby."

"You have to tell her how you feel. If you want her to stay, ask. Maybe she'll surprise you."

Maybe she would. She'd basically said that last night, hadn't she? Or had I just heard what I'd wanted to hear? Our conversation was becoming a blur and the growing throb behind my temples wasn't helping.

"What if she doesn't?"

"Then you know," he said. "You can let her go."

Would I ever let Eva go? "Well, I'm sort of fucked at the moment. She's on her way to London."

"And?"

I gave him a sideways glance. "And, what? I work here. My

home is here. Once I get a break in my schedule, I'll plan a trip or something."

"Or you could go today." Maddox stood and rounded the coffee table to stand in front of me. "Family first, Tobias. Take it from a man who has struggled with that concept. You'll regret anything else."

"I am picking family. Mom. Dad. Heath. Now you're moving home."

"We'll always be family. But we're not *your* family. Yours. The one you're making. I love Mom and Dad. You and Heath. But *my* family is Violet. And for my daughter, there's nothing I wouldn't do."

My family. There was only one person I wanted to build that with. "Shit."

"Yep."

"I need to get to the airport."

"Let's go." He strode for the door, swiping his jacket from the hook.

I ran to grab my keys and wallet from the kitchen counter, doing a frantic scan around the house. What else did I need? Clothes? Toiletries?

"Passport," Maddox ordered like he could read my mind.

"Right." I jogged to the safe in my walk-in closet, punching in the code. With my passport in hand, I left the rest behind. There were stores in London. I could snag necessities like a toothbrush and soap on a layover.

I passed the dresser, thinking I could at least shove a clean pair of boxers and socks in my coat pocket. I ripped open the top drawer and froze. There was only one thing I needed.

A ring. Maybe I'd kept it all these years because, deep down, I'd hoped for a second chance to put it on Eva's finger.

I pulled on a coat and put the box in the pocket closest to my heart. Maddox was already in his SUV when I stepped into the cold. The moment I was in my seat, he tore out of the driveway and down the road.

"My jet is in a hangar," he said. "Do you know her flight itinerary? When she touches down in London?"

"No. I'm guessing she's off to Seattle first." I frantically switched between airline apps, checking my options. "There's a flight there in an hour. Then a three-hour layover."

There were only two flights from Seattle to London today. Hopefully I picked the right one. Hopefully she was going to Seattle first, not Denver or Salt Lake.

"My pilot will fly you to Heathrow. You'd only have to stop for fuel."

"But if I can catch up to her, then I'll be on her flight to London." Even if she was pissed at me, we'd be on the same plane. "Let me see what I can do when we get to the airport."

He nodded and hit the gas pedal.

We parked in the loading zone, Maddox not caring if he was towed. He stuck right by my side as I ran to a clerk and begged her to find me a flight to London.

Her nails were long and they clacked against the keyboard as she typed. Then a slow smile spread across her face. "You're on the next flight to Seattle. Then I've got you on the connection to London. There's one seat left. It's not cheap."

I passed her my credit card. "Book it."

"Call if you get stranded," Maddox said. "I'll send my pilot to pick you up."

"Thanks."

He grinned. "Go get her."

"I will." My heart raced. This was happening. I was leaving it all behind to chase my woman.

And with every cell in my body, I knew it was the right choice.

With a wave, my brother started for the doors, but I stopped him before he could get too far.

"Maddox?"

He turned. "Yeah?"

"Glad you're home."

"Me too." One more wave and then he weaved through people before he disappeared outside.

The clerk handed me my tickets and I bolted from the desk, taking the stairs toward security two at a time. I stripped off my belt and fumbled to remove my shoes. Then I waited in line, shifting my weight between my feet, as the four people ahead of me walked through the scanner at a snail's pace.

Come on. I was in a hurry to get to my gate and . . . wait.

Adrenaline coursed through my veins and the pace was torture. But finally, I was marching through the terminal.

I scanned the displays, making sure I was heading toward the right place. I passed an empty seating area, seeing only one person against the glass. Her legs were tucked into the chair as she stared outside and across the runway. Her red coat hugged her slight frame.

My steps slowed.

I knew that red coat.

"What the—" I changed direction, moving straight toward the window. Was this real? "Eva?"

She jerked, whipping toward my voice. Her hazel eyes were full of tears. "Tobias?"

"I thought your flight was at ten."

"It was." She wiped furiously at her cheeks, sitting straight. "I missed it."

Was that why she was crying? "There's another one in an hour."

"Oh. I'll try—wait. How do you know that? What are you doing here?"

I sat in the chair beside hers. "Taking the flight to Seattle in an hour. Then making a connection to London."

"What?"

"Why'd you miss your flight?"

She lifted a shoulder. "I'm stuck."

I took her right hand in mine, curling our fingers together. Then I tapped my thumb across her index finger. "One. Two. Three. Four."

She sniffled. "I declare a thumb war."

"Shake." Our thumbs touched. "Winner asks the first question."

She didn't even put up a fight and my thumb trapped hers instantly.

"Why are you stuck?"

"Because I'm not sure if I'm making a huge mistake."

"Go again." We did another thumb duel, again she let me win.

"Do you want to go to London?"

"No. Yes." Her eyes flooded. "I don't know."

"How about if I go with you?"

Her chin quivered. "Really?"

"Really. If I went with you to London, would you want to go?"

"Yes. But . . . then what?"

"I don't know, babe." I let her hand go to frame her face. "I don't know. But we could start with this trip. Then the next. What I know is that I can't let you go. So if that means I go with you, then here I am."

"Tobias, I—" She shook her head. "What are you saying?"

"I love you."

Another tear dropped. "I love you too."

I slammed my lips onto hers, swallowing a moan. Her tears continued to fall, dripping onto my face, but as I kissed her, she started laughing, clinging to me as I clung to her until a throat cleared from the gate agent tore us apart.

"You'd really go to London with me?"

"I'm not going to ask you to stay," I said. "Not because I don't want you to stay, but because I think you would. You'd stay for me and the baby even though you're not ready. You want London. So London is what we'll do."

"I would stay."

Yeah, she would. But I wouldn't make her choose. I wasn't going to be the man who smothered her dreams and delivered ultimatums. She deserved better. "How about one more adventure? We tackle London. Then we'll decide what's next. Together."

"Are you sure? What about your home? Your family?"

I tucked a lock of hair behind her ear. "I'm looking at my family. I'm staring at my home."

"I haven't had a home, a real one, in a long time."

"You do now." I kissed her forehead, then took her hand again. "Thumb wrestle to see who gets my first-class ticket."

She gave me a wicked grin. There'd be no letting me win this time. "You're on."

EPILOGUE
EVA

O ne year later . . .

"Since we're early, can we swing by a project site real quick?" Tobias asked as I drove us toward town. "I want to see how the exterior lights look at night."

"Sure. Which way?"

"At the stop sign, head north."

"Whoa." I shot him a scowl. "Watch your language."

"What?"

"You said north."

He chuckled, shaking his head. "Take a left at the stop sign."

"Better." I smirked, then cast my eyes to the rearview.

Isabella was asleep in her car seat, her tiny lips in a perfect pout. This would be a long night for her, considering it was already past her bedtime.

Tonight was the annual Holiday family Christmas party and she was dressed for the occasion. Her red velvet dress was trimmed with white. Her slippers wouldn't last because she hated shoes but I'd put them on over her tights regardless.

"Did you grab the earmuffs?" Tobias asked.

"Yes," I muttered. Those freaking earmuffs. "They're in the diaper bag."

His parents had hired a live band, like they did most years, and it was going to get loud at the venue. So Tobias had found a pair of baby-sized earmuffs. Except instead of finding a cute pink or purple pair, heaven forbid something that would coordinate with her dress, he'd found orange.

Hunter's orange.

When I'd asked him why he'd picked such a heinous color, he'd told me they'd been the only ones with adjustments so she could wear them as she grew older.

My husband was nothing if not practical.

Tobias had proposed to me outside a women's restroom in the Seattle airport. The charmer. In all fairness, I'd botched his plans for something romantic. I'd leaned my head against his chest, and when my cheek had hit something hard in his coat pocket, I'd pestered him to tell me what he was carrying until he'd finally caved.

The same ring he'd bought years ago had been on my finger ever since. And as of last week, there was a wedding band to keep it company.

We'd gotten married the day after we'd finally moved home to Montana. The two of us had gone to the courthouse over lunch and made it official.

No dress. No tux. Just Tobias, our daughter and me.

It hadn't taken me long into the London project to realize I wasn't up for another move. By my third trimester, when my ankles had been swollen and my back had ached and the heartburn had been unbearable, all I'd wanted was to go home.

To Montana.

Dad had been right. I'd needed to run and run. But when I'd been ready to stop, we'd stopped. We'd waited for Isabella to

431

join the world, then when she was old enough, we'd moved out of our London flat and flown home.

Hannah and Keith were overjoyed to have us close. They'd kept watch over our house while we'd been gone, keeping it clean and fresh for our visits home this past year. They'd even flown to see us once. And Keith had made sure that Tobias had been able to continue his work, hiring another architect for Holiday Homes. So while Tobias had drafted plans from afar, there'd been someone in Bozeman to act as boots on the ground and help see the projects through.

"Okay, left here." He pointed out the windshield, directing us through a maze of roads until we pulled up to a house that stood proudly in a snow-covered field.

"Wow."

"Turned out well."

"That's an understatement, baby." I took his hand, smiling as I stared at the home.

The owners had wanted a barn-style house with a gable roof and sliding front door. When he'd told me about it, I'd been skeptical, but leave it to Tobias to create something enchanting and unique.

A small whimper from the backseat meant we needed to keep driving, so I took my foot off the brake of my new SUV and headed into town.

The Baxter Hotel was like a golden beacon, standing tall on Main Street. The moment we stepped into the ballroom on the second floor, we were mobbed by friends and family here to welcome us home.

Then the band started and Tobias instantly retrieved the earmuffs.

"Could you have picked a different color?" Hannah asked as he fit them over Isabella's head.

"What's wrong with orange?" he asked.

I rolled my eyes. "It doesn't go."

"She's a baby. She doesn't care." He lifted Isabella from my arms, kissing her cheek, then set her in her favorite place in the world—the crook of his arm.

I'd fallen in love with Tobias years ago, but watching him with our daughter was like falling all over again.

"Let's dance." He clasped my hand, dropping a chaste kiss to my mouth, then steered us through the crowd to the dance floor. With the baby in one arm, he swept me into the other.

"I'm glad we could be here for this." I rested my head against his shoulder as we swayed. "And for Christmas."

"Me too," he murmured. "No regrets?"

"None."

My boss hadn't been happy when I'd told him that London would be my last project. He'd offered me a huge raise to stay on but I'd turned him down. Because I'd already found another job.

After New Year's, I'd be joining the crew at Holiday Homes as their newest project manager. I'd be working for the family business.

There was a chance that Tobias and I would kill each other, working in the same office. Or there was a chance we'd have quickies on the regular after hours.

We'd figure it out. Together.

"How about a holiday classic?" the band's lead singer asked into the microphone as they rounded out a song. "We've been doing this sing-a-long all year and it's a blast. What do you say?"

The room erupted into cheers of agreement.

And then the lead guitarist began to play. "On the first day of Christmas, my true love gave to me."

I glanced at Tobias.

He threw his head back and laughed.

Then we sang along. And at the end, when we got to our version, we both changed the lyrics.

Two turtle doves,

And a partridge and a pregnancy.

ABOUT THE AUTHOR

Willa Nash is *Wall Street Journal* and *USA Today* bestselling author Devney Perry's alter ego. After working in the technology industry for a decade, she abandoned conference calls and project schedules to pursue her passion for writing. Now she has over forty published stories. She was born and raised in Montana and now lives in Washington with her husband and two sons.

Don't miss out on the latest book news.
Subscribe to her newsletter!
www.devneyperry.com

Printed in Great Britain
by Amazon

15024458R00257